nailed it

nailed it

CINDI MADSEN

Entangled Publishing, LLC
2614 South Timberline Road
Suite 109
Fort Collins, CO 80525
Visit our website at www.entangledpublishing.com.

Amara is an imprint of Entangled Publishing, LLC.

Edited by Stacy Abrams
Cover design by Liz Pelletier
Cover art from iStock

Manufactured in the United States of America

First Edition October 2017

To Mountain Dew. Come on, we all knew it would happen someday, and this book totally would've never happened without you.

Chapter One

"How could you not want to fall in love?"

I clenched my fruity, embellished-with-a-heart-swizzle-stick drink tighter, wishing I'd mixed it myself so it'd have more than a splash of alcohol. *Damn. My plan to be invisible has failed.*

Without looking, I knew Aunt Velma would be to my right, basking in the success of the engagement party she'd set up on the sprawling lawn behind her house. She wasn't technically my aunt, but once Savannah introduced you to her family, you were kind of part of it. No matter how hard you tried to resist it happening.

The Gambles were nosy and opinionated, which was one reason I'd tried to resist so hard. It was also why my attempts to keep them at a distance were futile.

I steeled myself for what would inevitably come next—something about how amazing love and marriage was, naturally.

Velma gestured to the betrothed couple. "I mean, how could you not want someone to look at you like that?"

I glanced at Velma, then followed the crisscrossing

strings of light overhead. They cast a soft glow on the tables and chairs overflowing with well-wishers and hung lower over the merry couple, leaving them in the spotlight.

My cousin Linc and my best friend Savanna were freshly engaged and disgustingly in love. Since I adored both of them, and they truly were perfect for each other, I was happy for them. Considering I'd introduced them to each other in college, I was taking credit for the match, even if it took a few extra years for them to get their happy ending.

Just call me Cupid.

Was it a prerequisite for Cupid to believe in love?

Technically, I didn't not *not* believe in it. It just didn't have any place in my life. I'd seen the havoc and destruction love left in its wake. I'd witnessed the unsteadiness of it, the self-reliance on another person, and the sharp, slicing words fired at will by people who claimed to love each other.

I liked my feet on the ground and my head in the logical cloud-free space it belonged in.

As a dating guru and creator of the 12 Steps to Mr. Right program, my best friend didn't understand my commitment aversion and possibly even believed that someday I'd meet my very own Mr. Right and change my mind.

But I had my own set of rules that I lived and died by. Well, there'd been no dying in the literal sense, obviously, but before I'd started following them, I'd had days where I definitely didn't feel alive, and I was never going back.

I referred to them as 13 Ways to Avoid a Broken Heart (and other loveborne illnesses). One more step than Savannah's program totally meant mine was better. For me anyway. Plus, I'd always liked the number thirteen, black cats, walking under ladders, and anything else people were superstitious about. It made people nervous, and I liked making people a little nervous.

I flashed Velma my best grin. "Girl, I have guys looking

at me like that every night in the bar." Honestly, the looks I received while bartending at Azure didn't have that my-world-revolves-around-you edge Savannah's and Link's did, but the unabashed lust, I got plenty of.

A scandalized gasp escaped Velma, turning the tables right back in my favor.

Way #1: Always be in control. In life, with people, and most of all, when it comes to love. Once you fall in love, you surrender control, and safety is most definitely not guaranteed.

And that's how it's done. I tipped back my drink. "This might not be the strongest, but it is super yummy. I think I'll go grab another. You want me to get you one?"

Velma lifted the drink in her hand. "Thank you, but I'm still working on my *first.*"

I ignored the implication that one drink was plenty and headed to the punchbowl for a refill. My skeptical side expected this party to be difficult to get through, not because I was sad that Savannah was getting married—because again, super happy, totally responsible for their meeting and giving her a push when she'd needed it a few months ago—but because I knew things would change.

Savannah was already so busy with her successful program, and Linc's sports reporting career was taking off, and everyone was moving on, and I was still tending bar. I'd always meant for it to be a temporary gig, but I made a killing in tips, and every time I went to apply for another job, I thought of the steady hours and sitting at a desk and then it felt like my skin was getting too tight.

I didn't want to be predictable. Didn't want to be boring. But I didn't want to be stuck, either, and for the past few months, I'd been in a rut.

No thinking about that. I'm in control and rocking this

party…

Only when I turned away from the table, I accidentally caught sight of Jackson.

Jackson, brother of the bride-to-be, guy who drove me crazy—both in the irritated and turned-on way—and, well, there might've been an incident where I'd slipped and had a one-week stand with him.

No, *incident* wasn't strong enough. I'd broken girl code, crossed lines with my bestie's brother, and momentarily let myself forget that sex would only complicate already-complicated things.

My sense of control had spiraled out of my grasp then, and as Jackson leveled his green-eyed gaze on me now, my grip slipped the tiniest bit. A shiver that I forced myself to cover traveled down my spine, and my sleeveless navy cocktail dress did little to conceal the goose bumps covering my arms. At least I knew the dark lace contrasted nicely with my pale blond hair, and my smoky eye was on pointe tonight. If a simple look was going to give me goose bumps, I needed the rest of me to be on its game.

It'd be so much easier to share the same space if I didn't remember what his lips felt like against mine, that mix of soft and scruff from his whiskers. If I didn't remember those big hands, callused from his contractor work, dragging across my skin.

Being in his arms.

I wasn't usually a girl who hung around. I left as fast as humanly possible or politely showed my gentleman caller to the door so I could be in charge of the leaving instead of waiting around for it to happen. Jackson was the only guy I'd let hold me afterward, and it killed me that I'd been so vulnerable in front of him because it made me feel vulnerable in front of him *all the freaking time*. Even more devastating, I hated how much I'd liked it there and occasionally longed to be there again.

Like when I lost my mind for a couple of seconds. Or before he went and opened his mouth.

Speaking of usually, I usually held back the memories better—my nights with Jackson were shoved away to the far corners of my mind. Unfortunately, they kept bobbing up, unbidden, to torture me. What I needed to do was remind myself of how ugly things turned afterward.

I lifted my chin, readying myself for a cool conversation peppered with verbal jabs, and he crossed the arms I'd just been reliving having around me, those damn muscles he got from all that manual labor popping out to taunt me.

He had this stupidly perfect hair, too. Nice and thick and longer on top, brown with a hint of copper that you only could see in the sun. It was styled as if he'd simply raked his fingers through it and let it do whatever it wanted, which was apparently to always fall flawlessly in place.

He gave me a tight nod. "Ivy."

"Jackson." Pre–blurred lines, we'd volleyed between passionately arguing and flirting with a daring, challenging edge, but afterward it was all animosity, and he'd been pretty clear that he wasn't starting a fan club for me anytime soon. I told myself that loathing was easier—his or mine, there was plenty to go around whenever our paths crossed. If I focused on that, I could keep hold of my control.

"I was thinking that for Savannah's sake, we could"—he dragged his fingers across his clenched jaw, looking like he was having trouble grinding out the words—"put aside our differences and play nice."

The phrase "play nice" brought on a barrage of images that were more dirty than nice and definitely not something I should be thinking about in the company of his family members, who were more on the proper debutante and southern gentlemen side of the fence. It was a side I didn't belong in, not by a long shot. Luckily, Savannah never cared about that kind of thing.

"I *suppose* I can manage to play nice. But with you…?" A smile tugged at my lips, and I went ahead and let it free, steering it into syrupy sweet range. "Only for an hour or so. Two tops."

An evil gleam lit his eyes. "As I recall, there's only one way to ensure you're saying more yeses than nos, and it was usually closer to two hours."

My jaw dropped as the blood in my veins boiled with a mixture of anger and desire that I never could properly sort out around him. I quickly snapped my mouth closed and muttered through gritted teeth, "You wish, you cocky jackass."

He clicked his tongue. "Is that any way to start our temporary truce?"

I glared at him. He glared right back. Then he had the audacity to grin.

I wanted to hold my drop-dead stare for longer, but no place was safe for my eyes. The guy always filled out his jeans and T-shirts nicely, the rugged look making it nearly impossible for my hormones to behave themselves. But the button-down shirt, casually open at his chest, and sports jacket combo was equally hot-flash inducing.

I'd scold myself for ogling him—a habit I'd tried really hard to quit—but his eyes dipped to take in my mid-thigh skirt before traveling back up to my face, so I wasn't alone. Fighting off a wave of heat that had little to do with the warm September evening, I reached up and twisted a strand of hair around my finger, doing my best not to remember the way he'd once driven his fingers through it and told me he liked it wavy and wild, the way it was right now.

Jeez. What's with me tonight? It didn't take a sex scientist (a job I was far more qualified for than the Cupid one, FYI) to figure it out. I was sexually frustrated. While I used to be onboard with mutual adult fun, lately when I met guys, I just couldn't get into it. Not the flirting and definitely not trying to turn the flirting into more. Sometimes it was because talking with them for more than a few minutes revealed the beer bottle in their hands had a higher IQ than they did, but I used to not need conversation.

Ugh, why did my brain have to function all the time?

Because that's how you stay in control. Now get it together and say something to Jackson, and don't you dare do the flirty voice thing. This is a temporary truce for Savannah's sake, that's all. It's not like it's admitting defeat or anything.

"So, did you do the big brother thing and tell Linc that he better take care of your sister or else?"

"While I do love a good threatening, I didn't bother. Velma already did it, and I'm man enough to admit that she's scarier than I'll ever be."

I snorted a laugh, which made Jackson laugh. I think both of us were a tad tipsy. Although I wasn't tipsy enough to keep from noticing the deep timbre of his laugh or how he shifted closer to me.

If I drank more, staying in control would be slightly more difficult, but for some reason, I was having a hard time remembering why I needed control so badly. Some of my best times with Jackson involved being totally and utterly out of control. All passion, no thinking…

Until it caught up with me.

Which was why I schooled my hormones and shoved away all thoughts of going down that painful, land-mine-filled path again. "Has Velma given you the 'don't you want someone to look at you like that' line yet?"

"I actually got the 'isn't it about time you find your other half and settle down' one." Jackson tugged at the sleeves of his jacket—clearly he wasn't used to wearing one, in spite of looking like he could model for Lumberjacks Gone GQ monthly, a catalog I'd absolutely subscribe to if it didn't only exist in my imagination.

"Ah, classic," I said. "As if you've just been walking around as half a person until now. I thought you looked lopsided."

"Hey." He ran a hand down his shirt. "I look sexy as hell."

"I'd like to argue, but…" I bit my lip. *Damn it. That crossed into flirty territory, didn't it?*

He leaned closer, his hand going to my lower back and his breath skating across my neck. "You don't have to freak out. I know better than to read more into comments like that from you."

It should reassure me, but instead my heart splatted in my chest. "I—"

"Do my eyes deceive me, or are you two actually having a civil conversation?" Savannah stepped up to us and eyed us with a healthy dose of skepticism, like it might all be a big ruse where we shouted "psych" and then went to town on each other.

Since my brain hated me, it flooded with images of kissing rather than punching.

"Consider it an early wedding present," Jackson said. "Don't expect anything else, though."

Savannah shoved him, and he wrapped his arm around her shoulders and pulled her in for a side hug. "Congrats, little sister."

"Thanks. Maybe now Mom and Aunt Velma will finally stop giving me crap about being a single dating expert."

Jackson nodded. "Probably. Next up, questions about when you'll be popping out a few kids."

Savannah groaned. "The hint about grandchildren has already been dropped. I just want to focus on how I'm finally getting married to my very own Mr. Right." She turned to me, and an embarrassingly strong wave of emotion hit me. I liked to keep that all bottled up, but it was dangerously close to exploding out of me. I lunged forward and hugged her tight.

Very little was constant in my life. I spent my entire childhood moving more times than people on the run from the mob did and had enough stepdads or almost-stepdads to create my own dysfunctional army of men I mostly couldn't trust. Life had been one big merry-go-round until I'd met Savannah.

She was my person and had been since we'd first met. I'd even tried to keep my guard up, simply because I'd learned to never get attached, but she charged right through like the Kool-Aid man.

I heard her sniff.

"Don't start crying, or I'll start," I said, choking back the tears clogging my throat. "And you know I'd rather eat worms than cry in public."

Savannah laughed. "I'd hate for people to think you were an actual human girl with feelings."

"Me too. That's exactly what I'm saying." I couldn't help but glance over her shoulder at Jackson, worried that I was giving him ammo to later use against me.

He'd taken a step back, allowing us some space, but he gave me a consoling smile when our eyes met, and then it was all I could do to stifle the urge to cry. If even he was taking pity on me, it was worse than I thought.

"If an engagement party makes me this damn emotional, I'm not coming to your wedding," I teased.

"I'm pretty sure it's required for the maid of honor to be at the wedding." Savannah pulled back to shoot me a serious look. "So don't even talk like that."

"Oh, great. You're going to be one of those bridezillas, aren't you?"

"Oh, for sure. Isn't that the point of a wedding? Forget happily ever after. I want to strike fear into everyone around me."

"Here, here," I said, lifting my palm so she could slap it.

We broke into laughter, and then Linc came over, also looking dashing but slightly uncomfortable in a button-up shirt and jacket. I gave him a hug for good measure. He was one of the other constants in my life, even though he'd gone and left me for minor league baseball for a handful of years before returning to Atlanta.

My two constants were about to marry each other and form two halves of one whole or whatever, and I told myself that I'd be okay. I was a grown up. I had years and years of experience in basically being on my own.

But I was afraid the past several years with my makeshift family might've made me soft.

Before we could get a decent conversation going, Velma called over Savannah and Linc, insisting they pose for more pictures.

Jackson stepped up next to me. "You okay?"

I exhaled a shallow breath and glanced at him. "Of course." He raised an eyebrow as if he wanted to challenge me on that, and I raised one right back. "You're not going to mess up our truce already, are you? The hour's not even done yet."

He held up his hands as if he were surrendering, a little too much amusement for my liking curving his lips.

A flicker of hope sparked—maybe we could go back to how it was before. We'd never really agreed on much of anything, but our exchanges used to be more like good-natured verbal sparring matches that sometimes ventured into fiery passion, each of us waving our red flags, taunting the other to charge like a bull.

These days, if and when our paths crossed, there was only arguing with barbed words meant to slice. Muttered insults like "succubus"—him about me, and "jackass"—me about him. I racked my brain for a neutral subject, but I wasn't very good at small talk, and he and I could manage to get into a fight over the weather.

I needed to say something, though. While our brains and mouths were always at war, our bodies were perfectly in tune, and if I continued eye-humping him and thinking of all the innuendos I'd like to make, I'd get carried away and undo our tiny bit of progress.

I opened my mouth and said, "I was thinking—" as he said, "Well, I'd better—"

He gestured to me. "Sorry, you go."

"No, you go."

For a couple of seconds, we both simply stared at each other, but then he obviously decided I'd win a stubborn-off any day—and he wasn't wrong—and said, "I was going to say I'd better go see where my date is."

My smile tried to fall, and I quickly propped it up. I couldn't do much about the similar drop in my gut, but at least it wasn't visible. And seriously, what the hell, body? So what if he brought a date? That meant less time for him to spend bothering and judging me.

"That's why I didn't get more grief from Velma about my single status. Naturally she and my ma are already thinking Caroline's the woman who could finally complete me and get rid of the lopsided thing you mentioned—"

"Ha!" I thought we'd determined he looked sexy as hell, something I bet his date also agreed with. Man, I hated the thought of him with another woman, even though I knew I didn't have the right to feel that way. We'd only been getting along for twenty or so minutes. Tomorrow we'd go back to glaring and snide remarks.

My stomach dropped even farther. *Damn engagement party turning me into an emotional wreck!*

"It's still really new, though."

"Still new" meant something more than a friend who'd

tagged along for the sake of keeping the heat off him with his family and their obsession for everyone to be coupled and in love. Possibly even something that could turn into a permanent thing.

Despite Savannah's and the rest of her family's worrying over him and his constant single status, I always knew Jackson was the settling down type. Since I wasn't, I'd done the right thing by pulling away when things between us started to go deeper.

"I'll let you go then." My hand drifted up to his arm without my permission, as if it needed one last feel before our goodwill soured and returned to whatever black hole it'd camped out in the past four months. "I can't believe I'm about to say this, but I didn't have a completely horrible time talking to you."

"Wow, Ivy Clarke. With compliments like that, you're going to find your other half in no time."

"Oh, I'm complete all by myself."

"I know," he said, so quietly that I thought I might've imagined it. He took a step toward the table and his most likely perfect date but then abruptly spun around. "By the way, that dress? It's…"

I waited for the insult and got ready to dispatch one of my own.

"…*dangerous*."

With that added emphasis on the word, I wondered if he considered me dangerous, too.

And so I wouldn't go thinking too hard about that and all things Jackson Gamble, I decided it was well past time for me to make my excuse and leave.

Preferably *before* people ended up remembering me as the girl who'd cried through her best friend's engagement party.

Chapter Two

After shoving my pesky and rather inconvenient emotions down as deep as I could, I'd made sure to say good-bye to Savannah and Linc. On my way to wait for the cab I'd called, I spotted Jackson and his date. Blocking my escape route, too.

Thanks for that, Karma.

She was a cute slip of a girl with brunette, shampoo-commercial hair, and I could just tell she was the bubbly type. She even had that debutante look, like she could throw a barbecue in the backyard and then run over and be in a beauty pageant, all without getting her string of pearls dirty.

No wonder his family is already in love with her.

The two of them looked cozy but not on the level of familiarity that implied they were in the comfortable phase of the relationship. With my defenses already crumbling— and okay, maybe I experienced a *tinge* of jealousy—I didn't want to have to force a smile through introductions.

Jackson glanced up, and I quickly spun on my heel and detoured, willingly heading toward Velma.

You know you're in a dire situation when you choose a prim, meddlesome woman over eye contact with a hot guy.

"Ivy, have you met the Halfords' son? He's a therapist."

"Yikes." That was supposed to stay in my head. I wasn't sure if Velma was trying to make a love match or if she thought I was a good candidate for therapy, but I wasn't ready to travel down either of those roads. I'm sure he'd be equally horrified to go on a date with someone who had my issues—if he could find the time to remove his eyes from my cleavage, that is. "I've, uh, got to go."

Velma's glare pinned me in place, her pursed-lip expression making it clear she wasn't impressed with my manners. I swear there was a hint of benevolence in the mix, too, like I was her charity project and should be kissing her feet for introducing me to someone so clearly out of my league.

Hell, eye contact with Jackson couldn't have been *this* uncomfortable.

With a thrown out "Good-night," I made my escape. Since luck was so not on my side tonight, my away-from-Jackson route was now blocked off.

As I passed back by the drink table, I grabbed a glass and downed it, like the classy broad I was. It was much stronger this round, leading me to believe they'd recently added more liquor and hadn't mixed it very well.

Be invisible, be invisible…

My gaze accidentally drifted and locked onto the green eyes I'd been trying to hide from. The emotional turmoil that churned through me made me want to crawl out of my own skin. Concern creased his forehead, and he looked like he might step my way, so I waved good-bye, hoping he understood that meant *Just stay with your cute-pie date, because this hot mess is so out of here.*

Control, control. I need control.

Apparently, the karma gods thought I'd suffered enough, because my cab was pulling up to the curb right as I reached it. I climbed into the back and rattled off my address. We were ITP—or in the perimeter of the 285—but just barely, right on the north edge of Brookhaven, which left me with too much quiet time to think.

I spent my entire childhood, all the way up until the age of eighteen, with very little constant in my life, except that my mom and I would be constantly moving. I couldn't control where we moved or how long her relationships would last with her various boyfriends or temporary husbands or how many times she'd get her heart broken. You'd think after so many failed relationships, there wouldn't be any pieces left to break, but she kept on putting them out there.

That was why I didn't just crave control. I needed it like Kanye West needs attention.

Nowadays, *I* decided where I lived and where I worked, and I was keeping all the pieces of my heart. Except for that piece I foolishly gave out in college, when I thought a guy might be able to give me the steadiness I longed for.

I'd settled into a boring, predictable pattern, though, and I needed something more. Something to give my life a shakeup, yet not so much of one that I felt unsteady and lost the stability I craved. The right balance was hard to find, unfortunately.

"Wait." I shot forward in my seat, and my seat belt yanked me back. Surely, I hadn't seen what I thought I had. "Pull over."

"But the address you gave me is—"

"I know. I need you to pull over here for a minute." I thrust a handful of bills at the driver and then climbed out of the cab.

"You need me to wait?"

I shook my head as an overwhelming sense of desperation

hit me. I hadn't imagined it. There on the front lawn was a FOR SALE sign. My heels clacked out a staccato beat against the sidewalk as I walked toward the Victorian house.

Apparently, *everything* constant in my life was going away, all at the same time.

I walked up the porch and stared at the lockbox on the front door. For a moment, I wondered if the window on the second floor still had the broken lock and missing screen—sneaking in and out of there was a breeze. Anyway, it was when I was a teenager and not in a dress and heels and still experiencing a bit of a buzz from my last few drinks.

I peeked through the window, but with the curtains drawn, I couldn't see anything. From the looks of the outside, the property had been neglected. I'd vaguely noticed whenever I passed by, and I kept wondering what Dixie was planning on doing with it, but I never thought she'd sell her house.

Of all the places I'd lived growing up, this was the only one that ever felt like home. During the times Mom wanted to fully enjoy her honeymoon phase with her new fella—shudder—I was shipped here. When she was between men and mourning her breakup by spending weeks in her pajamas and crying, this was where we settled.

Dixie was Mom's best friend all growing up, and they were as close as sisters.

Until Dixie dared to fall in love with one of Mom's many exes. Dixie tried to reconcile, but Mom never could get over it. Luckily, by that time, I was seventeen and grown enough that I'd only had to endure another year before fleeing to college. That last year was a rough one, where we'd moved to a tiny town in Alabama with her flavor of the year.

I never told Mom that the summer before Dixie got married to Rhett and I started at Georgia State University, I lived with Dixie instead of at the dorms. I even helped her plan and put on her wedding. I was terrified Mom would find out and disown me, but I'd needed an escape. Even when I actually did move into the dorms, I came and visited often, up until Dixie and Rhett moved to Charleston.

I'd always hoped they'd come back and Mom would find it in her heart to forgive and forget.

If Dixie sold this place, that would probably never happen.

I knew it was late and past the polite time to call, but right now it felt like the world was spinning too fast, and I needed some type of closure before I simply let go of my last constant.

But when Dixie answered, her voice filling my ear as I stood on the porch, I knew what I really wanted was to not have to let go.

Chapter Three

When I'd set this appointment, I hadn't factored in my hangover. Honestly, I was embarrassed I even had one with how tame the punch was—all except that very last one—but I think the emotional hangover was making it ten times worse.

I slid my sunglasses up on my head and approached the balding real estate agent. "Thanks for meeting me on such short notice."

"Well, Dixie insisted."

Last night I'd asked her to let me have one final look at the place. She'd told me that she would appreciate that, as she needed to know how much work it would take to clear out after it sold. She'd mailed the keys to the real estate agent and hired a cleaning crew to come in and give it a good scrubbing, but everything that hadn't moved across state lines with her was still inside and needed to be put into storage.

Apparently, she'd barely put it on the market yesterday, and she'd been planning to call and let me know, but she didn't know that Mr. Eager Beaver Real Estate Agent had already put up a sign.

The instant I stepped inside, memories slammed into me from all sides. Of dancing in the living room, blasting music while we cleaned. The scent of habitually burned food that had us throwing open the windows, even when it was winter and freezing, which meant we sometimes ate our dinner while bundled up like Eskimos. Sitting on the floral couch for girlie movies. *The Secrets of the Ya-Ya Sisterhood*, and *Moulin Rouge*, and all the cheesy romances that made my mom decide she needed to keep seeking that kind of love, while driving home my theory that true love only existed in fiction.

With every one of Mom's failed attempts, she unintentionally convinced me to never fall in love.

Of course, I'd slipped that one time, but I figured first loves deserved a pass. The important thing was I'd learned from mine.

After I stripped away the memories that made me love every inch of the place, from the popcorn ceiling with gold flecks on the top to the dilapidated floorboards on the bottom, it was a bit rough. The days of bold, overly floral wallpaper were past, especially if said wallpaper was peeling and faded. The carpet had seen better days—like in the seventies. It'd always been older and well worn, but now there were several threadbare spots.

"It's definitely a fixer-upper," Mr. Real Estate Agent said—I really should've paid better attention to his name. "But the location is prime, and the bones are good."

Does he think I'm looking at the place because I might buy it? I certainly couldn't afford a house in this neighborhood, regardless of the state it was in, and even if I decided to pour my savings into it and forgo luxuries like groceries, what would I do with three bedrooms and a study that moonlighted as a craft room?

The phrases "prime location" and "good bones" bounced

around my head. Thanks to fixing up my condo and my side hobby of repurposing old or beat-up furniture, I'd watched a ton of HGTV. While I was good at finding antiques and turning them into beautiful pieces, my condo was forever a work in progress. Mostly because I always got halfway through painting my living room before deciding I hated the color. It started out beige and had taken turns at being an annoyingly chipper shade of yellow, a shade of blue that served as a tribute to 80s-era eyeshadow, and a misguided maroon that left a splattered smear on the wall when the paint tray fell off the ladder, making it look like I'd brutally murdered someone and decided to forgo hiding the evidence.

Savannah wouldn't stop giving me crap about how my commitment issues even applied to picking a shade of paint, but it was more than that. It was a place that was all mine, and I wanted it to be perfect and to reflect me. I wanted that *permanent home* feel. To finally experience the sense of being settled instead of constantly trying to reassure myself I was.

A house like this wouldn't hold that same pressure. I could fix it up with my knowledge on what worked in the market.

My HGTV training kicked in, my mind spinning over what I'd do if I were fixing up this place to sell. Solid paint colors that would emphasize the Victorian-era style yet with a modern edge. Trim done in white. Hardwood floors…

An idea began to take shape, one that might be crazy. But it also felt like exactly the kind of shakeup I needed in my life.

After all, I'd sanded and refinished every piece of furniture in my condo, along with a handful of pieces I'd sold on Craigslist. I knew how to wield a hammer, power sander, and a giant staple gun, and thanks to my ever-changing living room wall, I had too much experience with a paintbrush. Most of the changes this place needed were the types of things I could do myself.

The more I thought about flipping this house, the more I liked it. I had the marketing know-how. I wasn't scared of hard work. I had a good sense of design, one that came naturally. A huge DIY project like this would be a commitment, but only like a month-long one.

There was something so fulfilling about taking something old and broken and turning it into something amazing.

This would be like my furniture renovations on a much bigger scale. *Like refurbishing on crack.*

Maybe this was my calling—the excitement coursing through me seemed to think so, and if this went well, I could make a career of it. Sprinkle in some inspiration from Joanna Gaines and the chick from *Flip or Flop* and boom, I'd have my own show. *Flopper-Upper.*

Okay, so the name needed to be workshopped, but it had potential.

I was getting way ahead of myself, but the more I thought about it, the more right it felt.

"I'm going to go look upstairs." I put my hand on the wooden banister, and when Mr. Real Estate Agent started up behind me, I added, "Can you give me a few minutes alone?"

He looked like he wanted to argue, as if I might go upstairs and wreck something. It's not like I had a sledgehammer in my purse, and honestly, with the state of this place, I couldn't do much more damage than time had done.

The light fixture over the stairs dangled on a wire, one too-hard step away from crashing down. *That's an easy fix. I've always wanted a reason to shop for that kind of thing.*

Once I was clear of the concussion-inducing light fixture, I charged upstairs and turned down the hall, into the bedroom that had occasionally belonged to me. Dixie had told me I could paint it and make it mine, but we always moved on before I settled on a color and style.

Funny enough, while trying to decide what to do in my condo, I'd known exactly what to do with this room, because that was how projects and procrastination worked.

The walls would get pale aquamarine and white stripes, and the light fixture would be one of those fun flower spheres or something. Too young for me, but not for teenage me.

I sat on the bed, cringing at the squeal of the springs. *That's right, I called these the how-to-get-busted springs.* Once I'd snuck in at two a.m. and jumped from the window to the bed, and Mom and Dixie had come to see what the racket was. They excelled at deductive reasoning and immediately knew I wasn't just all dressed up in the middle of the night for funsies. Then there was the time my high school boyfriend and I were kissing, and the springs alerted Mom that our make-out session had gone horizontal. She came up, interrupted, and made us play *Monopoly* with her and Dixie.

Every inch of this room told a story. Over in front of the full-length mirror was a dark stain from the time I decided to go from blond to brunette—it looked horrible and washed out weird, but I got to feel like a different person for a while. I toed the crusty rainbow puddle of dried nail polish on the carpet to the right of the bed—my case had tipped over and several of the bottles broke. I'd used an entire bottle of remover trying to get the stain out, but it was no use.

Blips of my sporadic life here were scattered about. The mermaid I'd painted in junior high, a plastic champagne glass from prom and the accompanying picture with the very boy who'd been forced into family board-game fun. Not sure why I kept those mementos, because we'd broken up the week before prom but still went together, "as friends," and it was super awkward. Enough so that I'd called Dixie and asked her to come get me from the after-party.

And like always, she was there when I needed her, telling me that someday it'd make a funny story, the way the crappiest of days did. Thinking about it now, it did make me smile. The big gap between us in the picture showed we weren't exactly digging our magical night, but I rocked that strapless red dress.

My eyes skipped to the stack of CDs on the dresser. I stood and scanned the albums, most of which I'd be embarrassed to admit to ever listening to now. I powered on the dust-covered stereo, thinking it wouldn't actually play, but the CD made that whirring noise, and then Jesse McCartney filled the room.

Yikes. Just because I'd had my doubts about long-lasting love, even back then, didn't mean I hadn't understood the allure of a cute male singer with an unnaturally high voice.

I spun in a circle, soaking in the memories.

Ooh, if I was going to fix up this room, I'd build a bookshelf along the short wall. I'd hit my head on the sloping ceiling more than once while retrieving a runaway shoe or earring, and I'd always thought it would make a perfect little reading nook. If I'd had it back in the day, I would've rarely left it. I was the nerdy girl who read not just fiction, but fatty non-fiction novels on whatever subject caught my interest. In my early years, animals—especially big cats like tigers, lions, jaguars, and cheetahs—and anything involving space. Then later, history, biology, and politics.

I majored in political science and, more shiny-eyed than I should've been, got my first job on a campaign. The older, married candidate hit on me again and again, and I tried to walk the right line, shooting him down without compromising my position on his staff. The night he'd cornered me and full-on propositioned me, following up with a threat about ensuring I would never work in politics again, I quit and concluded I'd wasted four years of college.

Of course I'd filed a report in an attempt to prevent him from treating other women the same way. You know, justice and all that jazz.

And of course he pulled enough strings with his good-old-boy contacts that nothing came of it. Well, nothing except for making me sound like a desperate hussy who threw herself at him. After that mess, I got the job at Azure, telling myself I'd tend bar while figuring out what I really wanted to do with my life. At one point, I toyed with running for office myself, but that was a commitment and a half, and I had a tendency to blurt out how I felt, unchecked, which didn't naturally lean toward being politically correct or well-liked. I hadn't completely ruled it out, though. It was in the Maybe Someday column and didn't feel right for the Here and Now one.

The squeak of the springs punctuated my return to the bed. I picked at a loose thread on the comforter as the renovated image of how amazing this bedroom could be overlaid the current one. Maybe it would never be mine, but whoever had it next—my hope was for a strong kick-ass girl who didn't have to deal with crap I had—would appreciate a quiet place to get away from the world.

"Excuse me," the real estate agent called up the stairs. "Are you almost done up there?"

"Almost," I said. Then I dialed up Dixie.

"Hey, sugar. My real estate agent told me that you had an appointment to look at the house this morning. Did you get the closure you needed?"

"Not exactly." I told myself it didn't matter if she said no, but my dampening palms told another story. "I actually have a proposal for you…"

Chapter Four

Water sprayed from the pipes under the downstairs bathroom sink, getting right in my eyes and soaking my shirt.

"Stop, stop, stop," I said over and over again, throwing one hand out to block the steady stream blasting my face—big surprise, the water didn't listen. I twisted the wrench on the part I thought needed tightening as the pipes gave another coughing creak and groan, as if telling me it was all my fault for expecting them to work after years of disuse.

"Oh, you wanna play like that?" I whacked the pipe with the wrench and was rewarded with another gush of water to the face. I scrabbled around on the wet floor, the liquid seeping through the knees of my jeans, and found the shut-off valve behind the toilet. It also complained and resisted doing the one job it had, but I finally managed to stop the flow of water.

Fat droplets clung to the strands of hair that'd come out of my ponytail and then slowly dripped down onto my already damp shirt. I exhausted every swearword I knew as I pushed to my feet and stormed out of the bathroom. Maybe if I let it be for a while, I'd magically know what to do about the leaky pipe and subsequent mess.

So far, the renovation process was going fan-freaking-tastic.

I was wringing out my shirt when a meow caught my attention. I looked down at the sleek black cat with the bright amber eyes. "You again? How the hell do you keep getting in?"

The cat's eyes narrowed to slits, and I swore she was judging me, like she had been every day since Dixie gave me the green light on my house-flipping idea.

What did I get myself into? I'd promised to not only clean out the place but also help Dixie sell it for a lot more, and in return, she'd reimburse me for what I put into it—which was already adding up quickly—and pay me a cut of the profit, which I'd invest in another property if this turned out to be my calling.

Dixie went for it, and I could hear the tears clogging her throat when she confessed she was overwhelmed by what needed to be done and that she couldn't thank me enough for giving her a solution to something she'd been stressing over for months. Finally, I'd be able to pay her back for everything she'd done for me. I'd also gotten a giant lump in my throat during our conversation, since apparently I was turning into an emotional, mushy person and was useless to resist it.

Case in point. This cat. Not Dixie's, not any of the neighbors, either.

"Well?" I asked the cat, because she and I had been talking for a few days now, even though I kept ushering her outside every evening, worried I'd come back to piles of cat poop.

She had the gall to look right back at me and meow like she wasn't doing anything wrong.

"Fine. I *might've* brought some cat food, but then you

really should find a more permanent residence. This one won't be empty for very long."

That was probably wishful thinking, considering I was almost a week into the project and in so far over my head I couldn't even see the surface anymore. Every single thing I tried to fix ended up more broken. Throwing in the towel and saying never mind wasn't an option, either, because in addition to a currently unusable sink, I'd already stripped a significant amount of wallpaper, which didn't come down as easily as the damn YouTube video told me it would. Not to mention the section of carpet I'd pulled up to see if there was hardwood underneath, just waiting to be polished—nope— and then there was the fact that I was too stubborn to give up. All my life my mom had gone back on her word again and again, and I prided myself on doing what I said I would. That was why I didn't make promises to guys I couldn't keep.

I grunted when I squatted down to grab the cat food and the plastic bowl I'd brought from home, well aware that as long as I fed the kitty, she was probably going to keep coming back.

With another grunt, I straightened, my hands going to my lower back.

Thanks to balancing reno stuff during the day and working my closing shift at the bar, I was tired and sore all the time. When Savannah showed up on my doorstep Wednesday night and accused me of skipping our weekly run in the park—which she was extra crazy about with her wedding coming up—I confessed to her what I'd done.

I could still hear her laughter as she'd said, "You're remodeling an entire house? You still haven't settled on a paint color for your living room."

I'd frowned at her, and she obviously read the exhaustion and stress in my features, because then she'd stepped forward and hugged me. "Sorry. I know that house means a lot to you, just like I know you'll do an amazing job fixing it up."

That was the nice thing about best friends. They busted your balls now and then, but they also knew when you needed a hug and some reassurance without your having to explain every little thing. Mostly because she already knew most of it. She'd promised to help however she could, but she'd recently started a new session of her 12 Steps to Mr. Right workshop and was balancing a lot of personal clients as well, so I knew she was drowning in work herself.

I could deal with the messy wallpaper and the painting that would need to be done once I finally got every shred of it down. I could also deal with the cat who Houdini'd her way in every night, despite my checking the house over for signs of entry. What I couldn't deal with was the faulty electricity and how in addition to the pipes making this awful screeching noise like the water had grown attached to them and didn't want to leave, now they were bursting right open. Then there was the attic. I'd opened the door and taken one step inside, only to spot a web that rivaled the one Frodo got entangled in on *The Lord of the Rings*. I'd quickly backtracked and jerked the door closed, deciding the monster spider who lived up there could have that space.

I shuddered and swiped at my shoulders, feeling ghostly spider legs crawling across them.

How had I let myself forget about this house's many problem areas? I'd thought of them as quirks, but I doubted buyers would fondly think of waiting ten minutes for hot water, only to have three-point-five minutes of it, as a quirk.

It's going to need a new hot water heater.

I wasn't delusional enough to think that I could install one myself, but when I'd priced them as well as the installation fee, I started wondering if my bank account could take the repairs.

I'll make it back. And then some.

I glanced down at my renovation cohort. "I don't suppose you know how to install a water heater?"

The kitty meowed, which I took to mean *she* didn't know how, but she knew a witch who could, and then I decided the fumes from the wallpaper remover were eating away my sanity.

Speaking of insane, I'm pretty sure I was beyond delusional when I decided I could do something like this in the first place. I thought of the shows I loved, how they'd flash the horrible before image onscreen and then the magical swipey effect would leave the new and shiny room in its place, making the transformation even more impressive. It always gave me a bit of a contact high.

I wanted that magical after. I wanted the high firsthand.

While I would love for it to be as easy as a magical swipe, I'd learned long ago that simply wishing didn't do any good, so it was time to get back to work.

Bonus, my clothes were nearly dry. Since I still wasn't ready to deal with the bathroom—that would probably take Google, YouTube, and some kind of ritualistic chanting involving mostly swearwords—I surveyed the kitchen, wondering whether to resume stripping off the wallpaper in here or the living room.

I frowned at the noise coming from underneath the sink. *Oh, no. Not another leaky pipe. I didn't even use the water in here today.*

Cautiously, I approached, registering it was different from the usual complaining pipe noise, more thumping than creaking. I flung open the cupboard and let loose a scream as a mouse darted out.

It skittered across the floor.

"Get it, get it," I yelled to the cat. She glanced at it, then turned to her food and continued to chow down. "Really?"

Looked like I was going to have to pick up a mouse

trap, because my temporary cat was now spoiled on food I'd brought her. She was pretty fat, too, which made me wonder if I wasn't the only one feeding her.

I went to close the cabinet door but caught movement. In a wad of newspaper, insulation, and other substances I couldn't quite make out were squirmy, pink, hairless mice. "I so didn't sign up for this." I turned to the cat. "You're not getting any food until you eat those."

She simply stared back at me, like she knew I'd cave.

I leaned on the counter opposite the mice nest, and as if to spite me, the island creaked under my weight.

Sick of trying to be optimistic, I called Savannah. "So, um, I'm having a meltdown."

"Oh, no. What's wrong?" she asked.

"It'd be shorter to tell you what's *not* wrong when it comes to this house. I'm pretty sure the electricity is going to give out any second, and I've got at least one leaky pipe that I made worse instead of better, because that's the kind of luck and skill I have. The wallpaper won't come off the walls no matter what I try, so it looks like Freddy Krueger visited and left his mark, and I just found a nest of baby mice. We're talking the disgusting kind with beady black eyes that look like embryos who need longer in the womb."

"You're not really making me want to rush right over," Savannah said, her voice on the teasing side. "Spoiler alert, I'm not good at dealing with critters."

"Okay, so I'll call Linc. How's he with plumbing and electricity repair?"

"Linc's out of town this week, and I'm pretty sure both of those things are beyond his skillset anyway. But you know who *would* be good at knowing exactly what to do? Like so good you'd think he even did it for a living?"

Jackson's face flashed before my eyes. It wasn't like I hadn't thought about the fact that he'd know what to do and how to fix everything, but I'd called him for help once and that was when lines got crossed and tangled, and I wasn't going there again. "Don't say it."

"Call Jackson."

I groaned and sagged against the nearest splotchy wall. "No, I got this. I mean, HGTV is a freaking liar who brainwashed me into thinking I could do it, so I just need to lower my expectations and realize I can't be as fast as a team of people." I also didn't have the resources or the experience, but thinking about that might give me a panic attack, so I was going to pretend those problems didn't exist. Like a grown-up.

"Ivy, come on. I thought you guys kind of made up or whatever."

"We called a truce for one night, and it was super touch and go."

"Are you ever going to tell me what exactly happened between you two? It's always been rocky, but it's definitely reached a whole new level in the past few months."

"Nothing happened," I automatically said, almost wishing it was true—it was the almost that stopped me from calling him more than anything. I couldn't trust my emotions or my memory reel around him, and I couldn't put myself in that situation, especially right now, when I felt so raw and vulnerable about life in general. "We just clash on every level, and I sometimes dream about strangling him with his own self-righteousness. And the feeling is mutual."

"Mm-hm. It would be easier if you guys could get along at least until after my wedding."

Another point for not calling him. He and I had two settings—crazy attraction and crazy irritation, and once either of those blew up in our faces, it'd make it harder to get along during the rest of the wedding festivities. Since I couldn't explain that to Savannah, I simply told her I should get going.

"I'll be over after my appointments to help however I can," she said. "Until then, will you at least think about calling Jackson?"

"Fine." Thought about it and rejected it. I said good-bye and attacked the kitchen wallpaper with renewed fervor.

About thirty minutes in, I peeled away a large section only to find it was covering a significant hole with wires, some of which weren't connected to anything. I wondered if electricity still flowed through them, but since my hair was naturally crimpy enough and I didn't think my insides would be improved by a little frying, I stayed clear.

I'll deal with that *later.* A lot of things were being put off for the mythical time when I suddenly knew how to fix them, which meant it'd all catch up with me, but I'd also worry about that later. Later was really going to suck.

Chimes rang out, and I froze, wondering if the fumes were making me hear things. When I strained my ears, I heard the scratching of baby mice in their home under the sink, and logic told me that since that was real, I wasn't, in fact, hearing things.

The several knocks that followed confirmed it. As I exited the kitchen, I checked the time. Savannah said she'd be tied up with work for a couple more hours at least, but maybe someone canceled. Or maybe a neighbor was coming to complain about the noise or tell me I'd catnapped their pet.

As soon as I swung open the door, I knew it was Savannah. Not *her* in the flesh, but her doing for sure. Her brother stood on the other side of the rickety screen door, scruff in full force, clothes deliciously dirty, toolbox in hand.

"Heard Ivy Clarke found herself in need of some help, and I thought now that's something I've gotta see for myself."

Chapter Five

I was going to kill my best friend. In fact, I was even reconsidering her title.

I crossed my arms. "Actually, I've got everything covered, so I'm sorry to say you've been misinformed."

"Mm-hm." Jackson barged right in, his big body brushing mine as he stepped inside. I smoothed a hand down my hair, painfully aware that I looked like a mess, and I wasn't even sure it was a hot one.

Not that I cared. I was plenty confident and had no trouble snagging men's attention, so I couldn't care less what Jackson "Overinflated Ego" Gamble thought about me. He'd already seen me in pretty much every stage anyway, everything from post-workout to glammed up, including a few times when I'd been wearing nothing at all. Plastered by water from a broken pipe might be a new, slightly more disheveled low, but I was a what-you-see-is-what-you-get girl.

"I know that words aren't your strong suit," I said, speaking loud and slow, because I knew it drove him crazy when I talked to him like a simpleton, "but 'I've got everything covered' actually means don't barge in here like some gorilla with a toolbox."

A muscle flexed in his cheek, but he just kept on surveying the living room, taking in the mostly stripped walls and messy carpet. Then, without a word, he headed toward the kitchen. He set his toolbox on the counter and spun a circle, his eyebrows crinkling then smoothing as he muttered under his breath. He stepped toward the wire-filled hole I'd unearthed.

"Where's the breaker box?"

"Um…It's…" My eyes bounced around the room, like I'd find clues taped to the walls.

A smug grin spread across his lips as he turned to face me, clearly proud he had something to hold over me. "You don't know, do you?"

"Not yet, but I can find it."

"I'm sure you can." His large frame loomed over me. "But I'm not so sure that you wouldn't claim the electricity was off when it was actually still on so that I'd get a nice jolt when I grabbed hold of one of those wires."

"Well, now that you've given me the idea, it does sound like a rather fun time."

"See." He tapped the side of my head, and I smacked his hand away. "I know how your twisted mind works."

"Oh, there's plenty you don't know about me and the way my mind works. So anyway, thank you for coming, but as I explained to your sister, I've got this." I nudged him toward the open archway that led into the living room. "I was just about to call an exterminator for the mice infestation, and—"

"Where did you see the mice?" he asked, dragging his feet and making it impossible to move him.

"One's running free after bolting out from under the sink, where she left her bald babies. I'm assuming she'll come back for them, but maybe she'll just leave them to fend for themselves. I haven't looked up how strong mice's maternal bond is yet."

That made the smile spread farther across his face.

"Research isn't amusing," I said, even though I knew he was far more amused by the mess I was dealing with and how flustered it—as well as his being here—was making me.

"It is when you're doing it." He gestured toward the sink. "They're under there?"

I nodded, and he opened the cupboard door and took a quick peek. Obviously, he wasn't icked out by them, because he also squatted and wiggled the pipes above their little bug-eyed heads. "This is loose, and I guarantee you need a new garbage disposal. This one looks like it might bust open any minute and send everything left inside to ruin the bottom of the cabinet."

"Not that I want that to happen," I said, "but I think I'm going to replace the cabinets anyway."

"What about the floors?"

I shrugged. It irked me that I'd failed to get a reaction by calling him a gorilla and talking to him extra slow, whereas his questions were making me feel stupider by the minute. "I haven't run the numbers."

He straightened and looked across the room at me, his steady green gaze boring into me.

My defenses prickled. "What?"

"What on earth are you doing here, Ivy? I'd ask if you're out of your mind, but I already know that you are."

"I'm going to flip this house." I paced across the room, nearly biting my fingernail before realizing that with the kind of work I'd been doing I didn't want to have that anywhere near my mouth. "Look, I know it might seem like I don't know what I'm doing, but I…" Panic rose, and breathing grew more difficult. "I do." There. That almost sounded convincing.

Jackson tipped his head, not buying it.

Yes, I'd had a moment of weakness when I'd called Savannah, but then I'd made some minor progress. "I can take out a loan, and I can do a lot of it myself. I'll hire out. It might take longer than I first thought, but I'm no quitter."

I ignored the low, doubtful sound he made in the back of his throat. I was going to finish this job if it killed me—and at this point, I wasn't all that sure that was the metaphorical kind of killing, either. But I didn't want to let down Dixie, and more than that, I needed to know I could do this. I'd quit my one other attempt at a serious career, and while I'd had my reasons, I should've attempted another job in that field. Back then I'd wanted to be in control, and right now I wanted to be in control *and* follow through.

I did pick up another rule when I started regretting my decision to quit over one skeezy politician.

Way #2*: Dreams over dudes. Never let a guy get in the way of your dreams. Pursue your own path, for one day you'll find yourself walking alone, and you should at least like where you're going.*

I'd seen my mom give up jobs, hobbies, where she wanted to live, and a slew of other things—time with me, for one—to make men happy. I'd seen them talk her out of projects she wanted to do, and I'd seen her believe guys when they told her she couldn't do something. I'd watched them crush her dreams until she didn't even seem to know what hers were.

At least Jackson hadn't outright told me I couldn't tackle this project, even if he might be (most definitely was) thinking it. "You don't have to understand, and I'd rather not hear that I'm in over my head, because I'm well aware, but I'm nothing if not determined, and if it takes every penny I have and every ounce of stubbornness and energy, I'll flip this house."

Jackson sighed and rubbed a hand along his jaw as he took another glance at the mess that was the kitchen. Then he turned back to me. "There's no reason for you to use up every penny you have, and you definitely have enough stubbornness to spare, but maybe hold it back for one little minute while I suggest something…"

I opened my mouth, and he arched an eyebrow, like he was challenging me to make it that one little minute. "Fine. You've got one minute."

"I'm actually finishing up a project, and my crew can handle most of it. I don't have another big one scheduled for a little over a month, and I was wondering what I was going to do with all my spare time. If you're open to an arrangement, I could…help you out."

Taking him up on the offer called to me, despite his obvious hesitance, but I was worried about attached-strings and crossed-lines. Then again, I was also worried about failing and messing up badly enough it ended up costing Dixie and me our life savings, which made me circle back around to wanting to say yes. "I'm not looking for a handout."

"And I'm sure as hell not offering one. I'd expect to be paid for my time and services, but I'll give you the family discount. I can promise you that I'll do it for less than any other contractor in the area, just like I can assure you that you need one. Ivy, this is a huge job. This isn't like those TV shows where they show you the before image, fail to show you how many people it takes to do the work, and then reveal the final shiny project. This house needs a lot of work."

My cheeks flushed at the mention of the TV shows that'd instilled me with too much false confidence in my abilities. Add that to their sins of lying and brainwashing. I needed the team of people, and Jackson practically counted as a team himself. "I'll admit it sounds like a good deal…"

"But?"

"*But* you and me working together? Wouldn't your family miss you if I killed you?"

"You're forgetting something…" He took a few long strides toward me, and I nearly backed up like a frightened little rabbit. Probably because there was a gleam in his eye that did seem almost predatory.

Or maybe those fumes were getting to me again. I lifted my chin, working to find the feisty attitude that usually kept me safe. "What's that?"

He braced a hand on the wall by the side of my head and leaned in, so close I could feel the heat radiating off his body. "Aunt Velma would avenge me."

A laugh slipped out, and then I mocked fear. I even grabbed hold of his shirt. "*Please*, Jackson. Please don't tell her I said that. I'll do anything! Even…" I made a big show of gulping. "Work with you."

"Without killing me?"

I acted like it was the hardest decision I'd ever made and let out a huge exhale. "Jeez, that's asking a whole lot. I'm going to have to think about it." I bit my lip. "And let's say I was thinking about it. What kind of terms are we talking?"

Jackson glanced around, his gaze back to assessing. "I need to take a look at the rest of the house, and then we'll discuss the nitty gritty details over dinner."

"Dinner?"

"Yeah, you know. Food that's typically eaten around this time of day. Especially if someone worked a long, physically grueling day only to give in to his sister's beck and call and come see what kind of mess her best friend had gotten herself into. You're probably already full from all the guys' souls you've been devouring, but I need to eat actual food."

I rolled my eyes at the succubus slam and slipped out of the cozy little pocket his body had formed. I needed as much air as I could get, especially if I was going to suppress the temptation to strangle him. "Well, I certainly can't subsist on the kind of vapid girls you go for—I'd starve."

"Ooh, that was a pretty good insult before you were one of them, but now it's a little self-deprecating for my taste. Sorta takes the fun out of my job."

I clenched my jaw so hard I thought I'd crack a molar. Clearly our temporary truce had expired, our war back on. But he could go ahead and bring it, because it'd take a lot more than a few jabs to make me wave the white flag. "Fine. Let's order dinner. Your treat since you're applying for the job."

"You're shit at saying thank you, Ivy Clarke."

Oh, I knew. I also knew us working together had disaster written all over it.

Watching him get hot and sweaty as he did all that manual labor? Fighting off sexual frustration as my ovaries did their best not to implode?

Arguments around every corner, ones we'd have while armed with tools like hammers and crowbars…?

Yep, it was going to be a disaster.

But I was smart enough to realize that at this point, it was also my only choice if I wanted to fulfill my promise to Dixie and to actually make a profit for my efforts. In a way, not letting Jackson help would be another way of letting my feelings about a guy get in the way of my dreams.

So disaster or not, here I come.

Chapter Six

During last night's dinner, Jackson and I played twenty questions, where they were all about the house and my vision for it, and by the end, it was probably more like forty questions. We also played twenty jabs and argued about what the most important features of the house were, but somewhere in the mix of all that, we formed a plan and a rather ambitious time table—six weeks, which was when his next job started. He was going to work up a budget as well (I was big enough to admit that he was better with numbers, but not like to his face or anything), and that in and of itself allowed me to relax and get a good night's rest. After my shift at the bar, of course.

I pulled my car up to the house and killed the engine, telling myself that today was a new day and I had backup now, so I was going to take the bull by the horns and tackle this renovation. Laying it out day by day, one project at a time, made it feel less overwhelming.

My step was even a bit lighter as I walked toward the house.

My black kitty greeted me, and like the sucker I was, I

headed to the kitchen and filled her food bowl. I petted her as she dove in. "I can't believe I'm feeding you even though you didn't take care of the mice for me. Isn't that the whole benefit of having a cat?"

Jackson had texted while I was working last night and told me the critter problem was taken care of. And I'd had this moment where I felt kind of bad for the baby mice, so I focused on the diseases they carried and how an infestation would hurt the resale value. I'd been so grateful that I even texted Jackson a thank you, all caps and *three* exclamation marks. What can I say? It was easier in text form.

He didn't reply with shock and awe like I'd expected him to, but no doubt I'd get teased about it when he came over later. My task for the day was to finish peeling the wallpaper off the walls of the bottom floor using the steamer Jackson had left for me, and this afternoon he was going to tackle the electricity and the rest of the plumbing if he had time, since he'd already fixed the leak in the downstairs bathroom. That was the other nice thing about the schedule we'd worked up—he left a bit of wiggle room for the bigger jobs, even though we didn't have much to spare.

By the time he showed up, I was pulling the last few stubborn strips down. I glanced over my shoulder at him. "I hate wallpaper with the fire of a thousand suns, in case you were wondering."

"Wouldn't you know it? I was up all night pondering that very thing." Jackson studied me like he was waiting for something—possibly for me to throw stuff at his head. Then he slowly lifted a white bag. "Figured you'd be hungry."

I wanted to wave it off, but my stomach growled as the scent of fried goodness filled the air, making it hard to claim I wasn't.

"I also figured keeping you well-fed would increase my odds of survival."

"Or maybe it'll give me just enough energy to kill you."

He shrugged. "I'll risk it."

He sat on the floral couch, one of the few pieces of furniture left behind, and you could tell the space had been mainly occupied by females because he looked utterly out of place on it.

"What?" he asked around a handful of fries.

"Nothing." I pulled my burger out of the bag he handed me and dug in. A moan accidentally escaped my lips, and considering the attention it brought on from Jackson, I was going to have to be more careful about making those kinds of noises. No matter how much my traitorous body enjoyed his body, I was never crossing that line again. I'd learned my lesson, thank-you-very-much. "Um, thanks for the food—I owe you, though. You paid for dinner last night."

"You can put it on my tab." He looked like he was fighting back a smile.

"What?"

"Two thank yous in two days. The fumes must really be getting to you."

I tossed a fry at his head. "They must be."

We scarfed down the food and wiped our fingers on napkins. I crumpled mine into a ball and flung it aside. "Do you want a Cherry Coke? I have a case in the fridge."

"I would *love* one." His grin was a bit maniacal and made unease dance across my skin.

"Oh-kay." I glanced back at him one more time before I stepped into the kitchen, but he was just cleaning up the bags of food. Guess I just didn't know how to react when he treated me civilly.

Shaking my head at myself, I pulled open the fridge door, my gaze still hovering behind me as I reached inside. My fingers wrapped around something fuzzy, and I whipped my head forward.

I let out a scream as my eyes locked onto the dead mouse. I jumped back, shaking my hand like that would make the icky sensation traveling up my arm go away.

Jackson's deep laugh drifted toward me, and I whirred around to find him leaning against the curve of the archway. "You wanted to keep the mama mouse as a trophy, right?"

I clenched my fists. "I'm going to murder you. And the judge will let me off for extenuating circumstances."

"I don't know. I think he'll find it funny."

"Oh, so you just assume the judge will be male?"

"I assume that most judges will find it funny. Are you saying you want preferential treatment because you're a female?"

I shook my head, and Jackson obviously didn't understand how much I wanted to wrap my hands around his throat, because he approached me instead of running away.

"I'll grab my own Coke." He reached around me, wrapping his hand around one of the cans. "I suddenly don't trust you not to spit in it or poison it."

"Both brilliant options." I threw my elbow back, catching him in the gut. His grunt sent satisfaction through me.

He picked up the mouse by the tail, and I ducked around the open fridge door, using it like a shield.

"So help me God, if you—"

"Relax," he said. "I'll give her a proper burial."

I packed as much wistfulness into my voice as I could. "Someday I'll say the same thing about you after I've dragged your dead body into the woods."

"Until then," Jackson said, tipping an imaginary hat and then taking the mouse out the back door.

I washed my hands and then retrieved a cold can and wiped it and the shelf off for good measure. I took a large swig, letting the fizzy bubbles course through me. "Agreeing to work with him is the dumbest thing I've ever done, even dumber than that time I drank my bodyweight in beer and then rode a mechanical bull."

The door swung open, and Jackson stepped back inside, sans mouse but with the same annoying grin on his face. "Did you say something?"

"Let's just get to work so we can get this over with as soon as possible." I left him to the kitchen and moved on to the baseboards in the living room that were so old that they'd become one with the walls and didn't want to leave. The multiple layers of paint acted as glue, and the wood was old enough that it often split in several pieces. I almost wished for wallpaper-stripping work again.

"Stripping work," I muttered with a laugh. *If this becomes a permanent gig and people ask me what I do for a living, I can say that I'm a stripper, and it'll make them so uncomfortable and be super entertaining for me.*

About an hour in, Jackson called out to me, asking if I could "come here for a quick sec."

"I don't know," I called back. "Last time I went in there, it didn't go so well, and I'm not in the mood for another prank."

His sigh carried through the walls. "No pranks. I just don't have enough hands for this job, and if you want the electricity fully functional, you're gonna need to get your ass in here and give me a hand."

With a sigh of my own, I left my tools on the floor, forced my cramped legs into motion, and walked into the kitchen.

"Hold this." He lifted pliers that were pinched around the bundle of wires I'd unearthed yesterday. "The wires don't have much give. I can't quite keep 'em all in place, and I'm having trouble getting hold of a wire that slipped down in the hole."

I eyed the tangled mess. "You can see where I'd be hesitant, considering you mentioned electrocution yesterday."

Making a big show of it, he touched the ends of several

wires. "I shut off the power. Thus no lights, and if we don't get them on soon, it's going to get dark in here fast." As soon as I took the rubber-gripped pliers from him, he added, "Besides, I'm saving electrocuting you until *after* I get paid."

"Ha-ha."

He started around me one way, then moved the other. I tried to flatten myself as much as I could. "Sorry. I just..." Jackson wrapped his arms around me—no, not around me, but one was on either side, and as he wiggled the wires, the firm planes of his chest pressed into my shoulder.

The tip of his tongue came out as he fiddled with the bundle, giving him a boyish edge that made my stupid heart flutter.

"There." His gaze dipped to mine, and the air changed, suddenly thicker and higher-charged than the electricity not currently running through the wires I was holding on to.

I cleared my throat, silently cursing my sexual drought and how on edge it'd left me. "So I can let go?"

He nodded.

I stepped aside and watched him fiddle with the wires, then rubbed a hand on the side of my neck. "Do you need me for anything else?"

He glanced back at me, eyebrows raised, and I cursed myself for phrasing the question that way. I held my ground, though, daring him to make an innuendo out of it—or daring him not to, I wasn't really sure.

He twisted some kind of cap on the bundle and dropped it into the hole in the wall. "Come with me to the basement and I'll show you the breaker box so you can see how to turn it off and on and what to do if you blow a breaker when I'm not here."

"A please wouldn't kill you now and then, you know. I'm not one of your employees."

He ran a hand through his hair, his muscles tight with

tension. "*Please* let me show you how this house works, since *you'll* be the one here most of the time, and it could come in handy for *you*."

This time I was the one who plastered on a maniacal grin. "You're welcome that I'm letting you demonstrate your handyman skills."

He tipped up his head to the heavens like he was asking for strength. Then he whipped a tiny flashlight out of his tool belt and extended it to me.

"Look at you with your cute little tool belt, all ready for action."

"Oh, I'm always ready for action." He nudged me toward the basement door, and he wasn't exactly gentle about it. I opened the door and hesitated at the threshold. Like in the attic, the darkness was so heavy it pressed against my skin. Or maybe that was the chilly air coming from the unheated space, but either way, the tiny beam of light didn't do enough to assure me that I wouldn't encounter a spider infestation or barrage of any other disgusting critters that liked deep, dark places. My logical side knew that I was bigger than spiders and they should be more afraid of me than me of them, but that didn't stop me from fearing the eight-legged creatures of doom.

"You go first," I said, extending the flashlight back to him.

"Afraid there are monsters in the basement?" he teased, his fingers curling around mine as he took the flashlight out of my hand. "Or that there's a serial killer who's bided his time for years, just hoping someone would wander down?"

I considered telling him yes and that I was far more willing to sacrifice his life than mine, but I figured we'd done enough endangerment jabs today. "Spiders, okay? So I'm going to use you as a shield against the webs."

"You realize I've already been down here once today.

Plus, the spiderwebs will drape over me and crawl down my back, right onto you."

I shoved him, repressing a shiver. "Ugh, stop it. You're making it worse."

"Careful, woman." He dramatically gripped the doorframe. "You're about to shove me down a rickety wooden flight of stairs."

"Call me woman again and I'll go ahead and do it."

"Okay, dude," he said, taking the first step into the dim, stuffy-smelling basement.

I shoved him again, making it on the barely-qualifies-as-a-shove side so he wouldn't lose his balance for real.

He chuckled. "Okay, nonentity."

"Better."

The farther we descended into the depths of the basement, the heavier the darkness became. I'd tried to keep a few inches between us, but now I crouched closer, using Jackson like a shield, my fingers curling into his T-shirt.

At the foot of the stairs he turned, and since I wasn't expecting it, I bumped into him. I gripped his biceps for a moment so I wouldn't fall, then quickly let go when the urge to hang on for a while filled me.

"Okay, so here are all the breakers," he said. "If you blow one, it's usually red."

Something about being in the mostly dark heightened my senses. His voice sounded deeper and my heart beat harder. I moved closer, partly because I was still thinking about spiders, but mostly because I could feel the warmth coming off his body and it was cold down here.

Yeah. For survival purposes. No southern girl could survive when the temperature dropped below sixty degrees, so why should I be any different?

He flipped the large switch on top, turning the electricity back on, but the only light in the basement was a bare bulb with a tiny string hanging down. It highlighted Jackson's hair and how much taller and bulkier he was.

"I think we're good to go," he said.

"Awesome."

"What on earth possessed you to take on a huge project like this, anyway? Seems like a bigger commitment than your norm."

I tilted my head. "It's like you never want me to stop shoving you." I kicked at the dirty floor with my tennis shoe. Last night I'd danced around the topic a bit, guiding the conversation to home repair facts and figures. I didn't want him to think I'd been driven by emotions, because I prided myself on the fact that I usually wasn't. "I just thought it was something I might be good at. Turns out I'm probably wrong, but I'm going to see it through anyway."

When I went to turn around and head back upstairs, he stopped me with a hand on my arm. "Why this house?" Of all the things he could've followed up with, for some reason I hadn't expected that, and it threw me off. "I know that once you set your mind to something, it's just about impossible to change it…"

I wondered if that was another jab at my fear of commitment. Toward the end of our amazing nights together, he'd said something about how maybe things could be different with us. That maybe two commitaphobes could make a right. Or a couple. Anyway, it was enough for me to know that I had to cut it off.

Not to mention that I knew fear of commitment wasn't why he hadn't settled down yet, and several of my rules had been waving at me in the rearview mirror, dragging my safety net along with them. So I'd shut it down, and when he didn't simply give up like I'd expected, I'd pushed even harder. Things spun out of control, anger overtaking everything else and turning to hate so quickly.

We'd hurt each other, which was what I'd been trying so hard to avoid. It just proved that once certain lines were crossed, you couldn't avoid it, and the experience left me that much more determined to never cross them with anyone again.

"Last night, when you said that you didn't want to do anything differently structurally but to keep the classic style while throwing in modern touches, I could tell this house means something more to you. More than just an opportunity to flip a house and make some money, the way you implied."

"You caught me," I said. "I guess…" The dim lighting made it easier, even if my spider paranoia was also kicking into high gear—I shuffled a few extra inches away from the wall. "Well, I guess you could say this is the closest place to home I had growing up. You know enough about my mom…"

That was another landmine subject. In a way, she was also the reason I'd not just come close to breaking my rules with Jackson, but to full-on breaking one of my biggest ones with him.

Way #3: Never rely on a guy too much. They're not life preservers. One day you'll jump only to find he's not there anymore, and then it'll feel like you're drowning without him.

The truth was, I'd broke more than one when it came to Jackson, but that was the realization that'd scared the crap out of me and shook me the hardest. I couldn't go back to that. Couldn't wait for him to pull the rug out from under me one day and be weaker for it. As I'd realized the other night at the engagement party, even just being friends with Savannah had left me weaker than I wanted to be.

That's a bad path to go down right now. Focus on answering his question.

"Anyway, whenever my mom was sick of me or needed

space or when her relationships fell apart, we came here. Dixie was practically my aunt, but she was like that cool aunt who has loud parties, lets you play hooky from school, and listens as you pour out your secrets, then tells you exactly what you need to hear."

A mixture of yearning and longing tightened my lungs. I remembered learning to bake in the kitchen upstairs while we blasted music, even though with Dixie, it was like the blind leading the blind. Funny enough, she was also who taught me to mix drinks, and she was a master at those.

"She and my mom had a falling out," I said, "and honestly, if my mom finds out that I've so much as stepped foot in this house, much less committed to fixing it up…" I shuddered at the thought. Mom was a master of using guilt and a sense of betrayal as weapons, and despite being aware of that, they still pierced the armor I wore around her, every single time. It was one of the reasons I hadn't kept in touch with Dixie—and even Rhett—like I wanted to. "I'm not sure she'd ever forgive me."

I looked up to find Jackson's eyes on me. It threw my senses out of whack, but then they immediately calmed, making it easier to continue. "But when I found out Dixie was selling the place, I just wanted to give it a proper good-bye and for it to be the house I loved instead of a rundown shack someone snagged for a steal. After everything she helped me with through the years, I also hoped I could make Dixie some extra money in the process."

Jackson blinked down at me, his expression unreadable in the dim light. Not that light would help much, because after everything went down, he always had his poker face on standby. Not that I blamed him. I deserved to be locked out.

I ran a hand through my hair, breaking eye contact so I wouldn't start thinking about that too much. "Before I come out sounding all magnanimous, I also wanted something that was mine. These days, I'm looking for something a little more fulfilling than bar tending. In my professional life," I quickly added, not leaving any room for him to go thinking that I'd change my mind about my personal life.

At this point, he probably wouldn't even care or give me another chance at…well, at more. Especially if he was still dating that super cute, bubbly girl he'd brought to Savannah and Linc's engagement party.

I was sick of telling myself it was for the best—I sounded like a stuck record—but it didn't make it less true.

The scuff of his shoes and press of his hand on my hip meant he'd stepped closer, but I didn't dare look into his face. It felt like my thoughts were written across mine, and dark or not, I was afraid he'd see them plain as day. Yet another reason that he was more dangerous than most guys.

"I get that," he said. "Wanting to do something bigger. Wanting to say good-bye to a place that meant something to you. You know that this is an impossibly huge job for one person, right?"

I shrugged. "I guess I thought that it might be for most people but that I was different from most people."

His low laugh stirred my hair. "You are definitely different from most people. What I'm saying is that needing help doesn't mean you were wrong about being good at this. You've got great ideas and enough stubborn to fuel a job this big, for sure." He nudged me with his elbow, a grin curving his lips. "We'll get everything fixed up the way you envision it, and I guarantee the house will sell for a lot more once we're finished."

My heart quickened at the *we'll* and the *we're*, half excitement, half fear. "Yesterday I realized I was in way over my head. I told myself it'd all be okay after our meeting, but today it feels like I've bitten off more than I can chew again. Plus, I'm starting to freak out about still being down in the possibly-spider-infested basement. How am I supposed to do it all, especially when there are two areas of the house that I'm afraid of?"

"That's why I'm here." He straightened and thumped a fist against his chest like the gorilla I'd accused him of being. "I fear nothing."

I laughed.

"Come on, let's get upstairs."

"Oh, thank goodness." Past playing it cool, I rushed upstairs, taking a big breath once I hit the landing. From this spot, I could see the mess of the kitchen to my left and the deconstructed living room to my right, and the exhaustion hit me, all at once.

"Did I ever tell you about my first job after breaking out on my own?" Jackson asked from behind me, placing his hands on my shoulders.

I shook my head and fought the irrational urge to lean back into his embrace—my body always managed to forget he was my bitter rival, which only proved doing this renovation together wasn't my brightest idea ever. But you know, beggars couldn't be choosers and all that.

Except a tiny part of me knew I'd choose him over a hundred other contractors, every time.

"Total disaster," he said. "Everything that could go wrong did. Permits, faulty wiring. The wrong order of lumber delivered. Since you can't exactly build a house without the framework, it set us an extra two weeks behind schedule. The clients were so pissed, and of course when fingers got pointed, they got pointed at me. One night after an especially hard day, I decided that starting my own business was the stupidest thing I'd ever done."

I spun around to face him. "So you're saying this project isn't the biggest disaster ever?"

"I...wouldn't go that far." He shot me a teasing grin. "I'm

saying that job didn't mean I wasn't good at building houses. I'm the best contractor out there—"

"And so humble, too."

"Right?" He reached up and braced his hands on the top of the doorframe, the muscles in his arms flexing in the most hypnotic way. "But there's a part of every single job that goes wrong. You're just getting your bumps out at the beginning."

"I'd say thanks, but I don't want to see the shock on your face and have to shove you down the stairs. You'd be no good to me with a broken leg."

"I want to say you'd be surprised what I can do without use of one leg, but I'm afraid you'd take it as a challenge." He stepped into the small hallway, closing the door behind him and holding it shut, like that'd keep him safe from me.

Right now, with the way he was staring at me, a cocky slant to lips that had traveled over most of the curves of my body, I was thinking I needed a door to hide behind so *I'd* be safe. One minute he was pranking me and we were tossing insults back and forth, and the next he was trying to reassure me and throwing out innuendos. The guy was an enigma wrapped in an eye-candy package, and if I wasn't careful, I'd slip and forget all about my carefully structured broken-heart prevention plan.

Chapter Seven

A meow accompanied the black cat who slowly came around the corner, dodging bags of trash and debris.

"There you are," I said, dropping the scraper-thing-a-ma-bobber I'd been using to remove baseboards.

Jackson stopped the hammering I may have been watching a little too closely this afternoon, thanks to the way it brought out the muscles in his back and arms, and looked over his shoulder. His eyebrows drew together. "You have a cat?"

"Don't sound so surprised. I mean, technically she's not *mine*, but she seems to have come with the house, and I'm considering her mine for right now, so you can hold back your commitment jab."

"I'm not going near that giant landmine. I prefer my guts inside my body, and since the reason I'm so surprised has to do with you not being the particularly nurturing type, I have no doubt you'd let me bleed out if I set it off."

"'Holding back' means not saying things like that, FYI. We've really got to work on your vocabulary."

"Sorry, can't hear whatever you're rattlin' on about over the sound of how hard I'm working," he said as he resumed his hammering on the archway that connected the living room to the dining room. It used to be a narrow, stubby archway but he'd widened and heightened it, and it opened up the entire space and made it look a lot bigger. If he could go more than an hour without saying something insulting, I might even tell him how much I liked it.

I suspected the people in Hell would be shivering and asking for jackets first.

Over the past five days, I'd been trying to work in the rooms he wasn't in, but somehow the only baseboards that needed removed were in this one, and to be honest, I didn't really know how to do anything else. I had too much pride to ask Jackson, so I had to YouTube each new project I took on, and after fighting with the fireplace in the living room for two long days—another thing the *Property Brothers* didn't properly prepare me for, by the way, *in spite of* being really good at "picturing the possibilities"—I was back to baseboard removal.

I hadn't seen the cat for a few days—and only after Jackson had left for the day—but the food I'd left in the kitchen was always gone, and I was trying out optimism and telling myself it was her, not mice or raccoons or some other horrible critter. "Jeez, you must be finding the food I'm leaving, because you're getting kind of fat. No offense," I added as I scratched between her ears.

The tap of the hammer slowed, and Jackson cast another glance our way. "I think that cat is pregnant." He pointed at her with his hammer. "She's really just fat in the stomach area, and the way it bulges out fits that diagnosis."

"How do you know what a pregnant kitty looks like?"

He folded his arms across the top of the ladder. "When I was a kid, I had a cat that got pregnant. I thought she was just fat, too, but then she had kittens in the corner of the dining room. Mom was not so happy about that."

I laughed, imagining that did cause quite the stir at Casa De Gamble. "It was your cat?"

"Men can have cats, too, okay?"

I held up my hands, like I was giving up, but I was far from it. "I guess I just thought of you as more of a dog person. I picture you having one that drools and grunts a lot to help make you feel right at home." Okay, so maybe it was my slightly sexist idea that cats were more of a pet for lonely women. Considering I'd recently decided to claim one as my own, I wasn't sure I wanted to hold on to that theory, either.

"And most witches own cats, so it makes sense that you have one."

My smile turned to glass, the better for cutting him with. "Watch what you say, because I've got a potion brewing in the basement as we speak."

Jackson smiled right back, his grin even bigger, since apparently even that was a competition. "Can't wait to try it out."

I'd exhausted my insult bank, and I figured we were only a few more away from swinging whatever tools we had within our reach, so I'd be the bigger person and let it drop. For now.

I sat back, my thighs done with being crouched down and in desperate need of a break anyway. My kitty climbed up on my lap, nudging her head against my hand so I'd continue to pet her.

Jackson stepped off the ladder and dug around in his toolbox. He looked my way, and I steeled myself for a dig about me being lazy and sitting down on the job. "You want to know why cats are better than dogs?"

I still wasn't sure this wasn't some kind of trap, but I bit anyway. "Why yes, yes I do. Because I know for a fact that *certain nameless cats* don't even catch mice, even when they're right in front of their nose."

"Cats bury their own shit," he said. "No walking after them with a baggie and scooping up their poop."

I looked down at the midnight-black cat. "We better get you a litter box, just in case. Our relationship will go downhill if I start finding poop everywhere."

The cat meowed as if she was offended that I thought she'd do something so uncivilized.

"Don't look at me like that," I said. "You're the one who got knocked up. No judgment on the extracurricular activities, but we need to talk about safe sex."

Jackson snorted a laugh. He crossed his arms and casually leaned against the wall opposite me. "Kitty sex-ed? This I gotta hear."

In spite of it obviously being a joke, heat settled in my cheeks. Not that I'd let that stop me. "You see, kitty, what happens is guys only want one thing—"

Jackson cleared his throat, obnoxiously loudly, and I amended my statement, because I supposed being amiable once in a while wasn't the worst thing ever.

"I mean, *some* guys only want one thing. Like, say, tomcats you meet in a back alley who promise you the world, but you know you've seen him out with other girls, a different one every night." I tsked and added a sigh.

"Don't you think you should give her a name before giving her the birds and bees talk?"

The cat's purr vibrated through me as I moved to scratch under her chin. Despite the lack of collar and striking out when I'd asked the neighbors about her, she still might be someone else's cat. Giving her a name meant admitting my attachment, and I had a rule about that.

Way #4: Attachments are the path to the dark side. Attachments lead to falling. Falling leads to crashing.

Crashing leads to suffering.
Therefore, resist the allure of the dark side, and avoid
attachments at all costs.

That was with men and to keep my heart safe. I hoped that letting a knocked-up kitty in wouldn't lead to too big of a crash, no matter how our arrangement worked out. I used to constantly ask for a pet growing up, but I'd had to make do with being around my stepfathers' family pets, and their hearts had already been given away to their owners, so it wasn't the same.

"I hate to agree with him—like, ever—but he's right," I said, addressing my feline friend. "You need a name before we have our chicks over dicks talk."

Jackson shook his head. "You're hopeless."

"Yep, that's me. A hopeless cynic. I'm the yin to Savannah's yang. Of course, I'm pretty sure she thought she could bring me over to the dark side, but leopards don't change their spots. Now, *shhh*. I'm trying to come up with the perfect name."

The kitty perked up her head, her whiskers brushing my hand.

"Black Widow. That's what I'm going to call you." I considered the happy purr confirmation she was pleased with her new moniker.

"I thought you were afraid of spiders," Jackson said.

I blinked up at him, adding a confused expression. "She's a cat, silly."

He shook his head again and ran a hand through his hair, which, of course, fell back in its perfectly messy place.

I leaned back on my palms. "You might as well save yourself a lot of trouble and give up ever trying to figure me out. I don't even get me sometimes."

A strange look overcame his features, serious with an

edge of determination. Then he pushed off the wall and paced toward me. Sitting way down on the floor, cat in my lap, suddenly seemed like a disadvantage.

"If you're about ready to pack it up," he said, his voice deep and measured, "I'll go tackle the non-feline spiders in the attic. I bought a couple of bug bombs to set off. We're talking nuclear arachnid annihilation."

Oh, that wasn't so bad. Actually, it's awesome. Nothing I needed an advantage for.

I gently scooted Black Widow off my lap and dubiously took the hand Jackson extended. Instead of letting go when he pulled me to my feet, he tugged me closer, my body bumping his. "By the way, I can be just as stubborn as you, and it might take me a while, but I'll figure you out yet, Ivy Clarke." His steady gaze bored into mine. "Count on it."

With that he brushed past me, picked up the bag he'd brought in, and walked upstairs.

While I just stood there, dealing with surges of heat and the inability to swallow, wondering what the hell had just happened.

And why, even though I knew better, I wanted it to happen again.

Chapter Eight

Friday nights at Azure were usually on the busy, hard-to-catch-my-breath side. The blue-hued lights added a calming touch that I rarely felt while working, although during the slow times, I often got caught up watching the water run down the glass-encased wall behind the bar.

I delivered an order of crab fritters—we had the best in the city, hands down—and moved to the other end of the bar for a quick breather.

Considering Savannah was going to bring her 12 Steps to Mr. Right workshop attendees here for their first field trip, where they'd learn how to spot red flags in person, it'd only get busier.

At least being busy meant lots of tips, because my side project was only getting more expensive by the day.

Thinking of the renovation led to thinking of Jackson, and I couldn't stop replaying his last sentence to me and trying to decipher exactly what he meant by it. *I'll figure you out yet, Ivy Clarke. Count on it.*

Why on earth would he want to figure me out?

I didn't even want to dive too deep into figuring me out. Somehow I also kept forgetting he was dating another woman, one with a lot less issues who didn't need decoding, no doubt. *He said it was really new, so maybe that means they're not serious.*

Not that I care either way.

Hopefully one day I would be able to sell that lie to myself, because it'd make working with him so much easier.

"Hey," a deep male voice said, breaking through thoughts best forgotten. Unlike the dozen or so heys I'd been on the other end of tonight, this one was friendly and familiar and a welcome reprieve to being hit on by guys who thought I was obligated to flirt back to get a tip.

I braced my palms on the bar in front of my cousin Linc and asked what he wanted to drink. As I placed a beer in front of him, I asked, "Is it weird to be on the other side of the bar?" Up until a month ago, he'd worked here part time, but with his sports reporting job taking off, he didn't have time to pour drinks anymore.

"Yeah. I kind of want to jump over and mix up some cocktails," he joked.

"If it gets busy enough once Savannah comes in, I might beg you for help."

Linc glanced at the time. "I haven't seen her all week—I've been in Baltimore—so I figured I'd come watch her work. Also figured I'd give some of the guys tips on what not to do when a large group of ladies arrives."

I clicked my tongue at him. "Skewing Savannah's hands-on lessons to make guys look better than they are? If she finds out, she'll have your head."

"I'm only helping out the ones I know are good guys, the way she helps her attendees. I'm teaching them to live up to their full, possible-Mr.-Right potential."

"So now you're a dating coach, too?"

He shrugged. "Sure. Why not?"

"Because the aforementioned off-with-your-head threat from your fiancée."

A slow smile spread across his face as he drifted off to some happy place in his head. "I have my ways of talking her out of being angry with me."

Of that, I had no doubt. Since we'd hit a lull and no one was waving their hand for a drink, I decided I could spend a minute or two camped out here at the far corner. Linc was a couple of months away from becoming an official part of the Gamble family, but he'd practically been inducted already.

"Did you happen to go to last Sunday's Gamble Family Dinner?" Every Sunday, Savannah and Jackson were required to be at a big, extended-family dinner, come hell or high water. I'd gone a few times, but I always felt a bit out of place.

Linc's eyebrows ticked together. "Yeah. I was asked about our plans for having kids after we get married no less than five times."

I dragged my finger through the ring of condensation Linc's beer bottle left behind when he lifted it to take a swig. "Did Jackson bring that girl he took to your engagement party?"

Linc slowly lowered his drink. "She was there. Why are you asking me instead of Savannah?"

"Because she'll read more into it, and it'll turn into the Spanish Inquisition, all rapid-fire questions about my intentions. I was just curious."

He studied me, one eyebrow arching. "Savannah once told me you and Jackson have a thing but that you don't really know what it is."

"We don't have a thing. We're working together to remodel a house now, but that's it." I straightened. "I'd better get back to work."

"Well, since you're 'just curious,' she was there, but I could tell Jackson didn't expect her to be. Pretty sure the invite came from his mom. Or Velma. Most likely both of them, actually. She's a family friend, and I know they're hoping it'll work out between them."

I wanted to point out that she didn't even seem to be his type, but what did I know about his type? That was further down this path than I wanted to go anyway. I was just psyching myself out about his comment, and he and I had spent a lot of time together, and it wasn't news that he was superhot. Also, I hadn't spent any time with another guy in a while, and clearly it was playing tricks on my brain.

That's it. I need to find a one-night stand guy, stat. After Savannah and her attendees have sorted them all out, it'll be that much easier. They'll take the long-term dating options, and I'll take my pick of the ones who run from commitment.

I once joked to Savannah that all I wanted was a smart asshole. A guy who I could have intellectual conversations with but who'd be as anxious to get back to his life after we hooked up as I was. I'd lamented the fact that they were hard to find, and she promised that he was out there, the same way she promised people their versions of Mr. Right.

A guy at the end of the bar snapped his fingers—evidently he had a death wish—and while I should probably get back to work, his rude gesture meant I was going to take my sweet time. I checked the customers at the other end of the bar and slowly made my way back to Mr. Impatient Snappy-Pants.

When the guy huffed and said, "Took you long enough," I gave him the shark-like smile that most people instinctually feared. A swirl of satisfaction went through me as his expression turned from impatient to trepidation.

"Did your mama not teach you any manners? You don't snap your fingers at people like they're dogs, and unless you'd like your drink shoved where the sun don't shine, you'll say

please and thank you. To be safe, you better add a 'ma'am.'"
I snapped my fingers, drawing his attention back to my face
when he tried to duck his head like a scolded puppy. "Do you
understand?"

He hemmed and hawed a little and then grumbled, "Yes,
ma'am."

"Great. And the etiquette lesson means I'll be expecting
an extra hefty tip."

I filled the reformed gentleman's order, and when I
noticed Linc stand up, I said, "Hey, that blond guy in the
back? He's a really good guy. While you're doling out your
heads-up to the nice dudes, give him one, too."

Linc saluted, and I felt a pinch of guilt for joining in on
his plan. After everything that had happened between her
and my cousin, Savannah was trying to be more open with
her Mr. Right definition, but she could still be a stickler for
her steps and red flags. Not that I blamed her—my methods
for avoiding heartbreak had kept me safe, and I clung to them
as well. But Adam was one of those smart guys I'd had great
conversations with, who'd also texted me way too many times.
He was sweet. Problem was, I'd eat a guy like that alive.

Not many guys could keep up with me or knew how to
handle me in general. Part of it was the vibe I worked to put
out there. Or, I guess, more what I *didn't* put out there.

Yep, I'd conceal don't feel, because Elsa was a girl after
my own heart and she had the right idea. She knew how to
keep people away.

I could use a big ice beast some nights at the bar. Since I
didn't have the ability to literally create ice, I went another,
similar route.

Way #5: *Go ice princess.*
*Close yourself off emotionally. No one can hurt
your feelings when you don't leave them out there all*

exposed and vulnerable. Don't volunteer too many details and don't ask for too many.

All my ways fed into each other. Closing yourself off emotionally involved control and avoiding attachments, but it was more than that. It was keeping the personal subjects to a minimum. When it came to theory or culture, that was where I liked to go deep.

There was nothing wrong with a little going deep, like, say, asking for what you wanted in the bedroom—just putting that out there—but pillow talk and cuddling after? Nope.

Letting him know that you're worried about your mother? Your future? Crying in his arms?

Nope, nope—and, you guessed it—*nope.*

I tried not to think about how badly I'd screwed up Way Number Five when it came to Jackson, because it was in the past. I couldn't change how much he already knew about my screwed-up relationship with my mother or that, in his arms, I'd actually seen what the cuddling fuss was about. The important thing was that eventually, I threw up my walls and Elsa'd the shit out of the situation.

In hindsight, possibly I'd gone too far, but I'd felt that sweet ache forming in my chest. The mixture of yearning and vulnerability that, left unattended, had the possibility of turning into a pit that sucked happiness out of your life and left you a broken shell.

I'd forgotten how hard it was to erase the good memories so you could focus on the inevitable pain down the road. The longer you let it go on, and the more intensely you cared, the worse the pain, too.

It was the right call. I needed to stop dwelling on Jackson and the curiosity about who he was dating. To keep up my walls, stick to a strictly business relationship, and be the best ice princess I could be.

I don't know why I'm even thinking about this anyway. We can barely stand to be in the same room.

Was it weird that I'd had the tiniest bit of fun keeping up with our antagonistic banter all week, even though it also made me want to pull my hair out? That probably didn't speak well to my mental state, but there was something invigorating about a daily challenge.

I delivered a drink and then turned to see Savannah and Linc's reunion after a week apart. He scooped her into his arms, and she kissed him with reckless abandon. A couple of her attendees made catcalls, and I smiled.

Savannah used to insist her clients and students only ever saw her ultra-professional side, but she'd gone and fallen in love, so she didn't have any control anymore. Obviously she was also super attached, and she wasn't even a little closed off emotionally.

It worked on her. She wasn't broken beyond repair by her past, even though I knew it wasn't all smooth sailing.

Despite my best attempts to smother it, it also brought on the slightest sense of longing, but I told myself that was for physical intimacy and nothing more.

Before I went and started thinking otherwise, I threw myself into work and didn't slow down until every one of Savannah's attendees had left.

I set a lemon martini in front of her—she'd loosened her grip on the need to be all professional, all the time, but she never drank until her job was done for the night. I'd seen enough people turn into idiots thanks to alcohol to respect that.

"Quick. What's a word for 'Alaskan native?'" Savannah twisted the *Atlanta Journal-Constitution* toward me, the crossword puzzle filled out in a mix of blue ink and what I instantly knew was Savannah's purple. "There were tons of sports clues in today's paper, so of course my part looks all pathetic, and I thought at least I could get this one, but it's not Eskimo, and it starts with an A if I'm not wrong about twenty-three down, so I got nothing."

Linc loved crossword puzzles, and they'd started to do them together, and did I mention they were disgustingly cute?

I'd been obsessed with Alaska for a brief period when I was younger, before I realized that I didn't handle cold well—I'd even wanted a penguin for a pet, and for some crazy reason, my mom kept saying no. "Aleut. A-L-E-U-T."

"I've never heard that word in my life." She counted the spaces and, when it fit, wrote it in. "I love you."

"Thanks, but I bat for the other team."

Savannah laughed, took a sip of her martini, then licked sugar off her lips and focused all her attention on me. "How's"—she pressed her lips together like she might laugh again, but this time *at* me instead of *with* me—"the renovating going? Choose any good paint colors lately?"

"I'm going to take that drink away."

She curled it closer. "No, I need it. I'm just still trying to put the girl who can't decide which color to paint the living room in her condo with the girl who's overhauling an entire house. Sorry I haven't been by to help, by the way, but this week was madness. I did, uh, send someone in my place, though." She twisted the stem of her glass between her fingers and winced. "How's it going with my brother anyway?"

"Let me give my guy who disposes of bodies a few more days and then I'll let you know."

"Very funny. I tried to call Jackson and ask him, but he's been conveniently hard to reach. Probably due to the fact that I sent him over there in the first place."

I leaned a hip against the bar. "Honestly, I was kind of pissed when you sent him over, but we brokered our deal, and as much as I hate to admit it, I couldn't do this big of a project without him. But don't tell him I said that."

"Come on. It wouldn't kill you to say something nice to each other once in a while, would it?"

"I'm not willing to take that chance."

"Well, I'm just surprised that you'll even admit it to me. I know you guys have a…rocky relationship."

I shot her a look.

"Okay. Closer to a toxic one."

I frowned for a second before gaining control and smothering the errant thought about that going too far. I'd almost defended our relationship, and now I wondered if the word "toxic" was a little too close to true.

Savannah bit her lip. "I did worry a little…"

"That I might maim him? I still haven't ruled it out, to be honest."

She shot me the same look I'd given her. "No. I know he's… He's trying to like girls who are better for him, ones who are on the sweeter side of the spectrum. Not so much drama, you know." I could tell she was beginning to stress out about what she was saying and how I'd take it, but she'd spit it out because we'd known each other well enough for long enough that we didn't pull punches when it came to something we thought the other needed to hear. "He's looking for long term."

I fought the urge to claw at my tightening throat. "Oh. Well, good for him. I'm sure it'll take a very sweet person to resist killing him."

Savannah studied me, her brown eyes narrowing.

I didn't think I had anything to feel guilty for, but with her studying me, I was suddenly forcing myself to be impassive, not even sure what I was trying to hide. "Seriously, if that's something he wants, more power to him."

I thought about her comment about his being hard to reach. We'd been working days, but he should have plenty of time to call at night. *I just want to know if he's dating that chick, for my own idle curiosity.*

It was something I should leave alone. Which was why I wouldn't. I'd never been any good at doing what I should. "What's-her-name from your engagement party probably fits the bill perfectly."

"Caroline? The Porters are family friends, and Caroline's sweet and energetic and has a life plan that would put mine to shame…"

Whoa. Considering Savannah's hyper-organizational skills and ever-present goals, even the thought of that much structure made my skin itch.

"I'm just hoping he'll give it a real chance. I'm afraid that he's been in so many screwed-up relationships that he'll decide she's not enough of a challenge or that stable somehow equals boring. He gets all pissed off when I psychoanalyze him, but I feel like the side of him that wants to fix everything is why he always chooses broken women. He wants to fix them. He claims he's done with that type, but I don't think he can help it."

Broken women. My heart sunk. He'd already said he wanted to figure me out. Did he see me as a project? Someone he wanted to fix?

I don't need fixed. I'm fine the way I am.

The constant antsy feeling and hollow sensation that'd recently plagued me said differently, but I'd repress that.

I was good at repressing things.

"Ivy?" Understanding dawned on her features. "When I said broken women, I'm not talking about you. You and Jackson are—"

"Never happening," I said, quick and firm. "I know you think we have a thing, but we don't. I mean, there's attraction, sure…" For a second, I accidentally got caught up in thinking about his eyes, his hands, his hard body.

"Please don't call my brother sex on a stick. You know

how I feel about that expression."

I refocused on my best friend. I'd respect her wishes, but the guy embodied everything any straight woman would look for when she wanted someone who'd be fun between the sheets.

Unfortunately, I knew just how fun, and right now I wished I didn't.

I reached up and twisted a strand of hair around my finger. "What I'm saying is that I'm not going to get in the way, if that's what you're worried about."

"I…" A raw, vulnerable expression flitted across her features. "I hope you're not mad. I just want the best for both of you, and both of you have the tendency to be a little self-destructive. I don't want to end up being responsible for something that'd hurt either one of you, and if you're truly set on avoiding a real relationship…"

Even after all this time, she still clung on to that glimmer of hope that I might change my mind, and I'd let her if it wouldn't end up disappointing her even more. "You know I don't do long term, and when I choose my guys to have fun with, I avoid messy complications like friends of friends and *especially* family of friends."

If only I hadn't slipped that one little time.

Okay, seven tiny times.

Well, seven times that weren't tiny in any sense of the word. Working with his hands meant he knew exactly how to use them, and endurance was the name of the game.

My pulse quickened, butterflies stirred, and my heart seemed to be expanding instead of staying in the shriveled ball I preferred for it to be in. Before I could fully enjoy the buzz of those deliciously dirty thoughts, guilt that I'd kept what'd happened from Savannah rose up and turned everything sour.

Warning. Shut down all emotions. Shut it down, shut it

down.

I cleared my throat and then grabbed a beer and downed half of it. I worked at a bar, so I had no such qualms about drinking on the job. In fact, it was practically a requirement.

"You've got that scary look on your face," Savannah said. "Somewhere between deadly determination and destruction, which usually means you drag me out dancing, and I'm so, so tired and Linc's been out of town all week and—"

"No dancing."

Her shoulders sagged with relief for a microsecond before she tensed and scrutinized me. "Now I'm getting the self-destructive vibe."

"Don't worry. I haven't been myself lately, but I'm getting back to me. And like your brother, I don't need you psychoanalyzing me."

She looked like she wanted to argue, but then Linc approached and asked if she was ready to go home. I could tell she was torn, her gaze moving from him—and her thoughts obviously moving to what she wanted him to do to her once they got home—and then to me, and there was far too much worry creasing her forehead.

"I'm good. I'll call you tomorrow." I tipped back the rest of my beer.

"Okay, and then we're scheduling a time to catch up without a bar between us." Savannah pointed a finger at me for emphasis.

"Deal." I put on my best I'm-all-good expression and waited until after she left to mix up an Absolute Bitch shot— vodka, Bailey's, Kahlua, and Tuaca. I tipped it back, rounded the bar, and approached the hottie who'd flirted with me when I dropped off his drink.

He'll do for a night.

I leaned in, displaying my assets to their fullest. "Got plans for after the bar closes?"

"Is that an invitation?"

"If you play your cards right."

He grinned, and I tried to be excited about it.

Then I ignored my best friend's voice and that comment she'd made about self-destructive behavior.

Chapter Nine

I rolled over in bed and looked at the empty space next to me.

I'd been so tempted to fill it with a hot guy who'd been clear he didn't want attachments. I'd even tried to keep conversation to a minimum, but I'd had this stupid flash of Jackson's face—obviously a brain malfunction I needed to look into—and then I couldn't go through with it. I couldn't even bring myself to kiss him.

Not because I had an attachment to Jackson or anything. Simply because I'd told my partner-in-home-repair that we needed to get an early start, and how could I do that if I took a guy home with me?

Sure, it was the flimsiest excuse ever, but I was also a big believer in not doing something if I wasn't into it.

The trouble was, I, uh, hadn't been into it since Jackson and I slept together, even though I'd rather drink glass shards than admit it'd been that long. It was like he'd broken the one part of me that wasn't broken.

I'll get it back. This is just a slump.

When I rescinded my invitation last night, Douchebag

McGee had gripped my arm and called me a tease, and I'd had to formally introduce his nuts to my knee. He wouldn't be having temporary fun with anyone for a few days.

The whole scene transported me back to my last year of college, when I'd scored the nickname Ice Cold Bitch from a group of frat brothers. Since I was too soft and naive my first year, it was a title I proudly owned.

I don't need anyone else. I'm complete all on my own.

I repeated that mantra as I showered, dressed, and grabbed breakfast. Even though working on the house left my muscles constantly sore, I couldn't wait to dive in again.

By the time I pulled up to the old Victorian, Jackson's truck was nestled against the curb. The dark gray Dodge Ram had built in toolboxes and basically looked like it could double as a bomb shelter. The combination was hot as hell, and that was coming from someone who barely paid attention to vehicles.

While his already being here wasn't going to help my constant sexually frustrated state, it'd be good for productivity on the house.

Banging—the hammer kind, not the good kind—greeted me first, and Black Widow greeted me second.

I bent down and scratched her head. "I don't need anyone else because I have you."

Of course, I didn't really have her, but sometimes you had to cling to what you could. Besides, at the end of this project, she was welcome to come home with me.

"You want some food?" I asked Black Widow, going the presumptuous route and heading toward the kitchen where the noise had switched from banging to a low hum.

Jackson stood there with his sander, sawdust coating his arms, and I recalled a post that called woodchips man glitter. Jeez, was the universe set on showing me what I was missing out on? Because I already knew, and if my determination to always be in control wasn't so firm, I'd jump him right here in the kitchen.

The counter looks like just the right height…

Jackson spotted me, shut down the sander, and lifted the clear safety glasses from his face. "Mornin', drill sergeant," he said with a smirk.

I licked my suddenly dry lips and bit back the urge to say that I wanted *him* to do the drilling today. "Morning, subordinate."

He jerked his chin toward the feline at my ankles. "I already fed your cat."

"Well, she is eating for two. Or more likely five or six." I dumped more food in her bowl, and she just looked at it, so she must've eaten plenty the first round. "Thanks for having my back, girl," I muttered.

When I straightened, Jackson had moved, his hulking presence taking up the entire room. Especially since there was a door in the middle of it now. I resisted the urge to reach out and brush the man glitter off his arms—no wonder he always smelled so woodsy and delicious. "Whatcha doin'?"

He swiped his hands together. "The back door wasn't closing right, which makes it hard for the locks to engage, and I want the place to be more secure."

Secure. Like how I'd felt in his arms back when I was letting myself feel emotions. Good thing I had that under control now.

"I'm about done, though," he said. "Want me to show you the attic?"

"Is it spider free?"

"That critter at your feet should be the only black widow that survived."

I shuddered. "Gah! You made it too real. Now I'm thinking about spiders."

"You named your cat after one, but *I'm* the problem?"

"Clearly," I said, and he chuckled. He put his hand on my back as he guided me out of the room. Awareness shot up my spine, and I might've leaned into his touch a little—it was early and I hadn't had caffeine yet, so I totally had a legit excuse.

He dropped his hand as we started up the stairs, which undoubtedly left my ass at his face level. I swayed my hips a bit, because why should I be the only one thinking about the other person's body?

This is probably more self-destructive than taking home that guy would've been. I reminded myself that I'd assured his sister that I wouldn't get in the way of his picket-fence possibilities with Miss Perfect and did my best to stop the swaying and move more like a robot in need of WD-40. *Now I just need to nail down the same emotional range of a robot, and I'll be back on track.*

Once we reached the attic, I gestured Jackson ahead of me—I planned on using him as a shield against webs and spiders, just in case. The air in the room was still on the dusty, stale side, but the cobwebs had been cleaned out. There was a pile of dirt and more insect carcasses than I wanted to know existed in the corner.

"You took down the webs and swept?"

"I didn't want to listen to you screeching and screaming as you tried to make it through the spiderweb maze," he said.

"You've really got to stop saying stuff like that." Goose bumps broke out across my skin at the thought of all those sticky spider-butt strings.

Jackson stepped forward and rubbed his hands over my arms, heat instantly building. "I don't know. It's kind of fun knowing you have one weakness."

"Oh, I have more than one. But I'm not about to tell them to you so you can exploit them." I was starting to worry he was one of them. No wonder I'd worked so hard to keep hold of the loathing and verbal attacks.

He mimicked being knifed in the chest, and I rolled my eyes. So I wouldn't laugh and get carried away staring at the stubble dusting his jaw, I stepped farther into the attic, studying the boxes and items pushed against the walls.

Jackson pulled a trash bag that I hadn't noticed out of his back pocket and bent next to the pile of dirt. "Do you want to see all the dead insects before I throw them away? See just how many I saved you from?"

"Um, that's a hard pass. You should totally add that to your dating profile, though."

He paused his cleanup efforts and crinkled his forehead. "That I collect spider carcasses? I think that's the kind of thing that gets you put on the FBI watch list."

"Ew, no. I meant you should put that you're good at killing insects and spiders."

"I'll have to remember that if I ever go the online dating route."

"Come on, you know Savannah will make you fill one out eventually. If she hasn't filled out one for you already." I glanced back at him, and we shared a laugh. And even though I knew I should leave it alone, just like I should've last night, I couldn't help adding, "Of course, if you're dating someone seriously now, she'll have to hold off."

I turned away so I could do a better job at acting indifferent, my gaze being pulled to the boxes labeled SCRAPBOOKS. *Be a robot, be a robot, be a—*

I nearly jumped when I felt Jackson right behind me, his voice next to my ear. "Why, Ivy Clarke, are you asking if I'm a free agent?"

I spun around and put a good foot of space between us, my crossed arms coming up as an extra barrier. "No."

He stared at me for a couple of beats, each second making the space smaller and smaller and him bigger and bigger. "Well, in case anyone else in this house is wondering, I haven't settled down quite yet. And I'm always up for a little fun."

The way his voice dipped with innuendo seemed like a dare, like he wanted to see if I'd flirt back, like we used to in the before period.

I froze, afraid to move or so much as breathe, because I didn't trust myself not to take the bait, even though I knew there was a hook hidden underneath it. One minute we'd be having fun, the next we'd both get sucked under the current of our constantly pulsing sexual attraction, and the one after that we'd have a major blowout and he'd be judging me and the way I lived my life.

Something akin to regret crossed his features, but I couldn't tell if it was regret over venturing into flirty territory or that I wasn't taking him up on it, or regret that we'd ever gone there in the first place. It disappeared as quickly as it showed up. He ran a hand through his hair and then hefted the bag in his hand. "I'm going to take care of this trash."

"I think that's a good idea." Then again, having a little fun seemed like a pretty good one too.

Bad thought. Bad, most definitely un-robot-like thought. How inconvenient that when Jackson wasn't being completely infuriating, he could be kinda charming. Or maybe that was just my dry spell talking.

That'd be easier to convince myself of if I wasn't standing in a swept-out attic. An awful notion hit me, and I stepped out just in time to see Jackson's delectable backside retreating down the stairs. "I swear, Jackson Gamble, if you put those spiders anywhere but the trash, you'll wish for death before I'm done with you."

He cast a devilish grin over his shoulder. "The thought never even crossed my mind, but now that you've given me the idea…You might want to sleep with one eye open."

His evil laugh carried up the stairs, and I shook my head, plotting ways I'd pay him back if he stooped that low. We're talking dismemberment, possibly after pushing him out a second-story window, and I was confident even Savannah wouldn't fault me for that.

I heard a door swing closed and crossed to my old bedroom window, where I could see him lower the trash bag into the ugly blue Dumpster taking up most of the driveway.

Looks like I'm going to have to beef up my resistance efforts…

. . .

Boxes surrounded me on all sides, obscuring the floral couch and the stripped-bare walls. I'd called Dixie and asked what she wanted me to ship to her and what she wanted me to give away or toss, and she told me I could get rid of everything except for her scrapbooks.

I was going to just throw it all in Jackson's truck to take to Goodwill when he returned from Sunday dinner at his parents', but then I'd opened up the boxes and dug around, looking for treasures.

A lot of old clothes that would probably never be in style again filled several boxes. One was filled with my high school clothes, and I ended up putting on a fashion show for Black Widow. Most of the items were on the tight side, and I'd attempted some fashion risks that I couldn't quite pull off— the generic Juicy Couture velour tracksuits, the ruffle skirts that I wore with also-generic Uggs.

I had nothing on my mom and Dixie's clothes, though. As I sorted through them, it was like scenes from my childhood flashing before my eyes, only the good times instead of all the bad.

I'd taken my first trip to the emergency room after roller

skating into the corner of the fireplace mantel and splitting the spot above my eyebrow open. Mom had been wearing a pink halter top that used to embarrass me, even though she'd looked amazing in it—that was probably why it was so traumatic. It attracted men like bees to honey, and I'd secretly been glad when the blood wouldn't come all the way out. Not sure why she'd kept it, but it was about time it bit the dust.

Dixie's favorite flannel shirt was in here, too. She'd worn it often, and one especially vivid memory came to mind, of her patting my hand and telling me that boys would always be intimidated by me, but a real man would know how to handle me at my best *and* my worst.

I'd just had my first breakup cry session on the rocking chair in the corner after Jimmy Walker told everyone he'd only gone out with me because I had big boobs but that I'd turned too clingy.

Yeah. Back in high school, I'd done the clingy thing. In my defense, he was my first, and I knew that Mom was getting close to marrying…Barry, I think? Which meant we were most likely going to move (we did), but I thought that if I had a serious boyfriend, Mom would let me stay and live with Dixie (I didn't get to test my theory, but doubtful).

In the end, it was a relief to move away for a while.

Barry was one of the better stepdads. He taught me how to golf, and he'd let me borrow his car a lot. In fact, for a little while, I'd dared to think that he might stick and that moving hadn't been so bad after all.

But of course, he didn't last—they never did—and by that point, I was so sick of hoping only to be more disappointed in the end.

Back in the present, I closed up the boxes, not sure I could take anymore memories. A picture frame caught my eye, and I retrieved it from the pile of photos that used to line Dixie's fireplace mantel. The frame held several photos:

a snapshot of Mom and Dixie and their dates at their high school prom, their dresses metallic pink and blue and their bangs exceptionally puffy; one from their college days; and another with the three of us, when I was four or five years old. Then the last one, a picture of me receiving an award at school my junior year.

Through the years and the moves and Mom's different guys, the one solid relationship I knew would always be there was Mom and Dixie's, and even they hadn't made it.

Because of a stupid guy.

I mean, Rhett wasn't stupid. He was smart and funny, not to mention loving and accepting, and my very favorite of Mom's exes. But she had cast him off, and then he and Dixie crossed paths a few months later. Dixie claimed she'd tried her best to stop it, but she fell head-over-heels in love.

More proof that if you didn't stop it in its tracks, it'd come and destroy everything you loved.

Yes, love destroyed love.

It was like those drug commercials where they show all the beautiful, happy people hugging and kissing and, like, frolicking and shit. But if you listen, in the background there's a person talking as fast as humanly possible, listing several serious side effects. Things like this may cause fuzzy vision, heart palpitations, severe mood swings, and vertigo.

Sound like anything else you know? Like, say, *love*?

All those side effects plus ignoring your family and friends who've been there for you your entire life, putting your daughter second, letting a guy you didn't even like all that much break up a friendship that spanned more than three decades, and being foolish enough to think that the payoff would still be big enough if you could just find the right one.

Okay, some of that might be projecting, but I'd seen my mom do every single one of those things. Which was probably why, during my first few relationships, I was so starved for attention that I clung to them like they were the only good thing in my life. Sometimes they were.

The high school relationships were easy enough to brush off. The college boyfriend was the one that really messed with my head. It'd made me feel stupid, too, because I knew better. I'd seen the side effects for myself, yet I still popped that love pill.

The rumbling of an engine dragged me out of the past.

I put the picture frame back in the pile, taped up the boxes of clothes that were still in good shape, and scribbled GOODWILL across them in black Sharpie.

Jackson knocked before opening the unlocked door and striding inside.

He had on a button-down, a sports jacket, and black slacks, and he looked good enough to lick. Er, shake hands with. My gaze snagged on the long fingers that would be rough and warm against my skin, and on second thought, maybe I should just keep my hands to myself.

I lifted my hair off my neck and pulled it up to help cool myself down. "How was Sunday dinner?"

In response, he let out the longest exhale ever. I wanted to ask if that meant a certain brunette had been there—the sweet one his family adored and his sister wanted him to give a real chance—or if the big sigh was because she hadn't attended, and he wished she had. But I'd already said too much yesterday.

Is he "having fun" with her? Was it hard for him to leave because they were having so much damn fun?

Not that I care.

I'm really working on not caring.

"Look, we've been putting in long hours, and obviously you're tired and could use a night off," I said. "I'm just sorting old boxes, and we can totally haul them to Goodwill later. Go home and get some sleep so that you'll have energy tomorrow."

"Don't you go worrying about my stamina." He flashed me a smile, but it was tight, like he had to work for it.

"Did something happen with your family?"

"You wanna talk families?"

I opened my mouth and then snapped it closed. Not only did it break a lot of my rules, my bittersweet memories were still swirling in the air, making me far too emotional as it was. "No."

"Me neither. It was just a long day, and I'm trying to… But I can't stop…" He shook his head and took a step closer, his eyes meeting mine. "I just want to forget about everything for a while."

"I could use a little forgetting myself." My lungs tightened. It seemed like an admission of weakness, even though he'd already said he wanted the same thing. Of all the places he could go to forget, I was surprised he'd choose here. Even more surprised he'd choose me. Although I supposed it just so happened he was here and so was I.

There was something in the air tonight, something that made everything feel different. Jackson was giving off an intense vibe, too, one I couldn't quite nail down but made my nerve endings stand on end. Instead of questioning everything, I wanted to relax and get swept up in the buzz of it all, just for a little while.

Jackson picked up a deck of cards I'd unearthed among the junk and tapped them against his palm. "How's your poker game?"

"I can hold my own," I said, excitement tingling across my skin. What can I say? My competitive nature needed feeding now and then. It often felt like Jackson and I were in our own sort of poker game, strategizing and bluffing and smothering every emotion so we wouldn't give away our hands. Might as well add cards into the mix so we could declare an official winner for the night.

Luckily I'd picked up some beer and chips at the grocery store earlier, too.

We decided on Texas Hold'em and set up on the tiny, barely-fits-three table that always looked out of place in the spacious dining room. Then we got to shuffling and dealing.

Jackson won the first round by getting lucky last minute with the queen he needed for his full house. I won the next with pocket aces. We went back and forth as we made our way through most of a six pack, our inhibitions a little looser each round.

Jackson leveled his gaze on me, his cards fanned out in one hand. "I think it's time to up the stakes."

"You feel like losing money tonight?"

"Not money…" He leaned back in his chair, the perfect image of casual, cool, and collected. "I was thinking we could make it a little more interesting and switch to strip poker. First person to end up naked or call uncle loses." He gave it a beat to sink in. "Unless you're scared."

The challenging gleam in his eye made my heart pick up speed. Judging from his smug expression, he thought I was going to back down.

Well, he was dead wrong.

Chapter Ten

Thanks to the tiny table, my knees brushed Jackson's bare ones every time I shifted. Not that I could feel they were bare per se, but I knew, and that made me more aware of every time it happened. A pile of clothes pooled on the floor next to us. His shoes, jacket, slacks, and shirt. My socks, shoes, and shirt.

The next card would reveal whether my pants or his socks would join the pile. Unless he went balls out—literally—and lost his boxers before the socks.

It wasn't like I hadn't seen him naked before, but it'd been long enough that I'd forgotten what it did to me. How the sight of his carved pecs and abs sent heat pooling low in my stomach. I was plenty confident in what I had going on, and it didn't escape my attention that his eyes grew darker with every item of clothing I lost, his breathing more shallow.

We were playing a dangerous game, and I hadn't had this much fun in weeks. Months, even.

I held my breath and leaned in as he placed his hand over the deck of cards to draw the river.

Two kings sat in front of me, a heart and a club.

Jackson had an ace of clubs and a two of diamonds.

The pot consisted of a three of spades, a ten of diamonds, a seven of clubs, and a jack of hearts.

Basically, the odds were in my favor.

With dramatic flair, Jackson flipped the card and threw it in the middle of the table with the others, then let out a holler loud enough to scare Black Widow into the other room.

"You've *got* to be kidding me," I said as I stared at the ace of hearts. Fifty-two cards—minus the nine on the table—and only three could screw me over.

And he'd drawn one of them.

I shook my head. "You had to have cheated."

Jackson held up his hands, displaying his bare arms and showing off all those muscles. "Where would I hide the cards? Clearly I don't have any up my sleeves."

He had a point there, I'd give him that, but that was all I'd give him. Besides a show. I stood, undid the button and zipper on my jeans, and shimmied out of them. I tossed them on top of the clothes pile and settled back into my chair, crossing one leg over the other. "I think I'm at a disadvantage. For one, my thong hardly even counts as underwear—"

"I'm pretty sure that's working *to* your advantage." His voice came out husky and sent a cascade of tingles down my spine. "I can hardly focus on anything besides the fact that you have a thong on." He dared a peek around the side of the table.

I slowly uncrossed my legs and then re-crossed them in the other direction, watching his Adam's apple bob in his throat. Admittedly, it made me feel powerful and more in control, but the heat in his eyes only sent my heart hammering that much harder, which spun me right back out of control.

The only thing I could think about was all the ways he could relieve the pressure building between my thighs.

There'd be no going home alone unsatisfied tonight…

I fought back the urge to clear my throat so I wouldn't give my shaky resolve away and renewed arguing my case. "But with your jacket, you also started with more clothes than I did."

"You've got a bra *and* panties. I've just got boxers. So as I see it, we're even."

I wanted to have the strength to say then maybe we should quit while we were ahead. Before we crossed more lines.

Basically, we were both one more win or loss away from winning big. Or losing big. I couldn't decide, and part of me just wanted to let it happen and think about the consequences later.

But we were only in the beginning stages of the renovation process, which meant another five weeks in tight quarters, not to mention he was my best friend's brother and she'd made it pretty clear that unless I was open to long term, her brother was off-limits. Hadn't I just been thinking about how stupid my mom and Dixie were to let a guy come between them?

Savannah wouldn't like me messing with her brother's head, especially if he had a real shot at a future with Miss Brunette Debutante. I'd be the temporary distraction, the one holding him back from a relationship that could go somewhere if he just "gave it a real chance."

Plus, I wasn't some broken doll for him to fix.

"I'm okay with who I am," I said.

Jackson's eyebrows drew together. Then he leaned forward and placed his hand on my knee as his eyes locked on to mine. I'd been right about the warm and rough fingertips, and my blood zinged through my veins, racing to where we were connected. "Good. I like who you are."

"You do not."

"Don't get me wrong, you drive me crazy, but it's an addictive kind of crazy." His fingers dug into my skin, and my stomach dipped and soared back up.

"You drive me completely insane, too," I said, feeling the need to one-up him even now, although my voice came out shakier than I would've preferred. "So what are we doing, then?"

Jackson's hand slid up the inside of my thigh, and I nearly let out a moan. He dragged his fingertips back and forth, his touch and the desire coursing through me torturous and exquisite all at the same time. "Just having some fun and relieving some tension after a long week. But we can stop if you want."

Holy shit, I so did not want to stop, even as my brain flashed *bad idea, bad idea, bad idea.*

His eyebrows arched in question, his hand frozen in place as he waited for the answer. My heart attempted to beat right out of my chest, and my internal temperature was rising faster and hotter by the second.

My phone rang, "Run the World" by Beyoncé blasting out, which meant Savannah. "That's your sister."

Jackson sat up in his chair and ran a hand through his hair. "Of course it is."

Whatever moment we'd had evaporated. We could get it back in all of two seconds, but now my brain was overtaking my hormones, reminding me that last time we'd had some fun it ended up turning more serious than that, and he knew too much about me, and I was best friends with his sister. Savannah was one of the most important people in my life, and while she might forgive one slip, hurting her brother again—accidental or not—would be much harder to overlook. Especially after our talk at the bar the other night.

I bent over and dug through the pile of clothes for my phone, biting back a laugh when Jackson let out a harsh curse. "Sorry," I said, flashing him a smile as I straightened.

"Yeah, I can tell."

He was right. I wasn't sorry, but I did get a bit distracted staring at his arousal, rather obvious with him only in his boxers. Before he scrambled my brain again, I turned away and answered the phone.

"Hey," Savannah said, her voice on the chipper, she'd-had-way-too-many-cups-of-coffee side. "I'm finally caught up with work, so I'm on my way to help. And I'm bringing leftover pie."

"Oh, you're on your way over *right now*," I repeated for Jackson's benefit. Guess it was a good thing that he and I had stopped our game before it'd turned into a super awkward session where his sister burst in on us. "Awesome. I'll see you in a few."

By the time I ended the call, Jackson had already pulled on his pants and was working on buttoning his shirt. Shame, really, although it was for the best.

"I'll let you two do your thing." He handed me my wadded clothes, and his woodsy, musky cologne flooded my system, revving me up all over again. "See you bright and early tomorrow morning?"

"I was going to head over to the home improvement store and get a feel for flooring and cabinets and all the kitchen stuff. Work up a budget for that part so I can figure out what I can afford versus what I'd like to do."

"Sounds like a plan. I'll pick you up and we can go together."

"Sure." Maybe by then, I could find a way to erase the sight of him in nothing but his boxers and the warmth of his palm on the inside of my thigh.

Chapter Eleven

I was going to kill Jackson Gamble.

The only problem was that there were way too many witnesses in the home improvement store.

"Do you even do the interiors usually?" I asked, throwing my hands up. "I thought you did mostly foundations and framing and all that other more structural stuff."

Jackson shifted his weight forward, his voice low and tight. "I mostly do structural jobs, but I've done plenty of interiors, and I also happen to have eyes. You asked what I thought and I told you."

I blew out my breath and leaned forward, too, determined not to let him think he had the upper hand. "Well, that's because I thought you would agree with me—clearly I was delusional."

He shrugged one shoulder. "That sounds like a you issue."

Angry heat wound through me, and I jabbed a finger at his chest. "I...*argh!* You drive me crazy!"

"Right back at you, babe."

For some reason, the *babe* stopped me and fired me up at the same time, and there was attraction in the mix as well, and why did he have to make me feel so many emotions at once? I was supposed to be emotionally closed off! How the hell did he always manage to break through my usually impenetrable walls?

"Can I help you?" a guy asked from behind me. He slid his thumbs along the edge of the maroon vest that signaled he worked here. "If I were you, I'd go with the sandstone tile. Hearty, hides dirt well. Very popular."

Of course he'd come over and agree with Jackson. Two dudes in the home improvement store who figured the little lady just needed told what was good for her. "No thanks on the help," I said through gritted teeth. "We're doing fine."

His eyes widened, and he slowly backed away—good choice on his part, regardless of his crappy taste in tile.

I turned to Jackson, the main target of my ire. On the bright side, I was no longer picturing him naked or thinking about the corresponding zip that'd shot up my core as he ran his hand up my thigh last night. Nope, my thoughts were all more on the strangle and maim side. "I need a minute to cool off." I pushed my fingers against my forehead, rubbing against the oncoming headache. "I'm going to go pick out a sink, then we can circle back around to the kitchen area and disagree on everything there."

Jackson crossed his arms, and I wished I didn't notice that stupid sexy line in his forearms. Or the way my pulse sped up because of it. "If you want me to just nod and agree, let me know, and I'll do that."

"Good! That'd be great!"

The smart-ass saluted me.

I stormed off, not sure how I'd gotten so fired up so quickly. It started when he'd wrinkled his nose at the apple green paint swatch I'd grabbed for the downstairs bathroom.

Evidently he was like those annoying people on *House Hunters* who pointed out one minor, easily changeable thing and threw up their hands and said *not this house.*

But I'd stupidly held out hope that once he *saw* the flooring I wanted to go with, he'd get it. So I showed him the tiles that looked like wood, the paint swatch up against it, thinking he'd be like "I see it now. Your vision for the house is amazing." (Okay, so the second sentence was highly unlikely and a tad optimistic on my part.)

Instead he'd said that tile should look like tile and wood should look like wood and then made sure to point out the vast price difference in a way that made me sound ridiculously frivolous. Then he'd suggested the "much cheaper, hearty sandstone," also mentioning the hiding-dirt factor. Never mind it wouldn't go as well with the paint I'd picked out and would look like every generic bathroom out there. And how much dirt did most people drag into a bathroom? If that was what they were so freaking concerned about, I should go with yellow, because it'd hide pee.

Ew. I backtracked when I realized I'd missed the aisle with the bathroom vanities. *Do we want a tiny vanity or just a pedestal sink?*

I scanned the vanities, stopping to check one out, but none of the words I read about it sank in. *I really love the look of that faux-wood tile. With the humidity factor, it'd be better for the bathroom than real wood.*

When I'd brought up that point, Jackson said, "Yeah, that's why I suggested the other tile and not actual wood."

I didn't know why I cared so much what he thought. *I* was the one calling the shots, and I maintained that most people who bought old Victorian houses bought them because they were different, not the same cookie-cutter houses that plagued new developments. But I also didn't want to make a decision that would hinder a quick, high-profit sale simply because I was stubborn. There was no accounting for poor taste, so I was sure that some people would agree with Jackson's assessment that tile should look like title and wood should look like wood, and generic sandstone might be the way to go for salability.

But Dixie's house deserved better.

Black Widow deserved better.

Not that she nor I would be staying to test out the tile, but if I couldn't imagine myself living there, it felt like I wouldn't be doing the house and everything it meant to me justice. Maybe it didn't make complete logical sense, but there it was anyway.

I stared at all the sink options, and damn it, I felt the need to consult someone, because I wasn't sure which way to go. The crumbling porcelain one barely standing in the downstairs bathroom was the pedestal type, with no room for makeup or hair dryers or any of the dozen or so items most females needed to get ready in the morning.

I'd used its brother upstairs way back when, and my makeup and hair brushes were forever falling on the floor. There definitely needed to be a vanity up there, but the downstairs bathroom was mostly for guests.

Putting in a vanity might also be a tight fit. Jackson had the measurements, but even texting him and asking him for them seemed like admitting defeat.

So I went for maturity, snapped a couple of pictures, and texted Savannah.

Savannah: *I like the espresso-colored one, but what color will the walls be?*

I pulled the green color swatch out of my pocket, took a picture, and hit send.

Savannah: *For sure the espresso, then. That's going*

to look amazing!

"Hah!"

The elderly couple next to me appeared to be concerned about my mental state, but I felt justified, so I didn't care.

Jackson wandered around the corner—apparently, he couldn't wait fifteen minutes to argue more with me. Seriously, the guy could start an argument in an empty house. He lifted the mini-notebook that was forever tucked into his back pocket. "Thought you might need the measurements."

Damn. He came for a nice reason, which made me the jerk. I told myself to force out the words I knew I should say—words that didn't come easy, yet I'd used them quite often on him lately. "Thank you." I extended my hand. "Tape measure, please."

He placed it in my hand, his fingers brushing my palm, and then I was back to thinking about them on my thigh.

I bent to measure the vanity.

"That one?" he asked, all incredulous-like.

I fired a few eye daggers over my shoulder, and Jackson clamped his mouth shut. For two seconds.

"I mean, looks like a great vanity. The measurements are usually on the box. And by usually I mean always."

I tucked the edge of the yellow tape on one corner and ran it across the length of the top. "I prefer the hands-on method."

"Oh, I know." He swiped his hand across the stripe of skin between my shirt and the back of my pants, and I fought to act unaffected. With him it was all heat, the angry I'm-gonna-lose-my-temper kind one second, and then the I'm-so-turned-on-I'm-going-to-jump-you-in-public kind the next.

"It's just that…" He settled his hand on the small of my back. "I'm sure that's going to be too big. Even if it technically fits, it'll look cramped in that tiny downstairs bathroom. If I were allowed to give my opinion, I'd say you should stick with a pedestal sink."

I rolled my eyes. "You're allowed to give your opinions."

"Am I?"

I straightened and spun to face him, the whir of the tape measure retracting ending with a loud *pop.* "It would make it easier if they were the same as mine, but I realize that's beyond unrealistic when it comes to you and me."

He hadn't moved his hand away when I'd turned around, and now it was on my hip, radiating heat. "And tell me...?" The swipe of his thumb just under the hem of my shirt sent my hormones into overdrive. "How bored do you get with all the guys who agree with you?"

I opened my mouth. Then closed it. Then opened it. "Depends." *Great come back, Ivy.*

Bored was one thing I'd never been with Jackson around. I just wasn't sure semi-irritated-and-constantly-turned-on was the gold standard.

"How about we do the espresso vanity upstairs?" he asked, his voice placating. "The green will look better with that big window, and if you want expensive-ass tile that looks like wood and takes a bite out of your profit margin, I'll put in tile that looks like wood."

"Okay," I said, ignoring the extra jab about the higher price. "I appreciate that." Since the touching method scrambled my thoughts, I stepped out of his reach, using the pretense of buying the vanity to cover. I tapped the top of the box that held a disassembled one. "Do I lift it up and put it on a cart or something? Or do I drag it through the store and lay it at the feet of the clerks at the checkout stands like the spoils of my latest kill?"

"One, I need to be more vigilant about disarming you before I take you out in public, or I have a feeling my head will be the next thing you throw at someone's feet..."

I pursed my lips, trying to hold a dirty look so he wouldn't go thinking he was hilarious while he gave me his most charming, false-innocence grin.

"And two, while I fully believe you could lift it, we're not going to buy the big stuff here."

"What? Then why did we come here?" And more, why did we have a huge argument over stuff we weren't buying?

"You said you wanted to look around and get a feel for what you wanted. I was trying to be agreeable." His grin widened, stretching the limits of his sexy mouth. "Some of the odds and ends, like paint, you can get here, but I'll order the cabinets and flooring from my vendors. It'll be a lot cheaper, trust me." He arched an eyebrow. "You at least trust me, right?"

Trust was a tricky thing for me.

Way #6: Never trust your heart with anyone. People lie, they change their minds, and feelings fade. No one will ever take as good care of your heart as you hope they will. The only way to keep it safe is to never give it away.

He wasn't asking for my heart, though. Just to save me money. And I realized that I did trust him—not with my heart, but with most everything else. "Yeah. I trust you."

"Good. We'll work on the agreeing thing." A wicked slant curved his lips. "Or maybe we'll just find a better way to work out our frustrations when we don't agree."

I reached up and twisted a strand of hair around my finger. "Like with strip poker?"

"*Wow.* You really want to get me out of my clothes again."

Set myself right up for that one. I couldn't even deny it. I was back to picturing him shirtless and seated across from me last night, his hand on my thigh. Too bad that couldn't happen again—I was glad Savannah's call had interrupted us before we went and made things super complicated.

Well, I was trying to be glad, and that should count for something.

He wrapped an arm around my shoulders and started toward the mock kitchens. "Let's go see what trouble we can get into picking out counters and cabinets, then I'll happily oblige your request."

I let him lead me over. But I was also calculating a way to regain my control before it slipped completely out of my reach.

Chapter Twelve

"What have you been up to?" my mom asked as we settled into a table at South City Kitchen for brunch Thursday morning.

Crap. Did I look guilty? A heavy dose of it pressed against my chest, making it hard to breathe. To some degree, I'd closed myself off emotionally to Cora, but I could never get all the way there. I mean, she was my mom. So even though she'd always chosen men over me, and even though I would inevitably get hurt by something she would say or do in the future, I couldn't help but try to keep our relationship as strong as it could possibly be.

Savannah claimed it was because I was a good person, but most of the time it felt more like a weakness than a strength. There'd been a lot of enabling through the years—growing up, I hadn't recognized that was what was going on, but now that I did, I still enabled her more than I should. I was still the adult while she made reckless, impulsive decisions.

"Ivy? Hello?" Mom raised her perfectly penciled-in eyebrows as much as she could, what with the constant trips to the spa for Botox. "I asked what you've been up to. You're even harder to get a hold of than usual."

Guilt flickered, but I smothered it before it could spread further. She rarely initiated contact, and when she did there were strings attached, as thick and sticky as the webs that'd been in the attic before Jackson took care of them.

"Just work," I said, repressing a shudder over the thought of spiders, immediately followed by a shiver of want as I thought about Jackson. "Lots of work."

"You work too much."

And you don't work enough. She'd always relied on men for everything. Where she lived, how much money she had to shop with, her self-esteem… It all came from outside sources, which was why it'd never be enough.

After a few disastrous turns of living with me, I told her never again. Not just for my sake, but for hers. I wanted her to be independent. Thanks to enough alimony checks to keep her afloat, she'd rented her own apartment (I'd had to move her in, naturally) and now had a job where she worked a whole fifteen to twenty hours a week. She would run out of funds eventually if she didn't work more, but she was looking for a guy instead.

"Since you're obviously not going to ask me what I've been up to, which is only polite, I guess I'll just have to take it upon myself to tell you." She shook out her napkin and draped it across her lap. "I'm dating someone."

My skin prickled, my appetite for the cheddar biscuits and gravy I was looking forward to fading. *And there it is.* Mom was in her early fifties but could pass for much younger. She spent a lot of time on hair, make up, and keeping in shape. Because how else were you supposed to land a new man?

"Don't give me that look," she said. "I know you want me to live alone forever, like some kind of nun."

I snort-laughed. I couldn't help it. The idea of her being

nun-like was laughable. Then the guilt I'd stabled broke free, and I worried that if I didn't act excited enough, she might decide she needed to go to desperate, dangerous lengths to get my attention, and last time that had happened it nearly broke me.

If it hadn't been for Jackson…

Which was why I'd relied on him too much in the past and couldn't make the same mistake. A suffocating sensation gripped my throat and lungs, and I tried to push past it. "Will you at least consider keeping your job?"

"I'm going to keep my job."

I let out a sigh of relief.

"I might have to cut down my hours, though. He lives OTP, so if I end up moving in with him, the drive will take longer than it's worth."

Commuting from outside the perimeter of 285 was a pain, but people managed it every day. "How long have you been dating him?"

She straightened silverware that didn't need straightening, delaying the inevitable, ridiculous answer. "One month. I wanted to wait until it was getting serious to tell you."

"If one month is the standard, I need to tell you about the cereal I recently discovered, because I've been seeing it longer than you've been seeing your boyfriend."

Mom let out an exhale, disappointment clear in her features—well, her forehead and eyes didn't crinkle, but the downturned mouth and years of experience meant I could read through her cosmetic procedures. "I guess I shouldn't tell you these things. Just keep it all bottled up." She added a chin wobble for emphasis.

I wanted to tell her that if she would just forgive Dixie for daring to date a guy she'd let go of, she could have her best friend back. Being the parent, her best friend, *and* her daughter was too much pressure, especially when she wasn't much of a friend or mother back. This brunch date wasn't to "just check in." It was the gateway conversation to how she'd need my help moving her belongings to a new house soon.

I had to shove away my emotions so that I could focus on Mom's and prevent them from spiraling out of control. "I want to know about your life, Mom. I just wish you'd date a while before moving in with the first guy you meet. And what about Savannah's workshop? She's offered you free admission countless times, and while I occasionally tease her about all her rules, she's helped a lot of women. Her classes could help you decide if this guy is the right guy. One who'll stick."

"Sugar, they're all the right guy until they're not. Love's a risk. I know you're good all on your own, but most people need other people. *I* need other people, or I just get so sad."

If only it were that easy. She needed to be adored, and the instant she felt like she wasn't adored enough, she threw that relationship away. Sometimes the guys ended it, too, for a myriad of reasons. Then she'd crash and cry, and I'd have to pick her up and support her for a few weeks to a month. We'd been doing this song and dance for over a decade, and I wanted her to learn some new steps.

I had. At one point in my life, Mom wasn't the only one who'd cried over the end of her relationships. I'd try my hardest to be strong for her, and then after she passed out, I would cry myself to sleep, grieving over the loss of stability, my makeshift home, and stepdads and stepsiblings.

The residual ache over the many losses through the years opened a pit over my heart, sucking the happiness I'd walked into the restaurant with a little at a time. I quickly shut down those thoughts and double-enforced my walls.

Needing people left you dependent, and I couldn't afford to lose my independence. And I sure as hell wouldn't let myself be reduced to someone who could hardly function without a man.

She'd gotten one thing right, though: love was a risk.

One I wasn't willing to take.

. . .

"What's wrong?" Jackson asked when I showed up at the house. I'd told him via text message that I couldn't get there until the afternoon, but from the looks of things, he'd started early.

I swallowed past the lump still lodged in my throat, cursing its existence. "Nothing."

Jackson tilted his head, but it would take more than a head-tilt for me to spill my guts. It'd take a crowbar and massive amounts of alcohol, and basically it wasn't happening.

I peeled off the jacket I'd put on due to the light rain. For the past few days, I'd tried to stay out of Jackson's path as much as possible to help with the temptation-to-cross-lines thing, which wasn't easy considering the house wasn't all that big. Choosing jobs that had taken me to the opposite end of wherever he was working had helped, but now I needed an all-encompassing one that would keep my mind and body nice and busy. "Give me something to do. Something challenging and labor-intensive."

"You wanna learn how to tear down cabinets?"

"More than anything," I said.

An hour later, my legs and arms burned from the squatting and lifting and lowering. I'd put on some music, and other than that, it was just the sound of our tools and the occasional grunts that managed to send my mind right into the gutter. Especially if I was also staring at Jackson as he moved a heavy box of wooden cabinet doors.

Drill in hand, I climbed onto the counter and fit the screwdriver bit on the screw of the last remaining section of cabinets. At first, all I got was grinding resistance.

"Careful to not strip the top of the screw or we'll have a hell of a time with it," Jackson said.

I shot him a look, conveying that was at least the tenth time he'd made that statement and I was on top of one stupid screw. I'd take a sledgehammer to this last section if needed. It'd be so satisfying to watch bits of wood fly. To do some major destruction.

Finally, the bit caught, and the screw came right out, a spiral of wood shavings along with it. I undid the last one, and the weight of the cabinet hit me, much heavier than I'd expected.

For a second, I got that free-fall sensation that proceeded a crash, but Jackson was right there, supporting the bottom and giving me a chance to catch my balance. "I've got it," he said, and then he took it from me and tossed it into the pile with the rest. He swiped his forearm across his forehead and extended a hand to help me down.

I supposed it'd be rude to refuse, and considering the mess on the floor, jumping down could end badly.

I slapped my palm in his and slowly lowered myself to sit on the counter. Instead of scooting back to give me room to get all the way down, Jackson stepped between my legs, wedging them open.

He dipped his head, leaving him right at eye level with me. "Now that we've gotten some of that anxious energy out with destruction, how 'bout you tell me what's up? You're still all tense."

"Am not." It came out weak, and his immovable stance proved he wasn't buying it. I didn't want to talk. I wanted to be in control of the guys my mom chose and ensure she wouldn't get hurt and end up in that dark, depressed place she lingered in longer and longer with each failed relationship. But that wasn't an option, and I hated it.

I hated feeling like we'd repeat this pattern until...well, I didn't want to think about how long. She'd probably be throwing weddings in the nursing home that we were both living in.

"Is it your mom?" Jackson asked. "Is she okay?"

I met his gaze, and my heart gave a painful squeeze. "She's okay when it comes to...all that stuff. As far as I can tell, anyway." The vice on my heart tightened as I remembered getting the call that she was in the emergency room because she'd taken too many pills. A possible suicide attempt they'd informed me, and while she had sad, blue periods now and then, I never thought she'd hurt herself. "I just worry. I mean, I've worried ever since that night in the ER, but I thought she was doing better and so well on her own. Now she tells me that she's dating again, and I'm so afraid that if it doesn't go smoothly, she'll spiral. And none of her relationships go smoothly. All growing up, I kept thinking surely this one won't end up like the last, but she chooses the worst guys, or if they're actually good ones, she dumps them—it's like she's got blinders on in her relationships."

"Want me to do some digging? Find out who this guy is and give him a shakedown if needed?" One corner of Jackson's mouth turned up, telling me he was joking, but I also knew that if I told him I wanted him to, he'd make good on his offer.

While we still couldn't agree on most anything, he'd always been a man of his word, and he was the kind of guy who'd defend people against bullies or step in if a situation got out of control. He wasn't easily intimidated or deterred, and that was why he was the most dangerous guy I'd ever met. Unable to help myself, I ran my hand down the side of his face. The scrape of his whiskers against my palm sent tingles dancing across my skin. "Not yet."

I reluctantly let my hand drop and gripped the edge of

the counter so I wouldn't be tempted to touch him again. "I can't stop thinking about how nice it would be to just shrug it off and say, 'Fine, date who you want. I'm out.' And then just be able to ignore her as easily as she's ignored me."

The truth of my admission flayed me open, leaving me way too exposed. I shifted, attempting to move off the counter because it was too much, but Jackson put his large hands on my thighs, holding me in place. "But you can't. And that's okay. I know you want everyone to think that nothing gets to you, but it's okay to have feelings."

I shook my head.

He caught my chin and lifted my face to his. "It is. But it's also okay to let go of what you can't control."

Shit. Tears were forming, and I couldn't cry in front of him. I decided that between bursting into tears and showing the tiniest bit of neediness, neediness was better than weakness—after all, guys ran from needy women. Holding on to that weak consolation, I gave in to my impulse, threw my arms around his neck, and hugged him for all I was worth.

It was so familiar, being wrapped in his embrace. In some respects, way too familiar. Him consoling me about my mom. Me losing my iron grip on my emotions.

I'd arrived at the emergency room that night all those months ago to find Mom attached to tubes and wires, so pale I could see every vein in her body. They'd pumped her stomach and said they had done all they could do and that it was just a waiting game. I'd been terrified I was going to lose her and had a full-blown panic attack. Savannah was out of town, and I didn't know what to do, so I picked up my phone and called Jackson.

I wasn't even sure why, but as soon as I saw his name in my contacts, I knew he'd know what to do.

He'd come to the hospital, and I'd flung myself into his arms, pretty much like I'd done moments ago. He'd held me as

I'd cried against his shoulder, lamenting the fact that I hadn't called her enough, and I hadn't paid enough attention, and I felt so damn helpless, and tell me what to do, just someone tell me what to do.

He'd held me until I was completely wrung out, not a single tear left.

Clenching my jaw, I forced myself to stop feeling and managed to stifle the urge to cry. I lifted my head and got lost in a sea of green for a moment…

Got lost in the way Jackson looked at me.

He didn't move, didn't breathe, almost as if he were afraid I'd freak out and pull away. I teetered on the edge of what I should do and what I wanted to do, and then I fisted my hand in his T-shirt and pulled him to me.

I brushed my lips across his. "I just need to not think for a while," I whispered.

"That can definitely be arranged," he said, tension vibrating through his muscles as he fought to hold himself back. "Are you sure?"

I nodded even though I wasn't sure of anything except that kissing him felt like the right thing to do in this moment.

I could feel the instant his control snapped, the change so palpable that electricity crackled in the highly charged air between us. He gripped my hips and pulled me flush against him as his mouth descended on mine. My legs automatically wrapped around his waist. One of his hands traveled up and tangled in my hair. Then he used his grip to angle my head and deepen the kiss.

As his lips moved against mine, his tongue dipping in for a quick taste, my thoughts went nice and hazy. Jackson kissed down the column of my neck and then pressed a sucking kiss over my collarbone. I arched against him the best I could, using the counter for leverage, but there still seemed to be too much space, too much clothes, too much everything and yet not enough.

His hands skimmed up the sides of my waist, his thumbs hooked on the hem of my shirt. We broke apart long enough for him to pull it over my head, and then I went to work removing his.

I sighed at the delicious skin-on-skin contact when we came back together, my desire flaring even hotter when he groaned.

Right as I reached for the button of his jeans, he pulled away. A protest was on the tip of my tongue, but then he undid my jeans, roughly yanked them off, and tossed them aside. He pulled me into his arms and crushed his lips to mine. I rewrapped my legs around his waist, and then we were moving.

"Where…?" Talking was more effort than I expected.

Jackson rounded the corner and started up the stairs. "Somewhere I can lay you back and kiss my way down your body."

"Well, in that case, take me wherever."

His lips found the sensitive spot under my ear, and his husky voice made goose bumps sweep across my skin. "I knew there was a way to get you to agree with me."

He lowered me to my feet once we reached my former bedroom, and the break in contact and kissing gave me two seconds too long to think. I desperately needed an escape, but I didn't want him to feel like I'd used him, even though I'd yet to meet a guy who cared about that when sex was involved.

"This…" I gestured between us and placed my hand on the center of his chest so I could keep him back long enough to get this out. It was entirely counterproductive, because his skin was warm, and I could feel his heart beating against my palm, the rhythm as fast and as hard as mine.

"We're only having fun," Jackson said, backing me toward the bed. He slipped his finger in the strap of my bra, and the exquisite drag of his rough fingertips robbed me of oxygen. "Enjoying it while it lasts. I've heard the speech, and this time, I get it. I won't make the same mistake I did before."

I wanted to argue that it wasn't so much a mistake and say it was me not him, which was overused enough to put it in the least-sexy things you could say category. But then he yanked the strap he'd been toying with down off my shoulder, his carnal side taking over.

He gave the other strap the same treatment, nipping at the exposed spot where my neck met my shoulder as he reached behind me and unhooked my bra.

Shivers of need cascaded through me, growing even stronger as his heated gaze ran over me. He gripped my hips, his fingers digging into my skin.

Then he tossed me on the bed, crawled over me, and started making good on his promise to kiss his way down my body.

I let go of my inhibitions, succumbed to the delicious sensations traveling up and down my body, and decided to let myself have fun and enjoy it while it lasted.

And with Jackson, I knew that that could be a very long time…

Chapter Thirteen

I woke up alone, and for half a hazy second, I was almost offended.

Then I realized it meant Jackson did understand. Maybe we really could just have fun, no strings or messy complications. Heaven knows I needed the release.

I sunk into the mattress, enjoying the tingly soreness and the memory of the kisses we'd shared. Of his powerful body moving over mine.

If we hadn't been alone in the house, the how-to-get-busted springs would've most definitely given us away. My smile spread across my face, reaching deliriously happy territory.

I'd forgotten how amazing sex could be. Like, I remembered it was amazing and I'd felt the lack of it in my life, but with Jackson it went so far above and beyond anything else I'd ever experienced. Last night was make-you-forget-your-problems-*and*-your-name sex.

I let out a contented sigh and then decided I should get up and moving. Since I hadn't been planning on staying the night, I didn't have any of my essentials here. Going home just to come back didn't seem like a good use of the few hours I had before my bartending shift at Azure, so I threw my hair in a bun and got to work digging through the boxes I'd pulled into my bedroom when the living room seemed too far, the stairs too daunting. I still needed to sort which of the remaining ones needed hauled to Goodwill and which were the ones Dixie wanted me to keep.

The first box I knelt beside opened up with a puff of dirt, and I coughed and waved a hand through the air before diving in.

These must be her scrapbooks. Now that I twisted the box around, I spotted the label.

Dixie had tried to get me into scrapbooking with her, always saving ticket stubs and little mementos that marked our trips. Like the one to the Tybee Island Beach and that misguided camping trip to the Chattahoochee Forest. *We so weren't roughing-it girls.*

The scenery was amazing, though. I recognized the maroon cover of one of the books and pulled it out—it had just the trip I was reminiscing about. I laughed as I studied the pictures: our fire pit with still-intact logs, marred only by a few scorch marks, as starting campfires wasn't in our repertoire; eating our non-melted s'mores; and one of Mom running from a cloud of bugs that must've loved her perfume or hairspray, our leaning tent in the background.

I ran my finger over the last picture—one taken using the timer on Dixie's camera—and tentacles of longing wrapping around me. It was the camping trip from hell, but the three of us were frozen in a moment of laughter. We'd had a lot of those in the good days—a.k.a., the days between Mom's men. They were my favorite memories. Mom hadn't been the same since the rift formed between her and Dixie. Nothing had been the same.

Instead of letting the sentimental wave pull me under, I lifted the book and studied the captions and cool effects Dixie added. She often spent hours perfecting one page. I didn't have the patience to cut borders and do all the gluing and decorating. She took it to the next level with funky rivets and grommets and other things I didn't even know existed before she'd pulled me up to the large oak table in her craft room one day. I always thought it was funny that we ate on a table that could barely accommodate the three of us, while the craft table was several feet long.

When I lifted out another book, a stack of loose pictures fell and scattered across the floor. As I gathered them up, I suddenly understood her fascination with recording everything. She had pictures of Mom and me squeezed into the tire swing that used to hang in the front yard—the neighbors thought it was an eyesore, which only encouraged us to use it more. Another set of pictures commemorated one of the yearly Fourth of July barbecues Dixie and Mom put on.

She even had pictures of me in a school play. The one where I was dressed like the palest Indian at Thanksgiving. *O-M-G, what was I doing with my hair?*

Half crimpy, half straight, and all WTH. I stacked them and set them aside, then lifted out a book I'd never seen before. It looked older, the material edges browned with signs of age.

The first few pictures were of Dixie and Mom, and judging from the styles and their age, it must've been from college. They'd lived in a small apartment near Georgia State University, where Dixie majored in English with a minor in photography—naturally—and my mom majored in attending school to find a man before eventually dropping out.

I flipped the page and came face to face with the man she found. My dad moved out of the house before I could talk in full sentences and relocated to the west coast when I was in elementary school. Phone calls between us were painful and closely resembled the type of jilted small talk perfect strangers would have, so we'd all but given up on them. I got the feeling kids had never been his thing, and from what I'd gathered from bits and accidental dropped hints, my mom thought a baby would save their rocky four-year marriage.

Spoiler alert: it didn't.

I sometimes felt like she had a hard time forgiving me for that.

I lifted the book higher and studied my parents. They looked so happy and in love. I'd seen Mom give plenty of guys the adoring, glassy-eyed look, but I'd never seen a guy return it quite that strongly before, like his every breath relied on her taking one, too.

Apparently, at one point, my father had returned her sentiment. There was even a cute photo strip of them kissing in a booth.

Just goes to show you that love never lasts, no matter how great it starts out. Thank goodness I knew better than to think it did.

For reasons I couldn't explain, I glanced at the crumpled sheets I'd spent the night tangled up in. Was that my brain trying to warn me not to get carried away? Because I was totally in control. I'd been completely upfront with Jackson, and he made it clear he understood and was on board with simply enjoying it while it lasted.

Which would be a month at most, because then we'd be done with this project and our lives would take us in different directions. That was just enough time to have lots of fun without getting too very attached.

Hell, maybe we'd still occasionally hook up when our paths crossed. Like we could sneak away to his old bedroom next time the Gambles forced me to a family gathering. After all, we'd done it in my childhood bedroom.

I smiled at that thought. The activities surrounding Savannah's wedding would give us ample opportunity.

Savannah. Crap. I'd done a good job of blocking out how mad she'd be if she found out I was sleeping with her brother for fun. My heart sank. I hated to disappoint her and do the very thing I told her I wouldn't do, and it'd make me even more of a jerk if I did it around her wedding.

I could see the looming disaster now. The bride and the maid of honor barely on speaking terms; the entire Gamble family interrogating me about why I had to get in the way of their plans to match Jackson up with someone who'd be so much better for him. I'd just sit there and shrug and hem and haw because I wouldn't have any counterpoints besides, "Well, I just really like having sex with him, and he's super good at it."

I doubted they'd sit around laughing, saying, "Classic Ivy," or, "No worries. Caroline can wait on the sidelines until he's done having his fun with you."

Last night I'd just jumped without thinking because I was sick of fighting my overwhelming attraction to Jackson all day every day, and as Savannah pointed out, I was occasionally self-destructive.

It didn't feel destructive, though; it felt restorative. More than a little addictive. Despite telling myself that what I should be doing was talking myself *out* of jumping into bed with him again, not indulging in fantasies of how much spontaneous sexy fun we could have as we spent the next month flipping this house, ideas and plans were stirring, the possibilities flooding my brain and giving me a residual high.

I was afraid that I was getting a little too close to breaking my seventh fail-safe, even if it was just hooking-up plans.

Way #7: *No making plans. Plans lead to expectations,*

and expectations end in hurt feelings, and hurt feelings lead to broken hearts.

There was no reason to have to make a decision now, when I didn't even know what tomorrow would bring. I'd just take things one day at a time. No set plans. No expectations or hurt feelings, and definitely no broken hearts.

Savannah would never agree with my methods, whether or not her brother was involved—she was a planner through and through, and being a dating guru on top of that, obviously she would only look at things from that angle. But *I* was the expert at avoiding messy relationships.

Apparently I wasn't that great at convincing even myself, because guilt still tried to bubble up. I did my best to push it down and turned back to the scrapbook to distract me from my jumbled thoughts.

Of course then all I could think about was how I was holding a physical reminder of everything you lost when you let a guy get in the way of a friendship.

Would Savannah be okay if I told her that this thing with Jackson was a little more than sex? As in mostly sex with a pinch of caring? Like I'd be sad if I ever followed through on my threats to his person, and not just because I'd go to jail?

I flipped pages in the scrapbook until I found another one of Mom and a guy who didn't even look vaguely familiar, which meant she was probably with him when I was too young to remember.

I wondered how many of Mom's relationships Dixie had documented. Were there dozens of happy couple pictures that needed ripped in two?

I'd bet money she didn't keep any of the pictures from when my mom and Rhett were dating. *Can you say aka-awkward?*

Conflicted feelings I didn't realize I still had drifted to

the surface. Loyalty said Dixie shouldn't have crossed that line with one of her best friend's exes, but it seemed unfair to deny her happiness when she'd been the one who'd cultivated most of it through the ups and downs of Mom's many, many relationships. Seven years later, and she and Rhett were still together, so they were obviously happy and working.

Or they'd settled for mediocrity, like most of the world did.

Pessimistic, I know, but it wasn't like I'd ever believed in the sunshiny optimism my best friend did. What was important was she believed it, and she'd achieved it.

I believed that I was just fine on my own.

And I'd achieved it.

Mostly.

· · ·

The next time I saw Jackson, I was elbow deep in paint, my music blaring through my earphones. Okay, so technically, it just felt like it, but I did have splatters clear up to my elbows. It'd only been two days since we'd slept together, but it felt like a lot longer, and before I could rein them in, butterflies erupted in my tummy.

"Hey," I said, tugging out an earbud and drinking him in from head to toe. His snug, dark gray T-shirt highlighted his firm shoulders and pecs and made his eyes greener somehow, and his jeans were distressed by hours of manual labor. My designated work pants had come faded and pre-ripped, but they were getting plenty of battle scars, as were my arms and hands.

Jackson gave me a nod. "Mornin'."

What was it about tool belts that made a guy that much hotter? In this instance, the guy had started out smokin' hot, so the combination was doing funny things to my insides.

I waited to see if he'd tell me why he'd been MIA the past few days, but he simply set his giant toolbox on the floor and opened it up. Friday morning he'd texted to tell me he had to take care of some things and that it'd take up the rest of the weekend, but not what things, and I hated how badly I wanted to know.

That's fine, I thought as I returned to my painting. *I'll just employ Number Five.* I wouldn't volunteer what I'd been up to (nothing except this and work, for the record) and I wouldn't ask for his whereabouts or what was so important it took two days.

Keep it all separate—the job, the sex, the personal stuff. That's how to ensure this doesn't end badly.

Last time we'd let all parts of our lives bleed together, and things got messy fast. I was nothing if not good at applying the past to avoid repeating my mistakes.

When I turned to ask what he was working on today, he'd already disappeared. I debated putting my roller down to go check and at least say more than "hey," but I heard the whir of the drill in the other room and decided if he wanted to just get to it, then fine.

Not like I'd been waiting for two whole days to talk to him or anything.

I channeled my frustration for good, focusing on my work like I was freaking Michelangelo painting the ceiling of the Sistine Chapel. Except for instead of a bunch of naked dudes I was rolling lines of a blue-gray color called Prelude. I wasn't sure what it was a prelude to, but I thought it was calm and soothing and modern.

I noticed Jackson didn't say anything about it. *If he doesn't like it, that just means I picked the right one.*

I attacked the wall with renewed fervor.

An hour or so later, my arms burned so badly that I promised I'd never lift them over my head again if they'd just hold on long enough for me to take care of the last wall. Unfortunately, it was the tall one leading up to the staircase, and I couldn't quite reach. I stretched for all I was worth…

And accidentally bumped the roller to the *white* ceiling, lost my balance, and barely got my hand out in time to catch myself against the wet wall.

The roller clattered to the floor, and it was a good thing the old floral carpet was going, because now there was a blue-gray blob on it. *Nailed it!*

Jackson poked his head around the corner of the kitchen. "Everything okay in here?"

I grinned extra wide. "Yep."

Instead of going back to whatever he was doing—building and hanging the new kitchen cabinets was my guess—he took a few steps into the room and picked up the roller. "Need me to get the top part?"

"I mean, you can if you want to. I can do it. I just need to get a step stool or a ladder." I was going to have to touch up the ceiling, too, damn it.

He refilled the paint and nudged me aside. "I got it, shorty."

I started to roll my eyes, but then he tested the limits of his impressive height, stretching himself as tall as possible. His pants hung low on his hips, and after going months without, I should be okay with going a couple of days, but all I could think about was the way his body pressed against mine the other night and how I'd like him to do it again.

"There," he said, extending the roller to me.

Our eyes met, and his pupils darkened, like he could read my very dirty thoughts. Before I got completely swept up in his orbit and things got carried away, I gripped the handle of the paint roller and took a large step back. My plan had been to take things one day at a time, but now I realized it just meant I hadn't decided anything yet, and I wasn't sure if we should follow our minds into the gutter or not. "I…I've been thinking…"

Jackson took a step toward me, closing the space I'd put between us. He swept the hair off my face and trailed his finger down and across my jaw. "I thought we took care of that thinking problem the other night."

"Jackson." Man, he was making it so hard to hold on to anything resembling resolve.

He leaned closer, his lips a mere breath away. "Ivy."

My heart thumped harder and harder in my chest. *Am I really going to do this? Say something that might stop our sexytimes fun in its tracks before I get my fill?*

Yes, damn it, it looks like I am. I really should've come up with a more solid plan so I'd know exactly what to say.

"While the other night was fun, I know that you're looking for something"—my throat tightened, and I had to force the words out—"more long term."

"You've obviously been talking to my meddling family— my money is on Savannah."

I shrugged. "It doesn't make it less true, does it?"

"I told you the other night that I knew we were only having fun, and I meant it."

"But you're dating someone." Guilt flooded me as I said it. I'd been so focused on how upset Savannah would be that I'd managed to forget that I had even more to feel guilty for.

"I've been on a few dates recently, yes, but I'm not in a committed relationship, or I never would've carried you to bed. You really think I'd do that?"

Now that I thought about it, no, but I still wondered if Caroline thought they were more serious. His family certainly hoped it would go in that direction. "I don't want to get in the way."

Jackson's intense gaze bored into me, making my heart skip a few beats altogether. "You've been in the way since the moment I walked through the door of this house—hell, maybe even since the engagement party. I tried wanting what's good for me, but wanting you is stronger."

Every ounce of air whooshed out of my lungs at once. "Then maybe we need to rethink our business arrangement. I can hire someone else to help me fin—"

"No."

There was the familiar irritation, leaking in and spiking my blood pressure. I tossed the roller down in the vicinity of the tray. "Okay, let's at least talk about it, because if—"

"No. We made a deal, and I plan on seeing it through. I'm also a grown man, and I'm perfectly capable of making my own decisions. I understand that this thing between us is temporary, and I don't care." He hauled me to him, his arm coming around my waist to secure me against him. "I'm not quite done having my way with you yet."

He crashed his mouth down on mine, and all my pent-up energy surged forward at once, common sense taking the backseat as lust took the wheel. I parted my lips, diving headlong into the kiss. I ran my hands up his firm arms, not realizing my left hand was still wet with paint from catching myself until I'd dragged it most the way up.

Jackson glanced at the smear of blue covering his biceps and the sleeve of his T-shirt, arched an eyebrow, and then backed me up against the wet wall, his hips bumping into mine.

I moaned as he ground against me. He felt so good I didn't even care about the paint or the fact that I'd need to redo the wall. I just wanted more of him on more of me.

I arched against him, satisfaction heating my veins at the rough groan that ripped from his throat. Groping each other became the best kind of competition, each of us seeing how riled up we could get the other.

His tongue stroked mine as he tugged at my shirt, and

not one to be outdone, I did some tugging of my own. One by one our clothes fell into a discarded pile on the floor. Jackson looped his thumb through the tiny string of my underwear, and a trail of color streaked down my thigh as he yanked them off me.

We came back together, a blur of lips and tongues and sweat-slickened skin. With all those pesky layers out of the way, it didn't take long before both of us were gasping for air and tumbling over the edge together.

Chapter Fourteen

Since she didn't have any client meetings, Savannah came over to help me paint Tuesday morning, something she'd done several times at my condo, even though we'd never gotten more than halfway finished before I decided I hated the color and needed to pick a different one.

Funny to think of that now, especially since I was so sure which colors I wanted in this house, even if Jackson didn't always agree on my vision. Although yesterday he *had* admitted to liking the blue-gray. He'd said it as he lifted strands of my coated, sex-rumpled hair, so I'm sure that had something to do with it.

I reached up and ran my fingers over the slightly crunchy strands the paint hadn't quite washed out of and bit back a smile.

"Who's the guy?" Savannah asked.

I quickly snapped out of it and returned to the paint tray to refill my roller. "No guy. I just like renovating. I think I found my calling."

When I turned around, Savannah had the hand not

holding her roller on her hip and a serious expression on her face. "One, I'm a dating coach who makes her living off reading body language, and two, I'm your best friend. That's not an I-enjoy-painting smile. That's an I-got-laid-and-it-was-amazing smile."

In spite of my best efforts to force my lips to remain in a neutral position, I made the mistake of thinking of the sex against the wet wall, and a smile broke free, accompanied by a swirl of heat. Yeah, I was busted—I really needed to up my poker-face game. "Okay. I did, and it was amazing, but I don't want to talk about it."

Savannah stared at me with a perplexed expression, like I was a familiar puzzle she'd forgotten how to solve. "Since when? Are you, or are you not, the same girl who told me that 'absence makes the vagina grow fonder'?"

I laughed and set my roller to the wall. "You're welcome for my little gems of wisdom. If I recall, I told you that as a cautionary tale, one to warn you to keep your distance from Linc if you didn't want to slip. How'd that work out for you?"

"I tried it. It wasn't for me." She gave her own I-got-laid-and-it-was-amazing smile, and the overwhelming urge to tell her all about it nearly overpowered me. I wanted to talk about the guy's amazing body and the many equally amazing things he did with it. Wanted to tell her that he kissed like he'd been born to kiss and that he and I had this addictive, crazy-strong chemistry that laid waste to every other experience I'd ever had.

But she'd only be happy for me until she found who it was with, and I felt bad enough about that, especially since I knew she'd always worried he and I would hook up and it would be a disaster.

After all, we did, and it had been. Luckily, she'd been out of town that week, far enough away that she couldn't read my emotions so easily. This time around was different, though.

We'd learned what worked for us and what didn't.

And *man* was it working for me.

"Earth to Ivy," Savannah said, right by my ear, and I jumped, my roller globbing the paint on so thick it dripped down in streaks. She laughed. "I've never seen you stare off into space all dreamy like that."

Shit, looking at her was the wrong thing to do; I realized it as soon as her eyes widened to the size of a cartoon dog who'd just seen a raw steak. "You like him!" She shoved my shoulder. "Don't even try to give me that I-just-love-flipping-this-house bullshit. I need details on the guy who's managed to take my pessimistic, doesn't-believe-in-love best friend and turn her into a smiley, twitterpated girl who stares off into space as she thinks about him."

"I'm *not* twitterpated."

"I'm reserving judgment until I hear details."

I did a fish-struggling-for-air impression for several seconds. Even though she'd be upset, I still wanted to come clean and just get it out there so we could try to deal with it, but throwing family and judgment into the mix would tip the disaster scales, and I wasn't willing to risk having to end things with Jackson earlier than I absolutely had to. I was sure he'd agree, and he deserved a say, considering it would mean his family getting even more involved in his love life than they already were. "It's…complicated. I'm not saying I don't like him—I like something about every guy I sleep with."

"Yeah, but you like more than this guy's penis."

Of course Jackson swung open the door at that moment, and I doubted I was lucky enough for him to have missed hearing at least the word "penis."

"Keeping girl talk classy as usual, I see," he said, and his poker face was much better than mine, enough so that I had no idea how what he was thinking or feeling about what he'd overheard.

Maybe I shouldn't have given him a key. It was something I'd never given a guy before, but it seemed counterintuitive to not provide my contractor with a way to get inside to work on the house when I wasn't there.

I prayed Savannah would drop it. Usually Jackson got all pissy when we talked about guys in front of him. Probably the way I felt pissy when I wondered if he was going to continue casually dating the debutante, and why wouldn't my mind drop that already? Ugh.

I also hoped he wouldn't say or do anything that'd give us away. As Savannah pointed out, she was way too good at reading body language, and she knew both Jackson and me too well for us to keep things hidden for long.

Although we had managed to keep our last fling secret.

"Fling" didn't quite seem like the right word for that week, but I didn't want to go into that, especially with the human lie detector in the room.

"We should take a break." I set my roller in the tray. "I need to talk to Jackson about what he's doing in the kitchen."

"Please say you have coffee," Savannah said, putting her roller next to mine.

I grimaced. Coffee was what I drank to have enough energy to get to my Cherry Coke, but if Savannah didn't have a regular supply, her woodland-creature-adorableness flipped to rabid animal mode. In the cutest of ways, while still being absolutely terrifying.

"Okay," Savannah said. "I'll go grab some sustenance from the Daily Grind and be back in like fifteen to twenty. With enough caffeine, I think we can knock out this room and the stairwell today."

"That would be awesome." My arms were now onto the fact that my promises to not keep abusing them were false, and they ached and burned with a vengeance. I couldn't wait to never see a paintbrush or roller again.

Sorry, condo wall that couldn't decide what color it needed to be—yeah, it was totally the wall's fault. I was just the paint messenger.

I looked over at Jackson, and he winked at me, a wink that said I remember what you look like naked and up against that wall over there. He was so going to get us caught.

"Okay, so who wants what?" Savannah picked up her giant purse and glanced from me to Jackson.

"Just get me a large cup of the blackest coffee they have," Jackson said.

"Black like his soul," I added, because if I didn't throw in a couple of verbal jabs, his sister would find us out for sure.

His eyes met mine, mischief dancing in the green. "And Ivy needs iced coffee to go with the temperature of hers."

Savannah sighed. "Really, guys? I thought you two were trying to get along. Do I need to take away any nail guns? Other tools that inflict damage?"

"Anything can be a tool of pain if you believe in yourself enough," I replied with an over-the-top grin.

She gave another sigh.

"And actually, an iced caramel macchiato would be awesome, thanks." I rubbed a hand on my neck and let it drift slowly down my body. "Guess Jackson knows just what I like."

Okay, now I was just begging to be caught, but the way his eyes flashed was worth it.

Savannah paused, her hand on the doorknob, and glanced over her shoulder at us. "Please don't kill each other while I'm gone. I was feeling all kinds of proud that you were getting along."

"Yes, Mom," Jackson said, and she shot him a look like she might kill him herself.

The second the door closed behind her, I released the laugh that'd been dying to break free. "Don't get me wrong,

I'm glad that we can nearly have an entire conversation without biting each other's heads off, but I kind of missed verbally sparing with you."

Yesterday we hadn't even bothered with words at all, besides things like *faster*, *harder*, and *don't stop*.

Jackson strode over, placed his hand on my hip, and slipped his thumb under the hem of my shirt, rubbing the skin there into a tizzy. "Same here. Although I think I might need to punish you for that black soul comment."

"I'd expect nothing less." I tipped onto my toes and planted a kiss on his lips. We didn't have time to do justice to any of the fantasies flickering through my brain, so I should probably keep the kissing to a minimum, but the way he kissed was a form of foreplay, so I figured it was still on the strictly sexual, not-emotional side of the scale.

He molded me to him, ran his tongue over my top lip, and then pulled back and pressed his forehead against mine. "To be continued later tonight."

"You bet your fine ass it will be." I ran my hand down his chest, getting a thrill at how quickly his heart beat against my palm. "We're in agreement that we shouldn't tell Savannah about any of this, right?"

"Do you see a future with a picket fence and two-point-five kids?"

My heart rate screeched into the danger zone, and my lungs stopped taking in oxygen.

He chuckled and dragged his fingertips across my collarbone, the panic easing as a dizzying swirl of desire took its place. "That's what I thought. Which is why telling Savannah would be a bad idea. If we explain we're just having fun, she'll be mad at both of us for doing that to each other, regardless of whether or not it's what we both want—mostly because she'll never believe us, since her brain doesn't work that way. And if we say we're just seeing how things go, she'll have visions of you in a white dress and me in a tux dancing through her head."

I swallowed hard, the panic overtaking the pulsing need coursing under my skin. "Okay, that's enough analogies that give me hives for a day." I bit my lip. "I just feel bad keeping things from her."

"I know." His hand came to rest on the side of my neck, his thumb pressed over the pulse point that quickened even more at his touch. "But we're doing it for her good. And this is about no complications, right?"

I slowly nodded, even though there were complication land mines all over the place. Denial seemed like the best way to address those right now.

"Okay, then." He dropped his hand and took a step back, and I immediately missed his touch and the warmth of his body. "Let's head to the kitchen. I realize you were just making an excuse to talk to me when you mentioned it, but I need to get your opinion on a few things."

"You're asking my opinion?"

"Yes, boss. Because unlike you, I'm open to suggestions." Apparently the verbal jabs weren't quite over, although the grin he aimed at me softened it.

"Well, here's something not open to suggestions," I said. "I'm going to make you pay for *that* comment later."

His grin only widened. "Bring it, babe."

I decided to let the term of endearment slide, because when he said it, it was more like a promise of naughtiness, which totally meant it hardly counted.

Chapter Fifteen

Four weeks into the project—three of which I'd had Jackson's help for—and the place was really coming together. I mean, the floors still looked like a paint and debris graveyard, but the kitchen had new white cabinets with this white backsplash that Jackson talked me into. Because I *could* listen to other people's opinions.

I leaned my forearms on the gray-swirled quartz countertop and ran a hand over its smooth, cool surface. I wanted to skate across it—I totally wouldn't, because the counters were flawless and I was scared to even test them by cooking anything, even though I'd been staying the night more and more. I'd even brought over some toiletries and clothes. And enough condoms to keep Jackson and me otherwise entertained when the need arose. Which was pretty much every night after we finished working. I'd be so tired that I'd think I didn't even have the energy for sex, but then he'd give me a look or brush his hand across my back, and all my energy renewed like a video game character who was ready for one more round.

Let's see, it's been…just over a week since we started fooling around.

Last time the walls started closing in right around this point. As if I'd summoned them with my memory, those metaphorical walls pressed against my lungs, increasing the pressure with each breath I couldn't catch.

It's not the same. For one, it hadn't been seven days in a row. We'd missed two in there when he'd sent that ambiguous text about being busy. Two, we had more defined boundaries this time around. And three, we *had* to be around each other all day, no option for space, or we'd never finish the renovations in time.

I thought about how we had to wrap up everything in the next few weeks, and a different kind of pressure built, like my heart was fighting with my lungs and then they decided none of them could fit in there together, so they all decided to battle it out for control.

Since I couldn't make heads or tails of that, I thought about the last time Jackson and I had started up our frenemies with benefits arrangement, looking for clues to help us avoid that same ugly outcome, where the end meant the loss of benefits and the friend part dropped from the enemies part.

Man, I'd been such a wreck when my mom was in the hospital, and he'd swooped right in like a flannel-clad knight on a white horse. The next night he came over to check on me, and after a heated kissing session on the couch, we'd fallen into bed and I'd asked him to stay.

I cringed at the memory, because I wasn't usually *that girl.* But he'd stayed, and then we just started spending every night together, like it wasn't a big deal. At first, it didn't seem like one. He'd sleep over and make coffee in the morning. Then he'd leave a warm cup on my bedside table before he took off for work so that—as he'd so nicely put it in the note he'd also left—I wouldn't terrify any children when I left my house un-caffeinated. He'd even drawn a little broom underneath to really drive home the implication I was a scary witch in the mornings.

Most girls would kill for that (well, maybe most would prefer a sweeter note, but I'd be offended, not to mention suspicious, if a guy called me sweet). And it wasn't like it wasn't amazing. Funny enough, being around Jackson didn't give me the same suffocating sensation I usually experienced when a guy overstayed his welcome—which was about an hour or so in most cases. It was just that I started to rely on his comfort at night and that cup of coffee that said he cared, and I didn't want it to turn into fights over who did the dishes, and why couldn't I remember to put the lid on the toothpaste, dammit, and why was I sleeping in when the house was a mess?

I didn't want to spend my evenings watching the time, each hour that ticked by another one that he hadn't shown up. Broken promises, hateful, sharp words that sliced to the core, and the inevitable crash where the dark side wasn't a funny metaphor but where you lived day and night, your chest aching because you missed people and they were gone, and why did we hurt the people we claimed to love most?

I'd seen so many of my mom's relationships go that way. Amazing to awful. Sure, there was a bit in between, but the ugly or sad ending—and sometimes both—came every time. Security became a myth, and I swore that once I moved out on my own, I'd have the stability and control I desperately wanted.

I'd told myself that I'd be smarter, but what did I do within months of living on my own? I met a hot, charming dude who I let sway me over to the optimistic side. I thought I'd experienced enough to know the good guys from the bad guys.

I was so naive. So sure I'd found a good one. That he'd

be different.

Embarrassment flooded me as I remembered how hard I'd clung to the first guy who actually seemed to see me. I heard this quote once, and it applied perfectly to my relationship with Tyler: *We all eat lies when our hearts are hungry.*

I'd gobbled up his lies about forever and bought into all his somedays—someday I'll take you to Paris, someday we'll have a place of our own so we don't have to go so long between seeing each other, and so on and so forth.

I let down every wall and he'd Trojan horsed me.

The honeymoon period faded toward the beginning of second semester. I'd fed him all the information he needed to make each attack on me personal. *You're as crazy as your mother—this is why no one ever stuck around. I can't deal with you when you're like this. You just don't know how a relationship is supposed to work.*

I was so determined to not be like my mom that instead of walking away, I dug in my heels and tried that much harder to make our relationship work. And for the record, "like this" was asking why he hadn't come over when he'd promised, where he was on a Friday night. It was daring to ask that he hold me after we had sex or that we have a conversation beforehand, since I hadn't seen him for a few days.

Then he'd pour on the guilt, because he'd learned that I was conditioned to give into it—*thanks for that, Mom.* He'd go on and on about how he was busy and trying to keep up with classes, and I was asking for too much. He'd even choke up as he told me how stressed he was, and I would think, *Wow, he really needs me. I'll bend over backward to make it better, because I love him and we're in this together, and it's the least I can do.*

I'd turned down an offer to be in the Bioscience Club, which probably would've made me change my career to focus on that. Not to mention several other clubs, activities, and parties I could've been a part of. Each time I'd chosen him over things I'd talked myself out of wanting, sacrificing myself in the process.

Hindsight made me feel even stupider, but I hadn't made any other friends, and Rhett and Dixie had just moved away, taking with them my last shred of stability. So I gave my all to my asshole boyfriend, and when he dumped me, I had nothing left.

I pressed my hand against my chest at the ache that bloomed there, almost wishing I could be that naive girl again so I could just enjoy the beginning stages of a relationship but knowing there was no going back.

People expected more, and I didn't have more to give.

I jumped at the feel of a hand on my back.

"Sorry," Jackson said. "I thought you heard me come in." He swept my hair off the back of my neck and pressed his lips there, and I wanted to fall into his arms and forget about everything else.

Which meant I shouldn't.

Way #8: Repeats equal reliance. Never see a guy two weekends in a row. Spending too much time together leads to attachments and relying on each other. Emotions inevitably follow, and once those are involved, it's that much harder to regain control.

I stepped away, rounding the counter and fiddling with the new drawer handles. They were pewter and had this carved flower detailing that was subtle and very Victorian. I loved them, even though Jackson had balked at how much they cost. "This kitchen looks so amazing that it almost makes me want to cook. *Almost.*"

Fully in control now—go me, circling back around to Way Number One—I glanced up, adding a smile to my cooking joke.

Only Jackson didn't crack so much as a hint of a smile. He was studying me like I'd grown the devil horns he'd once accused me of hiding.

Strike that—it was worse than that. He was looking at me like a problem that he was working out how to fix, like when the cabinets weren't level and he had to put in a few fillers and do some sanding so the quartz countertops would sit right.

I'm not broken. I don't need to be fixed. What I need to do is stick to my tried and true ways on how to avoid a broken heart and the other loveborne illnesses that come along for the destructive ride.

Stirring up memories of my relationship with Tyler left it too close to the surface. I'd wrapped up my entire life in him, and after he dumped me, it took a couple of months before I could sort out me from him and recognize myself in the mirror.

I'd sworn never again. Sworn not to brush myself off, only to dive into the wreckage with another guy, the way Mom did. I took it a step further, deciding I wouldn't get in deep enough to get messy at all.

Only here I was, assuming Jackson and I would spend Saturday evening together, even after a non-stop week together that felt longer than seven days. Sure, they'd been fun, amazing days, and suddenly it seemed like they'd flown by too fast and we didn't have enough time left. Another sign that I was getting in over my head. "I've got some things to take care of before my shift at the bar, so I've got to take off early. I figured we both could use an evening off."

"Okay," he said softly.

I'd kind of expected him to fight me on it or that I'd have to add another excuse for him to truly let it slide. The tension leaked out of me at his response.

Then I wondered if he needed a break from me. If *he* had other plans.

Because I was losing my mind. Losing it to Jackson Gamble and his irresistible irresistibleness. "I know you've got dinner with your family tomorrow, too, so we can just rest up and hit it hard again on Monday morning."

Jackson ran a hand through his hair, and it immediately fell forward as usual, and I wanted to take a turn at running my fingers through it. Wanted him to boost me into his arms and have his way with me on the new counter. We needed to christen the kitchen now that it was finished and the island didn't do the rocking, groaning-under-my-weight thing.

I started past him, then paused, a torn-apart sensation tugging at me, screaming at me to run. Whispering for me to stay.

I settled for something in between. I braced my hand on his biceps, tipped onto my toes, and kissed him on the cheek. "Thank you."

I didn't know if I was thanking him for being so understanding, or for the beautiful kitchen, or for a dozen other things he deserved to be thanked for.

And when he simply cupped my cheek, peered into my eyes, and told me to be safe, a tiny fissure formed in my heart.

Yeah, I definitely needed a break from Jackson Gamble. I didn't make a long-ass list of rules to get my heart broken all over again.

Chapter Sixteen

A beam of sunlight greeted my eyeballs first thing Monday morning, nearly blinding me—ironic, since the broken slats on the *blinds* were responsible. I blinked and sat up, moving around the penetrating ray that got me every morning.

I stretched, and instead of a mixture of stuffy dust and fresh paint, I got a whiff of dark-roasted coffee. I did a double take at the Daily Grind cup on the nightstand, right next to the frilly lamp that I used when I wanted to read past bedtime undetected back in the day—it was a much better accomplice than the noisy bedsprings.

I lifted the cardboard to-go cup. *Still warm.*

A light, steady tapping noise echoed through the house. *Jackson must already be here and working.*

Words were etched into the cup in blue ink, and I twisted it so I could read them.

Forget small children, I don't want you to terrify any handsome handymen this morning. My lips stretched into a smile, and I ran my thumb over the roughly sketched broom at the bottom.

I sipped the coffee, moaning at the bold taste and warmth on my tongue. Like his sister, he sprang for the good stuff. They'd make a coffee drinker of me yet.

I couldn't believe I didn't hear him come in, but I never had back when we were doing our whatever. I could sleep through most anything—as evidenced by the fact that he'd been hammering away while I'd been crashed out.

I took a quick shower, ran some anti-frizz curling mousse through my hair, and pulled on my paint-covered, tattered jeans and a T-shirt. I contemplated makeup and then decided against it. If Jackson was already working, I should get to it.

Gripping my personalized cup of coffee, I hurried down the stairs. And then paused to admire the view. Jackson was on a ladder, hammering the white crown molding to the top of the wall. It gave the living room a finished, framed look and complemented the blue-gray paint perfectly, if I did say so myself.

As nice as the room looked, the real sight for sore, still-tired eyes was the drool-worthy guy. That strong line of his back, visible through his T-shirt, arms flexing with every swing. He also had a pencil behind his ear for marking and a few nails pinched between his lips, and I found it completely sexy for reasons I couldn't exactly explain.

Actually, it wasn't that hard to explain. He was hot and using his hands to help me achieve this outrageous house-flipping idea I'd gotten into my head.

"Thanks for the coffee." I lifted the cup, like otherwise he might not understand what I meant. "If I spot any handsome handymen, maybe I'll be able to refrain from hexing them. *Maybe*."

The crooked smile that tugged at his mouth made him the most handsome of handymen, and the cocky slant to it proved he knew it. "I'm sure they'll appreciate that."

I scanned the room again, mostly so I wouldn't just ogle

him and give away exactly how much I'd thought about him during my self-imposed two-day break. "You must've started early."

"You know how much I like worms."

I scrunched up my forehead, trying to make sense out of his words.

"Because that's what early birds get," he said.

"Ah. Explains why I stay in bed. I prefer…not worms." I downed the last of my coffee and wiped my hands on my jeans. "Put me to work."

"If you want to hold the molding so I don't have to try to balance it and hammer at the same time, that'd be great."

I walked up the other side of the ladder and, once he'd fitted the molding where he wanted it, held it in place. "Do anything interesting over the weekend?"

Surprise bled into his features, like he couldn't believe I'd asked. Honestly, I couldn't believe it, either. This was why I should plan out stuff to say beforehand. Since that wouldn't be weird. He removed a nail from between his lips, stuck it in place, and swung the hammer. "Not really."

How annoyingly vague. Vague is my *job.*

"How about you?" he asked.

"Same." I kept glancing from the molding to him, then back to the molding. This was torture, being so close and trying not to focus on Jackson, and how good he smelled, and the varying shades of green in his eyes, and what did he do over the weekend, and what was he thinking right now, and why was my brain doing this to me?

I stuck to the plan and forced myself to pull back before I got in over my head. Why isn't it working better?

"You know, I could hammer, too," I said when he stepped down from the ladder to grab another plank. "Then we could go even faster." *And I'd have something else to concentrate on besides you.*

He opened his toolbox and handed me his spare hammer and some nails. Once we were in position again, we started at opposite ends, planning on meeting in the middle. I swung the hammer, better now that I could focus on the head of the nail instead of the head of the hottie.

But now not-talking was getting to me, all the words we weren't saying stacking up and making it harder to find that easy camaraderie we'd experienced last week. I took it upon myself to try again to get a conversation going. "I did manage to sort through more of Dixie's scrapbooks in my spare time."

"I saw those scattered on the couch," Jackson said, fitting another nail in place. He raised his voice to be heard over the hammering. "Anything interesting?"

"They're kind of like almanacs for which dude my mom was dating year to year. To be fair, some lasted more than one. Not to mention we didn't see Dixie as much when Mom had a boyfriend, so she mostly captured the beginnings. Then there are pages of just the three of us—me, Dixie, and my mom—doing crazy things that were supposed to help Mom over whatever relationship she was mourning." I paused to drive the nail I was working on home. "I'd forgotten about a few of them, though. Like Craig Watson, who made me take my shoes off by the front door and had a room no one could sit in. He was crazy about the lid being on the toothpaste, too." Enough so that he'd blown a gasket when Mom forgot. In general, she and I were too messy for his perfect, orderly life.

"Sounds like a fun dude."

I huffed a laugh, stretching as far as I could go without moving the ladder, since we were sharing it. "Then there was Chuck, who was a little too fun. Like the carnival would be in town, so we'd hit that, and then the second we got home, he wanted to go right back out to dinner or a movie. I remember thinking can we just sit for five minutes? His daughter hated me and we had to share a room, so that was extra fun.

"Then there was a lot of Rhett, way more than the other guys." I hesitated. I hadn't meant to go deeper than little anecdotes about the constant carousel of men. "He was different from the start—for one, I actually liked him. He treated my mom well, and more than that, I didn't feel invisible or like he was trying too hard to include me, like it was all just a show for my mom's sake.

"He gave me permission to read any book in his sizeable collection, and then we'd have these great conversations about them and playfully debate topics. He taught me to drive and insisted on getting me a reliable car after I got my license."

Over the year and a half we lived with him, I slipped and got attached, even though I should've known better by then. Some of Mom's other men were nice enough, but for the first time ever, I'd thought, *This is what it must feel like to have a dad. I see what the fuss is all about.*

Jackson stopped hammering and turned to fully face me. "What happened with him?"

"He's married to Dixie now." I rolled the remaining nails in my hand, then squeezed hard enough for them to dig into my skin and redirect the dull ache that'd settled in my chest. I didn't know why it was hitting me so hard, harder than when I'd seen evidence in the photos that Dixie liked him from the start. I bet it was tough for her, watching them together. "My mom dumped him before anything started between him and Dixie—Mom translated 'too nice' and 'reliable' into 'no passion' and moved on to a guy who yelled at her all the time…"

She went from too nice to verbally and emotionally abusive. Good call, Mom.

"Did he yell at you, too?"

Since my thoughts were still spinning on Rhett and Dixie, it took me a second to switch gears and figure out why

Jackson sounded like he was ready to murder someone. I shrugged it off. "Yeah, but he wasn't the first to yell, and it's not like I'm scarred for life because of it or anything. By that time I was seventeen and could take care of myself. I yelled right back."

I reached for another nail, but I'd already used them all and the molding was already secured in place, and my hands needed something to do. Now that I'd turned on the memory tap, I couldn't seem to shut it off. "The worst part about living with him was that I was stuck in this tiny town in Alabama, where I didn't know anyone and there was nothing to do, so I felt completely trapped. I begged my mom to let me move back here with Dixie for my last year of high school, and she was just about to give in when Dixie called to tell her that she'd started seeing Rhett. My mom went ballistic. It got ugly, and afterward the rift was so wide and deep there was no chance of closing it. Which I think made my mom feel trapped, too, because she refused to leave Alabama, no matter how bad it got. And it got bad."

I didn't dare look at Jackson, afraid the weak wall holding back my emotions would crumble. Yet I couldn't seem to stop talking, either. Besides Jackson, Rhett and Dixie had been on my mind all weekend. "All those years we just showed up on Dixie's doorstep, no warning, and she took us in again and again. I never could figure out why, since my mom didn't even love Rhett, she couldn't just let her best friend be happy. That was such a shitty period. Within a couple of months, I'd lost one of the few of Mom's boyfriends I actually cared about, Dixie, and my freedom."

I pulled my gaze off the spot on the ladder I'd practically stared a hole through to find Jackson's eyes leveled on me.

"Wow. That was a whole lot of talking and drama that I didn't mean to get into, and I'm totally holding us back from our work. Sorry." I jumped down and reached for another piece of the molding.

Jackson stepped up behind me, gently tugged my arm away from the pile and turned me to face him. "Ivy. You know that you can talk to me. About anything."

I waved a hand through the air, sure I'd lose it if I talked any more about my past. I wished I could go back and stop myself from admitting so much in the first place. Stupid desire to get a conversation going. Talk about backfiring. "I'm totally fine. It was such a long time ago. Those scrapbooks are like time traveling to my past, and I should probably just tape them up and ship them off to Dixie before I get sucked in again."

Jackson ran his fingers down my arm and gave my hand a quick squeeze. "I don't think a little time traveling is a bad thing."

"Where would you go?"

He rubbed his fingertips along his jaw. "In my past?"

I nodded, then took a guess. "Back to your football glory days?" I infused my voice with an extra dose of peppiness. "Where you scored lots of touchdowns and cheerleaders."

He scrunched up his eyebrows. "I was a linebacker."

"Oh. Do cheerleaders not like linebackers?"

That cocky smile of his spread across his face. "They definitely do, especially when we're talking yours truly—"

I rolled my eyes.

"But linebacker is a defensive position."

I shrugged a shoulder. "Yeah, sports were never my thing."

"How do you even know I played football in high school?"

I swore we'd talked about it, but come to think of it, it was probably information I'd gleaned from Savannah. The first time I'd seen Jackson, I'd nudged her and made an inappropriate comment about how I'd like to climb him like a tree. Then she informed me that was her brother and added,

"So down, girl." Here and there after our initial introduction, I'd asked a few casual questions about him while telling myself I couldn't go there, no matter how sexy the guy was.

Guilt rushed right up to remind me I was going against my best friend's wishes. In my defense, I'd resisted for a really long time, and as he'd pointed out, he was an adult who could make his own decisions, and now I was rationalizing way too much instead of thinking of a good excuse for knowing that tidbit about him. "I'm sure you mentioned it. And you're trying to change the subject about where you'd go in your past."

There. Perfectly smooth way of redirecting our conversation.

Except he grinned at me like he didn't buy it. "I like where I am now."

"With your job and life?"

He took a step closer, his arms circling my waist. "Yeah. Don't get me wrong, past me had some fun, but he needed to learn more patience and understanding. Hell, present me could be a little better at that, too, but I'm working on it."

I placed my hands on his chest, going the extra mile and copping a feel of his firm pecs. "Well, how very advanced of you."

"Right?" He laughed, and I joined in. Then his expression grew more serious. "I know that when it comes to the past, you didn't have the easiest time growing up. So if you want to box up those photos and never look at them, I'll get the tape and throw them in the back of my truck right now. But if you want to reflect on the good times and think about how amazing it is that you became such a strong, stubborn woman who insists apple green is a good color for a bathroom in spite of it all, then you can do that too. And I'll happily do it with you if you want."

"Do it with me?" I asked, waggling my eyebrows, because

serious conversations made me uncomfortable, and this was getting way too serious. "How generous."

"Mind out of the gutter, girl. On second thought, keep it there. But you're going to have to wait until we get our work done." He kissed me square on the lips, turned me back toward the stack of molding, and smacked me on the butt.

I let out a noise of protest, even though it was all for show.

As we finished working our way around the room, we unabashedly checked each other out, flirted, and threw out innuendos right and left. About banging hard and nailing each other and screwing until we were out of breath.

I told him that I was going to rock his world and make him forget his name.

He promised that he was going to make me scream his name so he remembered it.

And at the end of the day, we made good on all those naughty, delicious promises.

Chapter Seventeen

"Hey, baby."

I ignored the guy at the end of the bar who'd had too much to drink and rounded the counter, putting some much-needed space between us for his safety. It wasn't just alcohol making him forget his manners. He'd been inappropriate before his first shot of whiskey, one of those rich good ol' boys who thought proper etiquette didn't apply to him.

He snapped his fingers, and my spine went stick-straight as I took deep breaths, working to retain control of my temper.

More and more, I was sick of bartending. I'd been spinning my wheels here, afraid to commit to something more. I loved working on the house, but I didn't know how realistic it was to set my sights on flipping houses full-time, considering that I wouldn't find another situation like the one I was in now. Not every home owner would just hand me the keys and tell me to go to town on their place, and Jackson wouldn't always be on hand to help fix my messes.

I wanted to believe that the skills I was learning and the

money I would make from the sale would help launch me into a new career, but I couldn't possibly make *that* much profit. Not to mention some tasks were still beyond me, both know-how and physically, even though wild horses couldn't drag that confession from me. I needed a new life plan. I needed to stop waiting around to find the perfect long-term career and take control of finding one.

Usually I avoided plans, because I didn't want anything to control my life, even me. Plans just screamed stifling and unbendable, and I liked spontaneity, as long as I was also at the wheel. But if I made a plan and found my way to something more—to a life and a job I loved—I'd be in even more control of my life.

As I brainstormed options, I wiped down the bar, going away from Mr. Grabby Hands. I did a double take at the guy who'd sat at the far end. Jackson flashed me a butterfly-inducing smile, and I ditched the rag and moved over to him. "What are you doing here?"

"I was in the neighborhood and needed a drink. I hear the bartender here is super sexy, too."

"Yeah. Jesse is pretty popular," I joked, jerking my head toward the guy who was working the late shift with me tonight.

"Ha-ha." Jackson brushed his thumb over my knuckles, and warmth coursed through my veins. "You look nice."

"Thanks. So, what'll you have?"

"Just a beer. Whatever's on tap is fine."

I poured it and set it in front of him. He seemed off somehow. "What's going on?"

"Oh, I just have a big project that I'll be starting once we finish up with your place."

"Do you need to start it early? I can do everything else if I need to. Except the flooring. And any structural stuff. Okay, so I still need your help on some of the projects, but I can work around your schedule."

One corner of his mouth turned up. "Glad to hear I'm needed. And you and I made a deal and worked out a schedule, and I'm sticking with it. I'm just trying to balance that and some other things. And my family is calling me every five minutes."

"Ah. They can be…persistent."

"Understatement."

I leaned over, folding my forearms on the bar. "Go ahead and let it all out. Tell me your problems."

A gleam entered his eyes, the one that usually accompanied teasing. "I thought you didn't like getting too deep."

"Well, I'm not asking as the girl you're sleeping with. I'm asking as your bartender. I've heard it all, so go ahead."

He took a swig, then he talked about permits and this guy he had to work with who always made things way harder than necessary, and some other industry speak that I couldn't completely follow, but I could tell he was passionate about it. That was what I was looking for in a career. Something I cared enough about to get into fights over permits so I could make my clients happy.

Or, you know, a version of that.

"Feel better?" I asked.

"Yes, actually." He picked up my hand and slid his fingers between mine so that our palms met. "Thanks for listening, random bartender."

I grinned at him, then leaned a little closer, enjoying the zips of electricity that shot up my arm and traveled right to my core.

I was considering closing the mere inches between us and kissing him when movement at the door caught my attention. His sister and my cousin stepped inside, and I quickly straightened, pulling my hand free of Jackson's grip.

"What are you doing here?" Savannah asked, addressing Jackson—obviously she knew what I was doing here. "I just got off the phone with Mama, and she was wondering where you were. She said she thought you were going to be at the house. Caroline was there."

I told myself not to look for Jackson's reaction to her name, but I'd done it automatically. He remained impassive and impossible to read. "She asked if I'd come over…"

What? That hussy asked him to come over?

"…and I told her I didn't know if I'd have time with the stuff I needed to finish up at work, but you know Ma."

Oh. His mom. Not a hussy and now I feel bad for thinking that, even if I'm also annoyed that she's still pushing the Caroline thing. I had to uncurl the fist I didn't even realize I'd made.

"Why doesn't she understand that work is a valid excuse for not stopping by? Especially on a random Tuesday night?" Savannah slid onto the stool next to him and smiled at me. "Hey."

"Lemon martini?"

"She wants my famous bourbon peach cocktail," Linc said.

Savannah looked like she wanted to argue, but she finally gave in. "Actually, I would."

"Beer?" I asked Linc, who nodded, and then my gaze skipped to Jackson. "Another?"

"Sure, thanks."

The annoying drunk guy hollered at me as I filled the drinks, calling me "sweetheart" and making comments on my ass, but I ignored him—clearly he'd had enough to drink already. On my way over to my friends, I slid him a glass of water, which he balked at, but I was on the other side of the bar before he could form a proper complaint.

As I neared, I overheard Savannah trying to pry

information from Jackson about whether or not he was still interested in Caroline, and I perked up my ears.

"So how's the remodel going?" Linc asked me, making it impossible to hear Jackson's answer, but it sounded like he was freezing out his sister on the dating front. Not that I blamed him. I loved Savannah, but she couldn't help getting involved and adding her opinion.

Unfortunately, I already knew her thoughts on the subject. She thought they could make it work if he gave it a real chance. While my best friend was a bit overenthusiastic when it came to dating advice, she was rarely wrong about relationships. Unless it involved her personally—then she was a little blind and too stringent about her rules.

Not that I had room to talk. I was ignoring several of mine while fooling around with a guy who'd said himself that he was trying to want what was good for him, and I wasn't it. I'd said I wouldn't get in the way and I was, and I couldn't seem to help myself, even though I knew better.

"Ivy?"

Right. Linc asked about the remodel. "It's coming along nicely. You should stop by sometime. The place looks totally different."

"And working with Jackson?" Linc arched an eyebrow, and I wondered if I was caught. All this time I'd been trying to hide from Savannah when I should've been worried about my cousin. Especially since he'd tell his fiancée.

I treaded carefully, keeping my expression as neutral as possible. "It's going better than expected. He definitely knows what he's doing." I thought about his hands on my body and then worked to quickly redirect my thoughts. "He's infuriating as ever but good at his job."

That eyebrow arched higher, and I raised one right back. My time with Jackson was limited, and I planned on selfishly clinging to every last minute. I told myself then I could say,

Well, it's been fun, and let him go.

My body betrayed me, hopping the fence to cause lung-squeezing panic over us ending as opposed to its usual stance against commitment. Add the jealousy over thinking of him settling down with one of the Carolines of the world and my insides were revolting.

Savannah twisted toward Linc and placed her hand on his arm, while her gaze remained on the screen of her phone. "Remind me, did you like the ranunculus bouquet or the magnolia one for the centerpieces? Apparently it's vital that my mom and Aunt Velma know right this very second."

Speaking of panic, I could see it in Linc's eyes—served him right for using that eyebrow on me to try to make me spill my guts. "Um, the ones with flowers?"

The two of them started discussing pros and cons of each of the options—i.e, Savannah talked while Linc tried to keep up—and I cast a smile at Jackson, wanting a coconspirator to laugh with me about the floral drama. Only he was on the phone, shaking his head.

"...can't make it tonight, Ma. I told you that I probably wouldn't..." He pinched the bridge of his nose. "Because I have a job and a house of my very own that gets lonely without me...I know I missed Sunday dinner, but I'll be there next Sunday, I promise." He paused, then glanced up at me and caught me eavesdropping. "We'll talk about that later... I'm planning on it. As long as—" Resigned sigh. "Okay, fine. Yeah, love you, too." He nodded a couple more times and then hung up.

"Did you miss an important date?" I asked, unable to help myself.

"I'm where I want to be," he said, his eyes leveled on me, and heat uncurled in my stomach.

"Was that Mom?" Savannah asked, and I straightened and wiped what she would call a twitterpated smile off my face. "How can she be texting me every five seconds *and* be on the phone with you?"

"I'm going to go do my job while you guys discuss the mysteries of your mother and her powers of meddling in both of your lives at once." I tapped the bar and moved away from them. What I needed to do more than my job was distract myself from the overwhelming feelings I was experiencing before they went and got me in trouble.

I filled a few drink orders and then checked glasses, even though it was slow and I knew we had plenty. When I turned around, Savannah stood in front of me, but her attention was on riffling through her purse. Finally, she found whatever she was looking for and glanced up. "I've got an early meeting tomorrow, so Linc and I are going to call it a night. I just wanted to say good-bye."

"Okay, I'll talk to you later."

Savannah hesitated, something in her posture making the hair on the back of my neck stand on end. "We still need to have a talk about your new guy..." She glanced at her brother, and I was sure I was caught, and I hoped that she would forgive me, but I just knew a lecture was in my future at the least. "We really need a girl's night sometime to catch up without the guys around."

Oh. A girl's night. It was only a coincidence that she glanced at her brother, and obviously I have a guilty conscience.

"Totally," I said, my telltale heart thumping like crazy.

"But no dance clubs. Last time was..." She shook her head. "I'd just rather have a night in. Just us."

Last time I'd been in an awful funk and decided my life needed a shakeup. A big part of dragging her to that club with me had been an attempt to deal with my ugly fallout with Jackson. I'd told myself that once I met some other hot guys, I could forget about the one still on my mind. Sadly, it hadn't worked, not even a little.

What if I'm setting myself up for another funk? I couldn't help thinking I was trying a little too hard to convince myself this temporary arrangement wouldn't end the same devastating way. Spending longer together this time around might only make the after part worse.

"No dancing, I promise," I said. "Well, unless it's in the privacy of our living rooms."

"Deal." Savannah leaned over the bar to hug me. "Do me a favor?" she asked.

"Anything for you."

"Just…go easy on my brother. I can tell he's stressed out right now, which means he might be a little short tempered and grumpy, but he means well."

Dammit. I wanted to spill my guts like the guilty person I was. "I will. We actually work surprisingly well together, as long as one of us takes charge per room and the other is just the helper."

Savannah laughed. "I can see that."

Linc came over and wrapped his arm around Savannah's shoulders, and then they walked out of the bar, leaving me, Jackson, and a few leftover drunk people.

A quick glance at my watch also told me I had an hour left on my shift before balancing tills and the cleanup that'd take about another hour. I wanted to throw in my towel for the day, hop across the bar, and crawl into Jackson's lap.

But that would be frowned upon. Besides, it had only been about twenty-four hours since I'd been in that position. How could I be missing him, even with him right there?

I finally decided to stop being a wimp and go indulge in some more conversation with a guy who could keep up with me. Possibly even handle me, not that I'd ever admit that to him. "How you doing?"

Jackson exhaled and lifted heavy-lidded eyes to me.

"Wishing I was in a certain living room, pinning a certain blonde against a wall."

I swallowed, finding the gesture harder than usual. "I do like a guy who doesn't bother to mince words."

"No word mincing here." He scooted closer, his hand covering mine. "Now, where were we before my sister came in…"

"Hey, sweetheart! I need a refill!"

Oh great, Drunky McGee is getting belligerent. To punctuate my point, he slammed his glass down on the bar and raised his voice. "Are you deaf? I need a refill, toots."

Who knew guys actually used toots anymore? I glanced over my shoulder, hoping Jesse would step in, but he must've gone on his break or headed into the kitchen to talk with the guys.

"Need me to take care of that?" Jackson asked, the line of his jaw tightening.

"I got it." I sighed and pushed away. I told the guy I was calling his belligerent ass a cab—in nicer, customer friendly terms, of course. He swore at me, but that was nothing new. While I was in the vicinity, I decided to round the bar and go close out my other tabs. The nights when it was slow, where we covered both the tables and the bar, were always my least favorite, especially since they moved at that crappy molasses pace.

On the way back, mere steps from being back on the better side of the bar, Drunky McGee nearly toppled his stool so he could smack my butt as I passed by.

I whirred around and jabbed a finger in his face. "Touch me again, and I'll make you a soprano for life."

He was clearly too stupid to get my meaning, but before I could expound, Jackson was right next to me.

I put a hand on his chest, holding him back. "I told you, I've got this."

"But I *want* to get it."

I held firm. "This is something I deal with all the time. I can handle myself."

"I know you can. But it's okay to have help sometimes."

"If I *need* help, I'll let you know."

Jackson looked like he wanted to argue, every muscle in his body coiled and ready to spring, but when I applied a little more pressure against his chest, he gradually backed down. A whole two or three inches. He played sentinel as I convinced Drunky McGee to pay his tab—I hinted a generous tip was in order and, since his math skills were greatly impaired, helped him with his addition—and wrestled him into a cab.

I tried not to be irritated that Jackson followed me outside for that last part, but at the same time, it was nice. But I couldn't get used to it, and I *could* handle it myself, and it definitely fell on more of the boyfriend side of the line than the hookup side.

As the cab pulled away, I smoothed a hand down my shirt, caught my breath, and slowly turned to Jackson. "You can't just loom like an overprotective, jealous boyfriend while I'm at work."

Jackson's eyebrows drew low over his eyes. "This isn't jealousy; it's concern." He swept his arm toward the bar. "I don't understand why one of the other guys couldn't have handled it. How often do you end up alone like that?"

There were plenty of nights Jesse or Dan goofed around out back or in the kitchen, leaving me to mostly go it alone. They came if I got busy enough to text for help, and it meant more tips so I didn't mind. While I hadn't even seen him tonight, I was sure Tony was in his office as usual, not paying attention because it was quiet. But there was no reason to explain any of that to Jackson, because that wasn't the point. "This is part of my job, and I can handle it."

"Oh, so now you're a bouncer, too?"

I crossed my arms. "Yes."

He crossed his right back. "Fine. Then I'll be your back-up bouncer."

"You can't be here every night."

He took a step closer. "Wanna make a bet?"

I opened my mouth, but before I could figure out what to say, the door swung open and Jesse looked out at me. "Just checking on you."

"Oh, *now* you check on her," Jackson mumbled.

"I'm fine," I said, a little too loudly and too defensively, but I was done with whatever was going on, especially since I didn't even understand it. How could we get into a fight over me doing my job?

I strode past Jesse, pushed into Azure, and checked on my last table on the way to the bar.

And when I finally reached my post, I hated how everything inside me still felt too heavy and thick and wrong. Hated that I'd fought with Jackson after having such a great start to the night. So much for understanding he was stressed and giving him a break like Savannah asked me to, and so much for him being here every night.

Not that I wanted that anyway.

Chapter Eighteen

I didn't know exactly how to act the next morning when Jackson came in. I knew he was upset about last night because he was gruff and short with his words, but when I tried to bring it up, he'd held up a hand and said, "Let's not get into it."

So we didn't. We didn't talk at all. Just went to work in different rooms. I took the upstairs while he tiled the downstairs bathroom.

Black Widow followed me as I moved from task to task, meowing back when I talked to her. She seemed antsy, which wasn't something I thought a cat was capable of portraying, but she was up and down and constantly meowing at me, and if she were a dog, I'd ask if Timmy fell in the well.

"What is it?" I squatted and scratched under her chin. "Is your boyfriend driving you crazy, too? I mean, I don't have a boyfriend, but calling him a tomcat seems a bit mean, since he was trying to be chivalrous, I suppose. But girls like us, we don't need chivalry, do we?"

Black Widow meowed, but I couldn't translate if she was agreeing or disagreeing.

"Maybe certain guys need to be chivalrous, whether ladies appreciate it or not." The deep voice made me jump, and I dropped the putty knife I'd been using to patch the master bedroom wall. "And I'm not going to just stand by and let some guy treat my girl like that, even if it means she's gonna throw a damn hissy fit."

I shot Jackson a scowl. "I don't even know where to start with that. I'm not your girl, *you* were the one throwing a hissy fit, as I recall, and I can't believe you were eavesdropping on our private conversation."

He crossed his arms and leaned against the doorjamb. "I can't believe you get upset that I care about your safety."

Black Widow meowed.

"I care about yours, too," Jackson said to her, and affection swirled through the frustration.

I tried to bite back my smile, but I couldn't help it. Staying mad just for the sake of winning felt more like losing, and I decided it didn't have to be a big deal if we didn't make it into one. I straightened and walked over to him. His muscles tensed as I neared, his apprehension clear, which almost made me laugh. Then it made me wonder what he expected me to say or do.

I placed my hand on his arm. "Look, I don't want to be upset anymore. We don't have long to enjoy our"—I dragged my finger back and forth across that sexy line in his forearm—"benefits arrangement, and I don't want to spend it fighting."

Jackson peered down at me, his pupils darkening. "I'm thinking of another F-word I'd rather spend it doing."

"Why, Jackson Gamble, you call that chivalry?"

He hooked his finger in my belt loop and tugged me to him. "It's impossible to be a gentleman all the time." A spike of heat shot through me as he dropped kisses along my jaw. He dragged his nose across my cheek and captured my lips with his. But before I could fully catch hold and move the kiss to the next level, he pulled back and looked me in the eye. "Would it really be so bad for someone to care about you?"

"Yes," I automatically said as my lungs went to collapsing on themselves.

He sighed. "Ivy."

"Jackson." I smoothed a hand down his chest, trying to find the right balance to keep him close but not too close. "That's not what this thing between us is about."

He covered my hand, pressing it flatter against him. "I can't just turn caring about you off like a switch. Believe me, I tried…"

My throat tightened, but I told myself not to freak out. Just smooth over the situation instead of turning a molehill into a big-ass mountain. "Fine. I'll take it as a…friend."

He made a sour face, probably because that'd never described what we were to each other. But lately I felt like we were possibly dancing around something close to that, and there wasn't a better word for what I was trying to convey, so I stuck with it.

"It just can't go into possessive, jealous territory."

"Fine," Jackson said, and I let out a relieved breath. "As long as no other guy touches you."

I ignored the way he'd half-growled it, as well as the way it made heat pool low in my stomach, and tilted my head. My disbelief in monogamy was a hot-button topic, one I'd pushed when I'd been desperate to drive him away. It'd also led to the blowout of all blowouts and I didn't want to go down that path, even though giving in scared me as well.

"You don't get to make all the rules, Ivy," he said, his voice firm. Then he yanked me to him, gave me a hard, demanding kiss that made the room spin, and added, "By the way, I'm putting the light fixture that I picked out in the dining room. I know you don't think it'll look good, but it will, so you can thank me later."

With that, he readjusted his pants and gave a nod: "Ivy. Black Widow." He turned and strode down the hallway, leaving me grasping for control and then wondering if I really needed it all that much right now anyway.

. . .

The microwave beeped, and I pulled out the bag of popcorn, inhaling the buttery, salty scent. It was as close to cooking as I'd come in the pristine kitchen, and it was a pathetic dinner. But it was the only food I had here, and I didn't want to drive over to my condo or even to a restaurant where I could grab something to go.

Technically, where I really wanted to be was in a bed upstairs with Jackson, relieving stress with sex before unwinding for the day. He'd gotten me all worked up with that growly, possessive talk and proprietary kiss, and then he'd informed me he had to leave early. When I'd very delicately pried for information (told him it felt like he was punishing me for our fight last night) he'd grinned and promised me he'd punish me properly later.

Jackass. Hot, frustrating, good-with-his-hands jackass.

Since the TV wasn't hooked up, I set up on the floral couch that no longer matched the living room and opened my laptop. After tethering it to my phone, I clicked on the latest crime drama I was addicted to. Hard-boiled detectives, grisly case details—none of that romance cures all bullshit.

Normally the show held my attention, but I found myself shifting and glancing at my phone every couple of minutes.

I composed a text to Jackson about the light fixture in the dining room that I absolutely didn't like. No, I didn't like it; I freaking loved it. On his tiny phone screen, the industrial water pipe chandelier had looked like whatever came before vintage. I was sure the bulbs and black and bronzed pipe would look out of place, neither Victorian nor modern. Instead, it married the styles perfectly, catching accents from both and pulling the whole room together.

I backspaced, rewrote my sentence, then backspaced again and started over. I reread what I'd typed, my finger hovering over the send button.

I can't send this. He's going to see this text as what it actually is. A desperate cry for attention, because I miss having him here with me. Since it now seemed too needy and too telling, I deleted it. The cursor blinked at me, like it was daring me to type something. *I just need to stick to the sexual side of our arrangement.*

I considered telling him that since he was too busy, I was going to have to punish myself solo. I typed three variations, each one super heavy on the emojis. "Oh my gosh, what am I doing?"

I tossed my phone away from me, deciding any attempts to contact him, strictly sexual or not, might be misconstrued and were dangerously close to breaking Ways Three, Four, Seven, and Eight. Possibly One and Five, too. In other words, *abort, abort, abort.*

I glanced at the show playing out onscreen. I didn't even know what the hell was going on or why the detectives had arrested some burly guy I'd never seen before.

Still bored after five or so minutes of trying to catch up, my phone found its way back into my hand. I pulled up Savannah's name. Last night she said we needed some girl time, and she wasn't wrong.

Me: *What are you up to tonight? I don't suppose you want to ditch my cousin and come hang out? I'm thinking jammies, junk food, and whatever other J words sound like fun.*

Munching on another handful of popcorn drowned out

the show playing in the background, not that I had any chance of catching up at this point.

> Savannah: *Sorry. Out to dinner with the fam to celebrate Dad's retirement, but it's like this odd, huge group date thing since the Porters are here, too.*

> Savannah, a few seconds later: *Now that I'm engaged, it's rather fun watching my mama and Aunt Velma meddle in Jackson's love life instead. They're so busy trying to point out how well his and Caroline's hobbies match up that they keep interrupting the conversation they're having to add commentary. I should probably throw Jackson and Caroline a bone and divert the attention so they have a shot at talking to just each other. This is a perfect example of why I recommend waiting until the relationship is more solidified before throwing family into the mix. LOL*

I frowned at the message. Earlier Jackson declared no other guy could touch me, and now he was out to dinner, making nice with the perky brunette he'd been on at least a few dates with? Talk about hypocritical.

Irrational irritation pricked at my skin—after all, he could go out with who he wanted, and yeah, his family was there, and blah, blah, blah.

I turned the volume on my computer up as loud as it would go, hoping someone onscreen would get murdered soon and that it'd help take the edge off the bloodlust I suddenly felt.

Black Widow strolled over to the couch and meowed at me.

"Sorry, but I doubt popcorn is good for cats, so I'm not risking it. Did you already eat the food I left in your bowl?"

She meowed again, so I picked her up with a grunt—she was heavier than she looked—and set her on my lap. For a few minutes, she remained standing, dancing around in front of the screen so I missed even more of my show, but then she finally settled in. I stroked her fur, and she started to purr.

"It's just you and me." I'd accepted the fact that she was mine now, and I hoped she would as well, even though it'd mean a move once this house was finished. We'd relocate to my condo, and Jackson would go his separate way, and we'd probably both miss him but be too proud to ever admit it. "Great. Now I'm getting all sappy and worrying about the future. If I start driveling on and on about soul mates and true love, do me a favor and put me out of my misery."

The way Black Widow tucked her nose into the crook of my knee as she continued to purr made me question if she understood the direness of my situation. I didn't get jealous over guys, yet here I was, experiencing more jealousy than I'd ever felt in my life. Add in missing him, and it made for a crappy combination that my common sense was useless to fight, no matter how many good points it tried to make.

Since analyzing that mess would hardly be relaxing, I followed my adopted cat's lead and stretched out on the couch.

The next thing I knew, I was waking up to a cat who was panting like she'd run a marathon. Her entire body was convulsing, and she made a weird, grunting noise.

"Oh, shit. You're not…?" I scrambled upright, patting the cushions for my phone. How hadn't I seen the signs earlier today? Then again, it's not like I had a lot of experience with animals in labor, or even humans in labor for that matter.

I finally found my phone, and I glanced from the screen to the in-labor cat, back to the screen. I had rules about relying on guys too much, and this was a little too close to the night I'd called Jackson, crying over my mom being in the hospital and asking him what I was supposed to do.

Black Widow grunted again. *Screw it. This isn't for me; it's for her. I don't know how to take care of a cat in labor.*

The last thing anyone would ever call me was nurturing, and Jackson said his cat had delivered a litter of kittens, which made him way more qualified than I was. So even though it was just past four in the morning, I dialed his number. It rang and rang…

And went to voicemail.

It's probably on do-not-disturb mode so he can sleep. I dialed it one more time, praying he'd pick up.

"Ivy?" His voice was all husky and deep, and for a moment, I almost forgot this was an emergency situation.

"My cat's in labor. Or, not my cat, but you know what I mean. Black Widow is having her kittens, and I don't know what to do, and…" I glanced at the panting, convulsing cat, who let out this sad little whimper. "I'm freaking out. What do I do?"

I could hear the squeak of the bedsprings, or maybe that was just my imagination. For one brief, psychotic-girlfriend-type moment, I wondered if he'd taken Caroline home with him—if she was in bed next to him, asking why some crazy girl was calling him so early in the morning—but I shoved that away to be dealt with later, because I didn't have time for my complicated emotions right now.

"Get her a box," Jackson said. "There are several in the corner of the living room by the bookshelf. Lay down a towel and get some water."

"But you're coming over, right?" I held my breath. Maybe I should've just said thanks for the box advice and left it at that. The female species had been having babies for centuries, and Black Widow and I could get through this together. Probably.

"Of course I'm coming over," he said, making it okay that I needed him to.

Even though I knew that it was dangerous to need him at all.

Chapter Nineteen

Jackson put his arm around my shoulders as I gaped at the teeny-tiny blind kittens. They squeaked as they wobbled their way to their mom, who took turns licking each one off. "Congratulations," he said. "You're a...um, godmother to a bunch of cats."

I curled into his embrace, which was a bit trickier with both of us on our knees, but the way he tightened his hold made it all worth it. "Does that make you their godfather?"

Jackson put on a very serious expression and did his best Marlon Brando. "You're making me an offer I can't refuse."

I laughed. "I think lack of sleep's made you a little delirious."

"It's possible."

I covered a yawn with my hand and leaned my head on his shoulder. We'd been kneeling in front of the box for so long I wasn't even sure my legs would work if I tried to unfold them and move. Jackson tipped his head so it rested on mine, and I didn't want to move anyway. "Thanks for coming over," I said.

Luckily, we didn't really need to do anything—Black Widow was a pro, and it made me wonder if this wasn't her first kitten rodeo. I supposed in Cat Land, it didn't make you a bad mom to let your kids fight it out on their own after a year or two, but as someone who'd basically had to do that, I couldn't help but feel for the little furballs.

"There's no one else I'd rather stay up all night with." Jackson ran his fingers down my spine and then slipped his hand in my back pocket. "Now I'm just wondering if my boss at my day job will accept being-up-all-night-delivering-kittens as an excuse for being late."

"Guess it depends on if she's a cold-hearted bitch or not."

"She sometimes pretends to be, but she's not."

I lifted my head off his shoulder, my mouth dropping open, and he laughed.

"Oh. Did you think I was talking about you?" He lowered his lips to mine, dragging his thumb across my jaw as he deepened the kiss.

When he pulled away, I nearly fell on top of him. It had to be because I was still tired from getting up so early, not because he stole my breath and made my insides go all melty on me. Yeah. I was going with that.

He pushed to his feet and then extended a hand to help me up. My legs didn't want to work, but since I made them, they rewarded me with the worst case of pins and needles I'd ever had.

Jackson dragged a hand over his face. "I've got to go grab a shower, and then I'll pick up some supplies from the store on my way over. Let's say ten-ish."

I almost told him he could grab a shower here and then I'd go shopping with him. But that struck me as borderline clingy, especially after spending most of the night with him. Then again, maybe if I wanted to kill him in the middle of the home improvement store, I'd stop thinking about how much

I wanted to be around him every waking second of the day. "Okay."

I walked with him as he made his way to the front door. Memories of yesterday were starting to trickle back into my consciousness, about how he'd left early, and how his mom and aunt were going above and beyond with their matchmaker duties. "Were you alone when I called?"

He blinked at me, obviously surprised. I was too. I hadn't meant to blurt it out like that, but apparently in my tired state, I was incapable of holding it back.

"Sorry." I shook my head, then raised my gaze to his. "Actually, I'm not sorry. You basically threatened any guy who dared to put his hands on me, then you went on a date with someone else. How is that fair?"

"It's not," Jackson said, and the anger working its way through me fired hotter. "But as you might remember, you didn't agree to exclusivity."

My breaths came faster and faster, and I clenched my fists.

"Now"—he tapped my nose, a completely antagonizing move that came dangerously close to signing his death warrant—"before you go unleashing that rage building up inside of you, I didn't go on a date, and I was very much alone when you called. In fact, as I was drifting to sleep in my bed, I was wishing that you were next to me."

My mood did a disorienting 180, and I opened my mouth a couple of times before I managed to make it form words. "I texted Savannah, and she said you were having dinner with Caroline, and I know that your parents and hers were there, too, but—"

"Ma and Aunt Velma have been trying to play Cupid for the past month or so, which I'm sure is why they invited the Porters to my dad's retirement dinner. And yes, I've been on a few dates with Caroline, but we've also been friends for a while."

I ran my finger along the collar of my shirt. "The way you and I are friends?"

Jackson stepped closer and twisted a strand of my hair around his finger. "No one else is friends like you and I are friends." He added an eyebrow waggle for emphasis. "I do like knowing that you're capable of jealousy, though. I was starting to think I was alone in that."

"I'm not jealous," I lied. "I just…wanted to be clear."

"Okay, let's be clear." He crowded my space, his hands going to my waist, and my heart picked up speed. "While you and I are doing this…whatever you're allowing it to be called, I'm not sleeping with anyone else, and I don't want you to, either. Can we at least agree on that?"

It was a little more official than I preferred, but since the other option was having him sleep with other women, I couldn't agree to it fast enough. It wasn't like I was interested in other guys, anyway—Jackson had practically ruined me for that, and I didn't want to think about what it meant for my future. "Sounds reasonable."

His mouth kicked up on one side. "And you and I are going to go on an official date."

My stomach bottomed out. "I don't date."

Way #9: No official dates. Hang outs are fine, and sure, eat a meal or watch a movie together, but as soon as someone throws the dirty D word around, it's time to shut it down.

Jackson backed me up a few more steps until my back met the wall. "If you want my body, you're gonna have to spend an evening out with me." Amusement danced along the slant of his lips. "I don't want you thinking I'm easy."

I let my head drop back against the wall. "Seriously, Jackson? You're being ridiculous."

"All I'm asking for is one little date. If you won't go out with me just because you have a crazy set of rules about what you do and don't do, I'd say *you're* the one being ridiculous. Or are you scared that my charm will be too much for you?"

"Oh, I can handle your charm if I happen to come across any of it." I jabbed a finger at his chest. "And don't act like I'm offending your delicate sensibilities by using you for your body. Easy is what this arrangement is founded upon."

He straightened, and I wished that I didn't notice the absence of his body and warmth so acutely. "Well, I'll be playing hard to get until we go on a date."

I crossed my arms. "You're not saying that we're not having sex until after we go out, are you?"

He mimicked my posture. "That's exactly what I'm saying."

"You'll never last."

"You of all people know how long I can last."

A flush of heat traveled through my body, because it did remember, and it wanted another demonstration. But saying I'd go on a date with him felt like giving away my control, and I couldn't just hand it over on a silver platter like that. "You're asking too much."

"I'm asking you to have dinner with me, Ivy. It's a little thing, and you've been in control of most everything else." He uncrossed his arms, placed a palm on the wall right by my head, and leaned in, careful to not let his body bump mine, and I felt each torturous inch between us. "Show me you can give a little."

Oh, I'd show him, but not by giving in. "I'll consider it," I said. By which I meant, *I'll get you to change your mind, no matter what it takes.* He'd just declared a sex war, and I'd go to most any lengths to win.

His returning smile told me he thought he had this in the bag, but the poor guy had no idea what he was in for.

Chapter Twenty

Five days.

Five freaking long, frustrating days since I'd had sex. Three of which (since that was when Jackson made his ridiculous official-date decree) I'd done everything in my power to get him to break. I'd worn my skimpiest outfits to work in, like the daisy dukes I'd unearthed in my high school dresser and was slightly embarrassed to be currently rocking. Which meant I had paint everywhere, and thanks to yesterday's halter top, I also had a scratch on my back from an old nail. If I didn't die from sex depravation, tetanus would get me for sure.

If I'd known on Monday night that it would be the last action I'd see for a while, I would've…I don't know. Gone for round three before letting him leave? Mentally and physically prepared myself?

When I went to check on the status of the living room floor, I found Jackson covered in a sheen of sweat and man glitter. The buzz of the saw fired up as he placed the edge of a wooden floorboard plank on the cutting table. As he pushed it through, that man glitter flew everywhere and the muscles in his arms flexed and bulged.

My mouth watered; my knees trembled. It was one thing to go through a drought, but it was another when you could see the physical overabundance of exactly what you needed *as* you were dying of thirst.

The buzz of the saw died as Jackson lifted the piece to admire his work. That strong line of his back showed through his T-shirt, and his faded Levis hugged his ass just right, and suddenly my mind was so far in the gutter I no longer knew which way was up, but I definitely needed some air.

Deciding I wasn't ready for this interaction, I quickly backtracked. Only my eyes lingered on his body, which meant I rammed mine into the archway. "Ouch!"

Jackson casually glanced back at me. "Hey, Ivy. You okay?" he asked, way too much taunting in his voice and the curve of his smile.

I crossed my arms, ready to let him have it, and his eyes snagged on the ample amount of cleavage my low-cut tank-top displayed. He swallowed, his Adam's apple bobbing up and down, and I reached up and rubbed my hand across my collarbone. "My goodness, it's hot in here."

Every muscle in his body tensed, and the line of his jaw tightened. Then his features sharpened, and he looked at me like I was his prey.

Come on, big boy. Go ahead and try to catch me. I want you to.

"You know what? It is." Jackson gripped the hem of his shirt, and my heart skipped a beat. One slow, delicious-yet-torturous inch at a time, he peeled off his shirt. He tossed it aside and then flashed me a smile. "Benefits of being a dude."

He went back to his task, resting the floorboard against the other one and nudging it into place, and without his shirt in the way, I could see the way every muscle worked, and damn did they work.

"Oh, I could lose my shirt, too."

He spun around so fast that he knocked into the stepstool holding his tools, and they clattered to the ground.

I toyed with the bottom of my tank-top, and he groaned. "Why don't we just call this a draw and have sex?"

He laughed, a stuttered, choked laugh, and then he stood and took a few strides toward me. "How's that a draw? That just means you win and I lose."

I dragged my finger over his pecs, down his abs, across the top of his waistband. "I was thinking we could both win."

He caught my wrist. Then he tugged me closer. His rapid breaths sent his chest bumping into mine, and my heart beat so loudly it drowned out everything else. He backed me up against the wall we'd had sex against before, hungrily claimed my lips, and thrust his tongue into my mouth like he meant to devour me.

But just when we were getting to where I wanted us, he pulled back. He let out a harsh curse as he ran his hand through his hair. "I need a water break," he declared, and then I watched his fine backside retreat from the room.

With him gone, I sagged against the wall, no longer bothering to hide my reaction to his smoldering kiss.

I thought I'd get him to break, but I was a hair away from giving in to his ridiculous demands.

My phone chimed, and I dug it out of its precarious spot in my tiny pocket.

Jackson: *Go back to your side of the house, you siren, because I'm not giving in to your call. Now, if you'd like to finish what we started, I made dinner reservations for 7:00. I'll pick you up at 6:30, here or your condo. I'd rather not have to drag you into the restaurant kicking and screaming, but that or coming peaceably are your only options.*

I thought if I tracked him into the kitchen and made a few more bold moves, maybe I could get him to abandon this silly notion of going on a date first. But his resolve had held up so far—much to my dismay—and I was sick of fighting it and horny as hell, and I could deal with a dinner date. We'd had dinner together plenty of times. This didn't have to be any different.

In fact, I could have some fun with it. Pay him back for making me get all dressed up and going on the date in the first place.

Me: *Pick me up at my condo, then. I'll save the screaming for later tonight.*

Then I added a kiss emoji, and when his groan carried into the room, it no longer felt like I'd lost this round.

• • •

When the hostess showed us to a table, Jackson pulled out my chair. I settled into it, eyeing him as he pushed it back in. "This is totally over the top," I muttered so only he could hear. "I don't need you to get my chair."

"Well, I *need* to peek down your sexy red dress, and this way, it looks like I'm being a gentleman instead of a pervert." He winked at me, and worse, it sent warmth swirling through me and had me fighting a smile. Over the top, indeed.

His fingers brushed across my bare shoulders as he walked to the other side of the tiny square table. Whenever I peered through restaurant windows and saw white linen tablecloths and napkins, I always walked on, because it wasn't my scene, and I didn't belong in a place like that. *A place like this.*

The hostess told us someone would be right with us,

and then we both lifted our menus. I couldn't remember the last time I'd been on an official date—probably because I had rules against them. But here I was, wearing a dress and heels, and the prices on the menu were up in holy-shit range. I tucked the menu to my chest and kept my voice low. "You know that you're getting lucky tonight, right? You don't have to spend this kind of money trying to impress me."

Jackson set down his menu. "Just let me woo you, dammit."

"But I don't need wooed. I need—"

He leaned across the table and kissed me, the fancy wineglasses wobbling and making a light tinkling noise. He started to sit back, but I grabbed onto his fancy shirt and held him in place. I ran my tongue across his top lip, and he braced one hand on the table as the other drove into my hair and angled my head to deepen the kiss.

Yes. This is what I need.

Someone cleared her throat, and Jackson slowly released his grip on me and slid back into his chair.

A nervous girl with huge eyes looked at us. "Sorry. I can come back. I just…uh…"

"That's all right," Jackson said, his southern lilt and warm smile putting her at ease. I liked how he did that—saw that she was nervous and made an effort to smooth it over and make her feel comfortable. As someone who worked in the foodservice industry, I appreciated it even more, because I knew it was a rare quality.

We ordered drinks, and she asked if we wanted to hear the specials, to which Jackson responded he'd love to. Then he found my knee under the table, curled his hand around it, and flashed me his lady-killer grin.

He's in fine form tonight, displaying all that charm I pretended he didn't have when he accused me of worrying it'd be too much for me. It was a relief to not feel like I needed to prepare for battle every time we came within twenty yards of each other, but I also knew we'd never get to a point where we wouldn't push each other's buttons. I must be a little bit crazy, because I kind of liked the way he pushed my buttons instead of cowering at my strong personality, the way a lot of guys had.

The masochistic side of me even liked that he hadn't backed down until I gave in to his demands for a date. How could I *like* that?

The waitress left to get our drinks, and he covered my hand with his. "You look mighty fine tonight. Did I tell you that?"

"I picked it up from the staring down my dress comment, but thank you."

"Anytime."

"You, uh, look nice, too." I didn't know why it was so hard to tell him so in this formal setting—it was beyond true. The crisp white shirt, casually open a few buttons, was really working on him, the scruff on his strong jawline was in full force, and I wanted to spend some time running my hands through his perfectly styled hair, until it was perfectly messy.

We ordered and then talked a little shop at the table, what all we had left to do and the like.

"By the way," I said after taking a sip of my water. "I keep forgetting to ask, did everything work out with those permits?"

"I'll find out next week, but I crossed all the Ts and dotted all the Is." His thumb brushed over my knuckles. "How about work at the bar? Did you have to play bouncer any more times this week?"

"No. And for the record, it's not usually like that, just me and a belligerent, handsy drunk guy." Jackson's grip on my hand tightened, so I quickly charged on with the rest. "Admittedly, I usually let the guys handle it, but the point is,

I can when I need to."

He exhaled a long breath. "I know. You can handle it all, all by yourself."

"I can." I ran my finger around the rim of my glass. "But I'll also admit that the things I used to love about working at the bar—the freedom, the fact that it fit my night-owl tendencies, being able to meet so many different types of people, and the tips…" Part of me wanted to backtrack. Say it was fine, but too much was out there now. "I'm starting to feel a little…unfulfilled. But the thought of a set career still makes me want to run." I reached up and scratched at my suddenly itchy neck. "I'm a mess."

"I'd say more like you're a girl in need of a good challenge."

I folded my forearms on the table. "Oh? And you think *you're* a good challenge?"

"Little ol' me?" He placed a hand on his chest. "Well, of course, but I was talking about in a career. I can see how much you enjoy the work we're doing at the house."

"I love envisioning all the different ways to change a room. And even when it doesn't end up being exactly what I had in my mind, that almost makes it more fun." It was like the furniture restorations I did on the side—my favorite ones were often the pieces that turned out different than expected.

"I mean, that blackberry-colored wall in the bedroom might have been a mistake…" I waited for him to say that he told me it would look too dark because there wasn't enough natural light, but he simply waited. "But I'd rather say that I tried something bold before deciding to go a different way. And that was how I discovered Pashmina Plum, which is perfect." Dixie would love it, even if she'd sell the place before she could enjoy it for herself.

"You've definitely challenged me this job—and I'm not just talking about with your clothing options the past few days." Jackson nudged my foot with his under the table, and my stomach completed a somersault. "When you told me some of the things you wanted to do, I thought you were out of your mind. But the kitchen and living room look amazing. I'm especially a fan of the blue-gray paint."

His eyes heated. I had a feeling he was remembering the time we'd ended up covered in it, and then I was reliving it, too. He cleared his throat. "Aside from the obvious reasons. And don't tell anyone, but…" He glanced around like someone might be listening. "I even like the apple green bathroom."

I slapped a palm against the table. "I knew it!"

Several heads turned our way—oops, that's why I didn't belong in places like this. Along with being a little too rambunctious, I was also the one who went the "I told you so" route.

Our food came, and we dug in—remodeling for hours on end every day drained me, and after a few dinners consisting of popcorn, chips, or takeout, my steak tasted like I'd died and gone to heaven.

As dinner wound down, Jackson leveled his full attention on me. "So what are you going to do about your career?"

I shrugged.

"You can't just wait for one to land in your lap, you know."

Offense rose—and just when we'd been getting along so well, too. "I know. I got to where I am by a lot of hard work, thank-you-very-much. I went to college even though it was up to me to pay for every class, every book, every everything. It wasn't easy to earn that degree, either."

"And now you have it and you're not using it." He shifted forward, his hand returning to mine. "Before you get all pissed off, I know that you work hard, and Ivy, you're one of the smartest people I've ever met. But what I think is that sometimes you hold back on the things you really want because you're scared you won't get them, and you'd rather not go for it than go for it and fail."

I tried to sort out the compliments from the insults and the anger at him from the anger that maybe—just maybe— he'd come a little too close to the truth. It'd be easier to blow off everything he'd said if he wasn't also one of the smartest people I'd ever met. Most of society assumed guys who worked construction must be all brawn and no brain, and admittedly, I'd been guilty of thinking the same way before I met Jackson. When it came to cost analysis and figuring out measurements and budgets, he was faster at doing the math in his head than I was with a calculator. If only he could keep his big mouth closed sometimes.

"You're pissed." A statement, not a question.

I gritted my teeth. "I'm… Yeah, I'm a little pissed."

"Well, too bad. I'm going to tell you the truth, even if you don't like it. If you need someone to push you, I'll push you. If you need someone to hate so you can prove him wrong, I'll be that, too."

Grr. One minute I liked that he pushed my buttons, and the next it made me stabby. Right now, the scale was tipping heavily toward stabby. "I guess I was lying when I said I don't want to be wooed. Now I'd rather go back to the wooing part of the date."

Jackson pressed his lips together. He scratched his eyebrow, then lowered his hand and locked eyes with me. "Like I said, you're one of the smartest people I've ever met." He reached under the table and placed his hand on my knee. "Also, one of the sexiest." He slowly inched his hand higher and brushed his thumb across my skin, the callused roughness sending a swirl of desire through me. "And the most frustratingly stubborn. I admire you for getting through college and for dealing with all the shit you had to growing up, and I want you to go after what you want. I want you to be happy."

I propped my elbow on the table and tucked my chin on my fist, steadily staring right back at him. "It's hard to argue with you when you say you want me to be happy. But you think you know what'll make me happy, and I'm not so sure."

I was afraid that switching jobs without a safety net would only leave me feeling more lost and out of control, and it seemed like I was already just spinning circles. Well, it'd felt that way before taking on the renovation project, and I worried that as soon as it ended, I'd go back to drifting and spinning.

Jackson ran his hand through his hair, loosening the hold the gel had on it. "I'm saying you owe it to yourself to try it. To make a leap."

My stomach dipped at the thought, and I debated holding back my automatic question. But while I didn't have a safety net for my career, Jackson was my safety net right here and now, so I went ahead and let go. "What if I quit and then I hate where I leaped, and I want to go back?"

"You think Tony wouldn't take you back in an instant?"

"True. But what if the career I'm considering isn't an easy field to get into?"

"You're Ivy Freaking Clarke. You'll figure it out." His voice softened. "And I'll do whatever I can to help. Deal?"

"I've made way too many deals with you lately," I said, doing a crappy job of hiding my smile.

He chuckled, obviously thinking he'd won this round. His hand slipped farther up my thigh, breaching the barrier of my skirt. "Now, I believe there was mention of getting lucky?"

Chapter Twenty-One

I put on my best innocent act as we pulled up in front of the old Victorian house and batted my eyes at Jackson. "So, Mr. Gamble, would you care to come inside for a nightcap?"

"Oh, so long as I wouldn't be imposing too much, ma'am," Jackson said, tipping an imaginary hat and playing along.

I reached for the handle to get out of his truck, and he stopped me with a hand on my arm. "Give a guy a second to run around and get your door." I rolled my eyes, but he rushed around the hood, opened my door, and extended his hand. He remained the consummate gentleman as we made our way inside.

I'd chosen here for our "getting lucky" fun, because it was neutral territory, and I wanted to check on the kittens.

"You'll have to forgive my mess," I said, tossing my purse aside. "I'm in the middle of a huge remodel project." I gestured to the floral couch. "Just make yourself comfortable while I grab the drinks."

On my way to the kitchen, I took a detour to the dining room. One momma cat and four fluffy, squeaky kittens sat in the dog bed (it was bigger than the feline options). I'd set them up in the corner of the room, where they were tucked away from the noise and traffic.

My chest felt excessively mushy as my fingertips brushed fuzzy little heads—I was experiencing a strange maternal moment or something, and I wasn't sure I liked it. I wasn't sure I completely hated it, either. Emotions were complicated, pain-in-the-ass enigmas.

Black Widow eyed me, like she trusted me, but only so far when it came to her babies.

"Respect, girl. But I promise I'll take good care of them. While I'm here." One little kitten raised its head and licked my finger. "Okay, forever." I wasn't sure how—I certainly couldn't take on one momma kitten and four babies. That was crazy cat lady overnight, and I was in the market for a new career.

Because Jackson told me I should go for it instead of waiting for it to fall in my lap, and I'd needed to hear it. I just needed to figure out what exactly I wanted, so I could know where to jump.

After giving Black Widow a quick chin scratch, I pulled the chilled bottle of wine out of the fridge and grabbed the neon-colored plastic cups from the cupboard in my pristine kitchen. And by mine, obviously I meant for the very temporary here and now. More and more I was thinking of this place as mine, and I needed to stop. It would be hard enough to say good-bye as it was. I needed to focus on the fact that selling it meant I'd done my job well.

I hope the house doesn't end up going to some pretentious couple like a few of the ones on House Hunters, *where the husband's a freelance hamster trainer and the wife sells dreams and rainbows and they somehow make 1.3 million.*

While they were usually that same type who talked about paint color as if it were a make-or-break issue, it also bothered me to think of them painting over what I'd done. Of them changing *anything* Jackson and I had poured so much hard work into.

Don't think about that. Think about how this kitchen is the kind of kitchen that sells the house.

Since we didn't have many cleared surfaces in the other rooms, I opted to pour the cups in the kitchen, and balancing the drinks, I carefully walked across the fancy new hardwood living room floor. It was mostly finished but needed swept and cleared of debris, which was the only reason I was leaving the heels on. Stepping on a nail would really put a damper on the plans I had for tonight.

The creaky spot in the hallway announced my arrival, and Jackson looked up. My guy, on my couch, while my cats slept in the next room.

I was really starting to have a *my* problem.

Then I noticed the book in his hands.

"Oh, jeez, don't look at that." I should've known better than to leave the scrapbooks out, but I'd been making my way through them, one book at a time. I set down the glasses and reached for it, but Jackson held it away.

"This is you?" He lifted the book closer to his face.

"Some of them are me, yes."

He took a swig from his cup, keeping the scrapbook out of my reach the entire time. Then he flipped the page, and his expression morphed into the glee-filled one he wore when he thought he was about to secure the victory in one of our arguments. "You were a cheerleader?"

"Only for a couple of months, and I was pressured into it." I swiped the book from him. "It was when I was in Alabama, and not only was I…well, kind of desperate for a friend, I was desperate for an excuse to not have to go home until the last possible minute. The very first girl I met was a cheerleader, and hey, when in Pom Pom Land…"

Jackson placed his arm behind me on the back of the couch, watching and waiting, like he knew I wasn't quite done traveling in that time period yet.

"I told my mom it wasn't a big deal, and she had no desire to go to a high school game. Plus, I think the asshole was already pulling the strings and keeping her as isolated as possible." I didn't want to go down that path, so I focused on the other part. "Dixie and Rhett drove two-and-a-half hours to see me cheer at my first game. Evidently Dixie snapped this picture for posterity, and I'm not sure whether I should thank or strangle her for that."

The rift had just formed between her and Mom, but she told me it didn't have to affect our relationship.

For a little while, it didn't.

In fact, it was nice seeing Rhett here and there, too. But then they moved, and I was grown anyway, so it wasn't like I needed extra parental figures around. Which was good because Mom was the only one left, and she was far from parental.

"Well, I plan on thanking her," Jackson said, wrapping his arm around my shoulders. "And if it'll turn you on, babe, I'll dress up in my football uniform and you can do a cheer for me."

I shot him a look. While I could totally get down with Jackson in a football uniform, I sure as hell wasn't going to don my cheerleading outfit again.

"I'm a little surprised you never learned that a linebacker plays defense, but I'm happy to tutor you and give you a thorough demonstration of how to tackle your opponent to the ground and hold them there."

"I cheered for basketball, and I didn't bother to learn much about that, either. I just recited cheers."

Jackson circled my thigh with his hand. "While bouncing around in a tiny skirt?"

"The tiniest. As I'm sure you noticed."

He grinned. Then his gaze dropped back to the photo. He flipped the page, and my stomach bottomed out. In the picture, Tyler had his arm around me, and I was laughing. I'd sent the picture to Dixie, because at the time, I thought he'd be a permanent part of my life, the way I thought she'd be a more permanent part as well.

I was so stupid back then, thinking I needed a guy to complete me. I pried the picture out of the book, which wasn't easy with the crazy fastener things Dixie had used.

"Whoa," Jackson said. "What are you doing?"

"Getting rid of a picture of some asshole I once dated."

"Isn't Dixie going to be mad?"

"I don't care. I don't want exes-hall-of-shame scrapbooks like my mom has."

"I didn't know you even dated enough to call guys exes."

I wasn't sure he meant it as a dig, but it pricked my defenses like one. "I don't. It's a mistake I won't make again."

I crumpled Tyler's picture into a ball and tossed it in the general direction of the trash can. He didn't deserve to have so much emphasis in my life or the way I lived it. He was just a blip on the radar. It was more that for the first time in my life, I'd thought someone actually wanted me around. It felt so nice to be wanted, and add in the sense of security I experienced over not only finding someone who understood me, but also that I'd be staying put for four whole years, and it was the perfect catalyst to make me fall in love hard and fast. I wrapped my entire life up in him.

When he walked away, the crash...it was brutal.

Ugh, the tears I'd cried over him. Tears he so didn't deserve, and he sure as hell didn't deserve that piece of my heart that he took with him. Looking back, I realized I'd clung on that much tighter because Dixie and Rhett had just moved away, and instead of feeling like my life had finally started for real, the way I'd expected it to magically do, I felt more alone than ever.

That last glimmer of hope about love and relationships snuffed out after that. I accepted the fact that people always leave. *Always.*

Jackson was studying me way too closely, like he could see another piece of the puzzle falling into place. Over this past month I'd spilled tidbits of information, starting with little, seemingly insignificant things, and then bigger things, like when I'd said too much about some of Mom's exes. Probably enough that he could almost see what it'd look like if he fit them all together. Now he wanted to repair the remaining gaps and holes.

"I'm not a puzzle," I said, fighting...not quite full-blown panic, but a hint of worry and another foreign emotion that left me anxious and drifting closer to the edge. *I'm not broken.*

"I know." He curled his hand around the side of my neck and brought out the teasing smile. "You're a sexy woman who wants to do a personal cheer routine for me."

My anxiety eased off, and I gladly took the bait he'd laid out. "How can you be so very wrong so much of the time?"

He dragged his hand down, his knuckles brushing over one of my breasts and sending a corresponding shock of need through me. "You sound pretty sure of yourself for a woman who not only lost a sex-off, but propositioned me on our very first date."

I made an offended noise as my mouth dropped open, but it came out a little too breathy to be convincing. He ran his fingers back up, retracing their original path and leaving me dizzy with desire. Then he curled his hand around my neck again and guided my lips to his, erasing the last of the bad memories and tension with his tongue and the hand drifting higher and higher on my thigh.

He pulled back and rested his forehead on mine, our shallow breaths mixing in the air between us. "Still waiting for that cheer."

"Okay, fine." I shifted, crawling onto his lap and straddling him. I brushed my lips across his and rolled my hips. "Give me an O."

He gripped the sides of my waist, holding me tight to him as he arched against me, his arousal pressing right where I needed it. I shuddered against him, wrapping my arms around his neck to anchor me. He kissed me, stroking my tongue with his as he reached back and unzipped my dress. One strap slipped off my shoulder, and he yanked it down and dragged his thumb over the lace cup of my bra. I moaned and rocked against him again, needing more of that intoxicating friction.

He groaned, making it that much more satisfying.

Despite my internal grumbling about getting all dressed up tonight, I was glad for my skirt. Even with it, it felt like there was too much fabric in the way.

As if he could sense where my thoughts were headed, Jackson laid me back on the couch and tugged the rest of my dress down, down, until it fell to a puddle of fabric on the floor. He slipped his fingers into my panties and then I was lost in a sea of euphoria.

He increased the pressure as he captured his lips with mine, and I blame the drought the past few days for how quickly I tumbled over the edge.

I was still boneless and panting when Jackson pulled me into his arms. "Upstairs," he said, and I simply nodded and hooked my ankles behind his waist. I still had my heels on, and Jackson definitely had way too many clothes on.

Once we reached my bedroom—there I went calling things mine again—he laid me down on the bed. He dragged himself down my body, kissing and teasing while I went to work removing his clothes.

As he moved over me, I wasn't sure why, but everything felt different. I didn't know if it was the date or the connecting, but in the middle of the endorphin rush, he paused and cupped my cheek, giving me a look that was equal parts tenderness and possessiveness. In that moment, he branded my very soul, and I waited for the fear to come, but the only thing I experienced was the need for more.

More of him, more of this, more of everything.

And without having to say a word, he seemed to understand and gave me all of it and more.

Chapter Twenty-Two

Jackson scooted away from me, moving like he meant to get out of bed. I caught his arm and tugged him back down to the mattress, hooking my leg over his to ensure he didn't escape. "You don't have to rush off quite yet."

The noisy bedsprings squeaked as he rolled to face me. His mussed hair, lazy smile, and exposed—well, most everything—sent intoxicating surges of happiness through me. He traced a finger over my sensitized, kiss-swollen lips. "I don't want to break any of your rules or make you break out in hives."

"I can handle a little bit of cuddling," I said, even though the annoying voice in my head chimed in, reminding me that I'd already broken several of my rules with him, and I should stop myself before I got too carried away and things spun out of control.

"Good to know." He hauled me against him and squeezed me tight. Then, with that mischievous gleam in his eye that warned me he was up to no good, he rubbed his nose against mine and squeezed even tighter, my breath shooting out somewhere over his shoulder.

I wiggled against him. "I said *a little bit!*"

He chuckled and pressed his lips to my neck, and then I couldn't help melting into his embrace. I snuggled up to him, my head on his shoulder. He skimmed his fingers up and down my back, and while cuddling hadn't ever been my thing, he was just so comfortable and he smelled so good, and I fit so nicely against his side.

The idea was to get him out of my system with this have-fun-while-it-lasts arrangement, but I didn't feel even close to having him out of my system. If anything, I only craved more.

In the name of self-preservation, it was time to remind myself that this wasn't destined to be anything more than temporary. Head over heartache was the name of the game, even if my body protested the very idea of saying or doing anything that'd make him leave my side ever again.

Which just made it all the more important.

I ran my hand down his chest and rested it on his taut abdomen. "Earlier tonight we were talking about careers and goals, and it made me wonder…" I swallowed and forced the question past lips that didn't seem to want to cooperate. "Do you want that whole picket-fence-and-kids stuff?"

Jackson went perfectly still, his fingertips freezing halfway down my back. He narrowed his eyes at me like he suspected it was a trick question. It probably was. Red alarms flashed through my head, and I held my breath, wanting to take it back but not allowing myself to. After all, I already knew the answer, I was almost sure. But I wanted to hear it from his lips instead of taking his very biased family's word for it.

His inhale and exhale made his chest expand and dip. "Someday, I suppose."

I nodded, a dull ache forming in the center of my chest. While going down this path would tear me up inside, I needed to hear it, and so did he. I propped myself up on his torso so I could look him in the eye. "You could have it with her."

"Her?" Jackson lowered his eyebrows. "Who's her?"

"The girl you were with at Savannah and Linc's engagement party and the other night at dinner. The friend-of-your-family girl." I couldn't say her name. Just saying that much opened a raw wound somewhere deep in my heart. Maybe he only saw friendship now, but if he let himself, he could fall for her and have that idyllic life. That'd never be me.

I'm the girl you shouldn't want, the one you have one last fling with before you settle down. And I'm...fine with that.

He sighed.

I braced for impact.

"That would certainly make my mom and my aunt Velma happy," he said. "But I'm just crazy enough to believe that if it's right, the thought of settling down with someone should make me so excited I can hardly wait to get started. And when I think of a future with her, that's not how I feel."

I reached up and fiddled with my earring—funny enough, it was Savannah's and my sign that we needed help. The other person would swoop in and run interference. Obviously, she wasn't here right now—and it'd be hella awkward if she was—and I supposed I was the one already running interference in this situation. I could really use some help spitting out the rest, though. "But maybe you'd feel different if I was out of the way. Not that I'm in the way. I get that this is just temporary. I'm just saying..." My fingers went to my earring again. "Well, I guess I'm stating the obvious."

"That if I stopped sleeping with you I'd suddenly fall madly in love with Caroline?"

I flinched, the reaction too fast to realize I needed to cover it. I did my best to lift my chin and put conviction into my voice. "Yes."

"Damn it, Ivy…" He raked a hand through his hair and blew out a breath. He studied me for a moment, and then he placed his hand on the side of my neck, his thumb dragging across my jaw and sending my pulse zipping into motion. "Why don't you let me decide who I want to be with? In case it's not obvious already."

"But I'm not an option. We tried it already, and—"

"No. We slept together a few times during one of the roughest weeks of your life. We didn't try a relationship."

Shit. This was supposed to be cuddling so he didn't feel like I kicked him out the instant sex ended. This was what I got for even indulging in that much.

Time to bring out the big guns. I'd been hoping to avoid resorting to such extreme measures, but it was for Jackson's good.

Way #10: *Display baggage.*
Don't hold back. Open up the countless suitcases of issues you've got packed away and watch them run in fear.

My heart pounded faster as I got ready to start flipping open suitcases. I'd seen grown men flee when my mom did it—which was why she'd learned to hide hers better and also why she'd stopped introducing her suitors to me near the beginning. In my case—or out of it, as it were—it'd led to the breakup of the dude I had the awkward prom date with and was one of the main things that drove away Tyler. He told me I had too many issues, enough that he'd rather break up than stay together "just for the great sex."

"I don't do relationships," I said, trying to quell the vulnerable, exposed sensation that make my skin feel too tight. "I get bored quickly, and I smother easily. I like going out and hooking up with guys, no strings attached. I'm all about getting in, getting off, and then getting on with my life.

Is that what you want? To be one of my booty call options?"

The muscles along Jackson's jaw tightened. "You really want me to be cool with you sleeping with other guys?"

I lowered my gaze a few inches, staring at the base of his throat, because the look on his face was too much. *It's for his own good...*

"I'm saying that's how I live my life. That's who I am. I don't believe in love, and I'm sure as hell not the girl you take home to your parents. I'm not the girl you take home at all. I'm having fun fooling around while we're doing the remodel, and I won't sleep with other guys until we've finished it up, because that's what we agreed to. But fun and temporary is all this can be, and if you don't understand that, we've got to end it now."

The urge to cry overwhelmed me, and I slid off him, lying flat on my back and pinching the bridge of my nose, attempting to redirect the pain and stop the tears from breaking free. "We probably never should've crossed the line again. I don't know what I was thinking."

Jackson rolled over me, his hands braced on either side. "You were thinking that you and I have this thing between us that won't go away. I tried to ignore it. Tried to snuff it out, and I even tried to hate you for the way you abruptly ended things after our amazing week together all those months ago. I'm not asking you for forever. I'm just saying give us a chance."

A lump formed in my throat. Why did he have to push? Why couldn't he flee, like any sane guy would? "But I don't believe we have one, and I'm not going to pretend otherwise. It'll just lead to both of us getting hurt at the end."

I sat up, keeping the sheets over my breasts because I already felt way too exposed, and looked for my discarded clothes. Looked for an escape, really. The walls began closing in, and my breaths came faster and faster.

"Hey, hey." Jackson's arm came around my shoulders, and he pulled me to him, my back to his chest. Seconds ticked by, my breaths gradually slowing. "Fine," he said, his voice low. "We'll do it your way. I'm not pushing for more. I just thought we could try it out and see what happened, but I'm fine with this arrangement, too."

My heart knotted, each beat tightening it a bit more. "It's all I have to give. I'm sorry."

"No reason to be sorry," Jackson said, but I could hear the disappointment and frustration in his voice. He kissed my shoulder and then shifted away, a cold draft of air taking his place as he pulled on his jeans. "I've got to get going anyway. I need to take care of some things tomorrow morning so I won't be in till around noon. Then I'll finish the baseboards downstairs, and we'll tackle the flooring and whatever else needs done up on this floor."

"Perfect," I said. The house, the plan, him.

Too bad it just wasn't for me. Even though for the first time in years, I sort of wished I was the kind of girl who could believe in happy endings.

Chapter Twenty-Three

A mix of irritation and panic swirled through me as I paced the length of the upstairs hallway Monday morning. Black Widow watched, her whiskered face following my movements, her *judging-you* expression in full effect. My instincts had warned me against picking up the phone, but I was having a bit of a blue day—a few blue days, really—and that made me think Mom might be having one, too, and guilt from the time I hadn't answered a call like that had me answering this one.

And immediately regretting it.

"But why do you have to move in with him?" I asked, my brain spinning for something that might make her see reason, even though it should know better by now.

"Because it makes it so much easier to have sex all the time," Mom retorted, and I groaned, wanting to stab my ears out, even though that wasn't a thing. Fine, she wanted to play dirty, I could sling some mud of my own.

"Well, then why can't *he* move you in with him, since he's getting all the benefits?"

Her exasperated huff carried over the line. "I thought I

could ask my *only daughter* for help, but clearly I was wrong. I'll just use money I don't have and call movers. Will you be happy then?"

I glanced around at all the work I needed to do—work I couldn't tell her about, because she'd consider it an act of treason. I only had a couple more weeks with Jackson's help, and after our rough ending on Saturday night, I worried things would be tense and weird between us today. I fully expected him to show up, say he couldn't do this anymore, and collect his tools. To walk away from our project and get as far away from me as he could. I was trying to prepare myself and be okay with it, even though it made everything inside of me feel heavy and wrong.

One problem at a time, Ivy…

"No, don't do that," I said, focusing on the situation at hand. "I'll…I'll find some time and help you move."

"Well, don't put yourself out."

"Mom…" I didn't know what more to say. No matter how many times I'd expressed my concerns about her life choices, it didn't matter. Didn't change anything. I'd been so determined to stop enabling her, but then came the night that shook me to my core, and I'd rather enable her than live with a lifetime of regret. "I just want you to be happy."

"And right now, the idea of moving in with the man I love makes me happy."

Which was exactly what I worried about. What happened when he stopped? And don't even get me started on her saying she was already in love. She was more in love with love than she ever was with the men she dated.

Love. The word made me feel empty and cold inside, and this was a big part of why. I was sick of love before I was old enough to date, and my bitterness toward it had only grown since. Defeated, I said, "Text me the details, and I'll figure out something."

She gushed, thrilled her guilt trip had worked no doubt, and I told her good-bye.

When I hung up, I noticed Jackson hovering near the top of the stairs.

Great. On top of the weirdness and tension between us, he'd just seen a way-too-vulnerable snapshot of me. Or I suppose I could view it as keeping in line with Way Number Ten and refer to it as displaying more of my baggage. Not that he hadn't already seen this particular suitcase of crazy.

"Sorry," he said. "I couldn't help but overhear. Is everything okay?"

I debated telling him everything was fine, but instead I rubbed at the headache forming behind my temples, hoping to convince it to leave me alone for a little while, because I was all filled up on shit to deal with. "My mom's moving in with a new guy. He makes her happy, apparently, so I should just deal with it."

Jackson stepped farther into the hallway, the bare bulbs overhead highlighting his hair and ruggedly handsome face. "But you're worried about what happens when he stops making her happy. Because of what happened last time."

I pressed my lips together and clenched my fists so I wouldn't cry, but my eyes watered anyway. If he hadn't known exactly how I felt, I might've been able to hold it back. "Pretty much," I said, and then I sniffed, super loudly.

Within a couple of large strides, Jackson had me in his arms. I wanted the strength to push away. To tell him I didn't need a shoulder to cry on—last time I'd used his shoulder for that reason certainly hadn't turned out so well. But I couldn't bring myself to do it when it felt so damn good to let him hold me.

"I know I shouldn't enable her and jump to move her in or help her flee every single time. She'll never learn to be independent that way, but I think that ship has sailed anyway, and I can't seem to help it. I set up boundaries, and she just laughs at them and takes them out like Godzilla, not caring about the destruction she leaves behind."

Jackson smoothed a hand down my hair. "It's okay. I of all people know what it's like to try to set up boundaries with family members who treat them like silly suggestions."

I smiled at that. At least his family crashed through with love instead of more destruction. At least they did it because they cared so much about *his* well-being instead of only thinking about theirs.

"Tell you what. I'll help you move her into the guy's house, and I'll have a nice chat with him about what'll happen if he fails to make her happy."

I half-laughed, half-cried. "Poor guy. If he doesn't leave her, she'll leave him. It's like musical chairs; she'll just keep on bouncing until the music stops and she literally can't move anymore, and that'll be the guy who sticks. Even if he wishes he could run but that bum hip of his won't let him."

"Maybe this one will stick," Jackson said, and I looked at him like he'd lost his mind. "Hey, a little optimism never hurt anybody."

"Wrong. It's hurt me every single time I've tried it out." A sharp pain lanced my heart. Time to redirect before I lost my grip on my control and fell apart.

I pulled out of his embrace. "I need a Cherry Coke. Do you want one?" Sugar plus caffeine was always a safe bet. When Jackson didn't immediately answer, I said, "I'll grab you one, just in case."

As I rushed down the stairs, he muttered, "And the world record for fastest at running away from anything involving emotions goes to Ivy Clarke."

My hand gripped the banister, and my feet slowed. A big part of me wanted to turn and defend myself—I had a feeling he'd purposely said it loud enough for me to hear, probably to goad me into finishing our conversation. To keep from engaging and turning this into a shouting match, I reminded myself that he'd just so nicely offered to help with my mom's move. He wasn't exactly wrong, either. Even though it still kind of stung.

I took long strides through the living room and into the kitchen. The cool air that wafted over me as I grabbed two cans out of the fridge was a welcome relief. I popped the lid open to mine and gulped about half of it down so the energizing effects could kick in as soon as possible. If it could also drown out everything else, that'd be great, but that was super wishful thinking.

I heard Jackson's heavy footsteps approaching, and I steeled myself for a lecture about how much I sucked at being a quasi-girlfriend, but then they went the opposite way. I stepped through the archway that opened to the dining room and saw him bend down next to the kittens, checking on them.

Over the past few days, their eyes were slowly opening, little slits with blue showing through. They were seeing the world bit by bit, and I wished it was a better, less-complicated place. I still didn't know what I was going to do with four kittens who obviously couldn't live here forever.

"Noisy little things," Jackson said, patting one on the head. All of them squished over in the same corner, vying for his attention. I sometimes had the same urge, so I could hardly blame them.

"Maybe I'll take one as a housewarming gift when I help my mom move," I joked as I knelt next to him and extended the unopened Coke—my version of a peace pipe—and every nerve ending in my body stood on end, desperately hoping it'd be enough.

Instead of taking it, he curled his fingers around mine. "Listen up, Flash, because I've got somethin' to say, and I'm not above tackling you to the ground to get you to hear it if that's what it takes."

Apparently, he wasn't going to let go of my hand until he said his piece, either. "You're not responsible for her choices," he said, and everything in me froze, leaving me unable to move, even if he'd let me. "And you sure as hell weren't responsible for the one she made last spring."

"She called me earlier that night, and I let it go to voicemail." Much to my dismay, my voice cracked. "If I would've—"

"Nope." Jackson locked eyes with me. "You're not responsible. End of story."

Black Widow came over and checked on her kittens, making sure we were taking good care of them since they were squeaking their cute little heads off.

"See?" Jackson nodded at the momma cat. "She's taking care of them, not the other way around."

"When it comes down to it, I'm all she's got," I said. She'd pushed everyone else away, including the one friend she'd had since she was a teenager. That one hit the hardest, because I didn't think it was a possibility. I always thought she and Dixie were soul mates. Nothing romantic, just solid, always going to be there for each other, soul mates. I'd built my foundation with it, telling myself that at least that would never change. But it did, and it took the last shred of my sense of security with it. I supposed that was another reason I was determined to be okay on my own. I saw my future, and while Linc and Savannah were in it, things would change after they got married.

Jackson cupped my cheek. "And she's dang lucky to have you." He leaned in and brushed his lips across mine.

I closed my eyes, enjoying the contrast of his soft lips and scratchy whiskers. Just when I was considering sinking into everything Jackson and forgetting the rest of the world, he broke the kiss.

He pushed to his feet, retrieved his tool box, and headed upstairs while I sat there and let the mix of happiness and sorrow twist through me. Happiness that Jackson knew just what I needed; sorrow that my mom would never change. Another strand of sorrow to mourn the fact that I couldn't be the girl who believed in happily-ever-afters with the guy turning my insides to mush.

I lived in the real world now.

The real world, where if I didn't give my mom attention, she found other ways to gain it.

After dealing with the moodiness that'd accompanied more breakups than I could count, I'd instinctively known that was why Mom was calling me that night, and I'd let the call go to voicemail. I was at work, after all. When I had a break, I listened to the message, which confirmed my suspicions that she and her beau at the time were over.

I'd decided I couldn't keep swooping in and saving her. Without Dixie to help balance her out, her emotions and mood swings were oppressive, and she needed to learn to save herself.

Three days later, she took too many sleeping pills and landed in the hospital. Ever since that cry for help, I felt so obligated to answer every call. To try to do whatever it took to keep her happy.

Was it horrible that I wished she would finally find the one even though I didn't believe in that, just so he could take care of her so I wouldn't have to?

I knew it was, but that was how I felt right now.

I didn't want to end up pacing the halls of another hospital, the antiseptic smell burning my nostrils as I faced the reality of losing Mom—who was the only person I really had, too, even though it never seemed like I'd truly had her.

Usually, I tried to keep my friends away from my mother, especially when she was in a downswing, but that night I'd desperately needed someone. I have no doubt Savannah would've flown home from her convention in a heartbeat, but it would've taken a day, and she'd been talking about presenting in front of her dating coach peers for months. I didn't want to blow that for her, but I'd needed someone—needed someone more than I ever had in my entire life.

Jackson's name had flashed like a beacon in the storm my life had dissolved into. Sure, we constantly argued, our crazy strong attraction always underlying our interactions, but he was reliable. He was the kind of person who knew what to do in emergencies, and as he'd held me that night while I'd cried and spilled my guts, I knew I'd picked exactly the right person.

He was still there in the waiting room with me the next morning. I saw him in a new light, literally and metaphorically.

Once Mom was released and I'd settled her in at home, he came over to check on me. The magnetic pull between us was supercharged and stronger than ever, and instead of bothering to fight it, we gave in, crossing lines without thinking about the consequences. After all the stress of taking care of someone else, it felt so good to be taken care of that I let Jackson completely sweep me away to a place where none of my worries existed.

Night after night, until I could feel my heart strings getting all tangled up with his.

I saw the disaster we were headed toward and slammed the emergency brake, hoping that'd keep us from crashing and burning. Only I was me, so I'd been too harsh and things got ugly.

I pushed, I avoided, and when Jackson hunted me down at the club one night so he could push back, he found me dancing with another guy. A nobody, and definitely not anyone I was interested in, but I'd tried to tell myself I was. Or that I could be, because I couldn't deal with the other option.

Jackson had practically carried me out of the club, and I'd yelled and he'd yelled, and instead of the flirty challenge that came along with most of our fights, this wasn't flirty or challenging. It was harsh and devastating, and neither of us was good at losing, which meant we swung that much harder.

I told him he'd read way too much into our week together, and when I could see the words sink in, instead of fixing them, I purposely picked at the scab—it was easier than thinking I'd made a mistake.

So I'd shrugged and said, "Look, it was a fun week, but I'm not sure what you expected. I'm not a one-guy relationship-type girl, and I never will be. Sorry if you thought otherwise."

We'd thrown a lot of verbal punches in our day, and that was definitely a low blow, but I was too stubborn and prideful to take it back.

He'd shaken his head, his eyes going cold, his words coming out sharp. "I should've seen this coming," he said with a mirthless laugh. "I knew how you were. But don't you worry your little head about me—I'll sleep just fine. So go on back in there and have your fun, and good luck trying to look at yourself in the mirror."

That jab was the TKO kind, one that knocked me on my ass, even as I'd forced myself to stay standing.

I'd finally pushed hard enough for him to walk away, and it took everything in me to remind myself it was for the best as I resisted the urge to crumple onto the sidewalk and cry.

A pit opened itself in my chest that night, and I renewed my vow to never let anyone get that close or that deep again.

Now here I was, my heart strings tangled as ever, and he was going to get tied up in the mess. Then we'd have to cut each other loose, and the cutting would hurt. After that would come the downward spiral, and I instinctively knew this time would hurt more and leave me broken for longer.

He only likes you when you're broken and vulnerable anyway.

So that I wouldn't think about that stray, distressing thought too much, I forced myself to my feet and headed upstairs to see what the plan was for *this* week. I'd focus on the here and now, and worry about next week, well, next week. One day at a time—that was how I'd lived my life, and I'd made it okay so far.

Mostly made it, anyway.

I found Jackson eyeing the window in my bedroom. Er, my old bedroom. "Hey," I said, shoving the bad memories and complications away and telling myself it was fake-it-till-you-make-it time. Especially since when it came to time, we didn't have a lot left. "What's the plan, boss?"

He laughed. "That's rich, you calling me boss."

"I thought I'd try it out." I made a face. "I don't like it."

"I'm so shocked. Now, come 'ere. I want to show you something." He gestured me over and then positioned me in front of him. "What would you think about me knocking out this tiny window and turning it into a big picture window? One with a little reading nook, so you could sit and read in the big sunny window and look out over the street."

"But this isn't my house."

Jackson's eyebrows crinkled, and he tilted his head. "I mean a more metaphorical you. So I guess what I should've said was 'so someone could sit and read in the reading nook.'"

Of course I wanted that, but honestly, I wanted it to be me doing the sitting and reading. I wanted to pretend for just a little while that this house was mine and I had a reading nook, and...and that I had a guy like Jackson who'd build one just for me. I bit my lip. "What about the budget?"

We'd pretty much blown through most of my savings, and I couldn't justify expensing some of the upgrades because they were more for me anymore, even though I also hoped it'd make the house sell for a higher price.

Jackson skimmed his hands down my sides and rested them on my hips. "Well, I'll give you an amazing deal on the labor, considering you'll be doing part of it, and I already have all the supplies but the window. Which means a couple hundred, and since I got a deal on carpet for up here—as long as you agree on what I picked out, which you should, because like I said, it's a good deal—it would still keep us within the budget."

"What does the carpet look like? As I recall, we don't have very similar tastes." I glanced over my shoulder at him, and he flashed me a wide smile.

"Just let me build you a damn reading nook, woman."

I was about to argue again that it wouldn't be my reading nook, but then he nipped at my ear. "We can use it for other things besides reading."

A shallow breath escaped my lips. "Sold, to the guy with the dirtiest mind."

He laughed and then pulled out his trusty notepad and went to writing figures and numbers, and I found myself wishing yet again that I was different or he wasn't set on a conventional family. Or that I could jump into the fog without being too afraid of getting hurt.

But I knew there was no guarantee, and my battered heart couldn't risk any more heartbreaks.

See, I wished I could say I didn't understand my mom's desperation that infamous night, and how she could do something like take a bunch of pills in order to make it all go away, but I did. At my lowest, right after that relationship with Tyler ended and I found myself desperately alone, I'd had the thought that no one would miss me if I was gone.

Logically I knew it wasn't true, but when I was depressed and spiraling, logic wasn't involved.

It'd scared the crap out of me. And here I was approaching

the point of no return with the guy currently using a tape measure to widen the window I used to stare out of as I dared to dream Mom would stop serial coupling, and we'd finally stay for good this time. Back when optimism was a luxury I could afford.

But with this renovation project and my mom getting ready to move, and my life in upheaval in general, I wasn't sure I was strong enough to cut off our with-benefits arrangement early.

Just a little while longer. Then I promise I'll let him go...

If I was lucky, we could part as friends, the way we hadn't been able to the first time I cut things off.

But I wasn't particularly lucky.

And I didn't think it was possible for me to be friends with Jackson without accidentally wanting more.

Chapter Twenty-Four

I slowed my steps as I neared the lecture hall where my best friend was giving her 12 Steps to Mr. Right workshop. While I didn't exactly subscribe to her system to find the Mr. Right—because I was all about Mr. Right Now—I admired how strongly she believed in it.

She had an inspirational quote to use for any and every situation, and while I'd heard a few of them more than once, I was always in awe of how many she had at her disposal. I liked to tease her about it sometimes, as did her fiancé, but like I said, I was proud. Maybe a little envious that she'd found her true calling, but my happiness for her far outweighed it.

Her passion bled into her voice as the click of her heels told me she was pacing the front of the room, doing her thing while a PowerPoint slide with inspirational thoughts and most likely bright colors flashed up front.

I snuck in as Step Eleven flashed onscreen.

Step Eleven: *Don't let your past heartbreaks get in the way of your future. Don't hold potential guys* *responsible for the way you've been treated in the past—remember you've let that go. You believe a guy out there will restore your faith in love. When you find him, drop your walls, open your heart, and don't be afraid to fully love.*

I'd seen her steps before, but this one struck me harder than expected. What she didn't understand was that my past heartbreaks left me broken, and hell yes, it'd changed the way I looked at my future. I didn't think it was in the way, though. More like the building block to learning to be okay on my own.

Savannah gave me a subtle nod as she continued her lecture, and I slid into an empty chair—the only empty chair in the entire room. Her workshops sold out crazy fast and had become even more popular since the mayor married one of her former attendees. The announcement of Savannah's engagement to Linc spurred even more women to sign up and learn how to find their very own Mr. Right. So much so that she now taught two sessions, one for this group who came in on Wednesday nights and another group who met on Fridays.

"I get it, no one likes getting their heart broken," Savannah said. "Let's be honest, it sucks. And it's not easy to pick ourselves up again after someone hurts us, especially a guy who we thought we might spend our entire lives with…"

I couldn't help thinking of Tyler. I rolled my eyes at my naive college self, who thought she was breaking the cycle, not realizing she was already in it. It hadn't been his personality or even his looks or charm that'd drawn me to him. It was that he *wanted* me. And when it started to seem like he didn't want me as much, I clung to him harder, desperate not to have to go back to being lonely. Like this poor, defenseless girl who just wanted to be loved, even if the love was toxic.

Then Linc came to visit me. We'd grown up together, one

of my few touchstones besides Dixie. When he met Tyler, he immediately hated him, and Linc didn't hate many people. And when Tyler treated me like shit in front of him, the way he'd started to do more often than not, Linc threatened him. Because he was an idiot, Tyler took a swing.

While I was sitting on the couch, icing his blackened eye, Tyler told me I wasn't worth it. Then he'd added that gem about how I had too many issues, enough that'd he'd rather break up than stay together "just for the great sex," making it clear that for him, that was all it'd been.

Stupid me, I was heartbroken. And I did the one thing I swore never to do: I acted exactly like my mom, as if her genetics were strong enough to overpower all common sense.

I don't think I ever thanked Linc for standing up for me. Probably because I was too ashamed to admit to letting myself be treated that way.

I shook my head, returning to the present.

"Remember, a bitter woman says, 'All men are the same.'" Savannah paused for emphasis. "A wise woman decides to stop choosing the same type of men.'"

Was I being paranoid, or did my bestie glance my way?

I liked my type. Hot and unavailable, just like me.

"Next week will be our last session," Savannah said, "and we'll top it off with one last field trip to Azure." Doubling up on field trips meant alcohol sales were higher at Azure on Wednesday and Friday, which in turn made Tony less likely to kick Savannah out for scaring off his male customers who shared my same urge to flee from commitment. "This week, I want you to focus on the fact that you now believe there's a guy out there who will restore your faith in love. Dropping your walls isn't easy, but you can't find the kind of love you want if you keep them up. Love is a risk, but it's also worth it when you find the right person to open your heart to."

Man, the girl almost made me believe in happily-ever-after. Or maybe that was just my recent desire to believe, thanks to a guy I knew was one of the good ones. Even if he did occasionally make me crazy.

I can only imagine how upset she'd be if she found out I'd ignored her wishes and started fooling around with Jackson, too selfish to stay out of the way like I'd said I would. The guilt I'd gotten a minor break from drifted to the surface. Ensuring Savannah and I never ended up like my mom and Dixie was all the more reason to stick to my previous assertions that Jackson and I keep things light and temporary. And very secret.

Honestly, we should end it now, before Savannah somehow found out and the three of us ended up hurt and mad at each other. But my willpower was too weak with him under the same roof, looking sexy all the time and putting his hands on me and making me feel things I'd never felt before.

Physical things only. *Liar.*

Denial used to be so much easier. The close proximity wasn't the only thing making it impossible to shut it down. Not when he showed up to help with kitten births in the middle of the night and pushed me to have serious conversations about my career, and not when he knew exactly what I needed to hear after dealing with my mom. We'd drifted into full-blown relationship territory, and the waters looked deceptively calm on the surface, but I knew the sharks were circling. One bad storm could rise up out of nowhere and brutally tear us apart.

Savannah talked about letting go of the way I'd been treated in the past, but it wasn't that easy.

Sure, my breakup with Tyler left a scar and hurt more than my high school relationships, but the ones from every guy my mom dated were there, too. From Dixie and Rhett drifting out of my life. Once I'd told my mom not to worry, that if we teamed up, we could take on the world together.

When she reacted like she couldn't imagine a worse

fate, it taught me that I wasn't enough for her, and maybe I wouldn't be enough for anyone, but I'd made a goal to be enough for me.

I need to focus on my career. That'll give me the fulfillment I'm missing.

Savannah dismissed her attendees, and once everyone had cleared out, I made my way up front to help her pack. "Oops," she said. "I forgot to ask for the phone numbers of their smart, asshole exes. Did you want me to call them back in and get you some digits?"

I laughed. "I think I'm good for now." Especially since I already had my hands full with a guy who often fit that description.

"Sorry I went a little long. You know me when I'm talking about this stuff."

"I do," I said. "You're really good at your job. Have I ever told you that?"

"Usually I get more wrinkled noses over the monogamy talk." Savannah narrowed her eyes on me. "Did you already start drinking?"

I gave her a light shove. "I was trying to be a supportive friend. Last time I ever do that."

She grinned at me. "Sorry. Thank you. And you *are* a supportive friend. Have been since the very beginning, and let's not forget how you talked sense into me when I was about to let Linc get away for good. You told me that when you're in love, your head isn't supposed to be straight."

"And your head's been quite crooked ever since."

Savannah laughed, but I had the fleeting thought that my head hadn't been straight for just over a month. Which was a ridiculous notion, one I was shutting down right now.

I shouldered the bag with her projector. Linc was out of town, so we were headed to her place for girls' night in. Just her, me, a movie, and some spiked ice tea. "Let's get this show on the road, because I suddenly feel the need to start drinking."

"I'm so ready for some girl time. I just got this facemask that makes your skin feel amazing. Wait till you try it, you're gonna love it."

"Sounds perfect."

"Oh, and we can talk about that guy you like that you're sleeping with."

Sounds like a disaster waiting to happen.

Chapter Twenty-Five

Talking became more and more difficult. Savannah nicknamed the goop she'd put on me the "paralysis face mask," and it had tightened to the point we could hardly move our mouths, which made talking difficult and hilarious.

The Sweetest Thing, our go-to movie since college, was playing in the background. Which led Savannah to ask if I'd named the puppy, a line from the movie that basically boiled down to using a guy's name instead of calling him anything but to keep him at a safer distance.

"It's jus…temp-ary." Seriously, talking without the full use of my cheek muscles made me feel even more ridiculous. "No point in namin' him."

Savannah leaned forward, and even though her face wouldn't let her pull off a canary-eating grin, I could see that sentiment sparkling in her eyes. "But you have."

"Was this yer plan all along?" I circled a hand in front of my face. "Render me incapable of movement and then interrogate me?"

"Of course," Savannah said, then she laughed, and I

laughed, and I could feel the mask cracking.

"Thish is the girliest thing I've ever done."

"And you're loving every minute of it. Admit it."

I reached for my drink, which I now had to sip out of a straw. The sweet tea and Southern Comfort burned a little as it went down. Nice and strong, the way I liked it, and we were already on our second round. Or was it third? "Ish just what I needed. But what I'm more interested in talking about is my career. Only I can't do it with this on my faaash." Ventriloquism definitely wasn't my strong suit—I was butchering words right and left.

Savannah looked at her phone. "It's time to wash it off." She paused the movie, and we squeezed into the bathroom of her loft to rinse off the mask and free our facial muscles.

I leaned closer to the mirror, checking out my skin and running a finger down my cheek. "It does feel amazing."

"See? I told you."

We finished the beautifying process off with moisturizer and then returned to the living room. Savannah lifted the remote, then suddenly dropped it and turned to me. "I want cookies."

"Mmm, that sounds amazing." In the best of times, Savannah and I were more of the order-food-in than cooking type, and I doubted being tipsy would make us better bakers, but now that she'd mentioned cookies, I couldn't stop thinking about sugary, chocolate chip dough. "Now we have to make them."

As we mixed ingredients together in her kitchen, Savannah asked me to update her on my thoughts about my career.

I told her about feeling like I was stuck in a rut. "I want something more. I'm really loving fixing up Dixie's house. I just don't think randomly begging people who have homes for sale to let me have at them is a career, unfortunately."

"Let's see. There's interior design…"

"Pretty sure I'd need to go back to school for that one. Why'd I think I wanted a political science degree?"

"Because you could actually understand it, unlike most of the population?"

"Maybe. But now I'm thinking I should've gone into something more practical."

"We are not practical girls."

"True," I said with a smile, then handed her the eggs when she gestured for them.

She cracked one and then frowned into the bowl. "Oh, shit. The egg kind of shattered." We both went to look in at the same time and knocked heads.

I rubbed my forehead but couldn't stop giggling. "I think we're a wee bit drunk."

Savannah held her fingers up, about an inch apart. "Little bit." She chased out the shell shards and wiped them on a paper towel. She glanced at the recipe, pulling it closer, then holding it farther out. "I hate that cookies always call for softened butter, like you know when you're going to be craving them and have butter out all soft and ready to go."

"I'll just pop it in the microwave."

"What about like on *Leap Year?*"

"How do they microwave butter on *Leap Year?*"

Sputtered laughter shook Savannah's shoulders. "I mean for your job. Amy Adams—whatever her name was in that movie—she stages houses to help real estate agents sell them faster."

"Probably something I could look into. And I have a few spare pieces of furniture I could use."

"Ooh, like your coffee table? Once Linc and I decide if we're going to live here in the loft for a while or buy a house, I want you to make me one."

I nodded. "Consider it a wedding present." I tapped a

finger to my lips, thinking about the staging suggestion. "I don't have enough pieces to do that on a wide scale. I've loved the construction stuff, but it's not like I can do it without help, and I don't have the experience to get a full-time job with a bunch of dudes who I'd have to ask for help from—that's kind of my nightmare."

"You are the worst at asking for help. That's why I just had to send Jackson in."

"I'm still not sure I forgive you for that," I said, light enough she would realize it wasn't true. I sighed. "I don't know. Maybe I should look at other jobs in other fields."

"No way. If this is what you want to do, we'll find a way."

I took the butter out of the microwave—it was more boiling liquid than softened, but how much difference could it make? I handed it to Savannah, and she dumped it into the bowl.

"Jackson would probably know more about which career fields you could branch out into. Have you talked to him about it?"

I paused and schooled my features, since a flutter had gone through my stomach at the mention of his name, then said, "Yeah, a little bit. He was pretty encouraging about me finding a job that I'm more passionate about, actually."

"See. You guys *can* get along when you really put your minds to it." She paused and raised her eyebrows—she'd told me before that she wished she could raise just one, but that her eyebrows liked to present a united front. "So, you guys are…getting along?"

"We're managing. We might even be able to part as friends." My heart tripped over its quickening beats, and I worried I was about to get busted, and then our girls' night would take a bad turn.

Quick, change the subject. "Do you think you could do some research and make up some charts with possible career options?"

"Um, you know I love charts. And research."

"I do."

She beamed and even clapped her hands. "I'll work on it this week."

"Thanks." With the dough done, I scooped out a glob and popped it in my mouth. "Mmm. Cookies was the right call."

After we ate more raw cookie dough than the salmonella police would allow, we shaped the rest of it, stuck the cookies in the oven, then returned to our movie and another round of drinks.

Which led to not hearing the cookie timer. I was glad that we'd eaten so much dough, because our cookies were flat puddles that were burned around the edges. We still ate a few, of course.

Savannah pulled out the bed in her couch, handed me a blanket and grabbed one for herself, and we relaxed back on the couch and finished our movie. And when it was done, she put in another DVD.

Our talking gradually slowed as the mix of food and alcohol and the late hour caught up to us. Then we crashed out on the couch, just like we used to back in college.

• • •

I groaned at the ridiculously loud rattling of keys coming from somewhere in the vicinity of the front door. I reached out, patting the area next to me until I made contact with Savannah, which meant someone else was at the door.

"I'm getting this strange sense of déjà vu," Linc said, and I squinted against the bright light at him.

Savannah stirred and scooted up the sofa bed. She glanced around, clearly trying to get her bearings. Then she reached up and rubbed at her neck—mine felt pretty stiff as well. "Yeah, this is definitely a college throw-back."

"Speaking of college…" The newspaper under Linc's arm crinkled as he flipped it open. "I'm looking for something that means 'studied in a hurry.' It's not cram, because it's seven letters."

"It's way too early for crossword clues," Savannah said, and I agreed with a slow nod that still made my head hurt.

Linc left his small roller suitcase next to the door and moved toward the kitchen. "I'll make coffee."

"Good idea," both Savannah and I said. I smiled over at her, and she grinned back. Last night was just what I needed. Time with my best friend to discuss my career and laugh and take a night off from life in general.

Savannah stood and stretched.

"Wow," Linc said. "You, uh, baked, hon."

I covered a yawn. "We were craving cookies last night. The dough was so good."

"What are you doing?" Savannah asked, and I glanced back to see Linc pulling out his phone.

"Taking a picture to send to Velma so I can tell her why the wedding's off. I thought I was marrying a baker."

Savannah's mouth dropped. She walked over and smacked his arm, and he laughed and pulled her close, covering her lips with his.

Most of the time, lovey-dovey couples gave me a big no-thank-you reaction, but instead a traitorous thread of longing rose up. To have someone to joke around with like that. Someone who knew you that well and accepted you for who you were.

The stupid thing was I knew that I had a shot of having it for a little while. But I'd be me, and Jackson would be him, and we would constantly disagree, and eventually, everything would crumble apart. His family wouldn't want to accept me—the "broken" girl who wasn't good for him—in the place of some perky, composed debutant. Or I'd feel smothered and need to break free. We didn't want the same things, and drawing it out would only hurt more.

If I was smart, I'd end it now.

The torn-apart sensation that'd plagued me lately tugged at me, fear over getting in too deep and an equal amount of panic over it officially ending.

The plan will keep me safe. No matter what, I stick to the plan.

I could handle another week and a half of fun without falling in love.

I was almost sure.

Chapter Twenty-Six

"Wait," I said as Jackson pulled his truck and the attached U-Haul trailer up to the curb of a brick rancher that looked hauntingly familiar. "This can't be it."

"This is the address your mom gave me," he said, rechecking the map on his phone.

Surely the house just looked the same, like a lot of houses in this neighborhood did, or the GPS had steered us wrong… The sense of foreboding prickling at my skin increased, suggesting this was why Mom had been so annoyingly vague about her new guy. Why she'd given the address to Jackson instead of me.

He and I had spent the better part of the day loading my mom's belongings while she'd done a lot of pointing. Naturally, her fella couldn't help, because he was at work. (Meanwhile, Jackson and my work schedule was completely inconsequential to her, not that I could even tell her about it.)

"What is it?" Jackson asked. "Why do you look like you're going to punch someone?"

I realized my hands were fisted and worked to uncurl

them.

"I hope it's not me, because I didn't say a thing when you changed *my* radio to that super crappy song, and that took a lot of willpower." He reached over and took my hand, proving he wasn't even a little bit scared of being punched. "Hey, that was a joke. I mean, the song *was* crappy, but you can push my buttons anytime."

His voice sounded far away, and I gritted my teeth as I glanced out the window at the house. I'd only been here a few times, once to move her in, late one night for dinner, and once to move her out. Over the last few years, I'd gotten so used to using the navigation on my phone that I didn't bother memorizing addresses and hardly paid attention to street names, but I was ninety percent sure this was the same house. It was definitely the same neighborhood. "She can't be this delusional, can she?"

"Babe, what's going on?"

I turned to find Jackson's green eyes on me. All day he'd been a steady source of comfort, stepping in when I lost my patience with my mom, giving me reassuring squeezes, and hugging me when I needed it most. But this? This was some next level bullshit. "The guy that my mom was dating before she…before she took those pills and ended up in the hospital…"

Two creases formed between Jackson's eyebrows. Then dawning smoothed out his features. "I'm guessing this is his house?"

I nodded, my jaw starting to ache from being clenched so tightly. "When I told my mom I thought she was moving too fast, she informed me that she'd known the guy for a while, so it wasn't as fast as it seemed. She failed to mention he was one of her exes." I shook my head. "It's finally happened. She's run out of men to date, and now she's trying repeats. This is just like her, too. Choose the worst possible guy and then somehow be surprised when he's, in fact, the worst."

Mom's silver Camry pulled into the driveway, and I climbed out and slammed the truck door, my anger rising fast and hot. "Really, Mom? Stan?"

"Now, Ivy, I knew that you'd react like this, but he's different now, and so am I. You just need to give him a chance."

A chance? Jackson and I had spent an entire day that we could've spent working on a project I loved, and instead I'd enabled her to reconnect with the very guy who'd sent her into a depression spiral.

The guy who hadn't shown up, even though she'd called him from the hospital. Yeah, I'm sure she'd partially done it to gain his attention and make him feel guilty for dumping her, but the fact that he hadn't cared enough to stop by anyway solidified my stance against him. He'd used up all his chances.

Now I regretted not telling her she'd have to pay movers, because I wasn't foolish enough to think I could talk her out of this.

Still had to try, though. "I'm not unloading your stuff. We're going back to your apartment and putting it all back."

"I already turned the keys in to my landlord, and they have a new tenant moving in next week. It's done."

I paced the lawn, trying to keep from losing my temper. It wasn't easy when I remembered those nights I'd stayed with her after her stint in the hospital, and how she'd told me about her ups and downs with Stan, and how she'd thought he was really the one, and why didn't he love her?

"I can't do this anymore, Mom," I said, my voice trembling. "If you insist on moving in with him, I'm not going to come get you when it goes south, which we all know it will. Why don't we just save everyone a lot of time, effort, and pain, and skip to wherever you'll move next?"

Mom looked over my head to Jackson. "If you'll come on in, I'll show you where to put the furniture."

I pinched the bridge of my nose, that out-of-control feeling I hated overtaking my body.

"Give us a minute," Jackson said.

Mom sighed, like she didn't have time for us to dilly dally while we were giving up our whole day to help her move in with a guy who'd already crushed her once. She even pouted her lips a little and batted her eyes, but when she realized Jackson wasn't as easy to manipulate as most men—or her dutiful daughter, damn it—she headed into the house and gave us some space.

Jackson's hands came down on my shoulders, and I tensed, not wanting him to touch me. I was too scared I'd break, and I didn't want to cry over my mom moving in with some guy, the way I used to in private back when I was a kid. With each impending move, I'd beg for her to let me just live with Dixie, but she always said no, a daughter was supposed to stay with her mama, ignoring everything her daughter truly needed, like stability and security and emotional support.

"Ivy," Jackson said, so softly the breeze carried the word on past me.

I shook my head.

Using his grip on my shoulders, he turned me to face him. "What do you want me to do?"

My chest rose and fell with too big of breaths, but it was breathe or cry, so I inhaled and exhaled. Inhaled and exhaled. "Take him out."

Jackson moved one hand up to cup my cheek, a crooked, almost-smile tilting his mouth. "I think you're confusing me with your mobster boyfriend."

A sputtered laugh escaped my lips. "Where *is* that guy when I need him?"

"Probably serving time."

"Why are the best ones always gay or in jail?" I asked with a dramatic sigh.

"And here I thought the saying was gay or married."

"Same difference," I joked, and he laughed. Then he slowly pulled me close, like he was testing to see if I'd let him hug me, and I gave in.

What can I say? I needed to feel his strong arms around me for a moment before I gave in—yet again—to my mother's whims and demands, even knowing she was making a huge mistake.

"It sucks that she didn't give you a heads up," Jackson said, moving his lips to my forehead for a quick kiss. "It's a manipulative move, and it pisses me off, honestly. Do you want me to just dump all the stuff on the lawn? Make the jerk haul it in himself?"

I looked up at him. "You'd really do that?"

He let out a long exhale. "No. I can't help it. I hear my ma scolding me for not being the bigger person."

I couldn't help smiling at that. I'd already known he was too much of a gentleman, and no matter how tempted to dump the contents on the lawn and tell my mom and Stan to sort out their own mess, I would also feel too bad to follow through with it. And that was coming from a girl whose heart was 75 percent ice. Although with Jackson's arms around me, it felt more like 50 or maybe even 40 percent, and I worried I'd eventually regret not holding on to the numbing iciness.

"You're definitely bigger than Stan," I said.

"Good. That should help when I threaten him that he better take good care of your mom or else. I'm also planning on adding that if he so much as speaks a sharp word in your direction, he'll regret it."

I shook off the funk this discovery had caused and put on my game face. "Okay. Let's just get this over with."

"On it," Jackson said, and then we went to work moving

my mom into a house she'd moved out of not all that long ago.

The entire time I kept thinking my mom had to be delirious or in denial—or both—to think she could make things work with Stan the second time around, simply because she wanted to.

It wasn't until we were pulling away, muscles exhausted from hours of labor, Jackson's hand on my knee, that I realized I was doing the exact same thing.

• • •

Savannah came back from the full loop she'd done through the living room, kitchen, dining room, and back to the living room, where I was waiting—not super anxious or anything.

Okay, super anxious. "Well?"

"I can hardly believe it's the same house; it looks so amazing." Savannah ran a hand down the archway and then pulled a blue folder out of her bag. "If you and Jackson wouldn't kill each other, I'd say you should forget everything I put in this folder and go into business together."

I automatically scoffed at the idea, but for a brief moment, I paused and let myself wonder what it would be like. Finding old houses and flipping them into beautiful homes.

Arguing over fixtures, paint colors, flooring, and every other minute detail.

Kissing and christening homes across Atlanta.

Sounded like fun, especially that last part.

But it would never work. Jackson had his own successful business to run—a business I'd already taken too much time away from—and I had…well, my life to figure out. Plus, the girl standing across from me to worry about. "I did seriously consider strangling him earlier today. But there's still too much work for me to do alone."

"Ha-ha," Savannah said with a shake of her head, like

her brother and I were a lost cause.

Which we were, in more ways than one. I wasn't lying about wanting to strangle him, either. The carpet sample he brought in and proudly displayed wasn't even close to what I'd envisioned for the upstairs bedrooms. It was all wrong. Berber and scratchy (Jackson called that durable), a mix of brown, tan, cream, and—for some odd reason—green (the hides-the-dirt rational returned, and like with the tile, I still didn't understand where all the dirt was coming from. Was that *Charlie Brown* character Pig Pen coming to visit? Cause I'd hose that little dude down before he stepped foot in my house.)

P.S., I knew it wasn't my house.

Despite my reservations, I was about to hesitantly agree to "the steal" for the sake of my overburdened budget, but then Jackson huffed that he could get his guy to send over more similarly priced carpet samples, and I'd accidentally slipped and said, "Well, praise the Lord, because I can't even look at a foot of this stuff any longer," and I could tell that he wanted to strangle me. Mutual desire to kill all around.

With a side of wanting to rip each other's clothes off. Our partnership might not be easy, but it was far from boring.

Speak of the sexy devil, he walked in, carting a large box. "Hey, Savannah." His gaze moved to me, and he bowed his head. "Dictator Clarke."

I rolled my eyes so hard I hurt myself. "The joke's on you. I *like* that title."

"Oh boy," Savannah said with a sigh. Then she extended the blue folder I'd nearly forgotten about. "Here's a list of options. If I found open positions in the area that matched, I also put them in there, because I'm cool like that. And if you don't see anything that snags your interest, we'll widen the net. We'll find the perfect job for you, no matter how long it takes."

"Job searching, huh?" Jackson rested the box against the wall and moved over to us.

"I asked Savannah to work her magic and help me find the right career."

"Committing to a career? Sounds like a big step."

My chest tightened. It *was* a big step. Maybe working as a bartender at Azure wasn't some grand life-changing experience, but my life had security and stability now, and part of me wanted to stay in the safe place where I knew what to expect.

Savannah shoved her brother's shoulder. "Stop, or you'll freak her out."

Jackson shoved her right back, making her sway on her heels. "She can handle it. I'm the one who told her she should go for the career she wanted in the first place."

Savannah looked between us. "Really?"

"It's true," I said, and Jackson's expression turned smug. "But before you go thinking you're always right, you're also freaking me out. So point goes to Savannah."

Savannah grinned extra wide, like a kid who'd just earned a gold star. "Ooh, a point system. I approve."

"Kiss-ass," Jackson teased, and she stuck her tongue out at him.

That broke the tension, and I took a deep breath before opening the folder. There were tabs and charts, and Savannah had also placed hot-pink sticky notes with encouraging quotes on them. I smiled at her. "Have I mentioned how much I adore you?"

She sheepishly swiped a hand through the air. "Aw, stop. It was nothing." But before I could study the materials that were clearly *not* nothing, she launched into an explanation of what she'd found. "So Atlanta is one of the top markets for flipping houses, although a lot of the foreclosed houses have already been scooped up by big companies who can flip them crazy fast and get them right back on the market."

"Stupid big companies," Jackson muttered as he leaned closer and studied the information over my shoulder. "They can afford to undercut people like me, even though the work isn't as good."

I don't know why it amused me that he sounded so grouchy about the big companies, because I did feel for him, and I was sure that the work wasn't as good. I rubbed my hand up and down his arm, wanting to soothe him the way he always managed to soothe me when I needed it most. "Your work speaks for itself. I know I wouldn't hire any stupid big company."

The corner of his mouth turned up, that one little movement enough to send my heart rate zipping faster and faster.

Then Savannah's gaze homed in on my hand and quickly dropped it. *Gah, how did I manage to forget for a second that she was here?*

I held my breath, afraid she was going to comment on it, but then she turned the page and pointed at a list of company names. "You might not hire one, but you could work for one. That's your best shot at continuing to do this exact type of work."

"Work for the enemy?" Jackson scowled, and I wasn't sure what it said about me that I now considered his scowls a form of foreplay.

I did my best innocent shrug, and he looked to Savannah.

"Don't glare at me," she said. "Just the messenger here." Using her tab system, she flipped to the section labeled "admin." "These jobs don't so much involve actual renovating, but they're positions at companies who do them, which might eventually get you there. The truth is, unless you're a contractor, not a lot of people hire someone who…" I could tell she was searching for the right word, so I filled it in for her.

"Isn't qualified."

"I was going to say someone who doesn't have much experience and isn't licensed. They don't realize that when it comes to you, you figure out how to do whatever you set your mind to. That's why you'd work in their offices and show them. You probably wouldn't make as much as you do in tips at the bar at first, but you can juggle both for a while, and like I said, there's always room for advancement."

I let that sink in for a moment, and she turned to Jackson. "Actually, you'd qualify for a lot of the jobs I found. If you'd like, I could make a list of some of the companies who are looking to hire guys with your experience and qualifications. The pay is really impres—"

"I get plenty of jobs on my own, thank-you-very-much."

"Oh, I know. And heaven forbid you recognize that your sister might have some good advice, whether it be career or, you know, dating, at which I happen to be an *expert* at, in case you forgot."

"In the past day that you haven't mentioned it? No, I haven't."

"Okay," I said, diverting the conversation back to the subject at hand before I had to hear about the type of girl Savannah thought her brother should be with. Girls who had nothing in common with me, I was sure. She'd once told me that the way I viewed relationships was similar to the commitaphobe guys she warned her clients away from.

I couldn't disagree, but that didn't mean I wanted to hear about the kind of girl Jackson would settle down with someday. I might not want the picket fence and two-point-five kids lifestyle, but I couldn't help envying the woman who'd have that with Jackson.

"Okay, what?" Savannah asked, and I realized I'd gotten a bit lost in disliking a hypothetical girl.

"What are my other options?"

"Well, since you can sell just about anything, especially to men, there's always real estate. Not quite as hands on, but still a good way to make a living." Savannah flipped to the handy-dandy "Real estate agent" tab, where a bullet point list greeted me.

—COMPLETE A 75-HOUR SALESPERSON PRE-LICENSE COURSE

—TAKE THE GEORGIA SALESPERSON LICENSING EXAM

—APPLY FOR A LICENSE

—START SHOWING HOMES!

I pictured myself showing homes, helping people find the place they'd settle into with their families. It wasn't what I'd originally envisioned, but Savannah was right—I could make it work.

"The last section details interior design degrees. There are two schools down on Peachtree, the American Intercontinental University and the Art Institute of Atlanta, both with bachelor's degree programs, so it'd mean more school, but if it's what you want…"

"Four more years of schooling. Wow." I knew switching up my career wouldn't be easy, but I was antsy to do something *now*. Locking myself into a four-year program brought back that squeezing, suffocating sensation.

Savannah bumped her shoulder into mine. "Breathe, girl. How did you ever commit to a major in college?"

"I was determined to prove I could get a degree. It was sheer, stubborn determination." I dared a glance at Jackson, who had a contemplative crinkle in his forehead. "What?"

He shook himself out of wherever his thoughts had taken him. "Nothing. Just…thinking."

"Care to share?" I asked.

That familiar evil gleam lit his eyes. "Nah."

"You're infuriating."

"Thanks," he said.

"We're having a vocabulary issue again. You see, *infuriating* means aggravating, purposely provoking, or maddening."

"So basically what you are, then. Thanks for providing me with such a perfect example."

I grinned extra wide, baring my teeth. Yep, the foreplay had begun, and I telepathically told him to bring it. The desire darkening his gaze meant he understood and he was up for the challenge.

"You better be nice, or I won't show you what I picked up."

I glanced at the big box he'd brought in. "Wait. Is that the window?"

He nodded, and I fought the urge to clap and squee, which wasn't usually in my repertoire of reactions to…well, anything.

"You want to see it, Savannah?" I asked. "Jackson's putting in a reading nook, and it's going to be so cool once it's done."

"Sure," she said. "There are some other options in the folder that you can go over later, including a property acquisitions manager position that looked promising."

"I'll definitely check them out." I placed the file on top of the stack of scrapbooks I was still making my way through for a mix of reverie and torture reasons. "Thank you, Savannah. I super appreciate all the work you did, and I can't wait to figure out what I really want to be when I grow up."

Jackson told us it'd be better to open the window in the bedroom so we didn't break the thing before we got it in there, so Savannah and I followed him upstairs, then stood back for the big reveal.

The cardboard came off, and the three panes were

worthy of the dramatic buildup and more.

"I love it," I said.

"I'm going to do my best to get it installed by the end of the day so you can still sleep in the room, but you might have to move to another for a night."

Or I could go to my actual home, the condo I owned, where I had my more comfortable bed. But I didn't want to give up even a night in this house. I could make excuses about checking on the kittens and needing to be here early, which was so much easier if I could just roll out of bed, but I loved this house. Most of my memories here were good, from my childhood to the sexy times with Jackson.

Which I shouldn't be thinking about with his sister in the room. She was already watching our exchanges too carefully.

"You've been sleeping here?" she asked, and Jackson's eyes widened for a second before he seemed to realize she was talking to me.

"Helps me get an early start," I said. "Plus, with the kittens…"

"Oh, yeah! I need to see the kittens. How did I miss them?"

Just like that, the best friend was successfully distracted. I gestured her toward the door. "Black Widow moved them so they're partially hidden by the long curtains that'll probably be shredded soon."

She started down the stairs, and I called out that I'd be right there before turning back to the open doorway of my bedroom. "Thanks, Jackson. For the window. For… everything."

I almost added that I'd thank him properly tonight, because my thank you was dangerously close to crossing into mushy, not-sex-only territory. But I meant everything—his help with this place and for caring about a reading nook and whether I'd have to skip sleeping here for a night, and for his help moving my mom yesterday, and the list could go on and on.

I didn't want to cheapen it by turning it into an "only physically" joke.

But now it felt so heavy, out there in the air between us. Vulnerability and shakiness set in, and I was in serious danger of overanalyzing everything and blurting out that we needed to end things now, because I, Ivy Clarke, was starting to experience feelings.

Jackson crossed the room, glanced past me into the hallway—assumedly to check that his sister was out of view—then lowered his lips to mine. "You're welcome," he whispered, and a shiver ran down my spine. "For the record, this is the most I've ever enjoyed a job, and I'm not talking about the fun we have *after* work, although I'm enjoying that, too." His thumb slipped under my shirt and rubbed the skin on my hipbone. "I'm talking during the hours we're working, and yes, even arguing over things like flooring and paint. I'd take this over an easy, boring job—an easy, boring girl—any day of the week."

Starting-to-experience-feelings moved into officially-having-full-blown-feelings territory. It was a good thing his sister was downstairs, because if he and I were alone in the house, I might let myself be swept up in his words and forget that we had an expiration date, not just on the job, but on us.

As it was, I was thinking that forgetting for the tiniest while might not be the biggest deal.

Ah, denial, my old friend. Always there when I needed to figure out a way to screw myself over down the road.

Chapter Twenty-Seven

I'd displayed so much baggage over the past week that any sane man would've run. Unfortunately—or fortunately, I couldn't quite decide—Jackson didn't run.

And somehow, I'd let him talk me into going to Sunday dinner with his family. In case there was any question, it definitely broke one of my ways to avoid a broken heart.

Way #11: Never go into enemy territory. No getting close to his friends, no family events. They only serve as complications and more ties that'll screw you over when the end comes.

I told myself that this was different, because I already knew Jackson's family, but I also knew that my coming with him would raise questions. If Savannah brought me along to dinner, no one would think twice. Instead, I arrived in the same vehicle as Jackson, and while I'd eat slugs before admitting it, he'd held my hand the entire drive over and I'd loved every second.

"This is a bad idea," I said, withdrawing my hand and

looking toward the lit-up windows of the two-story peachy-colored brick house that was much nicer than any place I had ever lived. My stomach rose higher and higher until it was fighting it out with my lungs for space.

"They'll never buy us as just friends." I turned to Jackson to see if any of my concerns were sinking in, but he was miles away from worried, his heated gaze too busy traveling over my body. "Especially not with you giving me that look like you've seen me naked in the past hour."

"I *have* seen you naked in the past hour, and if I close my eyes…" Jackson shut them. "Naked Ivy."

I smacked his arm, fighting back the laugh that wanted to push through the panic and burst free. "Stop. You're going to give us away."

"So what? Would it really be so bad if they knew?"

A tight band formed around my chest. "Knew what? That we're fooling around? Um, don't you remember how we agreed that Savannah would get ideas, and your mom and Aunt Velma would freak and stage an intervention? They might tolerate me as Savannah's friend, but they'd never think I was good enough for you."

"That's not true."

"It's true, and you know it. And because of our temporary status, it doesn't really matter. I don't want them to hate me afterward. We're going to eventually cross paths at these kinds of shindigs and, oh, Savannah and Linc's wedding."

Jackson's hand inched toward my bare legs. "And I'm supposed to pretend that I don't want to whisk you into a bedroom and have my wicked way with you when we're at those events together?"

"Yes."

"You're asking for the impossible."

"You're being impossible," I said. "Which makes me repeat my original point. This is a bad idea."

"Well, as you see from the pulled back curtains and figures at the window, we've been spotted, so there's no going back now."

"Okay. But just…do a better job putting out the friends-only vibe."

Jackson saluted me, and I figured it was as close to an agreement as I'd get, so I pushed out of his truck and smoothed down my dress. What the hell was I thinking? I blamed being under-caffeinated, overly tired, and still feeling vulnerable from this morning's surprise stop in to check on my mom. Stan hadn't come home during the hours we'd spent unloading her stuff on Thursday, and when I told Jackson I couldn't stop worrying about her, he'd dropped what he was doing at the house and said, "Let's go check on her, then."

Stan didn't seem very excited to see us, but Mom went on and on about how happy she was as she fussed over him. Did he need a refill on his drink? What would he like for dinner? She was thinking of changing out the curtains but only if it was okay with him, etcetera, etcetera. She was trying so hard, and as far as I could tell, Stan was unmoved. He sure as hell didn't thank her or shower her with any kind of affection.

As we'd said our good-byes, Jackson pulled Stan aside and made good on his promise to talk to him about how my mother deserved to be treated. Then he patted Stan on the back extra hard and took me home.

Home to the Victorian, anyway. And after he'd used his body to make me forget my worries for a while—ah, yes, the other thing to blame for my congenial mood—he told me I could use a break and a good meal. I agreed, my mind conjuring an evening of takeout in bed with him.

One minor lapse in judgment later, I found myself here in my Sunday best, about to have dinner with the whole extended Gamble clan.

Jackson put his hand on the small of my back, and I

glanced at him, eyebrows raised.

He looked right back at me, his hand remaining firmly in place. We were *so* going to get busted. I hoped my best friend didn't hate me afterward.

The door swung open, and we were pulled into the melee of several families, multiple conversations going on at once, and a whole lot of hugging.

Jackson hugged his mom and then returned his hand to my back. "Ivy's had a long week, so I told her she should come relax and enjoy some good food."

Savannah looked from him to me but didn't say anything. I wasn't sure if that was a good thing or a bad thing. Linc gave me a nod that had an edge of "thanks for taking the heat off me" to it.

"Of course," Lucinda said, throwing her arms around me and giving me a tight squeeze. "You know you're welcome anytime." She asked one of the kids to set a place for me, adding, "Put her next to Savannah."

Jackson opened his mouth, no doubt to request I sit by him instead, but he took in my wide-eyed, don't-say-anything expression and let it drop.

His mom patted his cheek. "Can you be a dear and go into the garage and get an extra chair?"

"Sure thing, Ma."

A swirl of affection wound its way through me. I loved that he was this big tough guy who cared for his family so fiercely, even during the times they were also driving him crazy by constantly calling and meddling in his life. Through my years of friendship with Savannah, I'd occasionally experienced twinges of jealousy over her family, but I'd always told myself I didn't need the complications of people in my business, demanding my time and giving unsolicited opinions.

Case in point: the austere look Velma was giving the hem of my dress, her pursed lips making it clear she thought it was too short, even though it was my longest one.

It was the same way the grandmother of one of my step-siblings looked at me before saying, "Lawd, people will be able to see Christmas when you sit down." She'd been the one to insist Mom and I attend church with them, but she'd changed her mind mighty quick once she saw what we planned on wearing. Evidently, she'd decided that she'd rather people gossip about our lack of religion than our lack of suitable church-going outfits.

I waited for Velma to go with the usual and tell me how great love was and how I should get on finding it because I was missing out. Unless she'd realized that I might be trying to get my love on Jackson and wanted to steer me away. Next thing I knew, she'd probably start spouting the merits of being single and how it was the right choice for me.

Which I knew.

The doorbell rang. "Oh, I bet that's the Porters," Velma said. She walked over and swung open the door.

The name and why it sounded familiar clicked about one millisecond before the Porters walked in, Caroline included. Heavy awkwardness crept through the room. Although I was probably the only one who felt it, considering everyone else thought Jackson and I were just friends.

Which we were.

But I still had one more week with him, so homegirl needed to back off.

Savannah put her hand on my shoulder. "Are you okay?"

I quickly rearranged my features to hide my annoyance. "Of course. Sorry, I was just thinking about everything I needed to do this next week."

"Mm-hm. I'm starting to wonder about all the things you're *doing*."

Shit. Lucinda instructed everyone to "come take your seat for dinner" before I could figure out how to respond—I was going to have to come clean, and soon. Bobbing and weaving around the truth was one thing, but I couldn't lie right to Savannah's face. I just had to hope that she'd understand, even if she was also pissed. *I have a feeling the lecture she's going to give me is gonna make her workshop sessions seem short. At least Jackson will have to suffer through one, too.*

On the way over to the table, I saw eight-year-old Evan, one of my favorite of Savannah and Jackson's cousins. Probably because he was the kid who was forever in trouble for things like pulling out a sling shot or arriving for the family photo covered with a thick layer of mud that he'd somehow found in the five minutes the adults took their eyes off him. *Oh, maybe kids like him are why people are so obsessed with flooring that also hides dirt.*

Evan was tugging at his tie, grunting like he was on the verge of suffocating.

I cast a quick glance around and squatted down—carefully, so no one had to endure even more of my scandalous bare thighs. "Want me to show you a trick?"

Proving he deserved to be my favorite, he leaned in and asked, "Is it how to hide your vegetables? Because I sneak mine into my napkin, then when I lay it on my lap like a *proper gentleman*"—the mimicked tone made me suspect Velma was the one responsible for that nugget—"I just shake it out and kick them away, so it looks like my baby sister spilled them off her tray." He leaned closer. "Don't worry. She's too young to get in trouble for not eating vegetables. I'm not sure what I'm going to do when she gets older."

I chuckled. "That's when you make sure there's a dog around." I loosened the knot in his tie to give the fabric more slack, then undid the top button that was right up against his neck. "There. Still looks buttoned, but it should give you a little more air. Best I can do for now."

He sucked in a big breath, filling his lungs. "Yeah. I can

make it work. Thanks."

I straightened and found Jackson's eyes on me. He gave me a slow, secretive smile, and a swarm of butterflies took flight in my gut and spread the fluttering all the way up to my heart. Lately I was having so many feelings that my feelings were starting to come right on top of each other, and my body didn't know how to handle them.

Abort, abort, abort.

I glanced at the door. The heels and dress would slow me down, but I could make it in a few short seconds and then be out of the house and running down the street like a paranoid lunatic. Then the nosy neighbors would call the cops and *voila!* A ride home.

"Ivy," Lucinda said, nice and loud, leading me to believe it wasn't the first time she'd called my name. "You're right here, dear." She patted the back of the chair next to Savannah and, with so many people looking my way, I had no choice but to accept my fate. "Jackson, come on. You're in your usual place across from your sister."

This was what I got for breaking my rule about going into enemy territory.

We took our seats, and my gaze met Jackson's across the table. I tried not to let it show that I didn't exactly love that Caroline was seated to his right, enough chairs squeezed in that their arms occasionally brushed.

He raised a challenging eyebrow, as if to say, *Are you going to do something about it?*

I raised one right back that said...*I don't know what to do because I'm way out of my league here, so I'm just mimicking you and hoping for inspiration.* Anyway, that's what it meant to me, but I highly doubted he got all that.

Lucinda asked Ray to say Grace, and everyone bowed their head, so I did the same, though the sensation of not belonging here returned full-force. But as everyone started passing around the food, Evan caught my eye and motioned to his napkin like, *Hey, don't forget the trick I told you about,* and part of me wished I did.

Maybe even more than part.

I should've escaped while I had the chance. Even back in the day when I'd semi-optimistically tried to bond with stepdads or stepsiblings or new schoolmates, I'd never experienced the desire to fit in this strongly. Now I suddenly had this startling yearning to be a different person so I could have a shot at a real long-term relationship. I rubbed my neck, fighting off waves of panic.

As dinner went on, Velma kept directing the attention to Caroline, and while I wanted to hate her on principal, she was sweet and polite and all the things that would work for the life Jackson wanted some day. He'd claimed that he wouldn't simply fall for her if I was out of the way, but I couldn't help wondering if that were true.

She finished telling everyone what was going on with the charity that she helped run. I read between the lines and heard the things she was too humble to say, like the fact that she had enough money that she didn't have to work, but she chose to, to help those less fortunate than herself.

Like I could compete with that.

"What do you do, Ivy?" Caroline asked, right as I'd taken a huge bite of my roll—the plan was to carb load and see if it helped rid me of all these mushy feelings that I was inept at dealing with.

I shoved the food in my mouth over to one cheek. "I'm a bartender." I reached for my drink, hoping it'd help wash down the roll and serve as a signal that I didn't want to talk anymore.

"She's more than that," Jackson said.

Nearly spraying my drink right back out, I looked at him and worked on swallowing.

"You should see what she's doing to this old Victorian house. I'm helping her flip it, and she's got a real eye for design. She's almost making me a believer in apple green as a suitable wall color."

"Almost?" I automatically said. "You love that bathroom, admit it. I find you in there all the time."

A few snickers went around the table. Because while Caroline talked about her charity work, I was the classy broad who talked about him being in the bathroom a lot. *Nice one, Ivy.*

"Spending hours laying tile can hardly be attributed to the green walls," Jackson said, "although I think that's why I started to enjoy them—at least they didn't need to be tiled."

"You keep telling yourself that." I fake-coughed. "In denial."

"I've been thinking of updating my place," Caroline said, placing her hand on Jackson's arm. "Maybe you can take a look sometime? See what you think?"

I gritted my teeth. He'd pointed out that I had an eye for design, but she sure wasn't putting her hand on *my* arm and asking *me* for help.

"Sure, I can take a look," he said.

As dinner wound down, Caroline talked about the changes she wanted in her house, which of course was in this same neighborhood, right next to her perfect parents. Her and Jackson's kids would play out in the backyard—or even the front, with its perfect picket fence—and be able to walk to either grandparents' house. The kids would be adorable, too. Amazing hair, amazing family, all around amazingness.

She was perfect for him, and I was a bartender with a cute design hobby that would never be a full-on career, whose skirt was a good three to four inches above the demure range. I was the girl who called with mice and spider problems because despite trying to be strong and independent, I was a hot mess and would always be.

The girl who called him after her mom took sleeping pills, then used him to make her forget that fact for a while. Then, even though I knew I was wrong for him, I jumped right into bed with him again, because he was sexy and amazing, and he had this ability to make me forget the rest of the world existed for a while.

Ugh, why are my thoughts insisting on rubbing how wrong I am for Jackson in my face?

It was selfish to hang on, though. Foolish to look around and think I could ever fit into a family who ate on good china.

Everyone began to push away, and when there was an attempt to help gather the dishes, Lucinda insisted everyone leave them be and go into the sitting room for after-dinner cocktails.

I pushed away, too, preparing myself for what I needed to do.

I might've broken rule after rule with him, but it was time I stopped this impending heartbreak in its tracks. Time to pull out all the stops and employ the rule I only used in the direst of circumstances, to scare off guys who were dangerous in the way that they could break down my walls and do permanent damage.

Way # 12: Act bat-shit crazy.

Employing in three…
Two…
One.

Chapter Twenty-Eight

"So being just a bartender isn't enough?" I asked Jackson as he moved over to me with a glass of wine in each hand.

He gave me one of the glasses, his eyebrows ticking together. "Of course it is. I'm just saying there's a lot more to you."

"Because there definitely would need to be for me to fit in here."

"You fit in just fine, Ivy."

"Not as well as Caroline over there."

"I think you were fitting in pretty well when you were teaching Evan how to loosen his tie and whatever other nefarious plans you two were hatching over there." Jackson leaned closer and tugged on the knot of his tie. "Care to hook a brother up?"

Warmth tried to rise up, but I shoved it away. "I'm wearing a freaking dress—one that Velma disapproves of, by the way—and heels, so you have to deal with your tie like an adult."

His lips brushed the shell of my ear. "I'll show you all the adult things I can do with it later."

Heat pooled low in my stomach. This wasn't going the way it was supposed to. I needed to up the crazy. Needing some space and time to fortify my plan, I tipped back the entire glass of wine, then extended the fancy etched crystal toward Jackson.

"Another?" he asked.

"Now you're keeping track of my drinks? What, a girl can't enjoy two glasses of wine?"

The furrowed eyebrows reappeared. "What the hell is going on with you?"

"Nothing." I crossed my arms. "If you're going to cut me off, I'll just go get another drink myself."

Jackson put his hand on my arm, stopping me from heading over to where the wine bottle sat atop a fancy bar cart. "I'll get it."

While he went for a refill, I wondered how far I needed to take things. I wished we were alone, but not being alone was what brought this on in the first place. Acting crazy in front of his family would only help push him farther away, even if my stomach dropped at the thought.

Savannah appeared next to me. "So…"

Don't worry. I'm fixing it. Your brother and I won't be anything soon.

"Savannah, dear," Lucinda called. "We were just talking about the centerpieces for your wedding, and Augusta and Velma had an idea. Can you come over here, so we can figure out if it'll work with the flowers you already picked out?"

Savannah glanced from the group of women to me. "To be continued. You and I need to talk."

"How ominous," I said, unable to help myself.

"Nothing ominous," she assured me before walking over to the group of women. That's what she thought. As soon as she found out what I'd been up to this past month, she was going to be upset and hurt, and I could handle her angry lecture, but the hurt would slice me right open. Clearly, I'd been out of my mind when I'd entered the no-strings arrangement with Jackson. I knew it'd bite me on the ass eventually; I just had no idea that I'd get so wrapped up in him while I was making a huge mess of my life.

Caroline had stopped Jackson and was flashing a pearly-white smile that matched the pearls around her neck. He broke free and returned, handing me a glass that was refilled to the brim.

"Dude, this is the biggest glass of wine I've ever seen." I sipped it, worried the red liquid would slosh onto the carpet and give the Gambles another memento of the night I messed up their plans to set up their golden son with the perfect woman.

"And I don't give a damn if you drink the whole thing," Jackson said. "Want a shot of thirty-year-old scotch to wash it down? Go for it. I don't care if you get so drunk that I have to carry you out of this house at the end of the night."

Dang it. He was resisting the crazy better than I thought he would. But after seeing my mom unintentionally sabotage most of her relationships, I had an arsenal of crazy to pull from. *Time to bring out the green-eyed monster.*

"Oh, I bet you *want* me to get drunk enough to pass out so that you can continue flirting with Caroline. Don't think I didn't see you talking to her. Bet you're wishing that you'd left me home to mope about my mom's move now."

"Okay, that's it." Jackson took the drink out of my hand and set his aside as well. Then he turned to fully face me, closing us off from possible conversation with anyone else in the room. "I have no idea what's happening. What is going on with you?"

"What needs to happen before we both end up hurt."

He ran a hand through his hair, utter exasperation in his

features. "Do you want me to take you home? I'll make an excuse and—"

"I'm breaking off our arrangement, okay?" It burst out of me, and now my breaths were coming too fast, and it took more effort than it should to continue on and do what I should've done before reaching Way Number Twelve, which was more a failsafe than anything else. "It's gone on too long, and I'm breaking it off now. You're free to go be with Caroline."

The line of Jackson's jaw hardened. "No."

"No? You don't get to decide if I'm done with our no-strings fling."

He crowded my space, making me take a step backward, and my body met the wall. "I do, and I'm saying no. No to ending it, no to her. Just no."

Swallowing became impossible. It probably didn't speak well to my mental state that as my irritation flared, so did my desire. I wanted to throw my arms around him and kiss him with reckless abandon, our audience be damned.

"Hey, everyone," Jackson said, raising his voice. Alarm pinged through me, tightening every one of my organs. He took my free hand in his and spun out to face the room, and boy did we have everyone's attention.

I tried to pull my hand free, but he kept his iron grip. I lowered my voice to a whisper. "Whatever you're thinking of doing—"

"Ivy and I are dating. You all wanted me to find someone I'm crazy about, and crazy is definitely the word I'd use to describe how I feel when I'm with her."

Shock went through the room in a wave, bleeding from one face to the next as eyebrows raised and jaws dropped.

He did not. Just. Do. That.

There was no reason to act anymore—I was about to go bat-shit crazy for real.

"We're not dating," I quickly said.

"We are," Jackson loudly contradicted. "Have been for a few weeks now."

Everyone else seemed frozen in place, like they didn't know how to react, or perhaps they hoped if they didn't move, it'd all be a bad dream. I'd employ the same method if I thought it'd work. I looked to Savannah, needing to see her face.

She was the only one who'd moved, taking a few steps in our direction. There was surprise, but there was also a hint of smug *I-knew-it* in there as well.

"He's...having a mental breakdown," I said in her direction, even though I was pretty sure I was the one having a mental breakdown. "He knows I don't date or do relationships—I made it very clear."

"Anyway," Jackson went on, like I hadn't said anything. "I'm officially off the market and have no desire to get back on it, because as you can see, I already have a girlfriend who's smart and beautiful and the best damn bartender in the world, although she also gives me a run for my money with renovations. You should see her wield a paint roller."

"Jackson," Lucinda said in a reprimanding tone, and I braced myself for harsh words about why I wasn't right for him. *"Language."*

Yes. One little swear word was clearly the problem in this situation.

Jackson lifted my hand and kissed the back of it. "Sorry, Ma. The best *dang* bartender." He pulled me closer and then moved his lips next to my ear and whispered, "I mean it, Ivy. You're smart and beautiful, and I know you like to pretend that you don't care about anything, but I see you, every single part of you, and I'm still crazy about you. Nothing you do is going to change that."

Time stopped; the earth spun off its axis. The ice around

my heart thawed all at once, even as I tried to keep the protective shell in place.

"Well, I'm glad that you're finally settling down," Lucinda said, then she aimed her smiling face my way. "And, Ivy, you're welcome here anytime, hon. I hope you know that."

Settling down? Where'd all the air go? On the bright side, his mom seemed okay with the announcement, even though I wasn't sure I was. Knowing that allowed me a tiny sip of oxygen.

"To Jackson and Ivy," Ray said, raising his glass, and everyone followed, although I noticed the Porters looked confused and a tad on the pissed-off side.

It shouldn't make me happy, but I'd be lying if I didn't experience a little smugness of my own over it.

Everyone echoed the declaration and drank, and there was no way I could tell them they had it all wrong now.

Well. My attempt to take a wrecking ball to this thing just went down in flames.

And I wasn't even sure how to go about putting the raging WTF fire out.

I figured the most important place to start was with my best friend. I pulled Savannah off to the side when everyone else went to get dessert. "How mad are you?"

"I'm not mad."

"You've got to be kind of mad, especially after we had the talk at the bar about me not getting in the way. Just let me have it. I deserve it."

She glanced around, assumedly to check that we were alone, and I steeled myself for the worst. "I put together that he was the guy you were sleeping with—the one you actually liked—the instant you two walked in together." She shook her head. "I can't believe I didn't realize it earlier. I'm chalking it up to being distracted with trying to balance doing two workshop sessions a week and planning the wedding."

"But that's just the thing," I said. "We're sleeping together, and I do like him, but when he said we were dating, that's quite an exaggeration. We've only been on one date."

"You went on an actual date?" Her voice pitched with a mix of disbelief and excitement at the end, and I could've done without the grin the news caused, because she wasn't getting this at all.

I blew out a breath. "Only because he said he wouldn't have sex with me again until after we did."

Her grin widened. "Go Jackson. Who would've thought?"

"No. No 'go Jackson.' This is just a temporary thing that's going to end when we finish the house, and I don't know what he's thinking trying to cross into more." I'd already been feeling the pressure not to accidentally hurt him, and now I had to worry about his family, and the pressure was increasing by the second. "You need to tell him about my red flags. Don't you have experience in relationship interventions? I need help here."

"People have to want to change when they come to me, and I saw the look on my brother's face. He doesn't want to change. He wants you."

"No, he just *thinks* he does, because yes, we've had a great few weeks." Amazing more like it, but if I told Savannah that, it'd only give her unrealistic expectations. Since my words didn't seem to be making an impact, I decided to remind her of hers. "But like you pointed out, I'm a self-destructive mess, and like I keep saying, I don't do long term, so this is never going to work, and he's got to know that. He probably only announced it like that to…I don't know. Take off some of the pressure of having your mom and Velma trying to set him up with Caroline, who's lovely, and I told him he should go for her. That's obviously who he should be dating."

Savannah shook her head. "I could tell that something was holding him back that night at Dad's retirement dinner, and now I know it was because he has feelings for you. And you're not a self-destructive mess. You're just…relationship adverse."

"Understatement of the year, Savannah."

My best friend reached out and squeezed my hand. "Look, I always knew you and Jackson had some crazy strong chemistry, and honestly, at one point I worried you'd hook up and it would be a disaster. But after seeing the way you two interacted tonight, I'm fine with it."

"But it *is* going to be a disaster."

"It's better to have a life of 'oh wells' than 'what ifs,'" Savannah said, whipping one of her inspirational quotes out of her endless supply.

Easy for her to say. Yes, she'd had ups and downs like anyone, in life and in love, but the "oh wells" in my life were far closer to "oh holy shit, that was an epic fail, and now I hurt everywhere." Through the years, I'd learned again and again—*and again*—that most relationships ended. People changed or they left, or you changed and left, and if I kept everyone at a distance, it didn't suck as bad when the endings came. It was my go-to coping and defense mechanism, and it'd kept me safe and secure for years.

Lucinda poked her head into the room. "Don't you girls want cake?"

Um, hell yeah, I wanted cake. More than that, I needed something to take the edge off the fact that everyone around me was in denial. Usually that was *my* thing, and how dare they all take it from me and leave me to try to be the sensible one?

If I was sensible, I wouldn't be wearing this dress and five-inch heels to have dinner with my boyfriend's family.

Which, for the record, at the beginning of the evening, I didn't have a boyfriend.

I walked into the dining room, where the mess from dinner had been replaced with perfect slices of chocolate cake on little gilded plates. My not-boyfriend gave me a huge grin and patted his lap, like I was seriously going to pop a squat there.

I shot him an I'm-going-to-murder-you-later look, and his return expression said he was looking forward to it. He could sit there all smug now, but tonight, I was going to take great pleasure in making him pay for pushing me into relationship territory without so much as a life preserver to cling to.

"Here, take my seat," Velma's husband Dick said, and everyone scooted down one, leaving me a chair next to Jackson.

Caroline's family had tried to escape after the big relationship announcement but somehow had been convinced to stay for dessert—the Gambles obviously had some wicked powers of persuasion skills—so Caroline was seated on his other side.

But I noticed she didn't put her hand on his arm or even talk directly to him, and as I gave in to the urge to touch him and curled my hand around his thigh, the self-satisfied voice in my head said, *That's right. He's* my *man.*

Try as I might, sensible and me never did get on for very long.

Jackson draped his arm over my shoulders and leaned in for a kiss, and I met him in the middle. It was chaste as far as most of our kisses went, and he tasted of chocolate and cockiness, but even as angry as I still was at him for his stunt, affection over his display sang through my veins.

Okay, maybe he makes a pretty good life preserver.

When I pulled back, I noticed several smiles aimed our way, along with *aww, ain't that sweet* looks, and pressure, even stronger than before, built in my chest.

I thought not having their acceptance would be the worst thing that could happen, but I was wrong. Having it was. Because I knew that I'd screw things up and then they'd hate me, and now there was so much more at risk than just my heart.

Chapter Twenty-Nine

"What were you thinking?" I asked as soon as we were in Jackson's truck, away from prying eyes. Or at least with an extra filter, considering I wouldn't be surprised if they were watching us through the window.

"I was thinking that you were acting crazy and trying to push me away and that I was sick of backing down in the name of not scaring you off. I was also sick of pretending I didn't want to wrap you in my arms and kiss you. I mean, have you seen the dress you're wearing?" He tugged me across the bench seat until I was right next to him and skirted the hem of my dress with his fingertips.

Suddenly I was glad that it was three to four inches too short for demure.

Except, wait, I was still mad at him. Why did he make it so damn hard to remember that?

I put my hand over his before I got lost in the drag of his fingertips and gave in to the awakening desire thrumming through me. "Now they're going to be disappointed when it ends, and I'll never be able to hang out with your family again."

"Guess that means you'll just have to stick it out with me," he said, infuriatingly unfazed as ever.

"Jackson, be serious."

He slipped his hand behind my neck, guided my face to his, and gave me a hard, demanding kiss. "Babe, I've never been more serious."

I groaned. "You're impossible."

"Right back at you."

I hated to bring up old hurts, but he was clearly forgetting them, so evidently, I had to go against my nature and be the responsible one. "Don't you remember how hard we crashed last time, and that was after only a week."

He tensed, making it clear he did.

"You're right," I said, forcing the words past my too-tight throat. "I scare easily, and when I felt myself growing attached to you, I freaked the hell out. I hope you know that I didn't mean what I said that night at the club. I pushed too hard. I wish I hadn't, and I regret that I ever pretended that week was anything less than amazing—that *you* were anything less than amazing. But you said it yourself, you knew how I was, and you still do, so…"

He adamantly shook his head. "That's bullshit, Ivy, and I'm calling you on it. I was wrong to say that back then, and I won't let you believe it now. I was hurt and I lashed out, and I should've told you long before that I was sorry about that night." He ran his thumb over my jaw in the way that I loved as his intense gaze met mine. "That day we put up the crown molding and talked about the guys your mom had dated, the same day we joked about time traveling? I told you that past me needed to learn more patience and understanding, and I meant it. That was my way of telling you that I was sorry, and I was working on it."

"That was an apology? Just a vague statement I was

supposed to magically understand?"

He slanted me a look.

"Right, right. I'm a pot calling the kettle black. Guess that means I'm perfect for boiling this down. Basically, we're both sorry that we hurt each other in the past."

He nodded.

"And we're gonna try really hard not to do it in the future?"

His mouth curved into a half smile. "You said *future*."

"And apparently you want yours to only last another minute." I gave his shoulder a shove, and his smile drifted into outright cocky territory.

"Glad all that's finally settled." He reached for the gear shifter and put it in reverse, maneuvering the shaft between my thighs. After a suggestive look, he backed up the truck and then spun around. "Now, your place or mine?"

Why did the first thought to enter my head have to be *ours?*

I was so irrevocably screwed.

• • •

I wandered the aisles of the antique store, my gaze skipping over knickknacks, lamps, clocks, and china-filled cabinets. Usually I made these trips on a mission to find something in particular, but occasionally a piece spoke to me and said, "Pick me. I'll be awesome with the right amount of work and paint."

With all the painting I'd been doing, I'd taken a break from my side hobby of stripping and refinishing furniture, picking up a paintbrush yet again the *last* thing on my mind. But this morning, my thoughts were too busy, all mixed up with Jackson and his family and my mom and who she was, and who I was, and I'd needed to get out of the house.

The house where Jackson had stayed the night. He'd pulled me into his arms after we'd had sex and didn't let go. It was like he'd decided we were together and there was no talking him out of it. While the guy did amazing contractor work, every screw in the right place, clearly the same wasn't going on in his brain. There were loose screws up there for sure, leading him to ridiculously optimistic conclusions about us.

Man, I wanted to be an optimist.

I passed a side table that would be perfect for the entryway of the Victorian. It was silly to spend money on it since the house would be listed within a week or so, but I supposed a nice staging table might help it sell faster, and I could always Craigslist it later.

I bartered with the lady in the store, convincing her to knock off twenty percent, and then spent ten minutes trying to maneuver the thing into the backseat of my car.

I climbed in the driver's seat and banged my elbow into the top of the table. "Really?" I rubbed at the tingly, not-funny-at-all spot. "I save you from a boring life crammed in that stuffy room, and this is how you repay me?"

Hey, might as well embrace the bat-shit crazy, since that's apparently what my "boyfriend" was into. I drove the five blocks to the Daily Grind. The fact that the place was Savannah's second office made me hesitate. She'd been amazing last night—more amazing than I deserved, for sure—but she'd only remind me of the complications with Jackson, and I wasn't sure my brain could handle any more anxiety-inducing thoughts.

Then I remembered no one else's coffee was as good, and in order to survive today, I needed better than subpar coffee. And about a case of Cherry Coke, but I already had that at home.

Damn it, not home. *The Victorian house that is soon to*

be sold to someone else, so get that in your head already.

I grabbed the folder my best friend had made for me, thinking I'd peruse it while I sat and drank my coffee. Then I'd be an adult and go face the sexy guy who would probably be up and hammering away at something by the time I got back, making it impossible to remember why I shouldn't try a full-blown relationship.

After all, what would it hurt?

Besides me. And him. And his whole family.

My lungs deflated, and I pushed inside the Daily Grind. Savannah wasn't seated among the tables and chairs, and while I'd worried about running into her, now I found myself wishing she was seated in one of the wingback chairs so I could plop down across from her and spill my guts.

Nothing screamed desperation like actually *wanting* to talk about my emotions rather than going back to the house where I'd have to experience them.

I paid for two coffees but asked the barista to wait to make the second, then settled into a table near the window and opened the folder. I'd meant to look at it several times the past few days, but life kept getting in the way.

Now it was time to buckle down, make a plan, and figure out what direction to take my career. I flipped past the real estate agent information to the tabbed "sales section" at the very back. *This must've been the promising job Savannah mentioned.*

Basically, the company wanted someone who could sell, but they also wanted him or her to acquire properties so they could flip them for a profit. The listing said sales experience was good, but they were willing to train and that the better the person did, the more she'd get paid.

I liked that it was something I could control, and I was a born saleswoman. Or at least I could talk my way into being one, where I'd work to prove I deserved a shot. I knew enough to tell whether buildings had potential, and I could always use the phone-a-friend option and call Jackson if I needed a second opinion.

Except that would be relying on him, and I'm already doing way too much of that.

But whatever, this is a good lead. I input the number into the notes section of my phone, deciding I'd call this afternoon.

"Hey," a familiar voice said, followed by the scrape of a chair against the floor. Then my best friend sat across from me. "How you holding up after last night?"

"I'm fine."

"And by *fine* do you mean freaking out and hiding in a coffee shop?" Savannah shifted forward in her seat. "No judgment, because I've done that before. Except since Linc knew this was my usual haunt, I had to hide out in a crappy café with super gross coffee, and even my newspaper told me I was being a wimp by hiding from him."

"Your newspaper told you?" I thought she was the saner of us, regardless of her silly notion of true love and Mr. Right.

"It fell on the floor, right open to the crossword section, taunting me with the puzzles that Linc and I had started to do together. Trust me, I heard what it was telling me loud and clear."

I snickered. "Well, the man glitter on Jackson talks to me sometimes."

"Man glitt—" A light went on in Savannah's head. "Sawdust?"

"Yeah." I bit my lip. "It says things like, 'Don't you wanna be nailed by the guy who works with his hands all day?'"

"Chatty sawdust." Savannah casually swiped my coffee cup and took a sip. "Notice how cool I'm being with your talk of my brother 'nailing you,' even though I'm keeping a tight lid on any imagery?"

"Noted."

The barista called her name, and she hopped up to get *her* coffee. While she was fixing it up, I peeked at her notes.

Step Two: *Find hope. Believe there is a guy out there who can provide you with a relationship that restores faith in love.*

"Want me to print you a copy?"

I pushed them away from me. "Hard pass."

Savannah laughed. "My little Ivy, so grown up and officially dating. It seems like only yesterday that she was wrinkling her nose over the word *commitment*."

I tossed one of the sugar packets I hadn't used at her head, which only made her dodge and laugh harder. "Speaking of your inspiring notes, I was just looking at this acquisitions manager position. I'm totally going to give them a call."

"I think you'd be great at that. It's at least worth looking into."

I placed my hand over the folder. "Thanks again for putting all this information together." I glanced at the barista and signaled for her to make the cup of coffee I'd take to Jackson, then I returned my attention to Savannah. "I guess I better go get to work. Jackson and I only have one more week to finish up everything, and I'm not sure how we're going to do it."

"I have a handful of client appointments lined up, but I could probably swing a few afternoons if you need me. I'll rope Linc into helping, too. I'll call you later, and we can figure it out."

"Sounds good." I pushed out my chair and leaned over the table to hug my best friend. I'd been so worried she'd be mad after Jackson made that big announcement at her parents' house—and I had a feeling she still would be if I ended up hurting her brother, unintentional or not—but it was nice that things were normal between us.

"What was that for?" Savannah asked when I pulled away.

"Because you're you."

"Wouldn't be me without you," she said, and apparently, I was turning into a big old softie, because that made me want to hug her all over again.

Instead, I grabbed the to-go coffee and went to spend the day with the guy I'd also spent the night with. Because I was trying out a new, semi-optimistic version of me, one who kept the things I liked about myself but also embraced new things that might make me even better.

Chapter Thirty

I followed the noise and found Jackson in the upstairs bathroom, installing the tile in the rain shower.

He straightened when he saw me, and a slow smile curved his lips. Instead of trying to smother the butterflies stirring in my gut, I let them free.

"I brought you coffee."

"After you finished having a freak out over the fact that I'd told my family we were dating *and* stayed the night?"

I schooled my features. "I have no idea what you're talking about. If you don't want my caffeinated offering, I'll just drink it myself." I took a sip and then stuck out my tongue. "Gah, you seriously must have a black soul to drink it like this."

"You're just scared that it'll thaw your icy heart, but the fact that you brought me coffee means it's already too late, so you should just go with it." Jackson took the cup from my hand and tipped it to his lips. He set it on the counter and then leaned in for a kiss. "Thank you."

"You're welcome. Now that everything's painted in

beautiful shades that *I* think are perfect, what should I work on next?"

"So you're really sticking with that purple in the third bedroom?" he asked. I shoved his arm, and he chuckled. "Maybe it'll grow on me, like the apple green."

"If it doesn't, we'll just chalk it up to bad taste."

He wrapped his arms around my waist and pulled me flush to him. "How about light fixtures? Nearly every one on the second level needs replaced, and it's one of those little time-consuming things, but I could show you how to do one fairly quickly, then set you loose on the others."

"And what if I change out some of the light fixtures we bought for funky chandeliers instead? Just for funsies?"

"Hey, if that's what floats your boat, I won't stop you. Even if I would say that most people prefer their chandeliers above their living room tables only, and even then, they want modern and not too low hanging."

"I'll take that under advisement."

Jackson put the lid on the grout and wiped his hands on his filthy work jeans, and I thought again about how they were one of the sexiest pieces of clothing I'd ever laid eyes on. Besides speaking to his hours of working with his hands, there was the way they hugged his muscular thighs and were also snug enough to hint at what else he had going on.

"Ivy? My face is up here."

"I know," I said, then I continued to stare at the crotch of his jeans, adding an exaggerated lip bite.

Jackson put his hands on my waist, turned me toward the door, and nudged me into the hall. "There will be time for playing out all those dirty thoughts tonight, but for now, we work."

"Who's the dictator now?" I joked, adding some extra resistance, because it meant having his hands on me.

Within a few minutes, we were up on a ladder, the old

light fixture that served as an insect graveyard hanging down, wires exposed.

Since the shorter ladder was only one sided, I was up a rung higher, with Jackson on the one lower, his body pressed against the back of mine, which was distracting to say the least.

"Just match up the colors." Jackson pulled the black wire out of the new, sleek light fixture that complemented the bronze accents we'd put throughout the house, then he twisted it to the black wire hanging from the ceiling and put a plastic cap on it. He repeated the process with the white wire, and then he stripped the end of the green wire and held it out to me. "This will connect to the screw on the grounding bar. I'll let you try it, since this is the hardest part."

I glanced over my shoulder at him. "You're not trying to electrocute me, are you?"

His hand slid around my waist, his fingers splaying on my lower stomach. "I wouldn't electrocute you now that I've finally got you right where I want you—which is in a relationship with me, for the record."

"But if I would've refused and stormed out yesterday? Or, you know, if you would've just let me break it off like I tried to?"

"Then all bets would be off," Jackson said with a wicked smile. "Good thing I shut that down. Just like I shut off the electricity to the bedrooms this morning."

I touched the bare wire to the metal plate and mimicked getting shocked.

"Funny. Now twist the end around the screw."

I wound it around and then pushed the light fixture into place. My arms started burning from holding it up, but I wanted to prove I could do it myself, even though it was nice to know I had backup, just in case.

After all the screws were secured, I slowly let go, afraid

it'd come crashing down.

But it stayed. Jackson smacked my ass. "Good job." He hopped down and extended a hand, which I took, because well, I liked holding hands more than I thought I would. "Think you can handle the rest?"

"I know I can."

"I'll be finishing up the tile in the shower. Holler if you need me."

As he turned around, I smacked him on the ass. After all, turnabout was fair play. "Go get 'em, tiger."

His laugh echoed down the hall.

Day One of being in an official relationship after five years without attempting any kind of coupling was going remarkably well. Which I knew wasn't a huge milestone for most people and that the beginning was the happy puppy love stage, but for a relationship pessimist, I was feeling rather optimistic.

• • •

"Why do you have a giant table in your car?" Jackson asked as he stepped inside the house. He'd gone to grab dinner about twenty minutes ago.

I took the box of pizza from him, walked it into the kitchen, and set it on the counter. "I sometimes buy old furniture and fix it up. Repurpose it or whatever. Did you ever notice the coffee table in my condo?"

"Vaguely."

"It used to be that ugly dark-brown wood. It's why I knew how to fix up the vanity in the downstairs bathroom to give it more of that antique look."

"So you just do it as a hobby? Or when you need furniture?"

"Yes." I grabbed two paper plates and slid him one. "But

I've also sold some on Craigslist. It was one of the reasons I thought I could take on this renovation project. I thought it'd be like that, but on a bigger, higher-stakes level. And it was. Just bigger and higher stakes than I'd bargained for."

Black Widow came in, noticed we were eating without her, and whined like she was near starvation, even though I'd fed her this morning and she had dry cat food in her bowl. But she was nursing kittens and I was a sucker, so I set down my pizza, opened a can of wet food and dumped it in her dish, then washed my hands and returned to my dinner.

"Did you call about that job?" Jackson asked.

"Yeah. I have an interview on Thursday. The guy I talked to was, like, super excited. Almost freakishly so. Like those infomercial dudes who sell shit at three a.m. You know they can't possibly be *that* excited about a glorified vacuum or being able to chop vegetables really fast. But I'm trying to keep an open mind."

"Hmm." Jackson seemed to be deep in thought, and I nudged him.

"What?"

He leaned a hip against the counter. "I've been thinking about your job dilemma, and at one point, I thought I might be able to find you a position working for me. I could use someone to do admin stuff, but only part time, and I don't think that's anywhere near your dream job. I also worried that…" He ran a hand over his jaw.

"That you forgot how to finish a sentence? Because you did."

I expected a smile, but his expression remained serious. "Most of the jobs I take on are through companies who've already got set floor plans, so it's just carrying them out. I don't do that many reno projects, and while I'm not saying you're incapable of wielding a power saw or a nail gun, I couldn't turn you loose with one, either—especially a saw. I happen to like all your fingers."

"I hardly use this one…" I held up my ring finger. "But my pinky I need for lifting when I drink tea, and my middle I need for obvious reasons…"

Finally, I got a hint of a smile. He shoved the last bite of his pizza in his mouth, wiped his hands on a napkin, then wrapped an arm around my waist and pulled me closer. "I want you to find that dream career, and I'd like to help you, but I also know you have this stubborn personality that resists help. Or that you might think it's a pity job and get pissed I even offered it."

"Sounds like me," I said, and his smile broke free.

"I could give you a jumping-off point and some experience, but there's the other thing. It's hard enough not to suffocate you just doing the dating thing and spending so many hours in this house. Add working together, and I'm afraid you'll run for the hills."

I pressed my lips together, turning over his worries, and I couldn't say I disagreed. One of the reasons I hadn't killed him during our remodeling adventure was that I got to make the final decisions, since in the end, it was my project. That wouldn't be the case on other jobs. I'd like to say I was a big enough person for it to not get in the way of our relationship—hard to believe that was a valid worry I now had. Who had I become?

A recovering pessimist who really likes this guy holding me and looking at me like he'd give me the world if I asked him to.

The point was it was going to be hard enough to make this thing between us work as it was, and I still wasn't sure I could. That I was even capable of it. Add working together day in and day out, and that seemed like a recipe for disaster. "You're right. Except I'd run for flat ground. Hills and I aren't friends when running's involved."

He nodded.

"And, yeah, it would feel a bit like a pity job, and I can get my own job." Despite the fact that he full-on said that, I found myself fighting off feeling insulted.

"I was kinda hoping this project taught you that it's okay to ask for help." He gestured around the room. "Look at all we've accomplished together. It's because we were here to support each other and keep each other going. You don't have to take on everything alone." He locked eyes with me. "It's okay to need other people, Ivy. It's okay to ask for help."

I scratched the back of my neck, not liking this line of conversation, although I did see his point. "Yeah, yeah, yeah."

To Jackson's credit, he tried to fight his victorious smile, even though he didn't quite contain it. "So I've been wracking my brain for the last week or so, but as you were talking about the furniture refurnishing thing, it made me think of this lady I've worked with a few times. Her name is Betty-Joe Crocker, and—"

"Wait. Her name is Betty Crocker? Is she a culinary heiress? Because if you're trying to hint to me that I should become a chef, first of all, have you seen me cook? That's right," I answered before he could, "because I don't. And second of all, never gonna happen, so keep on dreaming, buddy."

Jackson tilted his head, his expression asking if I was done.

"Well, you never know. First you think I'm relationship material and the next you think you can make me a cook or a baker. Does the word *delusional* mean anything to you?"

"Betty-Joe's business revolves around estate sales," he said, clearly deciding he might as well charge on with it before I could make more jokes about becoming a domestic goddess. "I've been leaving her card behind for people who need furniture. You should talk to her. Maybe it'll end up being nothing, but there's no harm in meeting her, right?"

I wasn't sure how estate sales and my thing went together, but it was nice of him to think of me, and he was right. It couldn't hurt. "Sure, I'll talk to her."

"Cool. I'll get you her information."

That seemed to satisfy him, and I took a moment to think back to what he'd said about how much we'd accomplished together. From here I could see into the beautiful finished living room, and if I glanced over my shoulder, I could see into the dining room. The entire downstairs transformation was astounding, to where sometimes it still struck me that Jackson and I had turned an old run-down house into something so beautiful. It'd taken a lot longer than fast-forwarding through the tiring workdays to throw up a quick swipey effect, but it made me appreciate the jaw-dropping after that much more.

We only had a few final touches to make the upstairs match, and suddenly I wanted to slow it all down and find more to fix, because I didn't want to be done. "Do you ever find yourself wishing a job could last longer?"

Jackson slipped his hand into my back pocket. "Never. I'm always in a race against time, and then something goes wrong, and the schedule is screwed, and people get pissed or sad or sassed, which is a combination of both."

"Sassed. I like it."

"But this job…" He curled me closer, and his lips sought out mine. He pressed me tighter to him, until it was hard to tell where he ended and I began, and it still didn't feel close enough. I poured my longing for…I wasn't even sure what exactly…into the kiss, drawing it out. Rolling my tongue over his, running my fingers through his hair, savoring his warm body and the way his scent invaded my senses and made me so aware of every inch of him. He let out a shaky breath when we came up for air and whispered, "This job, I sorta wish would last forever."

Chapter Thirty-One

Jackson and I had just finished a run to the home improvement store—hopefully our last one, since after going there nearly every day for little items and exchanges, I never wanted to step foot inside it again.

Jackson grabbed the door we'd bought, and I was balancing all the bags, still laughing about Jackson's off-key singing to the radio—Zayn may be able to hit those high notes while being male, but Jackson most definitely could not— when I noticed my mom sitting on the steps of the porch. *Shit.*

"Mom. What are you doing here?"

"Me? What am *I* doing here?" She stood, hands on hips. "What are *you* doing here, Ivy Lynn?"

Busted.

Jackson stepped past her and set the door down. I thought he'd go inside and leave us to hash it out, but he came back down the porch steps and put his hand on my back, a little lifeline gesture that said, *I'm here if you need me.* I had a feeling I would, my desire to avoid needing someone be damned.

"I've been renovating the house so that Dixie can sell it for a higher profit," I said. "How did you know I was here? Did she tell you? Are you guys talking again?" A glimmer of hope shimmered through me, whispering that maybe this was a good thing. Maybe our patchwork family could be put back together.

Mom let out a huff. "I haven't talked to Dixie in nearly a decade, and you know that, Ivy. You know why, too. But apparently *you've* been talking to her."

Guilt pressed in, extinguishing the hope, and I had to remind myself that I hadn't done anything wrong. Or maybe I had. It was hard to know where to draw loyalty lines with their situation. "I hadn't talked to her in a few years when I saw the house was for sale, so I called her and told her I'd like to fix it up before she sold it. This house is the only place that ever felt like home to me, and I…" A lump rose in my throat. "I don't know. I just wanted to say good-bye, but to say good-bye in a different way, I guess."

"A few years? So you *have* kept in touch."

Out of everything I'd said, of course that was the thing she homed in on. "She was like an aunt to me," I said, but in a lot of ways, she was more like a mother than my actual mom. Maybe that was a disloyal thing to even think, but it wasn't the first time I'd thought it. "She was family, the only family I was sure I'd always have." *And not even that proved true.*

"And what about *him*? You're chummy with him, too?"

I didn't have to ask who. "Rhett was one of the few guys who actually felt like a stepdad, even though he never officially was one. That first semester of college they checked in on me, surprising me with groceries, or they'd take me to dinner. Sometimes Dixie called just to chat. She'd listen as I filled her in on my life, and I needed that. You were too busy to talk a lot of the time, and—"

"Oh. So it's my fault that you went behind my back?"

"Do you even remember why you're mad at her? What? She dared to fall in love with one of your castoffs. She felt horrible about it, and she apologized again and again. I could see how torn up she was about it."

"If she was that torn up, she wouldn't have done it. And I still don't buy that she waited until we broke up, because she sure pounced quickly. She was..." Mom's voice cracked, and tears sprang to her eyes. I'd seen her cry over a lot of guys in my life, but I'd never seen her cry over Dixie, whereas I'd shed plenty of tears over her. "She was all I had, and she betrayed me." She sniffed. "I guess that's not true. The both of you were all I had, and you both betrayed me."

She swiped away her tears and started past me.

"Mom. Come on. Let's talk this out. You should come inside and see what we've done with the place. Dixie has all these scrapbooks that are full of pictures of us over the years. It's been really nice looking through them and reliving some of our good times."

Mom shook her head. "I should've known better than to drive through this neighborhood. Usually I go out of my way, but today..." She sniffed and shook her head again. "Then I saw your car, and sugar, it broke my heart. I realize you and I haven't always had the best relationship, but I never thought you'd stab me in the back like this. Just like she did."

Her words hit true, radiating pain from my heart outward. I wanted to point out that that would be a whole different situation, one that icked me out, but she stormed away, a fan of the last word to the end.

Jackson's hands came up on my shoulders, and he rubbed at the tension that'd set in there. "She'll cool off."

"No, she won't. She'll hold this over my head for the rest of my life, bringing it up whenever she needs ammo in an argument." But the really depressing thing was that she'd still mostly ignore me until she called me up to help her move out of her current boyfriend's house, and I'd still go.

Maybe we were doomed to repeat the process over and over, learning nothing, neither of us ever finding what we wanted from each other. Out of life.

I wanted to break the cycle. I didn't know if I'd ever have the kind of relationship with my mother that I wanted to. Most likely, that ship had sailed. I just hoped that it wasn't completely delusional to believe that not all my relationships had to be crappy just because 90 percent of them had been.

But that dang statistic wouldn't leave my head, and I wondered again if a rift would form with Savannah if things didn't work out with me and Jackson. I didn't want to drive by her house someday, wishing I wouldn't have ruined things but not sure how to fix it and too stubborn to try anyhow.

Jackson squeezed my shoulder. "Babe?"

"I'm okay." I inhaled a deep breath. "Mostly okay. I guess a part of me always knew she'd somehow find out and be hurt. I knew the risk, and I took it anyway."

I put my hand over Jackson's. *Please be different, please be different, please be different…*

Chapter Thirty-Two

It was our last night in the house, and everything we'd done today had a bittersweet edge to it, not to mention I was mushier than usual. I'd almost cried when I sat in the reading nook, looking out over the neighborhood and imagining spending hours relaxing and reading as I soaked up the sunshine.

I'd also gotten super emotional over the antique doorknobs Jackson had found at a salvage store. He'd replaced the "perfectly good" doorknobs, muttering and shaking his head at himself, but I think he appreciated the finishing touch more than he would ever admit to.

He'd borrowed a projector from Savannah, hooked up Netflix, and turned our last night into a Netflix and chill situation. No doubt Savannah would claim that was a bad thing, because she was more of an Amazon Prime and commitment girl, but I fully planned on sexy times for the last night in our house.

I guess you could say I'd binged a whole season of Jackson's body, and even though I knew this was just the season finale of this stage or whatever, I didn't want it to end.

I placed the bowl of popcorn in my lap and leaned back against the headboard as the movie started up—some action movie with horrible dialogue but extremely pretty people and good special effects.

The bed dipped with Jackson's weight as he settled in.

"What are you thinking?" I asked, giving him an incredulous look. "You can't watch a movie with a shirt on. It's way too hot up here." Balancing the bowl of popcorn with one hand so we didn't end up sleeping on kernels, I tugged at the hem of his shirt. He assisted, gripping the back of it and pulling it up over his head.

"Sometimes I think you just want me for my ripped body," he said as he tossed his shirt aside, a cocky grin on his face.

"Um, that's because I do," I joked as I blatantly ogled him. "I feel like I've been very clear about that."

"Well, then you need to lose your shirt, too. Like you said, it's too hot up here." He peeled off my shirt and tossed it onto the floor with his. Despite the fact that he'd seen me in various states of undress countless times by now, he still took his time looking me over, leaving me with a tingly, floaty feeling.

Then he tucked me next to him, and we watched a few minutes of the movie.

I lifted my head from his shoulder. "What am I going to do with my kittens? I can't seriously keep five cats in my condo."

"Put out an ad and I bet they'll go quick."

That made me sad to think about, regardless of it being the logical thing to do. The little furballs had their eyes wide open now, and they bounced more than walked, never venturing far outside of their bed.

"You can give it a while," Jackson said. "They need to be with their mom for at least another month or so anyway.

If that's too overwhelming for you, they can stay at my place until we find better homes."

Yep, mushiness was happening, my insides going all melty on me. I rested my head back on his shoulder. Over the past few days, we'd spent a lot of time in this bed talking until one of us drifted asleep. My interview for the acquisitions manager had gone well, and the two guys I'd met with were so excited that I'd renovated a house that they wanted to set up a time next week to check it out for themselves. While I felt like I'd nailed the interview, I still didn't have a good grasp of what exactly the job entailed, so I needed to compile a list of questions and make sure they were all answered.

But there was always later for that.

After a few more pointless and highly unlikely movie explosions, I began tracing the muscles in Jackson's arms. Shoulder, biceps, the sexy line in his forearm.

When I reached his fingers, he toyed with mine, rubbing his calloused fingertips over them and then bringing my hand up to place a hot kiss against my palm.

Desire and affection melded together and streaked through my body. I skimmed one of the grooves that bracketed his mouth and stood out when he smiled, then continued with my tracing, moving to his torso, across the pecs and then tiptoeing down his abs.

When I reached the waistband of his jeans, I dragged my finger back and forth, listening to his accelerated breaths and watching his Adam's apple bob up and down.

I flicked open the button of his pants, and it was like flipping a switch. He rolled over me, his body pressing me into the bed. He gave me the same treatment I'd given him, running his fingers over my collarbone, across the swell of my breasts, down lower, and lower, and lower.

I gasped, arching into his touch. Then we shed the last of our clothes and continued exploring each other's bodies, making good use of every last hour, minute, and second in the house that I'd always think of as ours, even if it had only been ours temporarily.

Afterward, Jackson held me close and ran his hand up and down my back. I could hear his heart beating in his chest, right under my ear, gradually slowing its rapid rhythm. My pulse slowed as well, my heart beating in time with his as it filled up with him entirely.

A sensation I hadn't felt in a long time spread through my chest, dizzying and visceral, and so damn intoxicating I wanted to reach for it and hold on to it before it left me behind. As hard as I'd tried, I'd utterly failed to keep Jackson at a distance, and I was dangerously close to breaking my last, most fundamental rule to avoiding a broken heart.

Way #13: *Never, ever, fall in love. Like, EVER. It can only end in tears.*

I closed my eyes, scared to move, scared to breathe, afraid to break the spell, while afraid not to.

"Ivy," he whispered. "I want to tell you something…"

Shit, shit, shit. I remained perfectly still, pleading with him not to say it, even as my heart begged for it.

Maybe I was wrong. Maybe he wasn't going to say anything about caring for me, or…more than caring for me. But the anxiety shifting into overdrive and cutting off my oxygen told me I wasn't ready for it.

He either bought my already-asleep act or decided to let it drop, which made me feel like even more of a jerk when he kissed the top of my head and pulled the blanket around me. Before I knew it, I was drifting off for real, the worry gnawing at the back of my mind promising me that tomorrow, it would be right there waiting for me.

Chapter Thirty-Three

The past several days had been a blur of playing catch up. Tony had been complaining about my lack of shifts, so I'd taken on a couple extra. Jackson had started on his new housing project, and it meant our working hours were opposite, which didn't leave much time together. Or any, really.

On top of that I'd boxed up all but one of Dixie's scrapbooks and cleaned the Victorian from top to bottom. Then there was my neglected condo. It also needed cleaning, and Black Widow was still trying to dart out the door every time I came home, like she wanted her old place back (a sentiment I shared, as hard as I tried not to). But then she would realize I had her kittens and begrudgingly stick around—so much for the bond I thought we'd forged.

On Thursday morning, I forced myself out of bed, cursing the early hour and the sloppy drunks who wouldn't just leave Azure last night. I fed Black Widow, cracked open a Cherry Coke, and rushed out of my condo.

The madness I'd felt all week calmed as I pulled up to the Victorian. It'd become my safe place again, just like it had when I was growing up.

Then I saw the FOR SALE sign, and sorrow pushed in. I'd have to find a new haven. Which was what my condo was supposed to be, and I was trying to force myself to believe it was, even if it had never felt like it. *Maybe once I pick a color for the walls and stick with it…*

The rumble of a truck engine broke me out of my thoughts, and I looked up, expecting the guys I'd interviewed with, only to find Jackson's truck and his sexy face in my rearview mirror.

I climbed out of my car and pulled my jacket tighter—an impending rainstorm had the temperature cooler than usual. "Hey. What are you doing here?"

Jackson drew me into his arms, kissed me like he meant to make up for the nights we hadn't seen each other, and then slowly lowered me back to my feet. "I missed you and wanted to see you."

My heart expanded. "I…" *Come on, Ivy. Force it out—it's the truth, after all.* "I missed you, too."

"I also wanted to meet these guys you might work with."

My mushy feelings turned to cement, the rough kind that tore up your knees. "I don't need you checking up on me. I've been taking care of myself for years, and I plan to keep on doing it."

He let loose a long-suffering sigh.

I scowled at him. "Don't sigh at me. If you would've kept it at missing me, I would've stayed happy."

"Fine. I just missed you. That's the only reason I'm here."

"Awesome. Now you better get to work. I'm sure you've got a big day ahead of you."

He crossed his arms.

I returned the gesture.

"Since you're hell-bent on being mad anyway," Jackson said, "I might as well tell you that I started digging into this company that you're considering working for, and some of what they do seems sketchy, which made me like the thought of you being alone in the house with two men you don't know even less."

"Okay, so you call me up and tell me that like a normal person so I can decide what to do with the information instead of showing up like some kind of overprotective bodyguard."

He took a step toward me. "Perhaps I would've if you'd picked up the damn phone last night."

"I was working." I advanced this time, crowding his space so he didn't think he could control everything. "I wanted to call you back, but I knew you'd be asleep, and I was trying to be *considerate*, although I don't know why I bothered, since you clearly won't do the same for me."

"We just have different ideas of how to be considerate. I care about you, so I did a little digging, but I didn't have time to do as much as I wanted to, and since I knew you were meeting with them now, I figured better safe than sorry."

"I'm not helpless."

"I would never use that word to describe you. I can think of a lot of other words I'd like to use, though. Frustrating, exasperating, stubborn, obstinate…I can keep going all day."

"Looks like those vocab lessons have really paid off. Some of those words mean the same thing, though, you infuriatingly dogmatic…" Since he'd so nicely left out *succubus*, I didn't want to resort to slinging old insults from our straight-up-enemy days, so I struggled to find something less harsh than *jackass* that would also fit. "Caveman."

"Admit it, Flash, you're trying to pull away again."

For once, I was relatively sure I wasn't. Not purposely, although yes, I'd had a minor freak out during our last night together, but I was mostly over that now. To be fair, I could also see how it might look similar to last time, what with the going from constant contact to a slow trickle of rushed texts.

Not that I'd admit that right now, because I had a leg to stand on in this situation, and he didn't.

We were still locked in our stubborn stand-off when a car pulled up, and two guys in suits piled out.

I forced a smile and greeted Chris and Brad of Peachtree Property Management, begrudgingly introducing them to Jackson but acting my way through it so they wouldn't realize it was begrudgingly, although I'm sure Jackson did. "Would you like to see the place?"

"Yeah, let's take a look."

As we passed by the realtor sign, Jackson frowned. "Why didn't you go with the real estate agent I recommended?"

Because it wasn't my choice. Dixie had a relationship with the woman whose picture was smiling at us. But since I was annoyed at Jackson, I said, "Because I'm fully capable of picking someone, and I picked a woman."

He gritted his teeth in a big-bad-wolf smile. "It's not that I have anything against a female real estate agent, I just know Joe Hardy and he's always been fair, and he knows the market better than anyone."

"I went with someone else. End of story."

"Fine."

I unlocked the door and led the guys inside. "I should've taken more before pictures, but I can show you the ones I have." I'd printed them up and put them in a folder. It wasn't as organized or fancy as what Savannah would've done, but it got the job done. I handed over the pictures, and they compared them to the transformed rooms as we walked through them.

Pride beat out my irritation at Jackson for coming over after days of not seeing each other, just to be bossy. Of all the things I'd done in my life, this project was one of the best. I'd used both my mental and physical strengths.

"We do already have a qualified designer and contractor

to do the flipping," Brad said, glancing at Jackson.

"I understand," I said, fighting off irritation at Brad now, since he'd made it sound like Jackson wasn't qualified, and they'd never find a better contractor. "I figured showing you this place would help prove that I know how to evaluate a house's potential and that I understand what kind of work needs to go into a project."

"It does." Chris placed his hand on my shoulder, and Jackson tensed up beside me.

"Let's look at the upstairs," I quickly said, stepping out of Chris's reach and starting in that direction.

After finishing the tour, we paused in the living room to talk business. They glanced at Jackson a few times, like they weren't sure what he was doing there, but I didn't want to have a fight in front of them, so I just let it be.

My salary would be solely commission based, which was a little intimidating, and they informed me that I'd be traveling around thirty to forty percent of the time. As they detailed the job, I thought it was something I could do, even if it wasn't exactly what I'd first envisioned. Maybe I just needed to change the image in my mind.

Once I had a steadier income, I could also do side projects, either repurposing furniture or smaller homes. The travel would cut into that some, but there was give and take with everything.

"A lot of these types of houses are worth a lot of money, simply because of where they are," Brad said. "People get attached, so it'd be up to you to get them to see the big picture."

"And the big picture is…?" I didn't want to sound stupid, but I didn't want to just nod and agree when I still wasn't one hundred percent clear.

"That we'll give them a good, fair price, so they can settle into a nicer home on the outskirts of the city."

This time I did just nod. But I wasn't sure I agreed. I needed time to process.

"We'll let you talk about it..." Brad's gaze lifted to Jackson again, as if I'd need to discuss it with him first.

"*I'll* think about it and get back to you," I said, offended they thought I couldn't make a decision without a guy. But *of course* that's what they thought. If it wasn't too late to ask Jackson to wait outside, I would've. I didn't want them to think I couldn't make executive decisions myself, like I'd be calling my boyfriend to ask if I should acquire a property. Why would they even need me, then? They could just hire him.

Not that he'd take the job, but it was the principle of the matter.

I led them to the door by myself—only thinking of it as a hostess, wifey type thing when I reached the door—and, trying to shove that back, wished them a good day and promised to be in touch.

As soon as they reached the end of the sidewalk, I spun to face Jackson. "That made me look super unprofessional. Like I needed you to be here to conduct an interview or explain what we did to the house."

"I don't want you to take the job," Jackson said, aiming a frown toward the door. "I got a bad, slimy salesman vibe from them. There's something underhanded about the way they do business. I can just tell."

Clearly, he hadn't heard a word I said. "You just don't like big businesses, their salesmen, or basically anyone who's not you. They're offering a chance to make a lot of money, and it'd be nice to have more breathing room in my budget." If I could make enough sales. They gave me percentages, but without knowing how much the houses would sell for, it wasn't easy to turn that into a solid figure. But I could do some research, get a rough estimate, and go from there.

Jackson squared off in front of me. "Money's not everything, and while I'm not the biggest fan of big businesses, theirs sounds like they're scamming people out of their homes. Let me ask around a little more, see what I can find out."

"I don't need your help choosing my career. We talked about this."

"As I recall, we talked about how you'd resist my giving you a job and you agreed, and then I pled a pretty compelling case in favor of help and support. And this is different. This isn't me getting you a job; it's me trying to protect you from a sketchy situation."

"I was picking my jobs before you came into my life just fine, and I'm a big girl. I don't need you to protect me."

"Ivy, you're being ridiculous. At least let me—"

"*Ridiculous?* For wanting control of my own life?" I jabbed a finger at his chest. "You're the one being ridiculous, showing up here like I'm some damsel in distress you have to stop before I make a reckless decision that'll ruin my life. That's my mom, not me. I make my own decisions, and I'm perfectly capable of taking care of myself. I let you out us to your parents and force me into a relationship, but I've got to draw lines somewhere."

Jackson stepped forward, right into my still-pointed finger. "I wouldn't have to force you into a relationship if you'd just let me in a little. I swear, Ivy, sometimes trying to get through to you is like blasting through a brick wall, only to find three more."

"Well, that's how I am, and I'm not changing for some guy."

"Some guy? I'm just *some guy*?" Hurt coated his words, and that pain echoed through my chest. Why did caring about someone always mean inevitably hurting them, too?

"You know that's not what I mean."

"You mean that you don't give a damn about my opinion and that you're still too stubborn to take my help, even if it's the best thing for you. Have you even called Betty-Joe? I told her about you, and I think it would be a great opportunity, and I bet you haven't even called her."

"I have it on my to-do list. I've been busy."

"I get that. I've been busy, too. But I've still managed to squeeze in a few important phone calls."

My stomach dropped. The honeymoon beginning phase of us was already ending. This was where things turned ugly. When there were fights over stupid things. I wouldn't bend over backward to try to make it all smooth sailing ever again. I wouldn't sacrifice everything about myself to try to make things work, and I wouldn't retreat into myself and just hope it improved, either. I'd come way too far. "Look, I've got the early shift at the bar, and I know you took time out of your workday to come check on me, even though I didn't ask you to and I don't need you to. Let's just call this a draw and get on with our day."

"Fine."

"Fine." I threw open the front door and stormed out. It would've been more effective if I didn't have to wait for him to come out so I could lock up after him.

"Ivy…" Jackson rubbed his eyebrow, the way he did when he was frustrated or tense. "Are you ever going to let me in?"

I shrugged. Then I clenched my jaw against the tears trying to climb up my throat. An ache settled over my heart, and all my doubts rushed forward. I knew this wouldn't work. We couldn't even survive one week away from our house. The spell had broken, and now I was standing in pumpkin guts and rags, exposed for what I truly was: a girl who couldn't be in a relationship long term.

With a resigned, slightly disappointed expression on his face, Jackson leaned in and kissed my forehead. If that didn't say good-bye, I wasn't sure what did. "I'll call you later, okay? We just need to spend some time together, and we'll figure this out."

I couldn't speak. Couldn't agree, because I was afraid that more time would only result in falling harder, and I already saw the ugly crash coming. The resulting fallout would be wide-spread, his family hating me, my best friend torn between taking sides.

I thought of my mom and Dixie and how they didn't even talk anymore. My mom wasn't talking to me, either. While a tiny part of me was relieved by that, the other, bigger part stung at losing her, even if she only remembered me when it was convenient. And, of course, I couldn't stop worrying she'd fall into a depression and try another stunt that landed her in the hospital. Or worse.

My life was spinning out of my control, because silly me, I'd loosened my grip on it for one little month, and now it would be a bitch to get back.

But I was pretty sure it was the only way to avoid a crash that would wreck not just my life, but Jackson's in the process.

Chapter Thirty-Four

In case anyone was wondering what a commitmentphobe's worst nightmare was, the answer would be a bridal shower. That would've been enough to leave me in hives, but adding the female half of Jackson's family to the mix was an extra form of torture.

If it was for anyone besides Savannah, I would've skipped it and spent a lazy Saturday in bed. I still hadn't told her that Jackson and I'd had a big fight and that we hadn't really talked since Wednesday morning.

He'd called a few times while I'd been working, and I didn't know what to say, so I'd done the mature thing and let it go to voicemail. I'd sent a text so it wouldn't look like the exact same radio-silence treatment that'd proceeded our first crash and burn, but I knew as soon as we had a face-to-face conversation, it'd be over. While that would help me regain control and help minimize the pain from breaking up, I also couldn't help wanting to put it off just a little longer.

Because clearly, I *wasn't* in control.

"Deep breaths," Savannah said as she sat down next to

me. "You look like you're going to pass out."

"I wouldn't rule it out."

"Then I'd have to give you mouth to mouth, and while that would take our friendship to a whole new level, it might be an awkward one. Especially since I just ate half a bag of Doritos on the drive over."

A sputtered laugh spilled from my lips. "Okay, you've convinced me. No passing out."

"How's life?"

"Lifey."

"How very verbose of you." She crossed one leg over the other, showing off cute pink heels with a bow on the toe. "What about things with my brother?"

A string in my heart tugged, and it hurt like a bitch. "We… I…" I shook my head and shrugged.

Savannah's face dropped. "I'm sorry. I shouldn't have asked."

"Yes, it's your fault for asking your friend a perfectly normal question, not mine, for being a not-normal female who can't deal with emotions or relationships."

Savannah grabbed my hand. "You just need some training. I'm not sure you know this about me, but I have this twelve-step program…"

A laugh that was too close to a sob came out.

"All I know is that the night you came over for dinner, you both looked happier than I'd seen either of you in a long time. I'll resist talking about happily-ever-afters, since you're still on the skeptical side of the fence, despite my many attempts to drag you over…"

"You are relentless. I think I still have scars from it." I lifted my arm like I was examining it for leftover damage.

She clicked her tongue at me as she shoved my shoulder. "What I'm saying is I believe that there's a guy who can restore even Ivy Clarke's faith in love, but that requires you giving a little, too, and maybe—just maybe—I think that guy might be my brother. You know, not everyone's happily-ever-after ends here, at a bridal shower and a future that involves a walk down the aisle."

"I think you're failing at resisting happily-ever-after talk," I teased.

Savannah gave an innocent shrug. "So sue me."

The games began before we could talk much more, and while I wanted to tell my best friend that she was totally right, I couldn't. It wasn't that I didn't believe in love. I'd just seen the destruction it caused when it turned bad, and I'd seen it turn bad *a lot.*

Countless times through the years I'd had to hold everything together while Mom cried, unable to get out of bed for days. It ended that way again, and again, and again. She seemed to lose a piece of herself every single time, too. A mix of real memories and ones I'd only seen in scrapbooks flashed through my mind, of her in every era, always with a different guy, and her style and even hair reflected the changes she'd made for them. But the image my mind landed on and held was her in that hospital bed.

She still had the hope of happily-ever-after, but I'd lost it, and too much had happened for me to get it back.

I'd tried to tell myself otherwise, but I was broken.

I recalled Savannah saying that Jackson liked to fix things, and I was sure when he saw me, he saw a woman in severe need of fixing. But I was too far gone, and he'd be so much better off with someone else. Pretty much anyone else. I didn't want him to break me more, and even more, I didn't want to break him.

Lucinda smiled over at me as we transitioned to gift time. "Isn't this fun? Maybe soon we'll be having one of these things for you."

What?

"I mean, once you and Jackson are engaged." She patted my knee. "No rush, of course, I realize you guys just started dating, but I've been dreaming of grandchildren for a long time, so if you want to try to race Savannah and Linc, I wouldn't mind."

The air left my lungs in a whoosh, and no oxygen would return, no matter how much I tried to inhale. His mom was already planning our wedding?

Yeah, I was so out.

I stood, clawing at the fabric on the neck of my dress. "I need some air."

"But, hon, we're outside."

I wove around the guests and the table of food but then froze in place when I spotted Jackson. He was walking with a steady, determined stride, and he was heading right for me.

I glanced back, debating whether talking to him or sprinting back to my seat a few yards away would be worse, and I still couldn't get any freaking air. *I can't breathe, I can't breathe, I can't breathe.*

Was this what a panic attack felt like?

Jackson strolled right up to me, jaw set. "You've avoided me for three days—don't even try to count your one superficial text, because we both know that was just another evasive maneuver. I think the very definition of desperate is showing up to your sister's bridal shower." He muttered a curse, and I glanced back to see the females in attendance giggling and gasping at a piece of very tiny lingerie Savannah had pulled out of a gift bag.

Under other circumstances, I'd laugh, but laughing required use of my lungs, and I still didn't have that. The walls were closing in, and my brain screamed that this was all too much. "Jackson, please, not here. I need…" I fought against the dizzying wave that made the ground unsteady under my feet.

"I thought if I just showed you I planned on sticking this through, no matter how hard you tried to push me away, that eventually you'd let me in. I've tried to be patient and tiptoe around so I don't scare you off, but Ivy, I'm crazy about you."

I ran a shaky hand through my hair—apparently, we were doing this here. Time to rip off the Band-Aid and get all the pain over at once. "I told you this wouldn't work. I tried to tell you. We couldn't even make it one week without a big fight. We need to call it before either of us gets hurt."

Too late, my brain screamed as my heart bled misery at having to say good-bye, but I clung to that logic, because there was hurt and there was shattered. The fact that I was having a panic attack over the very idea of more, even with this guy who I cared about more than I'd cared about any other guy before, screamed that I could never make it work.

Jackson took both my hands in his. "Ivy, come on. People fight. They don't always agree—you and I won't always agree. In fact, knowing us like I do, we'll probably disagree a lot." He gave me a watered-down version of his usual smile. "It just means we'll get to make up a lot."

Making up. With kissing and arguing foreplay and sex—holy crap, I was going to miss all that, but I couldn't think about every amazing thing I'd miss about Jackson or I'd never have the strength to go through with what needed to be done. "You think I'm broken. That you can plaster over the crack, or find the right part to fix, and I'll be whole. But this is who I am. I'm unfixable."

"I don't think you're broken. I think your trust is broken. I think too many people in your life treated you like you were temporary. I know you lost pieces of your heart along the way, to each new stepdad or stepbrother and sister, and even to Dixie. To your mom. To whatever idiot guys weren't strong enough to love a girl as strong as you.

"I think your idea of love is broken, and I'm not trying

to fix you. I'm trying to show you that it doesn't have to be that way. It doesn't have to end…we can make it work." He squeezed my hands. "I know you don't have a lot of faith in love left, but put it in me instead."

Tears sprang to my eyes, and no amount of jaw clenching or blinking would hold them back, so I let them go. "I don't think I can—I'm just not built that way. Our time together was fun, and I'll always be glad we had that, but I'm not who you want. You think you do now, but you'll change your mind."

"I won't change my mind. You *are* who I want, and if you'd just push everything else away and let yourself focus on you and me and how much better life is when we're together, you'd realize you need me, too." He pulled me closer and rested his forehead against mine. "I'm in love with you."

He gave me a couple of seconds to let that sink in, but it only caused more pain, more misery that I couldn't go down this path.

"That's right, Ivy Clarke. I love you, and I needed you to know that. But I can't force you to be with me, and I can't make us work all by myself. I'll give you space or time if that's what you need to figure out you love me, too. Just don't give up on us before we give it a real shot."

The lump lodged in my throat grew and constricted even more of my air supply. "I'm so sorry, Jackson, but it's never going to work, and I don't want you waiting on me to change my mind, because you'd be waiting forever."

The muscles of his jaw tightened, but he didn't get mad or sad. He just kept staring at me, so steady. Then he lowered his lips to mine and kissed me, his hand going to my neck, his thumb tilting my chin up for better access. He poured every ounce of passion that'd ever passed between us into it, our arguments and pound-for-pound banter and our steamy nights spent together. Since I was greedy and afraid we'd never kiss again, I met him stroke for stroke, until the world spiraled out from under me, my grip on his forearms all that kept me from falling.

When he pulled back and peered down at me, I didn't even bother pretending I wasn't broken—I felt the split deep in my soul. "I guess it's a good thing that I have more faith in love than you do."

Chapter Thirty-Five

Nothing like fleeing your best friend's bridal shower in tears to solidify your strong dislike of them.

It'd been two and a half weeks. Long weeks and days that seemed like an eternity. By now, Jackson had surely accepted that I wasn't changing my mind, especially since I'd fought him on the relationship every step of the way. The thought of him moving on made my heart and lungs feel like they were crumbling into the sea of agony that'd overtaken my chest, but then I reminded myself it was for the best. For him, anyway.

For all my rules and clever ways to avoid it, I was experiencing a broken heart, no question. Guess that's what I got for breaking pretty much every one of them with Jackson. It was always doomed to end up this way, yet that didn't stop it from being so painful that I wanted to stop pretending I could still function, curl up in a ball and cry, and never get up.

I'd never wanted to experience this level of desperation, but there it was, staring me in the face, mocking me while also lulling me over and telling me to give in. To give up. To succumb to the darkness.

Heaven only knew how bad it would be if I'd let the relationship go on for longer.

My GPS informed me the address was on the right side of the street, and I maneuvered my car into an empty spot. I wished this trip wouldn't make it completely impossible not to think of Jackson, but after tossing and turning for several nights over the job as the acquisitions manager, I couldn't take it. Not only did I also get a bit of a skeezy vibe (which admitting to, even mentally, made me think of Jackson once again), it felt wrong to convince older people out of their homes where their children might've grown up, just to make a bigger profit. Maybe some of them would be happy to have the money or to downsize or even upsize, but knowing me, I'd tell them how they could flip it themselves and make even more money and refer them to Jackson if they needed help doing it. That was a surefire way to piss off management and end up fired, not to mention penniless. I'd rather not have that mark on my work background, and if that meant slinging drinks at the bar for the rest of my life, so be it.

At this point, I couldn't even summon up a bit of caring about my career, something I'd been so desperate to change for the past couple of months.

Shoving my feelings as deep as I could get them to go, I climbed out of my car and pushed into the store. As someone who frequented antique shops, I was surprised I hadn't been in this one before, although it was different from most. After a pleasant conversation on the phone, Betty-Joe Crocker invited me to come check out the place for myself.

"Ivy?"

"That's me." I extended my hand and shook hers. She was several inches shorter than I was, with a sleek gray bob and half glasses with a thin gold chain. "Nice to meet you."

"You, too. Just pull up a chair." She gestured behind me.

"You've got several to choose from."

I looked back at the various chairs and picked one that I loved. The wooden back had the great detailing a lot of older chairs did, with a flower carved into the top and swirls that ran across the arch and middle piece. Naturally it made me think of Dixie's house, and I wished for a moment that the new owners—whoever they ended up being—would let me decorate, because I could reupholster the seat and make a beautiful mismatched set that still somehow went together.

That'd look amazing with the light fixture Jackson put in there, too.

I really need to stop mentally decorating that place and pick a stupid paint color for my condo wall.

Betty-Joe explained how she'd owned the business for forty-two years but that she was finding it harder to keep up these days. "Jackson's always so nice to refer people to me. He's come over and helped me move furniture in and out, too. I try to pay him, but he won't hear of it. I already didn't know how to ever repay him, and now here he goes, sending me someone to help."

I almost replied that I needed to find out more before I agreed to the job, but she'd put it in a way that made it hard to contradict her. Plus, now I was thinking about Jackson and how he'd shown up and taken care of my rodent problem, even before I'd officially hired him at a fraction of his usual rate.

Of course, I paid plenty for that with the disgusting dead mouse in the fridge prank. I shuddered a little, but I also fought back a smile.

Shaking myself out of my Jackson-heavy thoughts, I focused on putting my best foot forward here and now. "I've been shopping for antiques for years, but I also like to refurbish old beat-up furniture and turn it into contemporary pieces that sort of marry the old and the new. If that makes sense. I brought examples..." I handed Betty-Joe a folder with pictures of the pieces I'd done. Lately I was someone who walked around with a folder of my work. I supposed I should go fancy and call it a portfolio, but that seemed more like something professionals did, not someone who painted old furniture as a hobby.

"These are..." She looked up at me, and I held my breath. "They're really good. I think you could sell them for a fortune. Become the next JoAnna Gaines."

I blushed, which wasn't something I thought I did before this moment. "Oh, no. Nothing as fancy or big as that." Obviously, I loved *Fixer Upper,* and while I'd been a bit hard on HGTV, I attributed some of my furniture inspiration to that show.

"I'm serious. There's real money to be made with stuff like this. The people around here eat it up." She pushed her glasses up her nose and studied me. "Between this and Jackson vouching for you, I'm ready to cut through all the bullshit and talk business."

I hadn't been aware we were bullshitting, but I instantly liked her for putting it like that, even though I also worried that Jackson might not be in the mood to vouch for me these days. Although I also knew he'd never call her and take it back. "Lay it out for me, then, Betty-Joe."

She grinned. "I like you." The position entailed accompanying her to estate sales, helping her sort through the crap, and bringing back the hidden treasures. If I wanted to work my magic with some of the pieces, I could "have at it." She informed me that neither of her daughters wanted to inherit the business, and if this arrangement worked out, she'd be looking at retirement in a couple of years.

Since we were talking *years*, my lovely commitment issues screeched to the surface, but I sucked in a deep breath and told them to cool it—silently, so I wouldn't look like a crazy person. We were talking in ifs and possibilities, and I could take it a day at a time and see how it went. The salary wasn't as high as what I probably would've made as an acquisitions manager, but I'd be able to sleep at night, and it was more than I made at the bar, with the possibility to make even more in the future. Plus, it meant turning my side hobby into more of a side job.

All in all, it seemed so perfect for me that I almost worried it was too good to be true.

We agreed to a start date and start time—it was revoltingly early, but I'd make it work—and then Betty-Joe told me she'd see me next week. "You tell Jackson that I said hello and that I'll find a way to thank him for everything yet."

"Oh. I…" Man, for someone who usually kept a tight lid on her emotions, I suddenly wanted to pour out everything that'd happened between him and me. I really needed to… get more sleep or something. "See you next week."

Later I'd have to drop a few hints that he and I weren't talking all that much. Right now, I didn't know if I could do it without crying, and surely once I had another week behind me that'd be all but gone, right?

• • •

For the first time in weeks, I felt an emotion other than resigned sadness. In fact, I'd dare say I was excited. I closed up my tabs at the bar and rushed out of Azure. I'd dropped the bomb on Tony that I needed to go to part time but withheld the fact that if things went well, I'd be turning in my notice.

I buzzed over to the Victorian, and another swirl of excitement went through me when I saw the rental car in the driveway. I practically sprinted up the sidewalk and almost used my key before realizing I should probably knock instead, what with it not actually being my house.

The door swung open, and Dixie and I crashed somewhere in the middle, our arms going around each other as we squeaked out high-pitched greetings. For someone half my size, she sure had a tight grip, and I'd never been so happy to be robbed of air.

"Let me get a good look at you." She pulled back and ran her gaze over me. "Pretty as ever."

"Thank you. You look amazing—obviously coastal life suits you," I said. I meant it, too. Her honey blond hair hung in loose waves, and her skin had that sun-kissed glow. Footsteps made me glance over her shoulder, and Rhett entered the room. He looked the same, save a few strands of gray peppered throughout his light brown hair. "Hey."

He surprised me by stepping forward and wrapping me in a hug. "Good to see you, Ivy."

"You, too."

There wasn't any furniture, so we sat on the floor and caught up. They were happy in Charleston and spent their free time gardening and boating.

I told them about my new job and how excited I was to start.

"You did an amazing job with this place," Dixie said. "When I first walked in, I thought I'd gone and stepped into the wrong house."

Pride flooded me, giving me a light, floaty feeling. "Thank you. It was so much fun transforming the place."

"And we've already got an offer. Just came in today."

Everything inside of me froze and turned to stone. "Oh. That's…great."

Dixie's forehead crinkled. "I thought that would be good news."

"It is. I'll just…" I pressed my hand to the smooth wooden floor Jackson had spent hours laboring over. "I'll miss it. Do you ever miss it? Miss the memories we had here?"

Dixie's eyes went shiny with unshed tears. "Of course I do. I…" She brought a shaky hand to her lips. "Some of my best memories were in this house with you and your mama. How is she?"

I glanced at Rhett, because it was a little weird to talk about her with him in the room, although I wasn't sure exactly why.

"I'll give you gals some time to talk," he said, leaving us to it.

Once I started talking, I couldn't stop. I told Dixie about the ups and downs, about the night Mom had taken all the sleeping pills, and basically spilled my guts about how hard it was for me to deal with her sometimes. Guilt pressed in, but I needed to vent to someone who knew her and loved her, even as hard as she made it sometimes.

"I wish I could've been there for you more," Dixie said.

"Are you happy? With Rhett?" I wanted her to read between the lines and tell me if it was worth it.

A smile spread across her face, her eyes going a bit dreamy. "*So happy*. I wish it hadn't hurt Cora for me to fall so in love with him, but to have someone who understands me and loves me, even when we're not getting along…" She flattened a hand to her chest and sighed. "There was a point I thought I'd never fall in love, never have someone I could count on. I loved you and Cora, and those times you lived here with me, but you came in and out, and admittedly, I had a lot of lonely times. Then Rhett and I started dating—"

"You liked him before, though," I said. She seemed surprised but didn't contradict me. "The scrapbooks. Those pictures told a story."

Dixie pressed her lips together and nodded, and a tear slipped out and ran down her cheek. "I always liked him. But I swear I never did a thing until he and Cora were through."

"I believe you," I said. And I did.

"I'll always love Cora, but she never chose me or put me first, and Rhett does. The loneliness went away with him. Everything in my life just clicked right into place, like he was exactly what I'd needed all along. When I'm down, he picks me up, and I do the same for him. We make each other better." She wiped at her tears, and her smile returned. "These past nine years have been the best in my life. I wouldn't take it back, I'll tell you that. If you find love like that, you hold on to it. You do whatever it takes."

I tried to swallow but couldn't. Then I started fidgeting, her words digging at me even though I tried to bat them away. "So you just came to get your stuff and for the sale?"

"Mostly for my stuff—I left my scrapbooks behind, because for a while, they were too painful to look at. But lately, I've been wanting them. I'm ready to look back and remember the good, even if the bad makes me a little sad. I'll probably have to fly over again when the house closes."

"Did you…?" I cleared my throat, but it didn't make the lump that'd lodged there go away. "You accepted the offer?"

"Not yet. They offered the full asking price, but our relator suggested we see if any higher offers come in. Rhett said he'll let me decide, and of course I planned to discuss it with you before I made a decision, since you put so much into the place. But to tell the truth, I kind of just want to get it over and done and get back home. I definitely want to see you as much as possible before I go, though." She put her arm around me in a side hug. "I have missed you. If your mama would've let me, I would've kept you here with me so that you wouldn't have had to go through all those ups and downs while you were growing up. I know it wasn't easy."

I shrugged, like it was no big deal.

"I think that after she lost your daddy, she was forever scared to lose anyone, and that always seemed to push them all away, making her fears come true. But she was always most afraid of losing you. She loves you, even if she doesn't express it like most people do." She rested her head against mine. "I hope you know that I love you, too. If you ever need anything, you can always call me."

I nodded, and a couple of my own tears slipped free. "I love you, too. And I do, thanks." I sniffed. "I'm just going to take one last look. If you don't mind."

"'Course not. Rhett and I were just talking about dinner. When you have several favorite restaurants that you miss, it's hard to pick one. You'll come with us?"

"Sure."

She left to talk options with Rhett, presumably, and I stood to take my last look. I started with the dining room, peering up at the light fixture that I still loved, and thought back to a night before it'd been put in, when there was just a tiny table in this room. Jackson and my knees had knocked together as we'd played strip poker—there hadn't been any losers that night.

I wandered into the kitchen and thought about our nights eating takeout while leaned against the counter. About how when I was going out of my mind with the news Mom was dating again, Jackson put me to work tearing down cabinets. And after I'd gotten out some of the tension, he'd guessed it had something to do with my mom because he knew me that well.

Then I thought back to even before that, to the first day he showed up with his toolbox. While his reluctance was clear, he hadn't laughed in my face or left me alone to deal with the mess I'd made. Time and time again, he always managed to show up when I needed him most.

Like the night I called him at four in the morning because Black Widow was having her kittens and I didn't know what to do, and he raced right over.

I made my way back into the living room, and of course

the first thing that greeted me was the "prelude blue" wall Jackson and I had passionate sex against when we finally gave in to our off-the-charts chemistry.

The hollow space in my heart opened up with the memories, but instead of shutting them down, I let them flood in. Maybe I was a masochist, but I just wanted to remember all the good times once more before I said good-bye.

I climbed up the stairs and studied the light fixtures I'd put in after Jackson showed me how. Every room was a story of arguing and compromise, none more so than the apple green bathroom with the faux-wood tile—that might've been mostly Jackson giving in.

Then there was the last room.

My room.

The reading nook brought more tears to my eyes, along with a clashing mix of sorrow and happiness and so much missing Jackson that I thought it'd send me to my knees. He'd built that nook for me, even though I only got to enjoy it for a little while. I recalled that last night, cuddling in bed, watching a movie, making love—

Holy shit. Did I just refer to sex as making love? I shook my head, trying to dislodge it, but it didn't work. *This* is *where I fell in love with him.*

With every coat of paint, every nail and swing of the hammer, every floorboard laid, we'd built something, and along the way I fell in love with him.

My phone pinged, and I automatically looked at it.

Savannah had emailed me. I almost ignored it in favor of opening it later, but I could use a distraction right now.

I'm trying to stay out of it, but I was going through my slides and thinking about you, and how when I was about to walk away from Linc, you were the one who talked sense into me. I didn't want to listen, but your words pushed me down the path where I realized just how much I needed him, regardless of what had happened in the past.

So don't be mad, but I couldn't help myself. Maybe my other steps don't apply to you, but I think this one applies to everyone, and I just want you to promise me that you'll think about it. And I'm not just saying this because Jackson is sort of miserable without you, although he is.

Step Twelve: *Realize there are ups and downs in every relationship. When you inevitably hit road bumps and wonder if it's worth fighting for, ask yourself if you're a happier, better person because of him. If so, love means accepting someone for who they are, the same way you want them to do for you. Strong relationships are built, not stumbled into.*

I love you no matter what. Let's get coffee next week and catch up, okay?

Damn her. Damn her for knowing me so well and pushing me when I was trying to keep my iron grip on my rules and not hers.

Now I was standing in the room, tears blurring my surroundings.

There was no doubt I was a happier, better person because of Jackson. Obviously I did need fixing, because anyone who'd give him up had to be insane. I was the one who had all the loose screws.

He made it clear that he accepted me for me, even though I frustrated him sometimes. Okay, a lot of times. He could frustrate the hell out of me, too, but that never stopped him from telling me what I maybe, kind-of, sort-of needed to hear. We pushed each other to be better.

I loved him for showing up and worrying about me working for those smarmy jerks, even though it also pissed me off that he'd stormed right into the middle of it, the same way it'd pissed me off that night at the bar. I loved that he was so smart and witty and challenged me in ways I'd never been challenged before, even though those qualities were also why I occasionally wanted to strangle him.

I replayed the words he'd said about no one else being strong enough to love a strong girl like me.

Strong. Which meant he didn't think I was completely vulnerable and broken. Speaking of strong…

He told me he loved me, even after I pushed and pushed and pushed.

He loves me.

And damn it, I love him.

I'd tried everything to stop it, but he'd ignored my super-reinforced walls and had me breaking all my rules, and honestly, I'd given over a piece of my heart that night he'd shown up at the hospital. I hadn't taken it back, and since then, he'd won over piece by piece, until my heart completely belonged to him.

I had no unearthly idea how to proceed from here. I'd never been good at relationships, mostly because I stubbornly refused to believe they could work out, but I did happen to be best friends with a certified expert. I hesitated, worried I'd get her hopes up along with my own. But this was too big to screw up. Again.

Even if he forgives me, how will his family? I broke his heart right in front of them.

That thought only steered me into scared-shitless territory, so I shoved it away to be worried about later and focused on the love part.

I love him, and he loves me. I never thought that was

enough before, but I found myself hoping that it was. *Please, please let it be enough, because now that I know just how much I love him, I'm not sure I can live without him.*

My fingers shook as I pulled up the contacts on my phone. I scrolled to the name I wanted and tapped the phone icon.

Savannah answered after the second ring. "Is this the mind-your-own-business call?"

I licked my lips and moved closer to the window, bracing my hand on the frame. "This is the call admitting that your years of attempting to brainwash me must've worked, and now I don't know what to do about it."

"Wait. *What?*" I rarely managed to surprise my best friend—she took my slams on love in stride, laughing them off and accepting me for me—but I could hear the shock in her words. I could even picture her, straightening and pressing the phone tighter to her ear, sure she must've misheard me.

"I…" I paced the length of the bedroom, my rapid pulse hammering in my head. "I want to believe in happily-ever-after. I want to believe in Mr. Freaking Right and The One, and that love can last if you find the right person, and all that stuff that I swore was sappy bullshit."

An excited squeal carried over the line. "I'm not one hundred percent sure this isn't a dream, but I'm going to choose to believe it's real, because I just pinched myself and it hurt like a mother."

I laughed.

"Where are you? I'll bring my slideshow over *right now.*" If I wasn't mistaken, I'd heard her laptop snap closed in the background, and I had no doubt she was seconds from packing it into her bag and climbing in her car to meet me.

"I don't need a slide show. I just need…" I glanced around at the many surfaces that'd taken on a new light since realizing they led to this excruciating yet thrilling torn-apart sensation in my heart that whispered once again how in love

I was. "Your infuriating, super-hot, surprisingly sweet and understanding brother. I need him, Savannah." There. I'd managed to admit it to my bestie, and I sure hoped that was half the battle, because it wasn't easy.

I wanted everything with Jackson—throw in the damn picket fence while we were at it, because as long as he lived behind it with me, I didn't care about anything else.

Living together.

Me and him, in a full-blown relationship with no end in sight. All of his family speculating over when we'd get married and have kids and…

My lungs tightened to the painful point, even as my heart did its best to cling to the hope and love part of things. *Come on, anxiety, just a little break would be great right now.*

"Need? Wow," Savannah said. No inspirational quote tacked on, speaking further to the fact that I'd stunned her practically speechless.

I paced back to the window, needing the physical reminder of the reading nook to reinforce how well Jackson knew me, in spite of how hard I'd tried to keep him out. "But I'm crazy set in my ways—you know that better than anyone. I've spent so long believing that love wasn't for me, that I was perfectly happy being alone, and that even if I wasn't, no one would love me for me. I *know* that long-term relationships inevitably end in tears and disaster and hating the person you swore you'd always cherish. I *know* they rarely last and that I have way too many issues for it to actually work. I know all of that, yet…"

I dropped to my knees, rested my head against the cool glass, and closed my eyes, feeling like my world was spinning out of control. I pictured Jackson standing in front of me, steady and strong, his green eyes matching the greenery in the background as he'd asked me to put my faith in him.

Savannah's steady breathing came over the line, but she

waited, probably afraid to say anything in case it scared me into taking it all back. I appreciated her patience as I worked through the mess of thoughts and emotions and tried to figure out how to put it all out there.

"And yet," I said, picking up where I left off, "here I find myself hoping that I'm wrong, because my heart keeps trying to tell me something else. I've never felt the way I feel when I'm with Jackson, and yes, I am a better, happier person with him."

At that, she couldn't help but let out a victorious, whispered, *"Yes!"*

"I'm also kind-of, sort-of, totally in love with him." I bit my lip, just saying it out loud sending happiness swirling through me, even as gnawing worry came on its heels—after decades of doubt, it refused to just go away simply because I wanted it to. "But what if I try, only to discover that my original theories were right?"

"Then I guess you have to make a choice," Savannah said, and I held my breath, waiting to hear my options. "Would you rather be right, or would you rather be in love?"

When she put it like that, it made it easy.

Love. I choose love.

While I'd flirted with optimism before, this time I was going to commit to it. Time to prove I was as strong as Jackson believed I was. I knew exactly what I wanted. I even knew what my first step would be. I just hoped that it would be enough and that I wasn't too late.

Chapter Thirty-Six

Are you freaking kidding me?

Can't the universe just do me a solid and make this a tiny bit easier instead of harder?

I'd hit snag after snag in my plan. After spending several hours at the bank yesterday morning, I'd failed to gain the one thing I'd so badly wanted to add to my declaration. I'd wanted that physical proof, because honestly, I could use all the help I could get.

Not all hope was lost on that front, but my gesture this afternoon wasn't going to be quite as big as I wanted it to be.

If I ever got there, that was, because the flashing red and blue lights behind me made me wonder how many karma gods I'd managed to piss off. It was like life was trying to beat the crap out of me before I could make things right.

This is what I get for waiting so long.

What I get for—

The knock on the window nearly made me jump out of my dress. I'd bought this one specially for this evening, going so far as to choose a longer hemline that hit my knees, which might work against me in my current situation.

I rolled down the window and flashed the officer my most charming yet innocent smile. For good measure, I twirled a strand of hair around my finger—I'd worn it wild and wavy, the way Jackson liked, although the officer seemed pretty unaffected, a scowl permanently etched on his harsh features. "What seems to be the problem, officer?"

"You were going fifteen over the speed limit."

Right. This is what I get for being in such a hurry to tell the man I love that, well, I love him.

Couldn't the powers-that-be see that I was trying? That I could use a break?

"License and registration," Mr. Not-so-friendly Officer of the Law said, extending his palm. He squinted at me and then frowned at the bottle of rather expensive wine in my front seat. "Have you been drinking?"

I fought back the urge to ask if it looked uncorked to him—there was also a slight temptation to offer it to him, just to see if we could speed this along. "No, I haven't. And I'm sorry about the speeding, it's just that…" Obviously flirting wasn't going to get me anywhere so I decided to appeal to his empathetic side, hoping he had one. "You see, I'm on my way to tell my…well, he's not my boyfriend, but he was a few weeks ago, but then I messed it up, but even then he told me he loved me—can you believe that? And now I'm on my way to make it right, because I love him, too. But I've never done anything like this before."

My nerves stretched to the fraying point, and I'm sure the wild gleam in my eye only made the cop more suspicious. I grinned, and that only made the distrust in his expression grow. "Never gone all out to tell a guy I love him, I mean," I said. "Not the speeding part. Not that I normally go around speeding—safety first, I swear."

"Have you taken anything? You're talking about as fast

as you were driving."

"Just caffeine. In liquid form, a la Cherry Coke." How had I ever thought of myself as smooth? That was the last word I would use to describe me right now, which only made me worry about the giant declaration I was about to make. If the officer would stop asking twenty questions and just give me a ticket already—I was past thinking I could talk him out if it, so now I simply wanted him to give it to me and let me go.

Better not say it like that, I thought, even though I wasn't about to ask him to hurry. I had a feeling that'd only piss him off and convince him that he needed to assert his authority over me.

"Sit tight while I go run this," he said, lifting my license and registration.

Sit tight. Like I could even do that at a time like this.

Great. Now instead of showing up before *dinner, I'm going to be crashing right in the middle, which won't help with winning over his mom and Velma. If I even have a chance of that after what they witnessed at Savannah's bridal shower.*

While tapping out a rhythm on the steering wheel, I mentally ran over everything I wanted to say to Jackson. Like every other time I'd tried to lay it out, it always came out jumbled, one thought merging into another before I could finish it. Last night in my condo I'd even practiced in front of my herd of cats, feeling like an idiot the whole time, and big surprise, their judgmental expressions didn't help. Hoping it'd magically come out better once he was standing in front of me was preposterous, so it was a good thing I'd fully committed to optimism. Even if the bitch was making it hard to stay faithful.

No one had been more in the way of Jackson and me than myself, so loan officers and uptight cops could go ahead and try, but I wasn't giving up.

My phone rang from its position in my console, and I

picked it up, answering when I saw Savannah's name.

"We're about to start dinner," she whispered, leading me to believe she must've stepped aside to make the call while everyone else was heading to the table. "Where are you?"

I rested my elbow on the top of my door and pressed my fingers to my forehead, trying to fight off the oncoming headache that was equal parts frustration and anxiety. "With a cop who has a stick up his ass. I'm pretty sure he's writing me a ticket."

"Actually, he wrote a warning after seeing that you didn't have anything on your record," he said, and I jumped, nearly dropping my phone in the process.

Shit, shit, shit.

"But it just got upgraded to a speeding citation," he said. "And now you get to walk a straight line for me, too. Let's see how you do considering all that caffeine you drank."

Spoiler alert: in these five-inch heels, between my nerves and the gravel on the side of the road, it was going to be wobbly.

"Can I just tell my friend—"

The officer swung open my door. "Out now, ma'am."

Well, at least the universe had answered my plea about doing me a solid and making this easier. Unfortunately for me, it was with a resounding *no*.

Chapter Thirty-Seven

After walking in a straight line while touching my nose and reciting the alphabet backward—which hello, who can do that quickly without the song?—I could think of a dozen better tricks to find out if people were over the alcohol limit. But he knew I wasn't drunk, so it was a power trip involving wasting as much of my time as possible. Anyway, to say my optimism and mood hadn't been beat up would be a lie.

I almost said screw it, turned around, and headed for home, postponing my attempt to win back my man another time. Like, say, when I felt less stabby. But I didn't think I could handle anything else karma decided to throw at me, so I decided I'd better fix things with Jackson ASAP. I couldn't think of the other option—I wouldn't let myself.

I thought I'd already been at maximum nervousness, but as soon as I parked behind the other cars lining the Gambles' driveway, the nauseating swirl in my gut upped it to the next level. *So glad to be proved wrong about that.*

My feet hurt from walking around in front of the cop, and if someone in the neighborhood hadn't seen me and reported it to either Lucinda or Velma by now, I'd be shocked. The headlights and flashing lights had done a great job of spotlighting me, after all.

Oh, crap. The wine. I backtracked and grabbed it out of the passenger seat. It probably wouldn't help as much now that I was so late, but I needed something in my hands to help with the trembling anyway.

Every window glowed a warm yellow, and I could imagine the Gamble family seated around the table. Considering my epically bad luck, Caroline would probably be there as well, along with her parents. And Jackson would've decided that he was done waiting for me to pull my head out and picked tonight of all nights to take my advice and go for her, leaving me an hour too late.

Savannah would definitely interfere before letting that happen. That thought, along with her pep talk two nights ago, gave me the strength to ring the doorbell.

I smoothed a hand down my hair, hoping I didn't look as beat up as I felt.

Savannah answered the door, and I nearly burst into tears at the sight of her—I had no idea how badly I needed a friendly face until I saw hers. "Oh, hon." She threw her arms around me and hugged me, and I squeezed her right back. "I thought it would be you. I'm glad I nearly tripped my dad in order to be the one to answer the door. Are you okay?"

"Well, after thirty minutes of proving I'm not drunk and getting a hefty speeding ticket, I'm not great, but I think I'm okay. I'm super nervous, though. Why did I decide to do this at your parents' house with your entire family here?"

"Because love makes us do crazy things. You're talking to the girl who climbed onto a stool in front of an entire barfull of people—some of whom were my clients—and poured out her heart to win back the guy she loved."

"At least I'm in good company."

"And if it makes you feel better, I'm an even better coach than a dater." She scrunched up her nose. "Is *dater* a word?"

"Focus, Savannah. I need you with me." I tried to peek through to the dining room, but I could only see the kids' table. On the bright side, Evan flashed me a thumbs-up. Even though he didn't know what I was about to do, I still took that as a good omen. "So your hot, infuriating, sexy, perfect brother is in there?"

"I'm not sure about all those adjectives, but yeah. He's in there."

I lifted my chin. "Here goes everything." I strode into the room, and several people looked up at me. I think they were expecting Savannah, who'd stopped a few feet behind me—either as a sign of support or blocking my exit or perhaps both—and some of them did double takes.

Jackson shuttered his expression, the warmth draining from his easy smile, and my stomach dropped all the way down to my shoes. *I'm too late.*

No, I can't be. I can fix it. I have to fix it.

I cleared my throat. "Hi, everybody. Sorry I'm late. Not that I was, um, officially invited, but I did plan to crash on time if that makes it any better. And I brought wine." I lifted it like they'd need proof, and with me, maybe they did.

Blinks all around. Except for Aunt Velma—she had a pursed-lipped expression. *Yeah, sorry not sorry for messing up your plans to set up your nephew with the perfect girl from the perfect family.*

I set the bottle on the table and turned to Jackson. My heart knotted, and adoration and attraction surged to the forefront. He looked so sexy, hair combed back, jaw fresh-shaven and kissable, and green eyes trained on me. From this angle standing above him, I noticed the top button on his gray button-down was undone but hidden by the navy tie I wanted to yank on to get him to stand up and wrap his hard body around me.

Which I supposed would be inappropriate considering the present company, especially the kids, who were taking advantage of the distraction by piling vegetables into napkins.

I nearly laughed, and I knew it would come out sounding completely maniacal. Laughing would be so much easier than words, though. I wrung my hands together, and if the heat in my face was any indication, it was bright red. "Do you guys think you could excuse Jackson for just a minute?"

"Sure, dear," Lucinda said. "I'll set a plate for you, too."

"Better hold off on that just yet." Because if this attempt to make things right went down in fiery flames, I was fleeing for sure.

Jackson slowly stood, and I tilted my head toward the other room. He led the way with long strides that I worked to keep up with, and as I passed by her, Savannah slapped my ass.

"Go get 'em, girl," she whispered, and I heard both her mom and Velma scolding her for such a rude gesture.

Jackson spun to face me, and I nearly ran into him—I didn't know we were stopping already. He put his hands on my waist to steady me, then yanked them away like touching me had burned him.

Why didn't he look happier? Why didn't he look... anything? *He changed his mind. I'm about to pour out my heart, and he's going to tell me he's over it. Over me.*

Wait. That's not very optimistic. Shit, shit, shit.

He crossed his arms, and it made his shirt pull tighter across his chest and exposed a few inches of his sexy wrists. Who knew wrists could be sexy?

Focus, Ivy. "Hey."

"Hey," he said, his voice not betraying what was going on in his head right now.

"So how've you been?" Ugh, why couldn't I get my mouth

to cooperate? This wasn't how I was supposed to start my big speech. *Come on. We practiced this.*

"Really, Ivy? To be honest, kind of shitty."

"I'm sorry."

His face fell, the first hint of emotion he'd let show.

"I mean, I'm sorry it took me so long." I started to reach for him and then pulled back my hand. "The truth is I was scared. Terrified, actually. I'm not good at relationships, and I've tried so hard to keep my heart protected. Then you come along, and I know you said that you knocked down one brick wall only to find another, but one wall was enough for you to get in." My voice caught, and I had to work to keep going. "Renovating that house with you…it was amazing, and I loved every second. Even though you also drive me crazy. Seriously, you're the most infuriating person I know."

One corner of his mouth kicked up.

"But you're also sweet and fiercely protective and way more patient than I deserve, and then there's the dead-sexy thing."

The other side of his mouth got in on the smile.

I stepped closer to him, so close only a breath separated our bodies, yet it was still too much space. I reached up and ran my hand down the side of his face, leaving my palm against his warm skin. "You asked me to put my faith in you, and you should know that it's not that I don't have faith in you. Because I do." Crap, how could the waterworks be attempting to break free already? I was barely started with everything I wanted to say. Blinking as fast as I could, I blew out a breath. "I just didn't have faith in me, and because of that, I knew there couldn't be an us."

"Ivy—"

I moved my fingertips over his lips. I was finally getting going, and if he spoke, I'd lose my momentum and everything I wanted to say and most likely the thin thread of control on my emotions, too. "Anyway, that *was* what I thought. But I couldn't stop thinking about you and how even though that house held most of my happiest childhood memories, the ones I'd made there with you over the past couple months were even happier. Then Dixie got an offer on the house, and I panicked. Because it's *our* house. It's where I fell in love with you.

"So I begged her not to take the offer and to let me buy it instead. I want to live there with you and to build a future with you. But I'd need..." I swallowed my pride and shoved every ounce of courage I had into the next word. "Help. I'd need your help. I really wanted to hold up a deed and show you that I bought our house and wanted to live there with you, but the bank won't let me buy it without an offer on the condo, since my salary also fluctuates so much, and to be honest, even with my new job, I'm not a hundred percent sure I can afford the monthly payments by myself."

My heart beat so hard and fast that I swore it was about to burst out of my chest, but finally my mouth was cooperating, so I kept talking just as hard and fast. "But it doesn't even have to be that house if you don't want to live there. My main point is that more than anything, I want to be with you and go home every night to you, and I just need you, Jackson. And also, in case I didn't say it already, because I'm starting to lose track of what I practiced saying, and what I actually ended up saying..." I inhaled a deep breath and let it out. "I'm in love with you. I love you so much it scares me, but I'm not going to let that stop me anymore."

A weight lifted off me now that I'd finally told him everything, and it felt like I'd taken my first full breath in weeks.

And like everyone had earlier when I crashed their family dinner, he just blinked at me.

"Am I too late? Is it crazy to think that we should buy a

house and move in together so soon? I know it's a big step, but I'm ready for a big step with you. If you are. If not, then I can just live in the house, and maybe eventually—"

Jackson yanked me to him and crashed his lips into mine. He kissed me like he meant to memorize every inch of my mouth, while his hands were working on getting reacquainted with my body. It immediately responded, wanting more while thinking this had to be a dream. I couldn't have everything I wanted, could I?

That was when I reminded myself I was optimistic now and threw myself more fully into his embrace and the mind-blowing kiss.

"You scared me for a second," I said when we came up for air. "I thought you were going to say I was too late."

"For a second?" Jackson reached up and brushed his thumb across my tingly lower lip. "You scared me for three long, awful weeks. When you told my mom not to set a place for you, I was sure you were about to reiterate that we were over for good."

"As I recall, I tried telling you that before and you didn't listen." I bit his thumb, and he groaned.

Then he glanced over his shoulder and whispered, "I better be careful. I bet my entire family's eavesdropping."

"Think they'll forgive me for being so stupid the past few weeks?"

"Only the past few weeks?"

I smacked his chest, and he laughed and pulled me in for another kiss. He was definitely holding back, though, and I couldn't wait until we were alone later tonight, just me and him, no one listening in. To think of that happening every night for the rest of our lives…

I waited for the hint of panic I'd have to shut down, but the only feelings the thought brought on were happiness and anticipation.

"Wait," I said, placing my hands on his chest. "You never said yes to moving in with me. Which is fine. If it scares you, and you'd rather take it slower, I understand."

A butterfly-inducing grin spread across his face. "I told you that you're who I want and that I needed you and loved you in front of most of my family. You think I'd do all that and be scared to move in with you?"

"Well…" I shrugged. "Kind of. You've got your place, and I didn't even ask before jumping in. Maybe it's a good thing the bank said I needed someone to co-sign on the loan." I slid my hands up and linked them behind his neck, bringing my body flush with his. "I just really love that house, and you and I put all that work into it, and I have so many good memories there, which is a bit unusual for me. And like I said, it's where I fell in love with you. Where I picture us years from now."

"Wow, Flash, you said that without even a hint of panic."

"No more Flash. No more panic—except for the panic I feel over you not wanting to take a risk on us."

"You and me? We're not a risk, babe." He enveloped me in his arms and squeezed me tight. "We're a sure bet."

"You think so?"

"I know so. Which is why we're going to that bank tomorrow and buying *our* house, whatever it takes."

I threw myself at him, kissing him with reckless abandon and letting happiness and love wash over me.

Until the loud throat-clearing.

"We're all really happy for you," Lucinda said, peeking through the doorway, and Velma and Savannah were beside her, wearing matching smiles. "Now why don't we skip to the drinks portion of the night and give you a proper toast?"

I took that to mean they also forgave and accepted me the way I was, and that was when the dam finally broke and the tears burst free.

The next several minutes were a blur of hugging and

toasting and being surrounded by more love than I dared to believe was possible.

I'd broken all my rules and fallen in love, and my heart still beat in my chest, fluttering and fully intact. I'd say something horribly cheesy, like the guy who'd fixed up a house with me had also fixed my heart along the way, despite my reiterating over and over that it wasn't broken.

But I'd done enough in the way of admitting today, so I decided to curl closer to the guy who'd done the fixing and simply enjoy the happiness buoying me up to cloud nine level. And just so there was no mistake how I felt, and because being able to tell someone I cared about them without being scared was a new sensation for me, I tipped onto my toes, pressed my lips to his, and whispered, "I love you, Jackson Gamble."

"I love you, too." He deepened the kiss, clinging on to me like he was never going to let go, and I knew he wouldn't. Not in the metaphorical sense, anyway.

Right there on the spot, I compiled a new list to ensure I enjoyed my very own happily-ever-after. (Someday I'd tell my best friend that I admitted its existence, and I was sure I'd never hear the end of it, but I had a feeling she already knew anyway.)

There was only one rule, one I swore I wouldn't break.

 # 1: Love fully, no matter what. It's totally worth it.

Epilogue

I stepped over Black Widow, who'd camped out halfway down the staircase and wasn't about to move for me. Then I hit the landing, nearly tripping over Loki, the trouble-making male kitten we'd kept because I'd turned into one of those girls with attachment issues.

The other three kittens had found happy homes as well, and Black Widow had been to the vet so she wouldn't bring us any more surprise litters.

My heels echoed across the hardwood floor. "Jackson? Are you down here? We can't be late or your sister, mother, and aunt will take turns killing us. And not to sound like a total diva, but I'm the only one who gets to threaten to murder you."

Jackson walked out of the kitchen, a steaming cup of coffee in a to-go mug in one hand and a Cherry Coke in the other. "Which is why I come armed with caffeine. If you're going to be stabbing me, I want you to be able to give it your all."

"So considerate," I said, taking the cold can. "I knew I

moved in with you for a reason."

"If you decide to forgo the stabbing, you should know that I'm good for more than providing caffeine. There's banging, screwing, nailing…" He waggled his eyebrows, then his gaze traveled up and down my body, taking in the sherbet-pink bridesmaid dress that left my shoulders bare. "Damn, you look hot." He moved closer, taking away the drink he'd just given me and setting it and his aside, then wrapping his arm around my waist as his lips met mine.

For a second, I forgot about the fact that I was going to be in a wedding in a couple of hours and got lost in kissing Jackson. The past three months of living in the house where we'd fallen in love had been amazing, and I fell a little more in love with him every day, regardless of ups and downs or the times he occasionally drove me crazy. I couldn't believe how much I loved living with a dude, and I knew that had a lot to do with the dude.

He parted my lips with his, deepening the kiss as he walked me backward until my back met the wall.

"Jackson," I warned, but it came out breathy and not nearly as stern as it needed to be. His lips moved to my neck, and I tipped my head to give him better access when I should have been shutting it down. "We don't have time right now."

"But this is my favorite wall, and you look really sexy." He pressed me flatter to said wall, and the desire flooding my veins turned molten. "Even sexier with the blue-gray contrasting that bright dress."

"A dress I'm wearing because I'm a bridesmaid at your *sister's wedding.*"

He sighed. "Fine. But later tonight, you, me, and this wall have a standing appointment." He nudged me with his elbow. "Get it. Standing."

I rolled my eyes, but a laugh slipped out. We retrieved our drinks, and Jackson placed his hand on the small of my back and guided me out onto our porch, where he'd hung a swing I'd picked up at my new job and repurposed. I *loved* my job. Loved how it was always different, and all the varying types of furniture I came across in a day. The estate sales were like a peek into people's lives, and there was something cool about taking their stuff and giving it a new life with new people who'd attach new memories to the pieces. Betty-Joe had also let me fix up her shop so the storefront drew more people in, and my pieces were selling really well.

The swing allowed Jackson and me to sit outside, enjoying the shade and gentle swaying as we talked about our respective days.

I also spent countless hours in the reading nook, and Jackson often came home, all deliciously dirty and covered in man glitter from work, and then the nook would turn into more than a reading spot—after drawing the shades of course.

Jackson opened the passenger door to his truck for me like a gentleman but smacked me on the ass like the Neanderthal he also was.

After he merged onto I85, he took my hand and laced his fingers with mine. "You nervous?"

I shook my head. "Nope. Just really happy for Savannah and Linc. Don't get me wrong, I'll be glad when the ceremony is done, but at least Savannah chose cute dresses"—I lifted one of the layers of chiffon on the skirt—"and it's pretty sweet how excited she is. I remember this time when even optimistic, inspirational-quote-spouting Savannah doubted there was a Mr. Right for her, and I'm so happy she found him."

I took in Jackson's profile and scooted a little closer. "I'm, uh, happy that I found mine too, for the record. Even though I was sure you didn't exist for a very long time."

Jackson lifted our entwined hands and kissed the back of mine. "Good thing I took all that time and effort convincing you that we were perfect for each other."

"I think being delirious from all the fumes worked in your favor, too."

"Hey, I'll take it."

A short drive later, we pulled up to his parents' house. Before I could even climb out of the truck myself, Jackson was there to extend a hand. I think it showed great growth that I no longer refused help, whether or not I needed it.

The next couple hours were a blur of last-minute wedding stuff and keeping Savannah from crying and ruining her makeup and laughing and hugging and both of us crying and needing to touch up our makeup.

Right before we headed to line up for the ceremony, Savannah pulled me into a hug. "Thanks for everything, Ivy. I never would've gotten here without you."

I squeezed her back. "Right back at you."

"Love you."

"Love you, too. And I think it's time you passed the dating coach flame to me. Just for the ceremony."

She grinned.

I gave her the same treatment she'd given me once, with a smack on the butt. "Now get out there and marry your Mr. Right, girl. You've been waiting forever for this moment."

"I really have." She took a step and then turned to me. "Um, actually, you have to go first."

"Right." I quickly rushed forward and lined up in my spot at the back of the aisle. Since Jackson was a groomsman, I'd jumped at pairing up with him. We walked down the aisle, together—*whoa, not like that*—and then took our places for the ceremony.

It was beautiful, there were tears—and I'm not saying whether or not some of them were mine—and the groom kissed the bride.

The crowd erupted in cheers, and then everyone transitioned to the tables for the reception. I was watching

Savannah and Linc, grinning as they beamed at each other and kissed every five seconds.

Someone walked up behind me, and I turned, expecting Jackson.

Instead, I got Velma. Her attention was on the happy couple, but then she glanced at me.

"Yes," I said, nice and firm.

Her forehead creased. "Yes, what?"

"Yes, I do want to be in love like that, and I am."

There was something about Velma's return grin that sent my nerve-endings on high alert. "Does that mean Lucinda and I can mention a future wedding? Maybe save some of the decorations from this one, just in case?"

I scanned the crowd for Jackson, finding him a couple of yards away, talking to one of his older uncles. He caught me staring and winked. Warmth flooded me, the love I felt for him radiating through my entire body. "Yeah," I said to Velma. "Go crazy."

I started toward Jackson but then noticed my mom near the back. I didn't know why, but I hadn't expected her to come. "Hi, Mom. Beautiful ceremony, wasn't it?" A few months ago, I might've added a jab about not getting any ideas, but now I understood her better. Sure, I wouldn't put up with a lot of what she did, and I didn't think she had healthy relationships, but I understood now how you could get swept up in someone and think with your heart instead of your head.

"It was," she said.

I glanced around, wondering if Stan had come along, but not wanting to ask.

"He's not here. He and I…we broke up."

"Oh, Mom. I'm so sorry." My lungs deflated, and I looked her over for signs that might tell me how she was handling it, while crossing my fingers it wouldn't be as bad as last time. "Are you okay?"

"It's okay, I'm okay. It was about a month ago."

A month? "But you didn't call. Are you still living with him?"

"No. But I know you have your life with Jackson, so I called someone else." She fiddled with the sleeve of her dress. "I called Dixie."

My jaw dropped for a second before I forced it back into place. "Wow. So you guys are…talking?"

"We are. She'd mailed me an old scrapbook with a note that said she missed me, so when Stan and I started fighting again, I called her up. It was stilted at first, but then we got to talking like old times, and I realized how much I missed her, too. We talked about you as well, and I know I haven't always been the best mother, but I'm gonna try to be better, even if it's too late."

For the second time today, tears rose to my eyes—okay, yes, I cried during the ceremony. I hugged my mom, and she hugged me back, and it was a bit awkward since we were out of practice, but it gave me hope that maybe someday, we'd be our version of okay.

The hand on my back made me turn, and Jackson slid his arm around my waist and tucked me next to him. He nodded at my mom. "Cora."

"Hello, Jackson." She dabbed at her eyes with an embroidered handkerchief and then flashed us a smile. "You kids have fun. I'm going to go give Savannah and Linc my best." She walked through the crowd of people, and I curled closer to Jackson.

He kissed my temple. "You okay? That seemed like one of your better interactions with your mom."

"It was, and I'm better than okay." I gave him a quick recap, and when I noticed Lucinda and Aunt Velma pointing at us, eager grins on their faces, I patted his chest. "Fair warning, Velma asked me if she could mention a possible future wedding—as in yours and mine. And I told her to go crazy. Honestly, I figured they were going to do it anyway."

Jackson's fingers tightened on my hip. "But it won't send you running?"

"Nope. No more running from you."

"Good to know." He dipped his head and kissed me. "So that means you're…open to it? Someday?"

I slipped my arms around his waist and brushed my lips across his. "I'm not letting you get away, and I'll do most anything to make sure you don't."

"Clearly, if you're open to wedding talk."

I laughed.

Then we were called over with a mild scolding for not being where we were supposed to be, with the rest of the wedding party. We ate and drank and ate and drank some more. There was music and toasts and dancing and cake.

Then my best friend was sent off on her honeymoon with the guy she loved, and I was finally left alone with my boyfriend. "Wanna go home?" he whispered in my ear.

Man, I loved that we shared a home. I nodded. "Yes, take me home."

By the time we made it back, we were completely exhausted. I kicked off my shoes, ready to force my muscles to climb the stairs so I could flop into bed and never move again. But my two cats meowed at me like they were starving, since we'd fed them so long ago—or, you know, this morning. Not to mention the bowl of dry cat food that I'd filled before we left.

"I got it," I said, going to feed the cats while Jackson went upstairs. I gave them some extra love, petting them as they ate so they didn't feel neglected, and then made my way upstairs.

Right as I'd reached the top of what felt like Mount Everest, I remembered Jackson and I had a date with the wall in the living room, and while my muscles ached, the idea of that made other places ache, strong enough that desire overtook my exhaustion.

"I was promised some wall action," I said as I pushed open the door to the bedroom, "so I hope you're not too tired to deliv—" The last of my sentence dropped off as I noticed the lit candles around the room.

Jackson walked over to me, his tie off, his shirt undone at the top, exposing a few tempting inches of his chest. Then he dropped down on one knee and held up a ring. "Ivy Lynn Clarke—"

"Wow. When you said someday, you meant, like…now."

"I've been carrying this ring around for weeks. I thought it might be a few more months before you'd be ready, but I love you, and I don't want to wait." He grabbed my hand. "I want to call you mine, and for me to be yours, and I want to marry you. So will you? Marry me?"

I looked down at him, thought of the rest of our lives stretched out before us and spending those as husband and wife, and I couldn't extend my ring finger fast enough. I nodded and said, "Yes, yes, yes," excitement making me repeat the word a ridiculous amount of times, but I also wanted to show him there wasn't an ounce of hesitation on my end. "I can't believe that I'm going to get married. Me. Married."

"Believe it, babe." He stood and kissed me, then he boosted me into his arms. "Now what were you saying about that wall?"

As he carried me down the stairs, my excitement spiked even higher, and instead of my usual desire to slow everything down, I found myself wanting to hurry up and get married so we could spend the rest of our lives kissing and laughing and getting all riled-up arguing, and then making up after we lost our tempers and threatened to kill each other.

Oh, yeah. We were totally gonna nail this happily-ever-after thing.

Acknowledgments

Some books are nice and easy to write, most are a little more roller-coastery, and some are hard. This one was hard. (Resists using romance writer brain to make an innuendo.) If it wasn't for Gina Maxwell and Rebecca Yarros, I'm not sure I would've survived. For reals, you girls save me and keep me laughing and as sane as possible, and man I love you guys! Same goes to Evangeline Denmark, who talked me off a ledge one night and helped me come up with the "Go batshit crazy" rule, which is still my favorite of Ivy's rules. Thanks to Stacy Abrams for seeing all the fiery potential between Ivy and Jackson and pushing me to make it bigger and better. That was when things stopped being so hard and started getting really fun.

Thanks to HGTV for making us all think we can flip houses, only to have harsh reawakenings when we're elbow deep in paint, debris all around us, wondering if we'll ever be able to use our kitchens again. My husband and I, along with our kiddos, did some renovating a few summers ago and it provided a little too much disasterous scenario inspirations, but we learned a lot and eventually, the madness ended. Mostly. Thanks also to my house for going the extra mile to provide inspiration, springing a leak in the ceiling in my newly remodeled family room while I was swamped with writing this book and behind deadline. Man, you know how to make a girl feel special—LOL.

Huge shoutout to my team at Entangled Publishing!!! With all the exclamation marks!!! There are so many awesome people there, and I appreciate every person who helps polish my books, get them into the hands of readers, and make sure people know about them. I appreciate the brainstorming meetings and the care you've taken with my career. Extra thanks to Holly Bryant-Simpson, Riki Cleavland, and Jessica Turner for all the publicity help. Big hugs to Liz Pelletier, Heather Riccio, Melanie Smith, and Candy Havens for everything you do for me, and for being fun people to hang out with. (Both my editors, Stacy and Alycia, also fit in that category.) I've also met a ton of awesome author friends there and just love being part of the Entangled family.

To my dear family, thanks for putting up with writer brain and burned dinners—people told me that I couldn't burn stuff in the foolproof Instapot and I'm proud to say I proved them wrong. Because I'm an overachiever like that. (I talk about our Instapot Fred and dinner disasters over on Facebook a lot if you'd like to friend me and see the disasters firsthand.) And still my family keeps laughing and encouraging me and they're always my biggest cheerleaders and my best inspiration for what love is. Hulk (my husband prefers me to refer to him as this on social media platforms, so everybody just go with it), I love you. Sometimes, like Ivy and Jackson, we have heated arguments and drive each other a little crazy in every possible way, but like them, we also belong together.

Huge thanks to my readers and to bloggers and reviwers

and librarians and just the entire book community. I'm so proud to be a member, because reading is totally where it's at. Thank you all for letting me share my stories with you.

About the Author

Cindi Madsen is a *USA Today* bestselling author of contemporary romance and young adult novels. She sits at her computer every chance she gets, plotting, revising, and falling in love with her characters. Sometimes it makes her a crazy person. Without it, she'd be even crazier. She has way too many shoes, but can always find a reason to buy a pretty new pair, especially if they're sparkly, colorful, or super tall. She loves music and dancing and wishes summer lasted all year long. She lives in Colorado (where summer is most definitely *not* all year long) with her husband and three children.

You can visit Cindi at: www.cindimadsen.com, where you can sign up for her newsletter to get all the up-to-date information on her books.

Follow her on Twitter @cindimadsen.

Discover more Amara titles…

THE NEGOTIATOR
a novel by Avery Flynn

Workaholic Sawyer Carlyle needs a "buffer" between him and his marriage-obsessed mom. But when the woman he hires turns out to negotiate like a pitbull and look like lickable sunshine, he's soon agreeing to things straight out of his comfort zone.

SAISON FOR LOVE
a *Brewing Love* novel by Meg Benjamin

Liam Dempsey isn't long for Antero. He's not interested in forming any attachments before he leaves in a month, but after a sexy hook-up with his sister's friend, he finds himself unsure where his future stands. The last thing Ruth Colbert needs is something else on her plate, but a steamy night with Liam was just what she needed. The problem is, now she wants more, if only she could find the time for him.

Hot for the Fireman
a novel by Gina L. Maxwell

When Erik Grady's chief at the fire department mandates therapy for supposed PTSD or a permanent desk job, Erik has no choice. But this doctor is not what he expected. She's curvy and hotter than a four-alarm fire. And he just happens to have firsthand experience with her curves. Of all the men to walk into psychologist Olivia Jones's office, why did it have to be her one-night stand? But she's a professional. And if he demands three dates before he'll change therapists, she'll date him, all right. It's time to see how much heat this fireman can take…

Worth the Wait
a *Kingston Ale House* novel by A. J. Pine

What does a girl do when the man she thought loved her steals her life's savings? She re-evaluates her life—and establishes a full-on cleanse to rid herself of toxins. No alcohol. No red meat. And certainly no—um—male parts. Jeremy Denning doesn't do commitment. But he can't stop thinking about the woman who's sworn off men completely. He's out to prove himself worthy of her love—without so much as a kiss—but in doing so, he may lose the one thing he's vowed to never give up. His heart.

Made in the USA
Columbia, SC
11 October 2020

36675030R00188

Made in the USA
San Bernardino, CA
23 May 2019